MERMIN™

BOOK THREE: DEEP DIVE

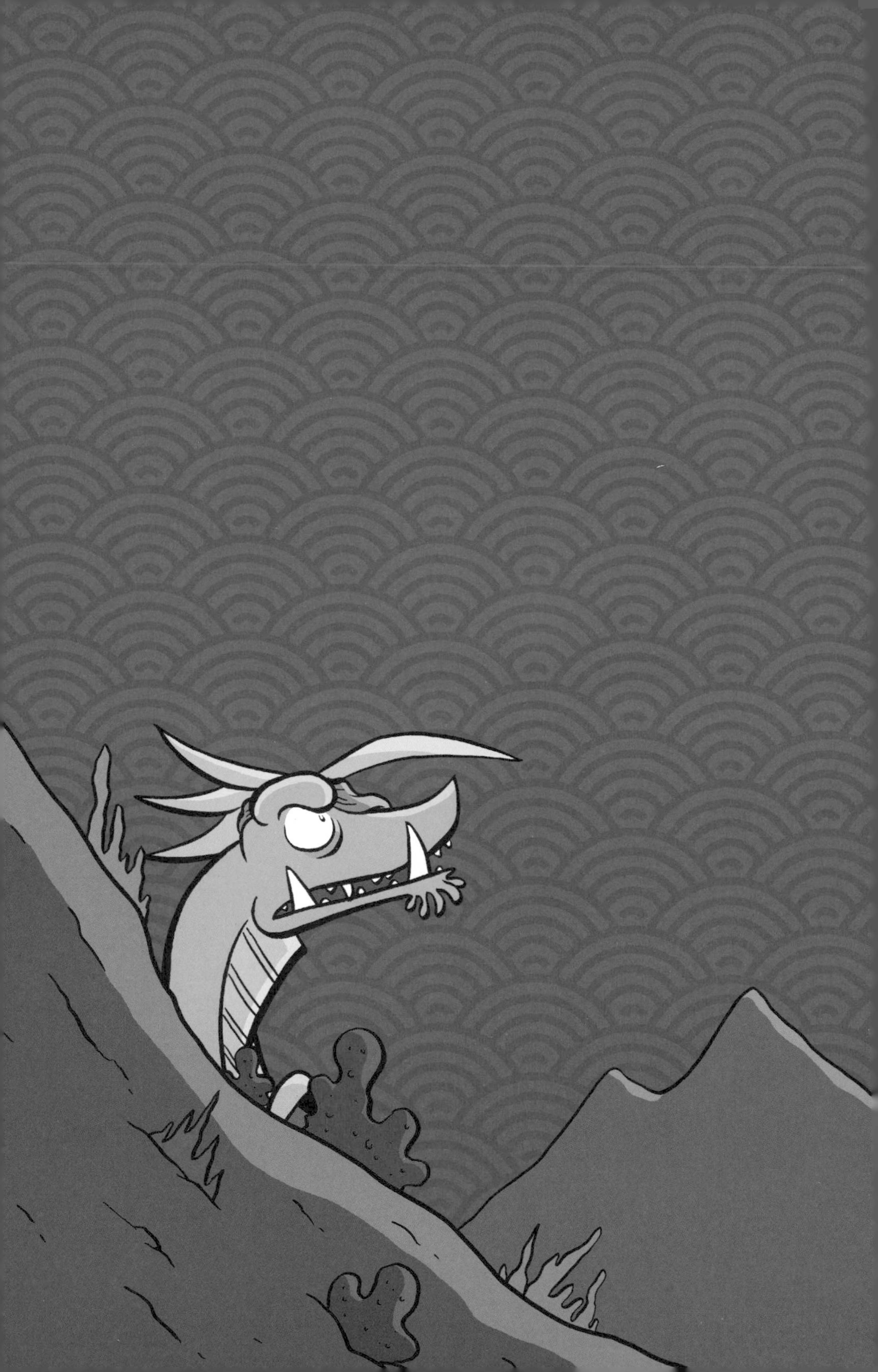

MERMIN™

BOOK THREE: DEEP DIVE

Written and illustrated by

Joey Weiser

Colored by

Joey Weiser and Michele Chidester

Edited by

Jill Beaton

with

Robin Herrera

Designed by

Keith Wood

with

Jason Storey

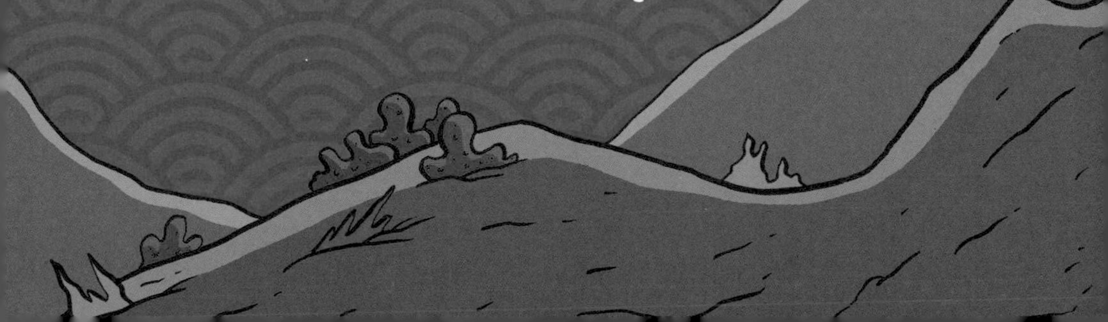

Oni Press, Inc.

publisher, **Joe Nozemack**

editor in chief, **James Lucas Jones**

director of sales, **Cheyenne Allott**

director of publicity, **John Schork**

editor, **Charlie Chu**

associate editor, **Robin Herrera**

production manager, **Troy Look**

senior designer, **Jason Storey**

inventory coordinator, **Brad Rooks**

administrative assistant, **Ari Yarwood**

office assitant, **Jung Lee**

production assistant, **Jared Jones**

1305 SE Martin Luther King Jr. Blvd.
Suite A
Portland, OR 97214

onipress.com
facebook.com/onipress
twitter.com/onipress
onipress.tumblr.com
tragic-planet.com

First Edition: September 2014
ISBN: 978-1-62010-174-2
eISBN: 978-1-62010-172-8
Library of Congress Control Number: 2012953664

10 9 8 7 6 5 4 3 2 1

Printed in China.

CHAPTER ONE

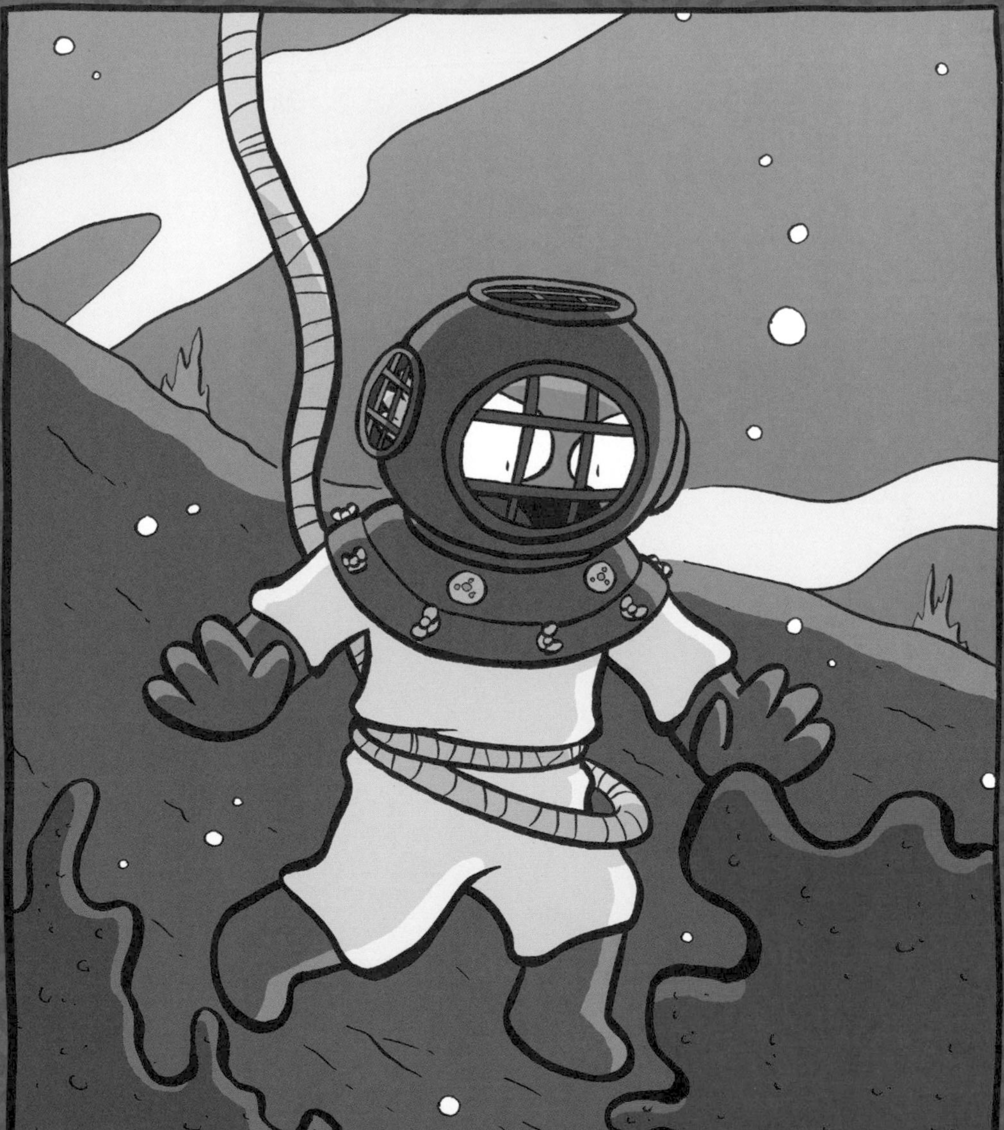

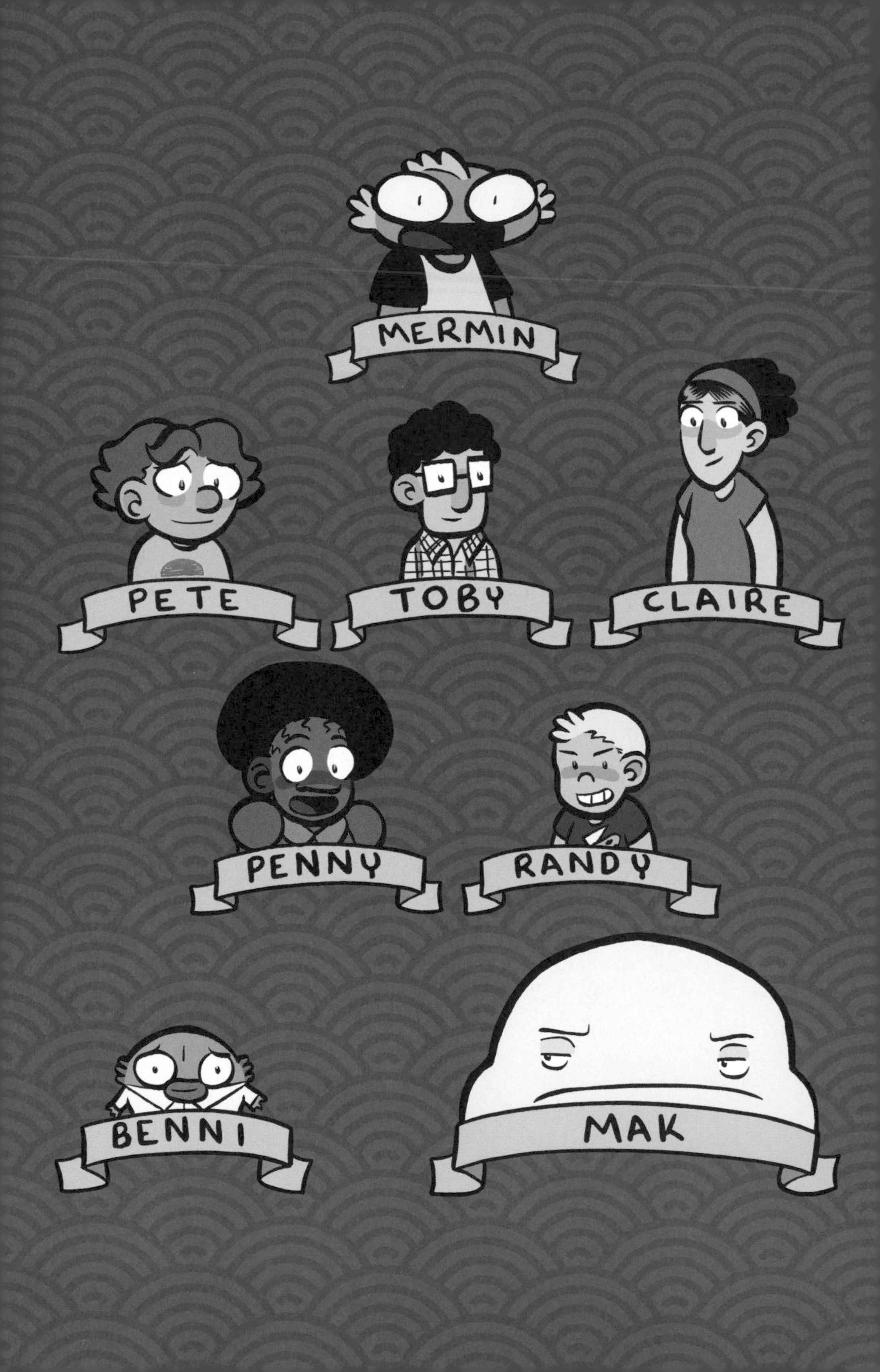

MERMIN
PETE
TOBY
CLAIRE
PENNY
RANDY
BENNI
MAK

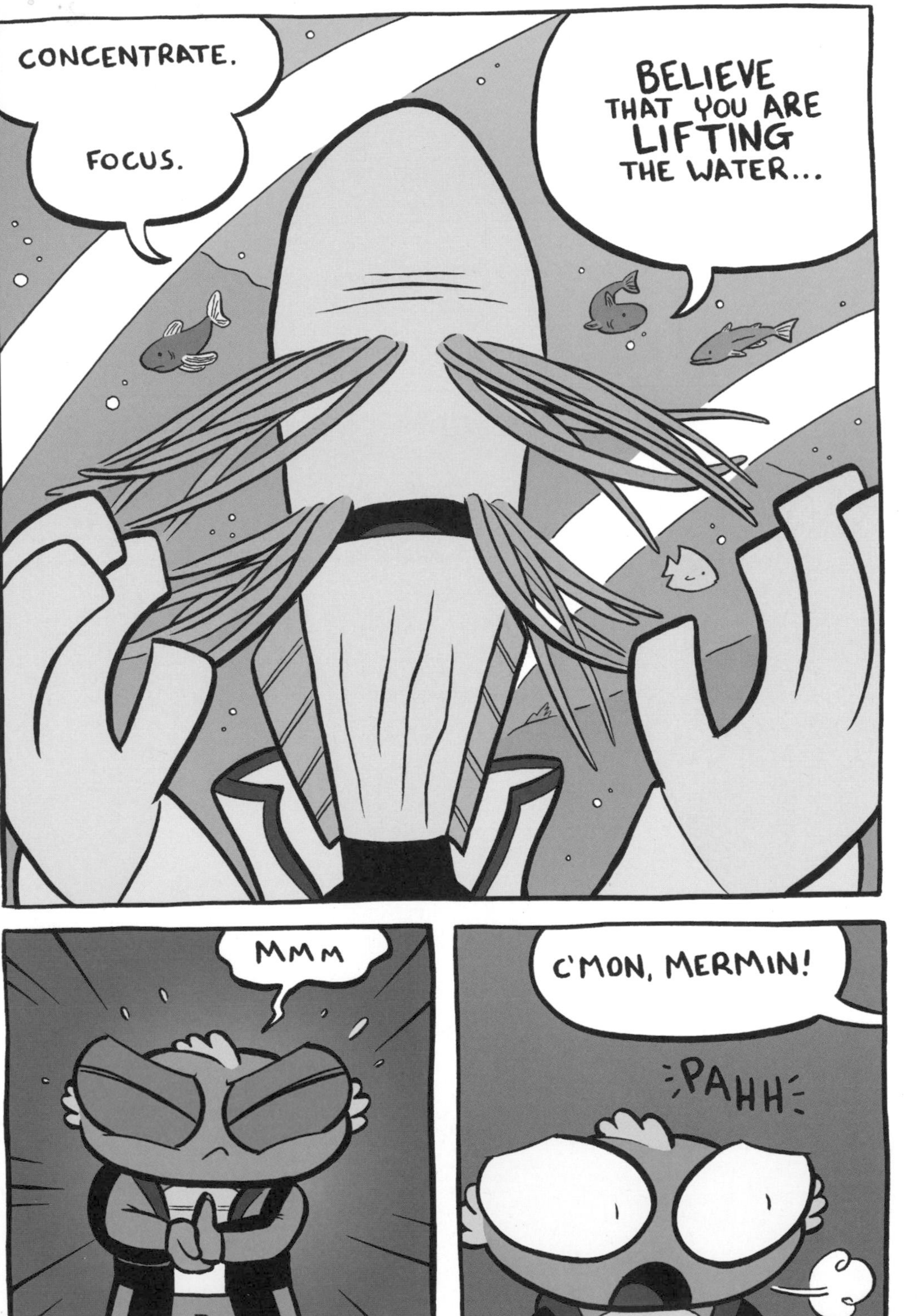
CONCENTRATE.
FOCUS.
BELIEVE THAT YOU ARE LIFTING THE WATER...
MMM
C'MON, MERMIN!
PAHH

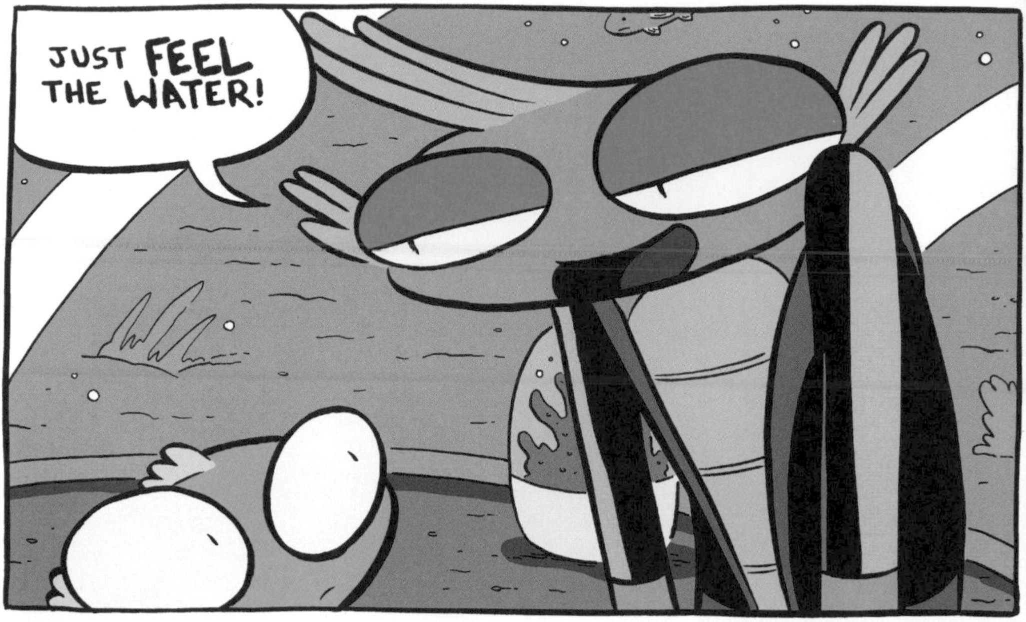
JUST FEEL THE WATER!

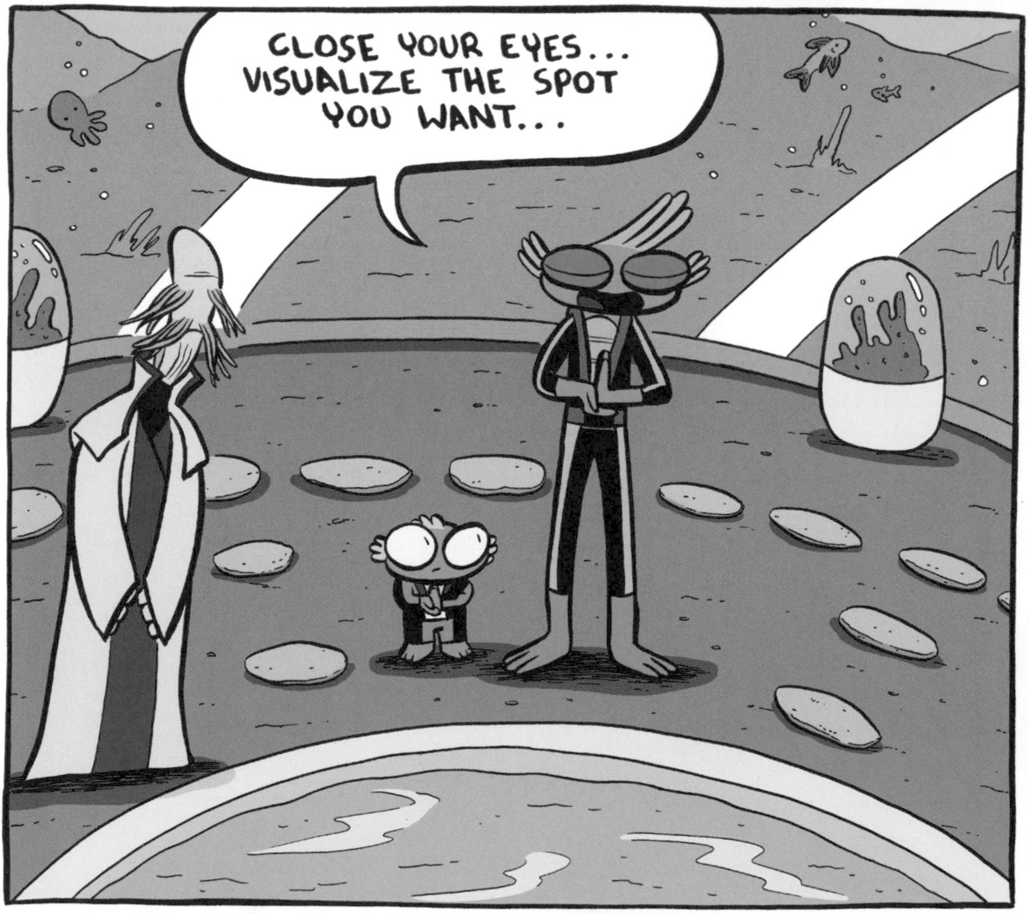
CLOSE YOUR EYES... VISUALIZE THE SPOT YOU WANT...

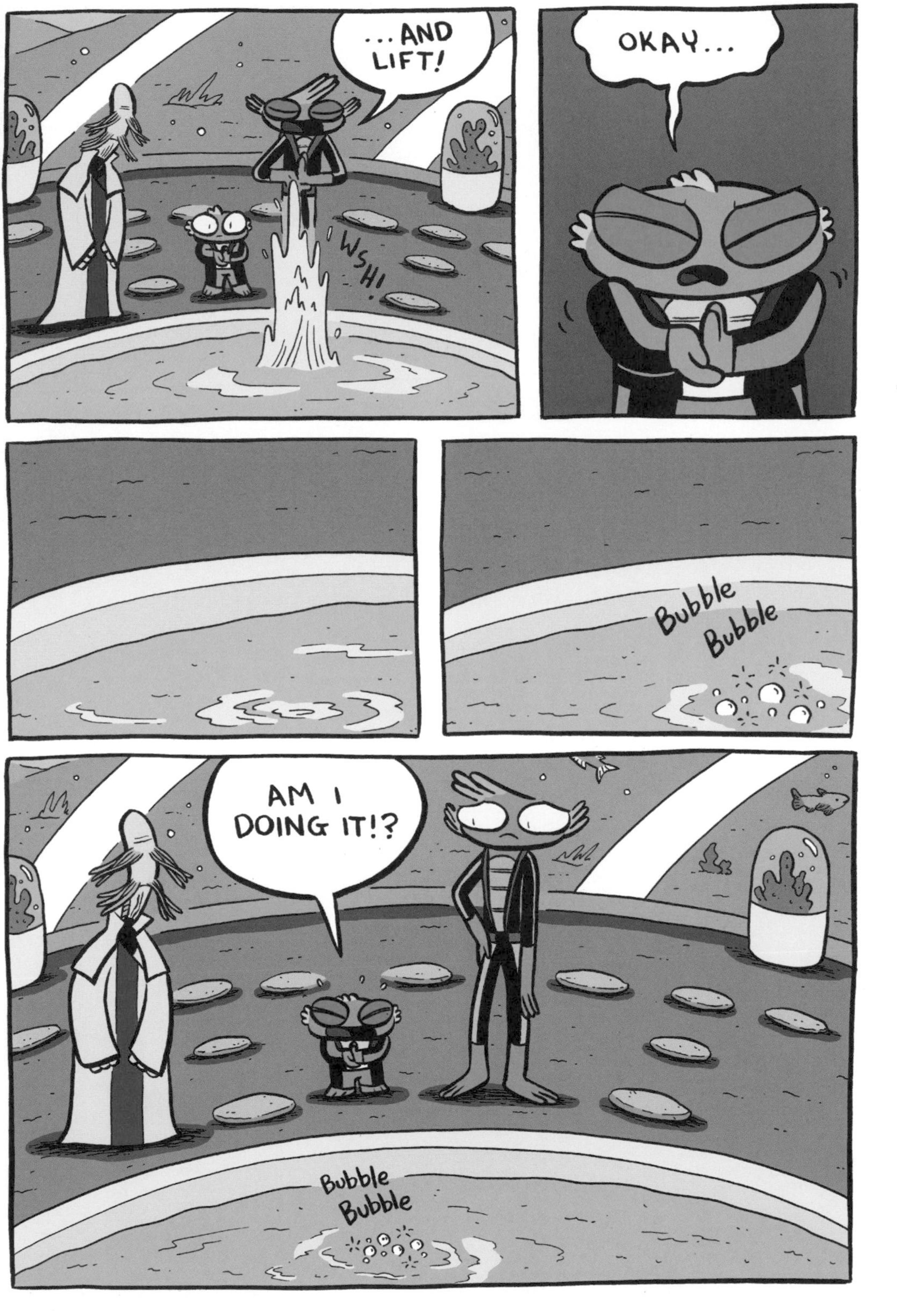
...AND LIFT!
WSH!
OKAY...
Bubble Bubble
AM I DOING IT!?
Bubble Bubble

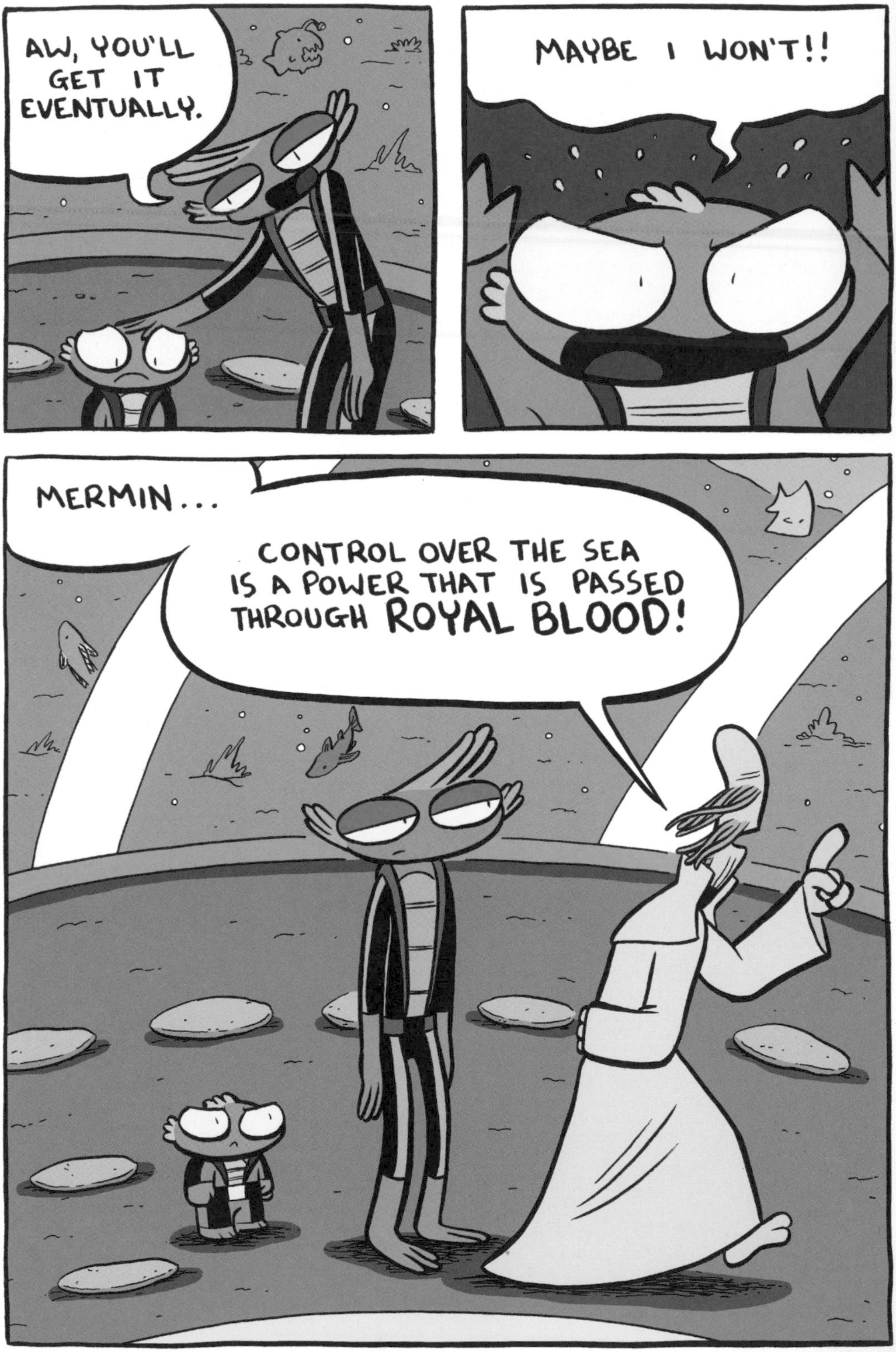
AW, YOU'LL GET IT EVENTUALLY.
MAYBE I WON'T!!
MERMIN...
CONTROL OVER THE SEA IS A POWER THAT IS PASSED THROUGH ROYAL BLOOD!

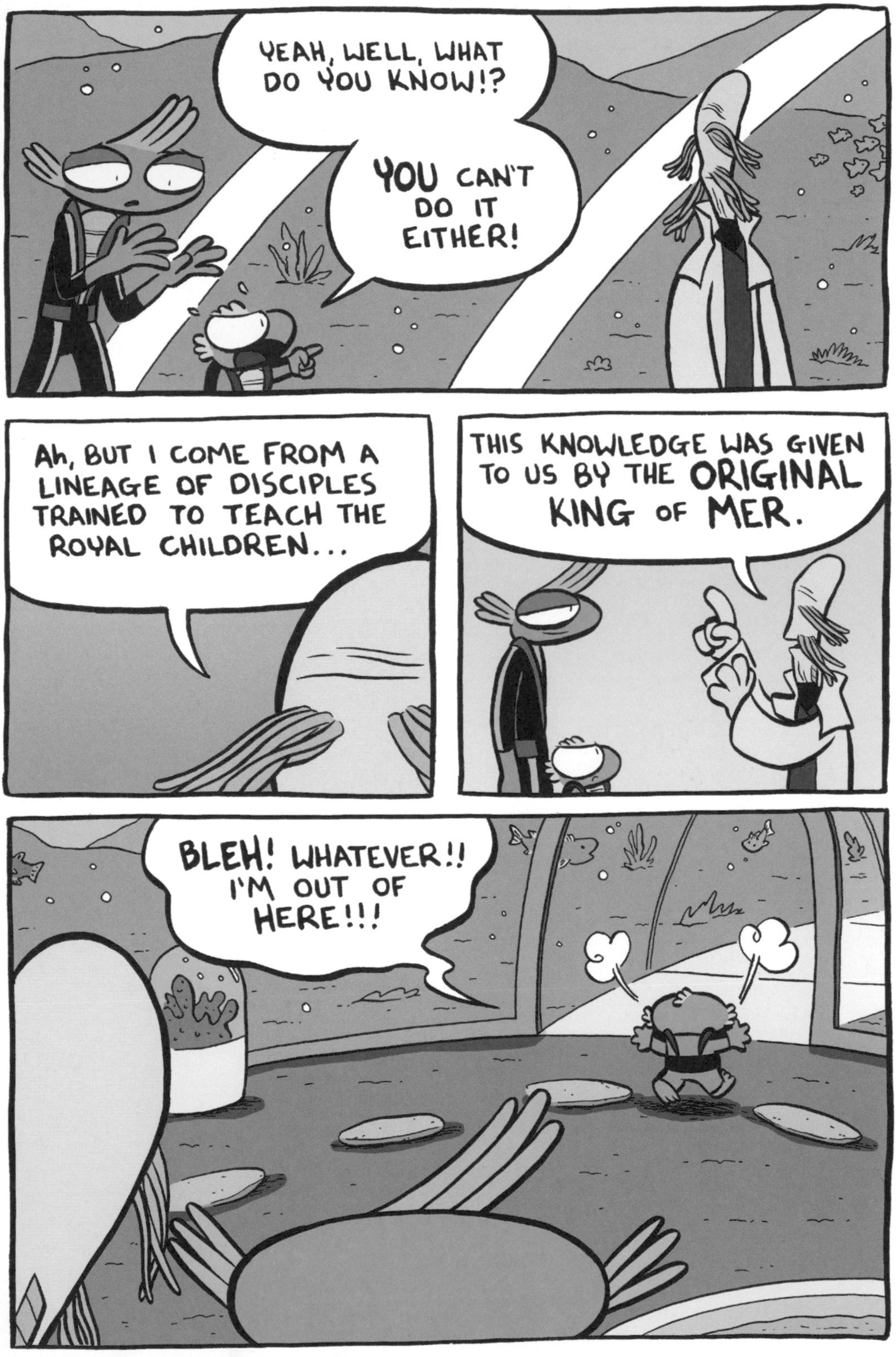
YEAH, WELL, WHAT DO YOU KNOW!?
YOU CAN'T DO IT EITHER!
Ah, BUT I COME FROM A LINEAGE OF DISCIPLES TRAINED TO TEACH THE ROYAL CHILDREN...
THIS KNOWLEDGE WAS GIVEN TO US BY THE ORIGINAL KING OF MER.
BLEH! WHATEVER!! I'M OUT OF HERE!!!

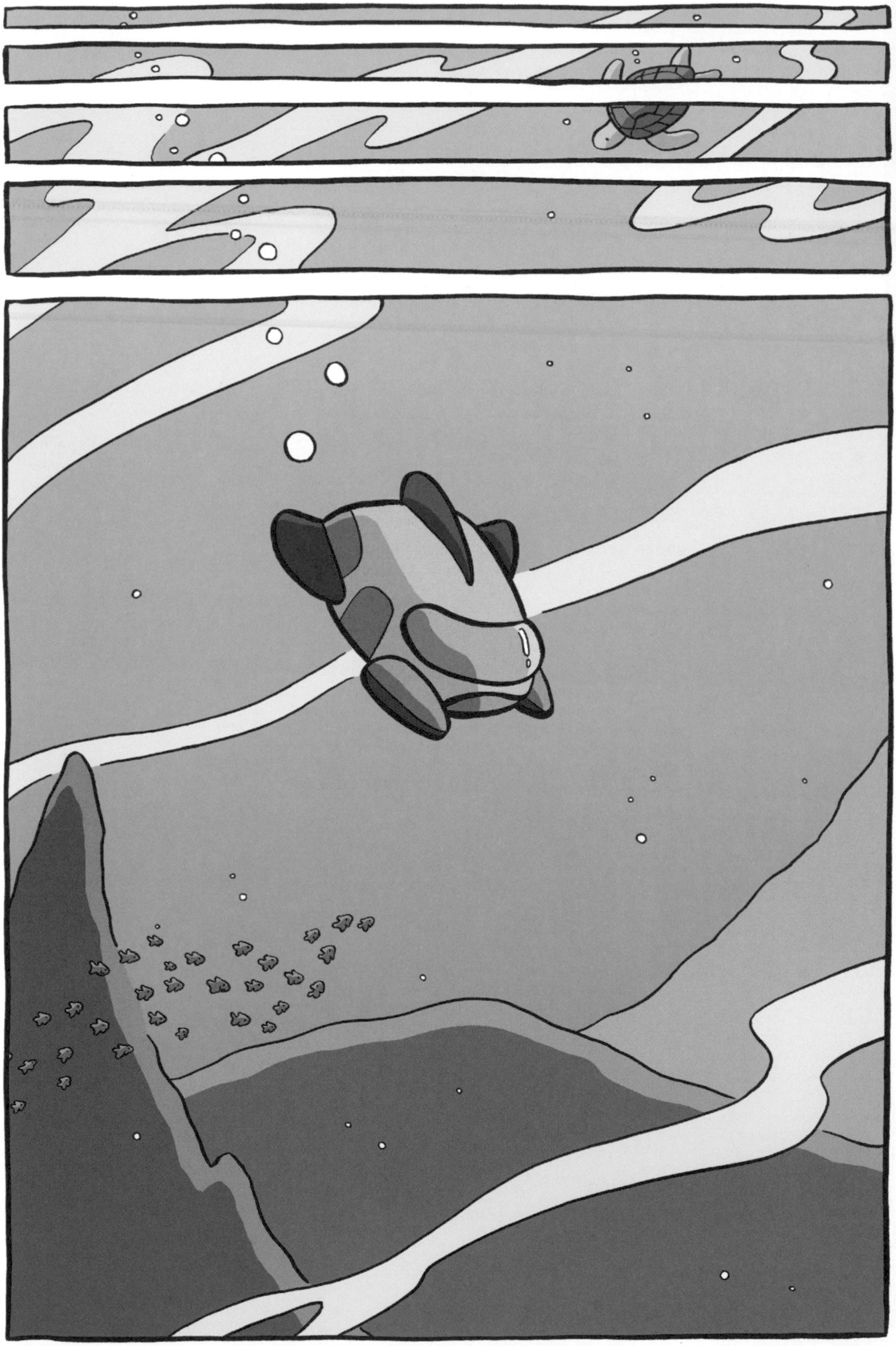

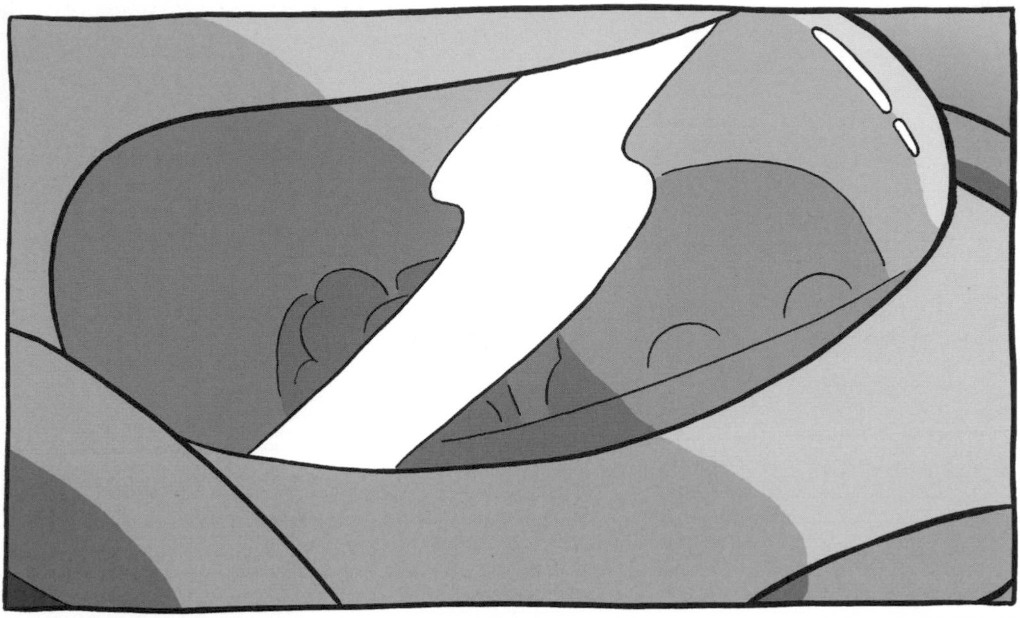

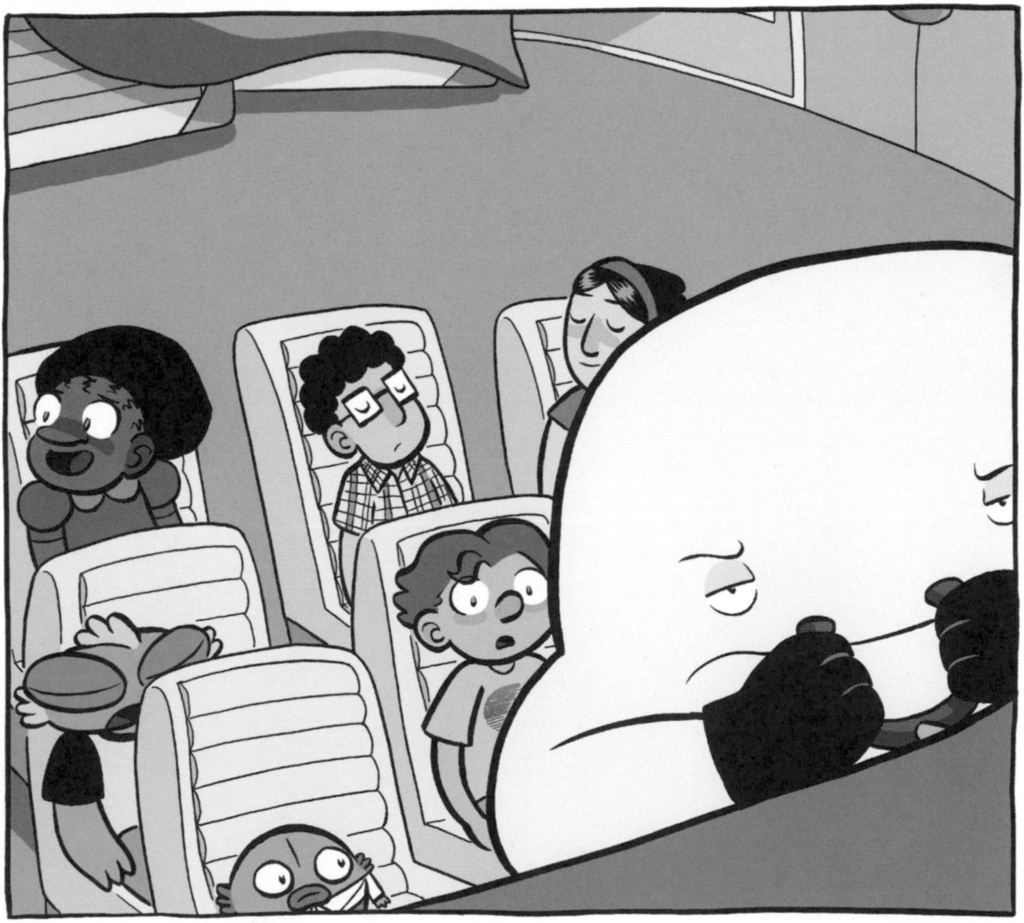

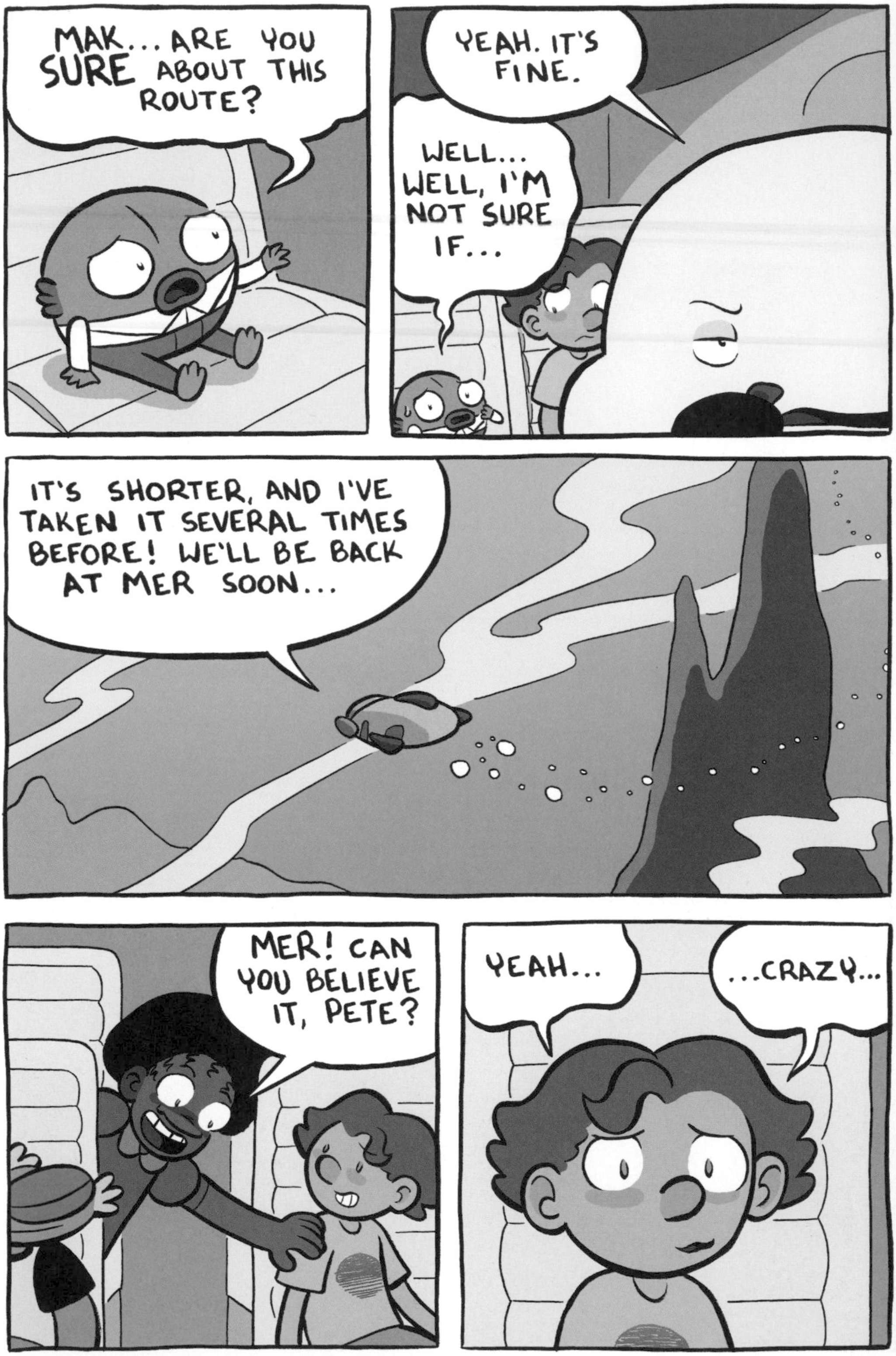
MAK... ARE YOU SURE ABOUT THIS ROUTE?
YEAH. IT'S FINE.
WELL... WELL, I'M NOT SURE IF...
IT'S SHORTER, AND I'VE TAKEN IT SEVERAL TIMES BEFORE! WE'LL BE BACK AT MER SOON...
MER! CAN YOU BELIEVE IT, PETE?
YEAH...
...CRAZY...

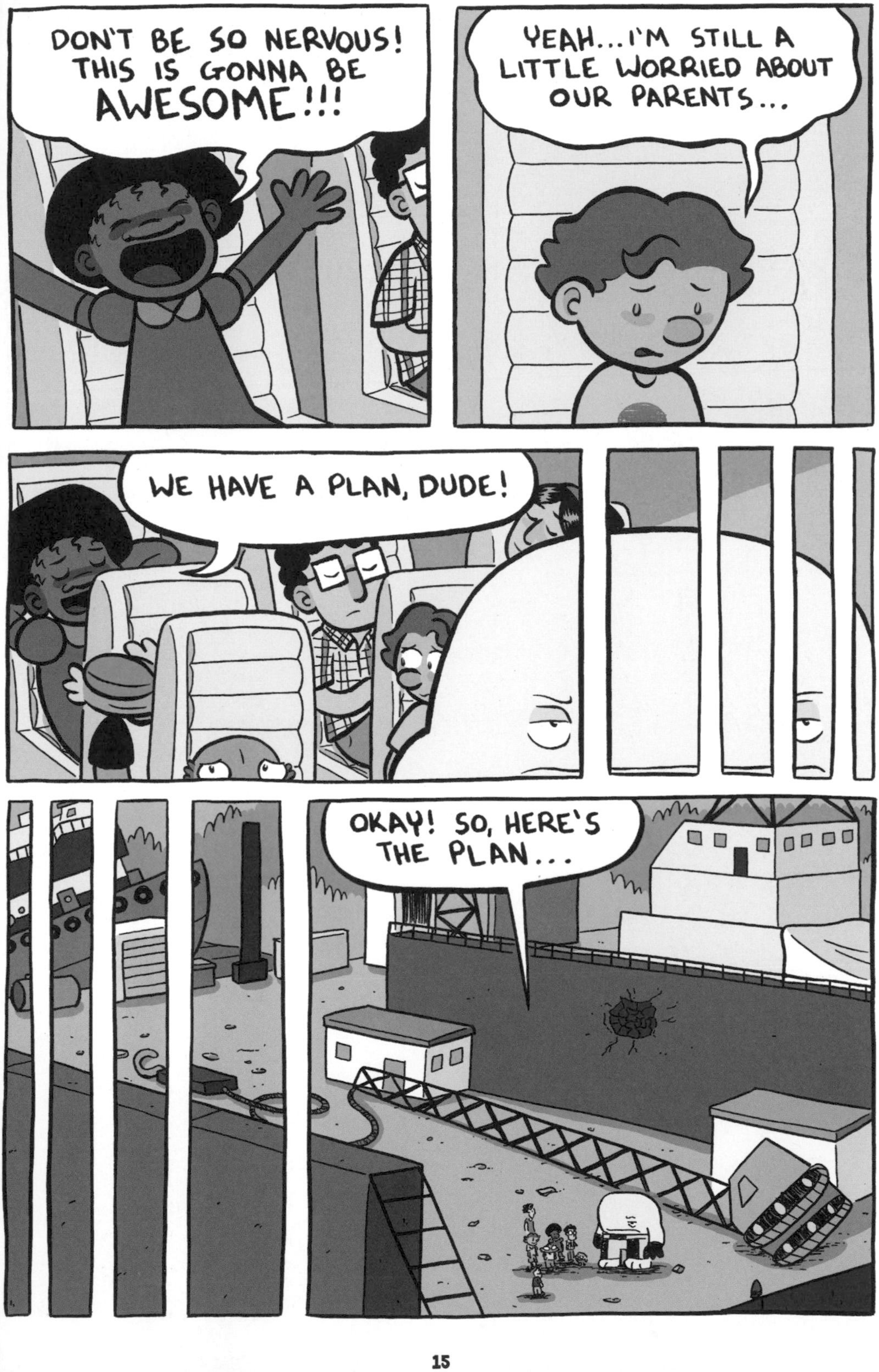
DON'T BE SO NERVOUS! THIS IS GONNA BE AWESOME!!!
YEAH...I'M STILL A LITTLE WORRIED ABOUT OUR PARENTS...
WE HAVE A PLAN, DUDE!
OKAY! SO, HERE'S THE PLAN...

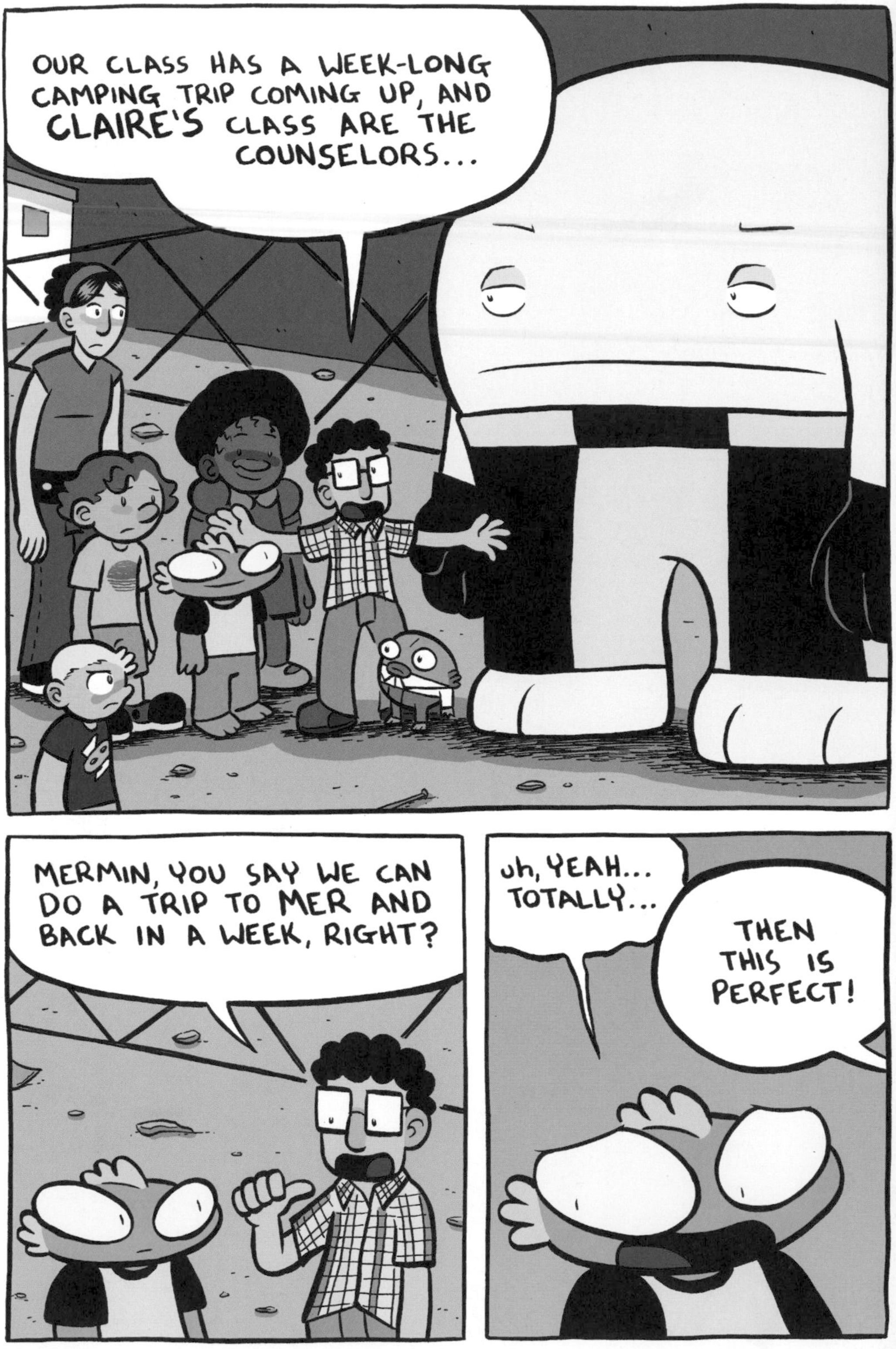
OUR CLASS HAS A WEEK-LONG CAMPING TRIP COMING UP, AND CLAIRE'S CLASS ARE THE COUNSELORS...
MERMIN, YOU SAY WE CAN DO A TRIP TO MER AND BACK IN A WEEK, RIGHT?
uh, YEAH... TOTALLY...
THEN THIS IS PERFECT!

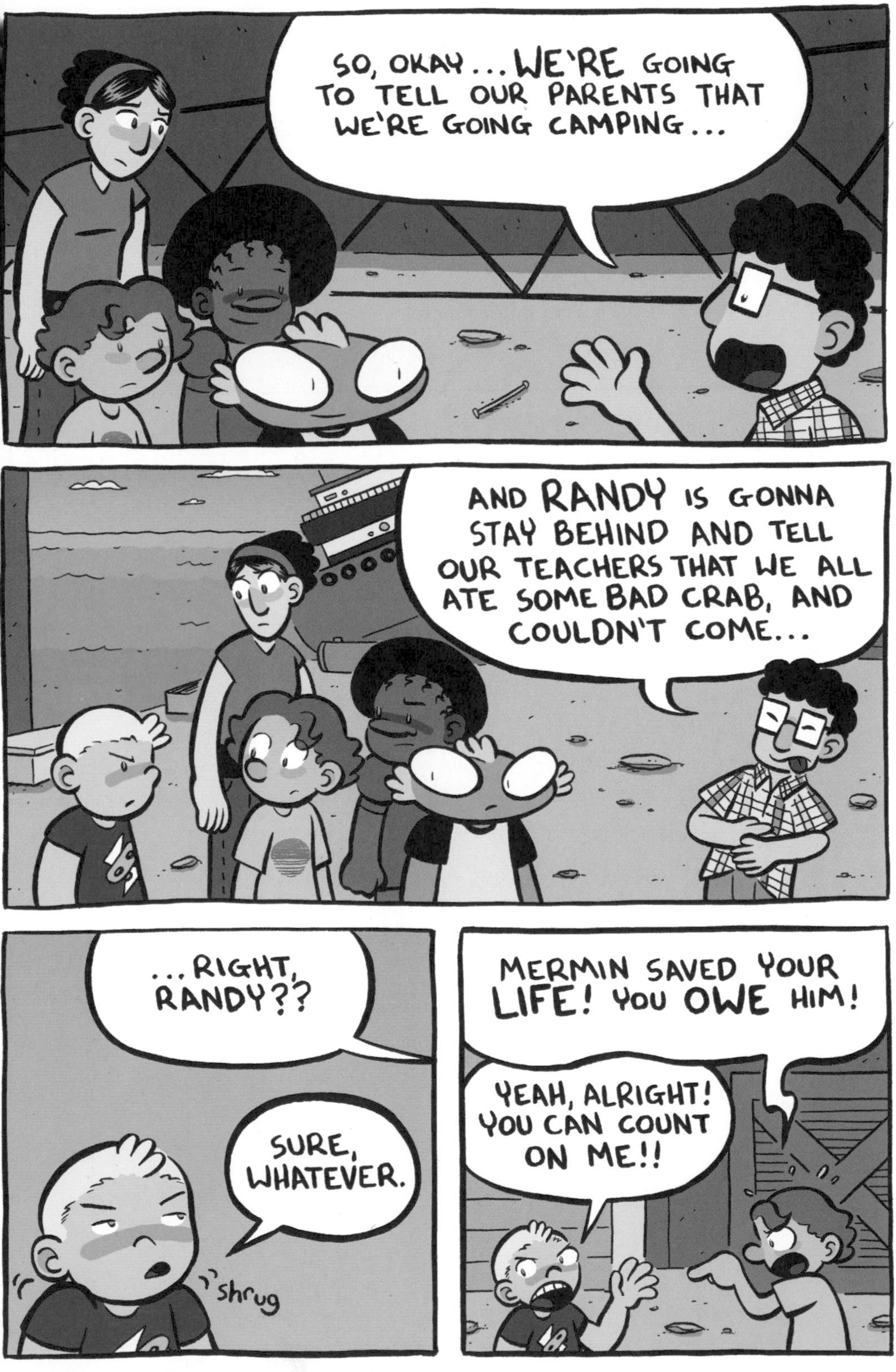
SO, OKAY... WE'RE GOING TO TELL OUR PARENTS THAT WE'RE GOING CAMPING...
AND RANDY IS GONNA STAY BEHIND AND TELL OUR TEACHERS THAT WE ALL ATE SOME BAD CRAB, AND COULDN'T COME...
...RIGHT, RANDY??
SURE, WHATEVER.
shrug
MERMIN SAVED YOUR LIFE! YOU OWE HIM!
YEAH, ALRIGHT! YOU CAN COUNT ON ME!!

I DON'T KNOW... THIS PLAN SOUNDS PRETTY SHAKY TO ME...

A-AND...I...I DON'T THINK IT'S A GOOD IDEA TO BRING HUMANS DOWN TO MER KINGDOM...

AW, C'MON YOU GUYS!!

ALL I NEED TO DO IS GO DOWN AND TALK TO MY **DAD** REAL QUICK--

YOU MEAN THE KING OF MER.

YEAH! YEAH! WE PROBABLY WON'T TAKE THE WHOLE WEEK!! IT'LL BE **FINE**!!!

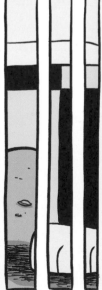

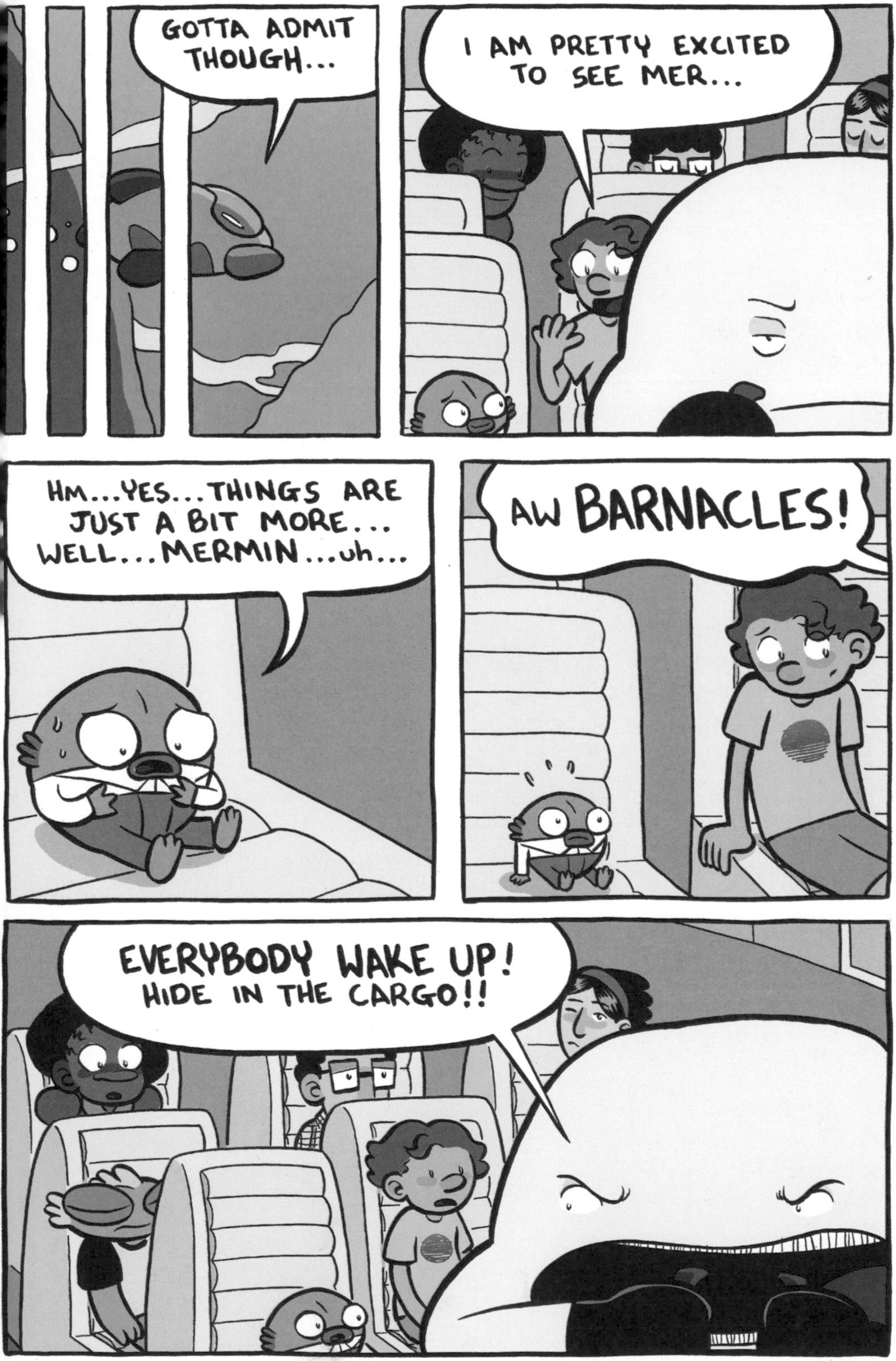
GOTTA ADMIT THOUGH...
I AM PRETTY EXCITED TO SEE MER...
HM...YES...THINGS ARE JUST A BIT MORE... WELL...MERMIN...uh...
AW BARNACLES!
EVERYBODY WAKE UP! HIDE IN THE CARGO!!

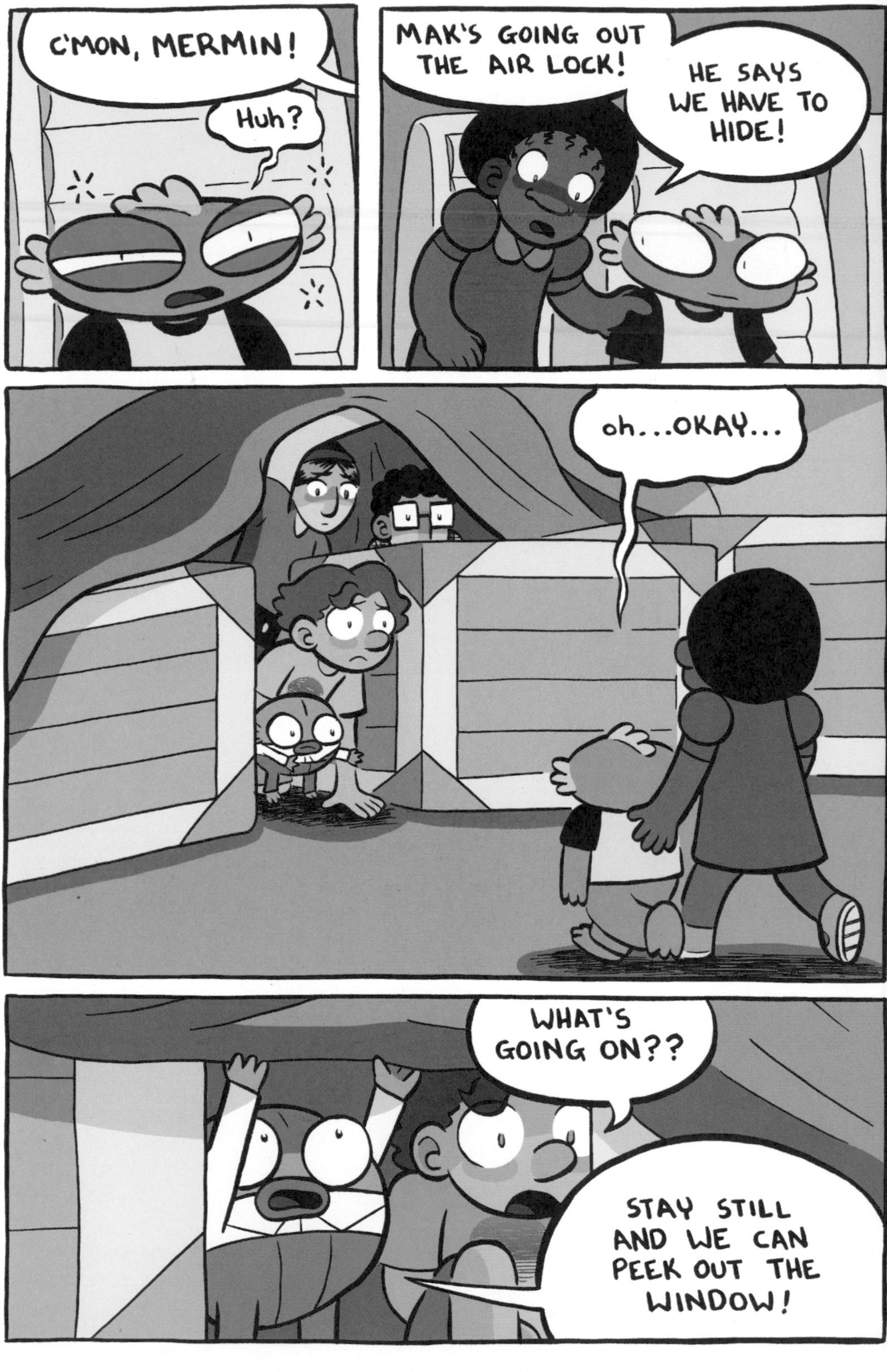
C'MON, MERMIN!
Huh?
MAK'S GOING OUT THE AIR LOCK!
HE SAYS WE HAVE TO HIDE!
oh...OKAY...
WHAT'S GOING ON??
STAY STILL AND WE CAN PEEK OUT THE WINDOW!

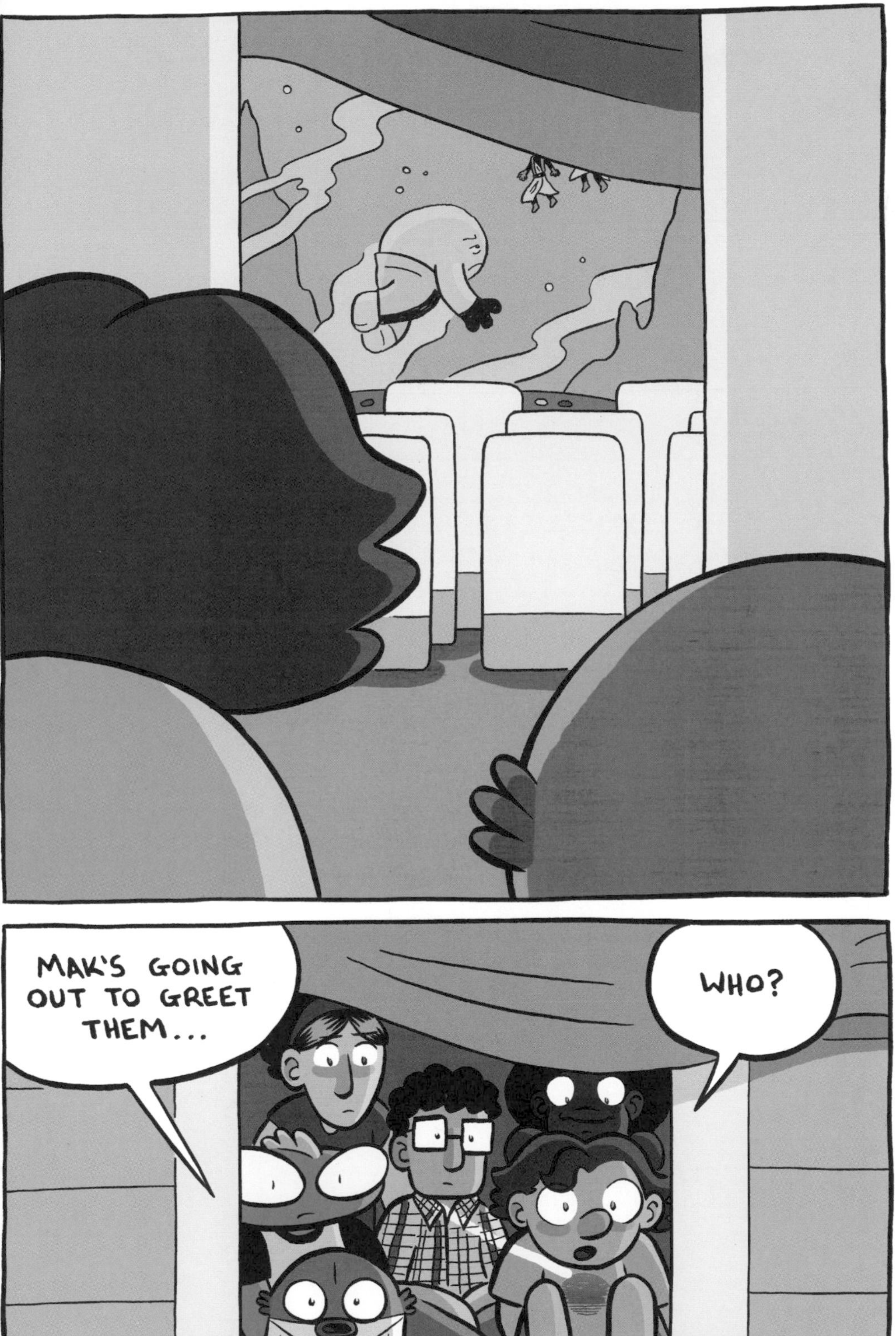
MAK'S GOING OUT TO GREET THEM...
WHO?

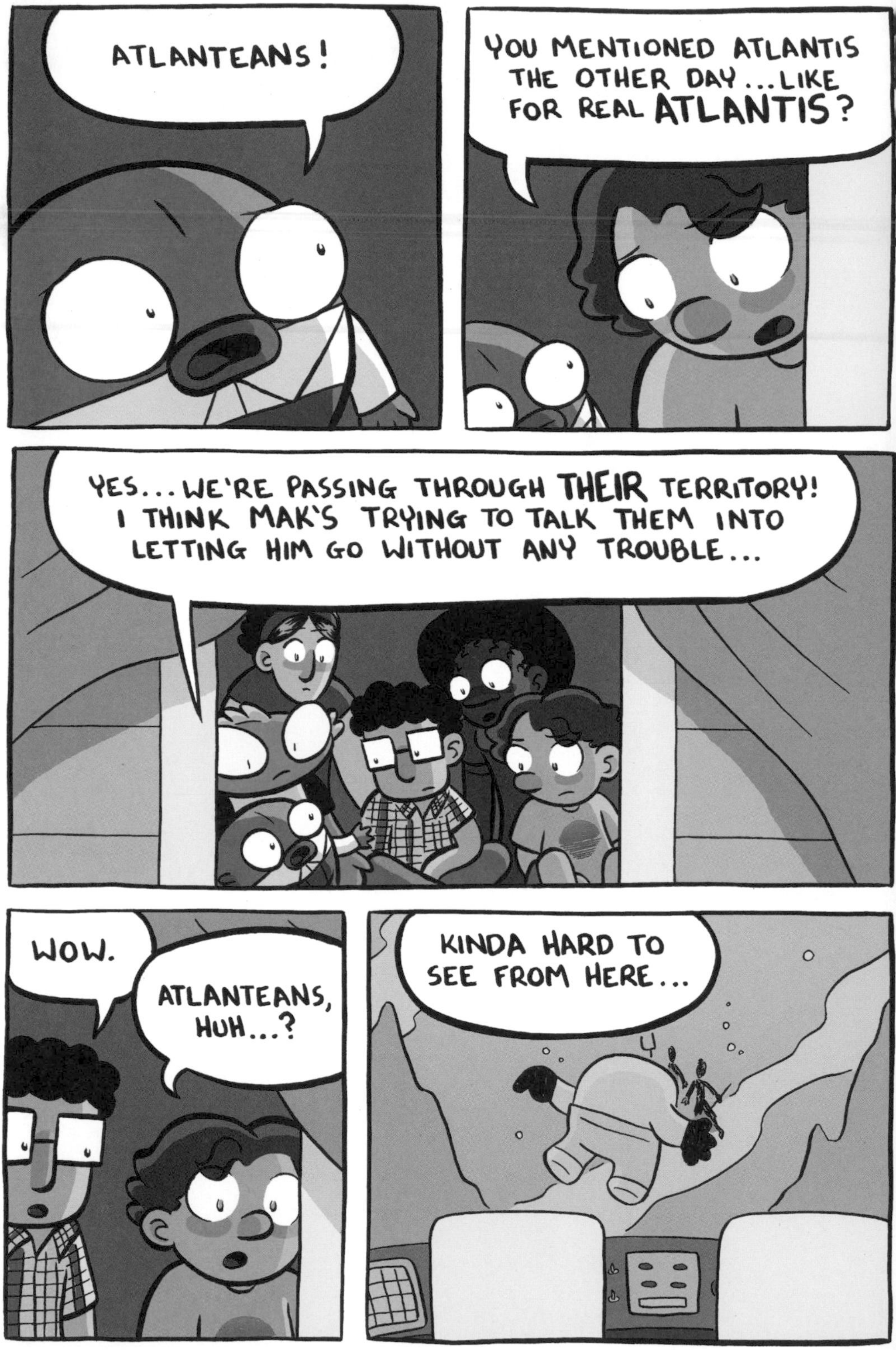
ATLANTEANS!
YOU MENTIONED ATLANTIS THE OTHER DAY...LIKE FOR REAL ATLANTIS?
YES...WE'RE PASSING THROUGH THEIR TERRITORY! I THINK MAK'S TRYING TO TALK THEM INTO LETTING HIM GO WITHOUT ANY TROUBLE...
WOW.
ATLANTEANS, HUH...?
KINDA HARD TO SEE FROM HERE...

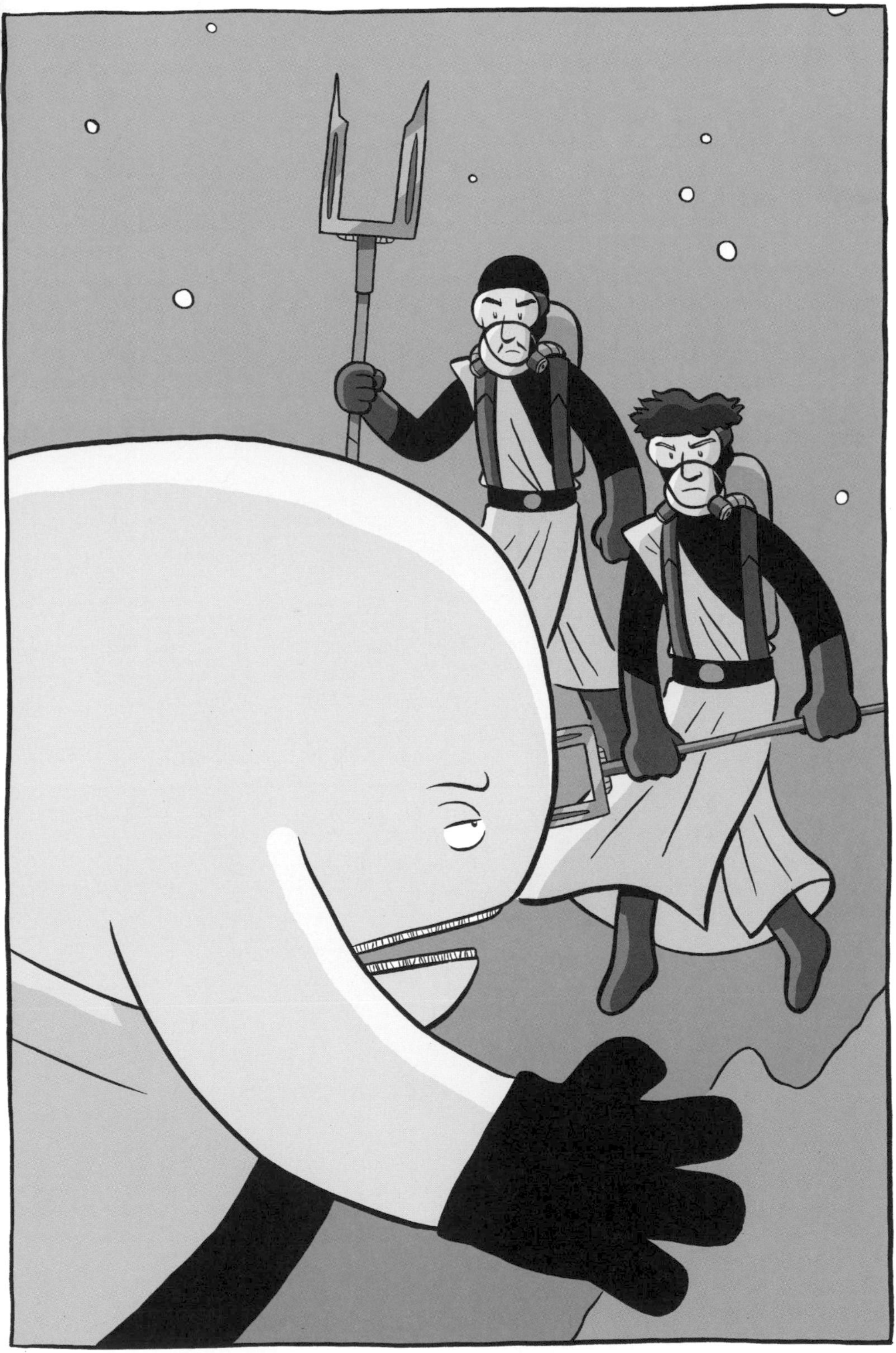

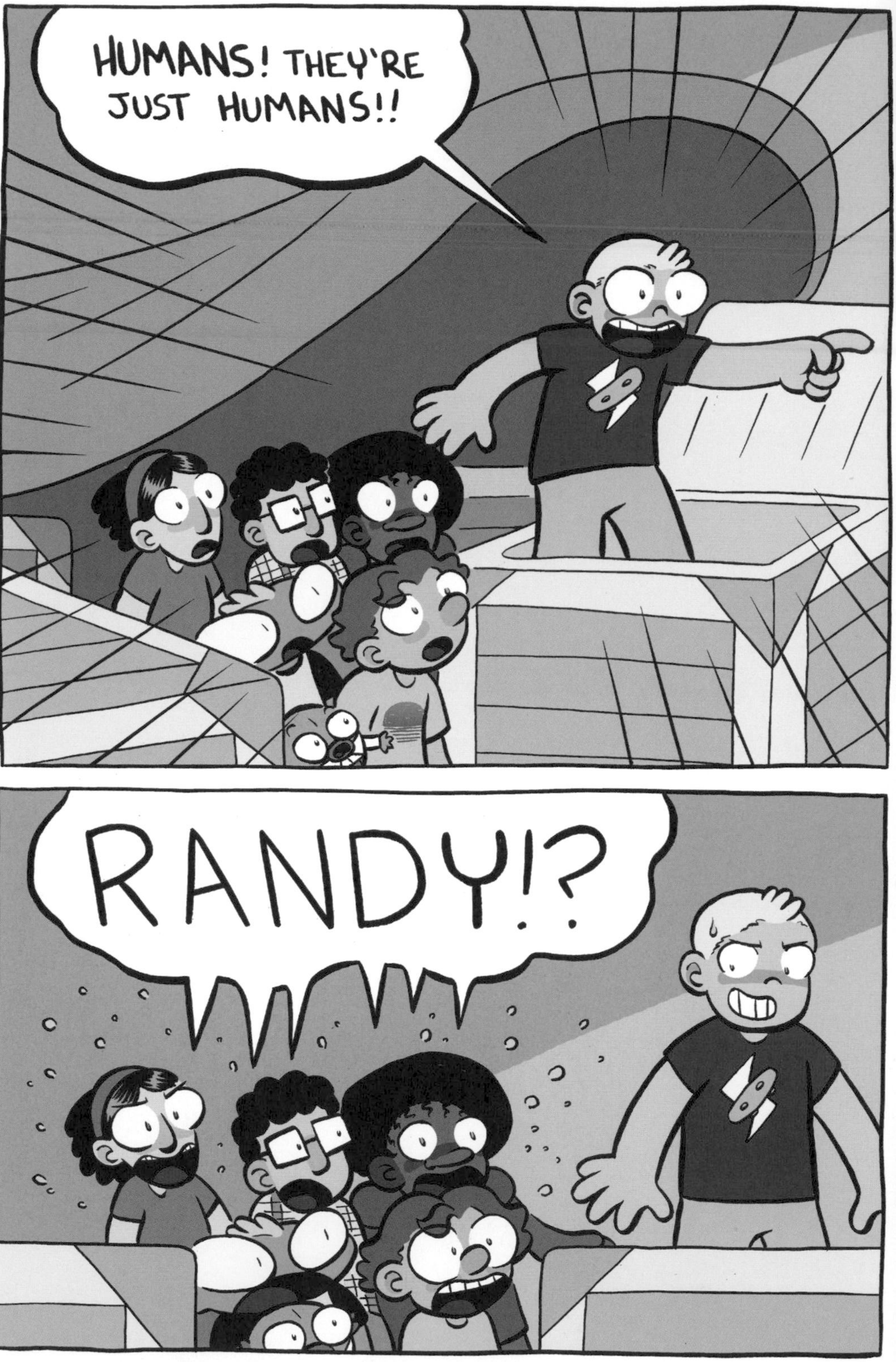
HUMANS! THEY'RE JUST HUMANS!!
RANDY!?

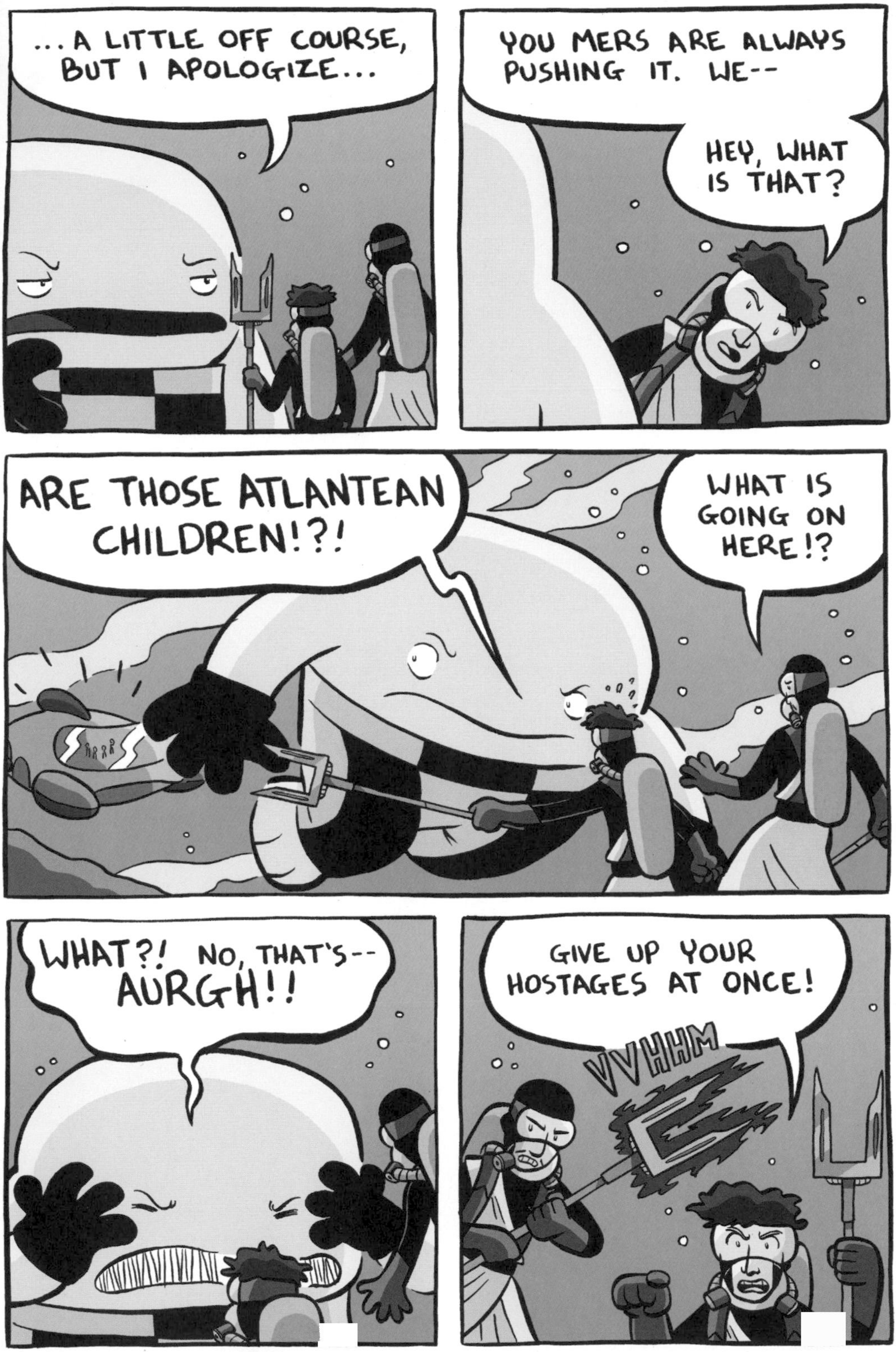
...A LITTLE OFF COURSE, BUT I APOLOGIZE...
YOU MERS ARE ALWAYS PUSHING IT. WE--
HEY, WHAT IS THAT?
ARE THOSE ATLANTEAN CHILDREN!?!
WHAT IS GOING ON HERE!?
WHAT?! NO, THAT'S-- AURGH!!
GIVE UP YOUR HOSTAGES AT ONCE!
VVHHHM

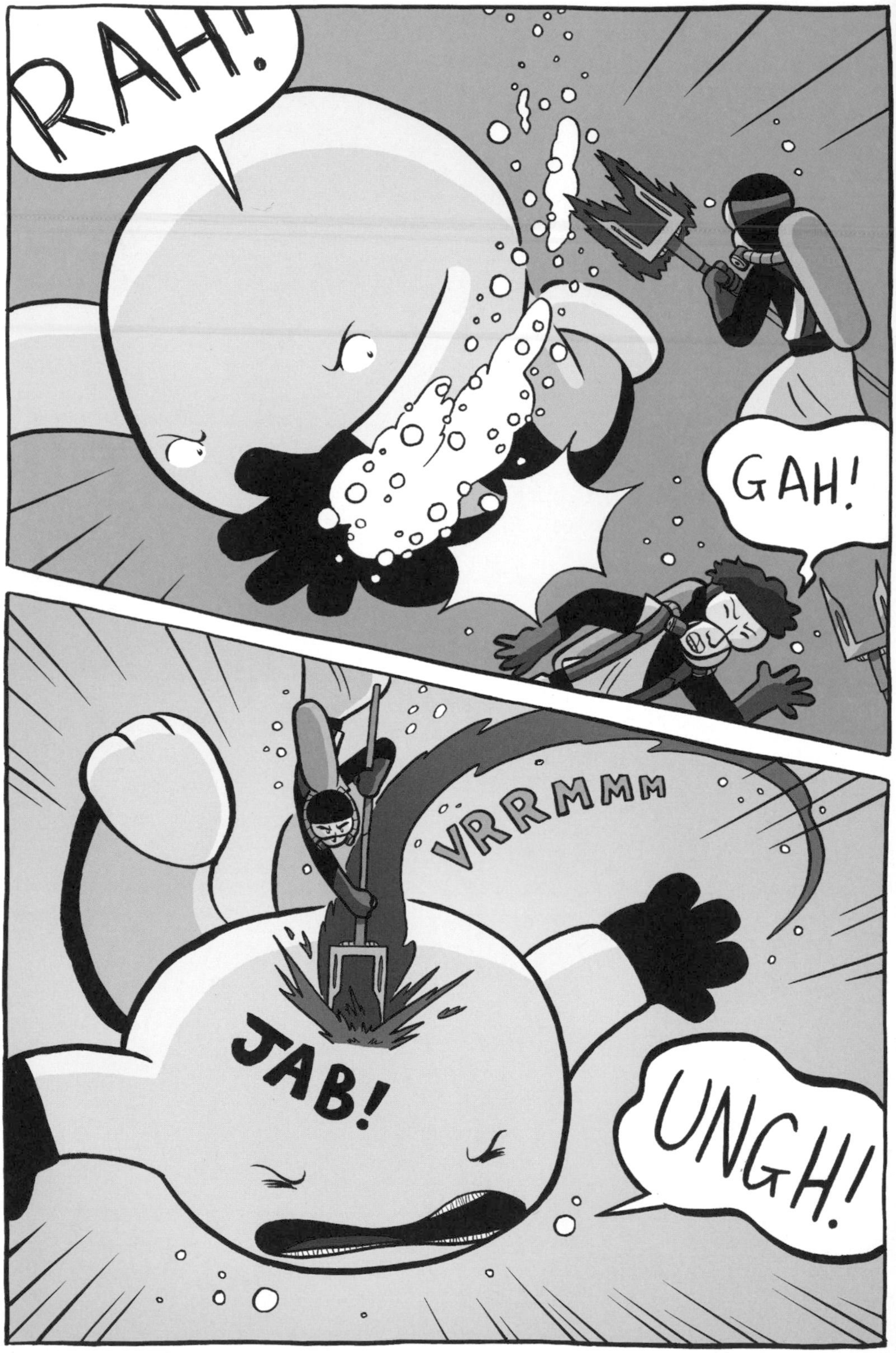
RAH!
GAH!
VRRMMM
JAB!
UNGH!

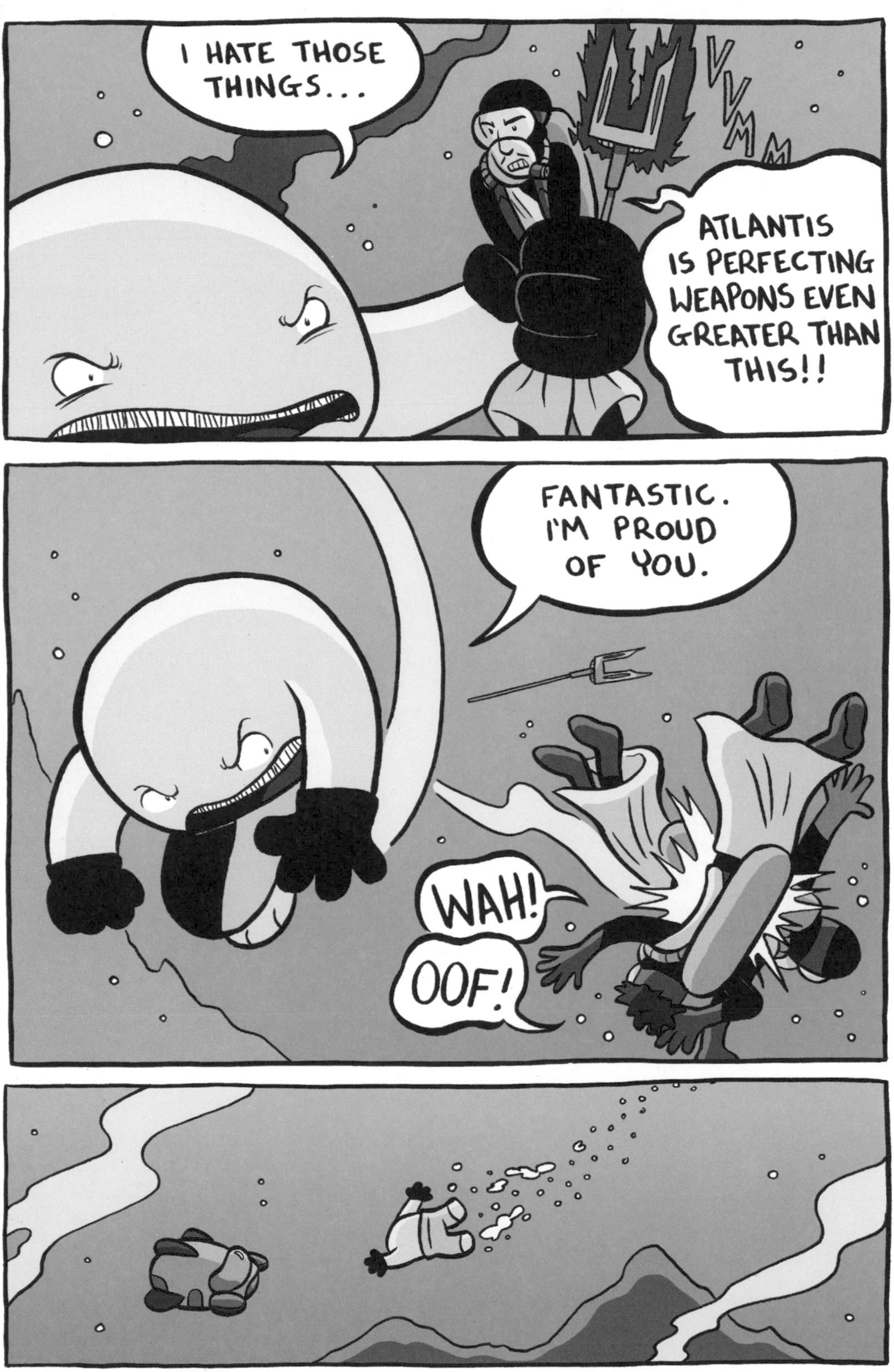
I HATE THOSE THINGS...
VVMM
ATLANTIS IS PERFECTING WEAPONS EVEN GREATER THAN THIS!!
FANTASTIC. I'M PROUD OF YOU.
WAH!
OOF!

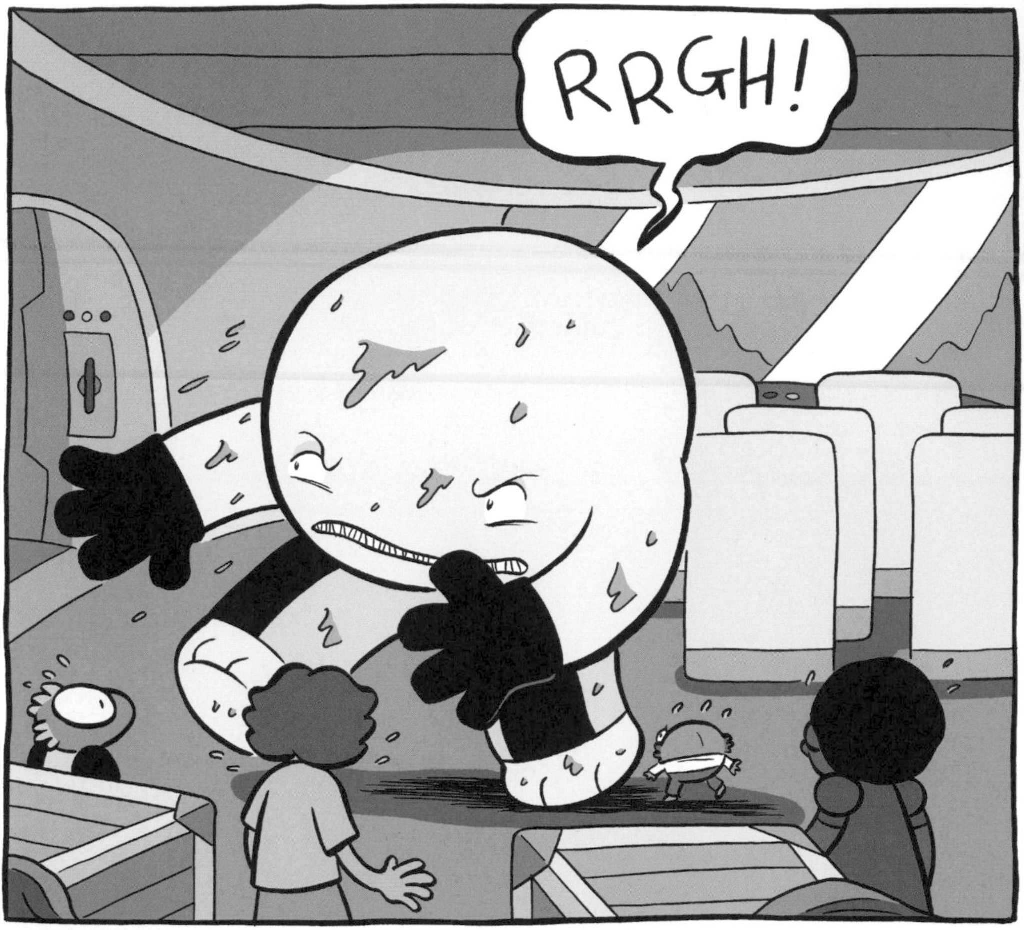
RRGH!

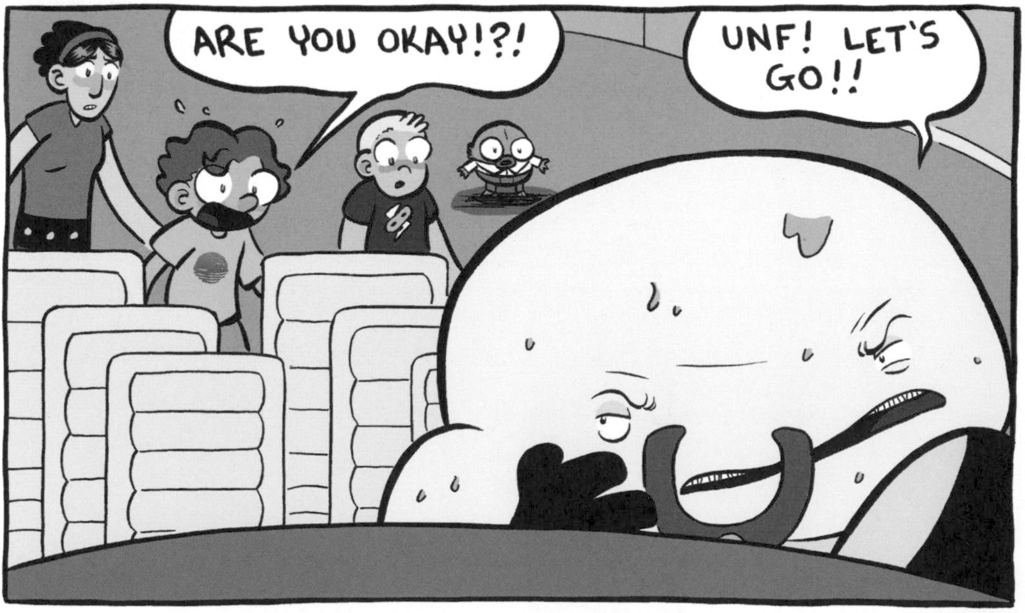
ARE YOU OKAY!?!
UNF! LET'S GO!!

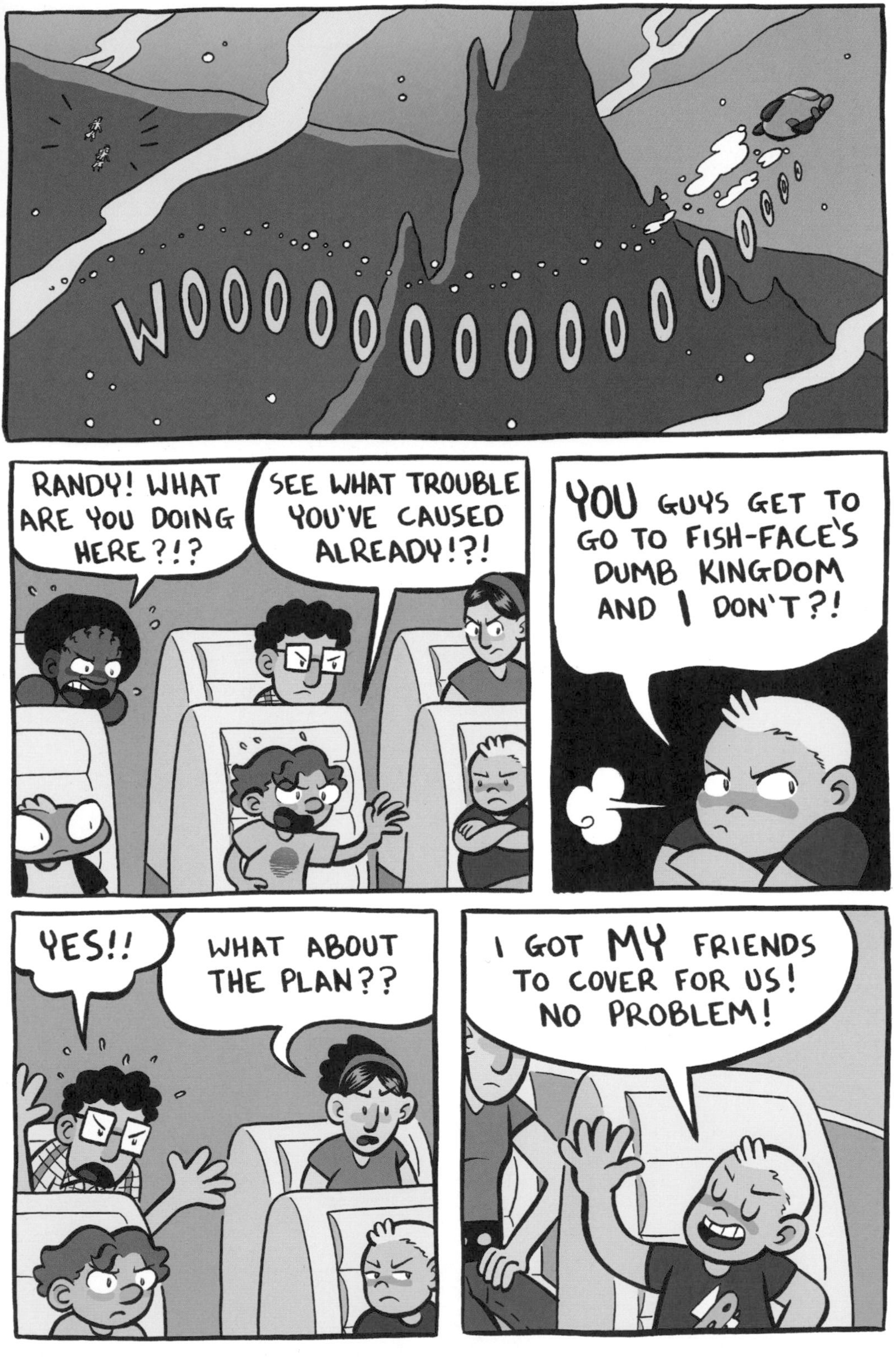
WOOOOOOOOOOOOOOOOO
RANDY! WHAT ARE YOU DOING HERE?!?
SEE WHAT TROUBLE YOU'VE CAUSED ALREADY!?!
YOU GUYS GET TO GO TO FISH-FACE'S DUMB KINGDOM AND I DON'T?!
YES!!
WHAT ABOUT THE PLAN??
I GOT MY FRIENDS TO COVER FOR US! NO PROBLEM!

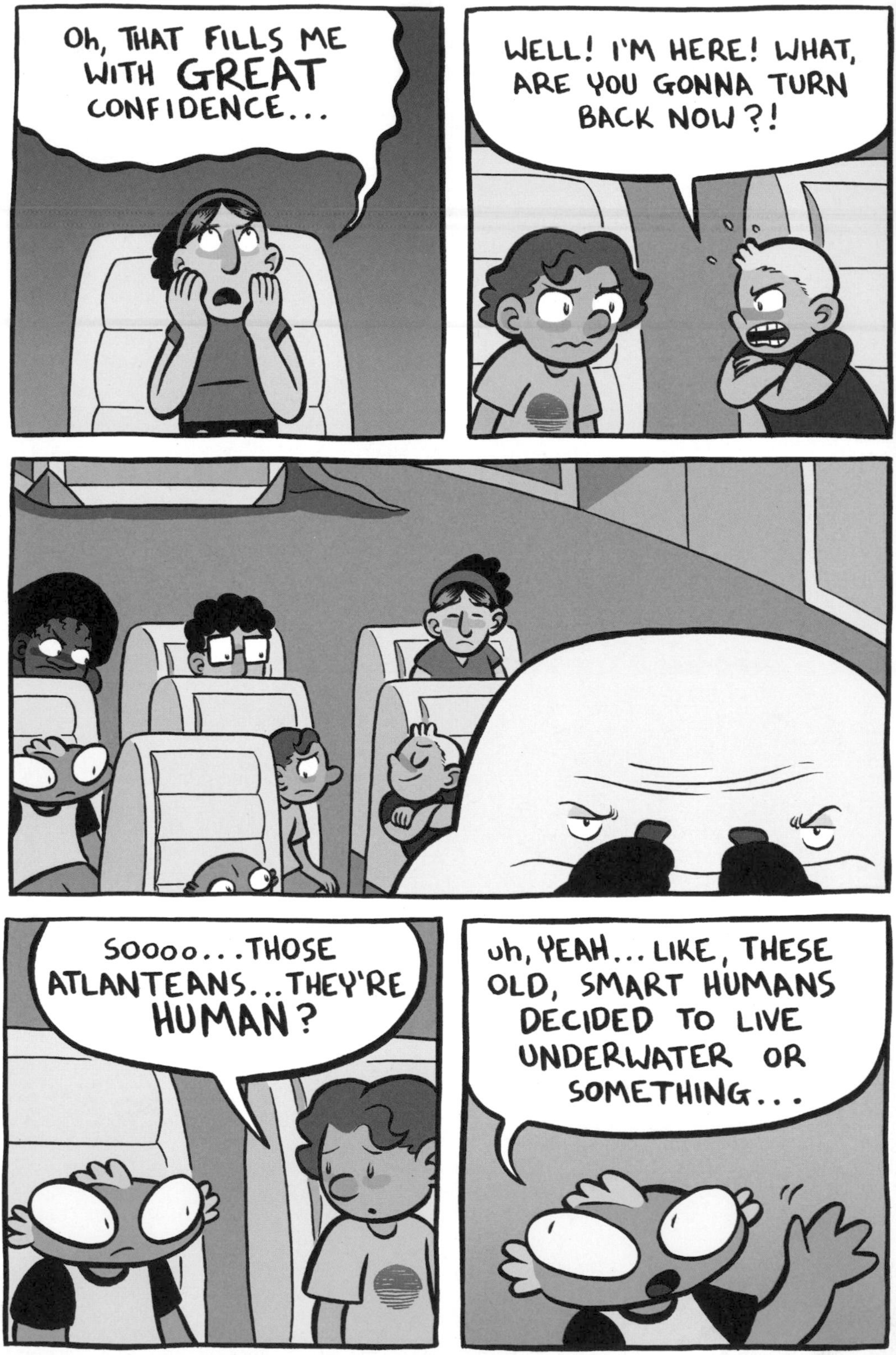

Oh, THAT FILLS ME WITH GREAT CONFIDENCE...
WELL! I'M HERE! WHAT, ARE YOU GONNA TURN BACK NOW?!
SOOOO...THOSE ATLANTEANS...THEY'RE HUMAN?
uh, YEAH... LIKE, THESE OLD, SMART HUMANS DECIDED TO LIVE UNDERWATER OR SOMETHING...

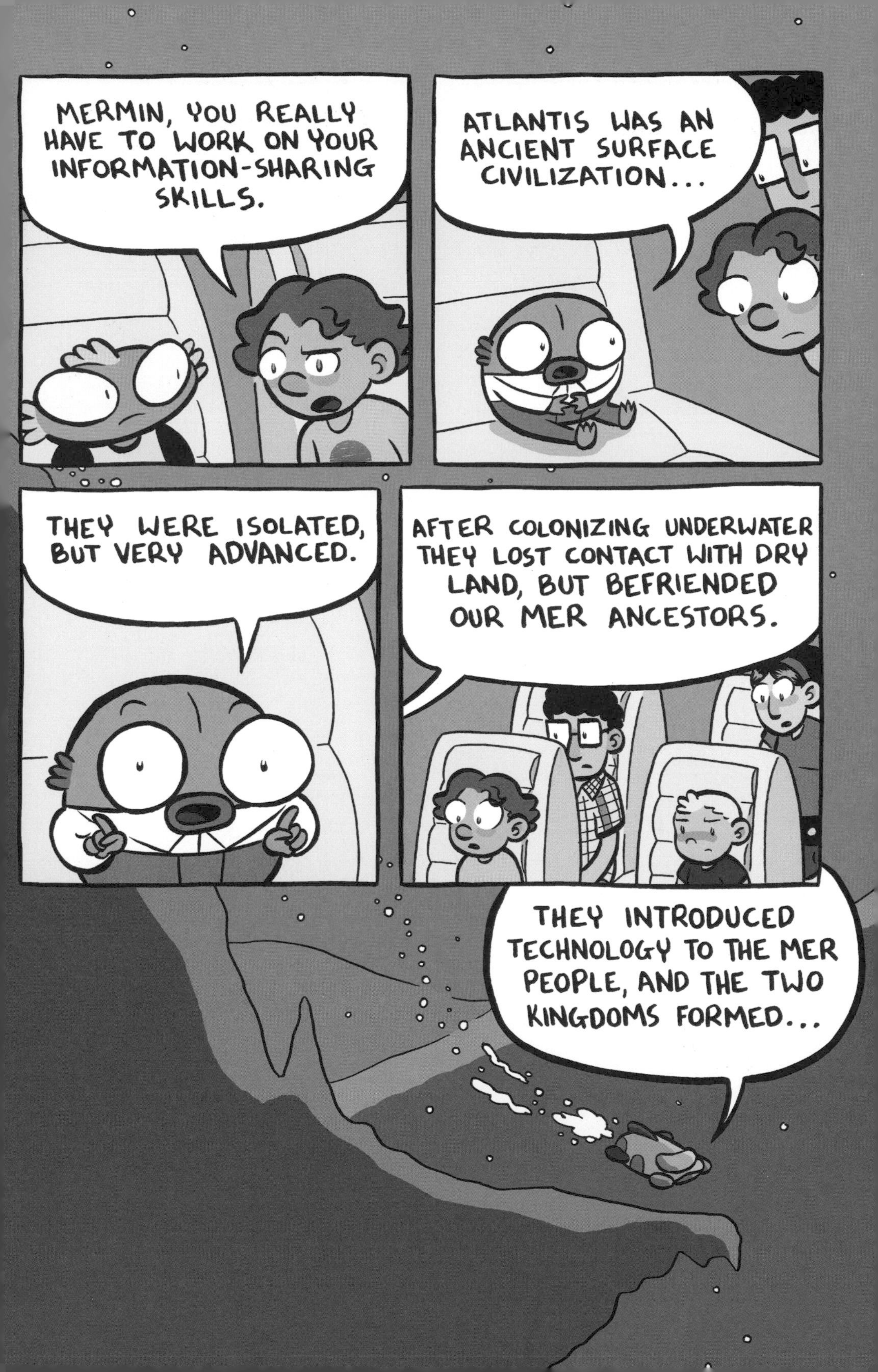
MERMIN, YOU REALLY HAVE TO WORK ON YOUR INFORMATION-SHARING SKILLS.
ATLANTIS WAS AN ANCIENT SURFACE CIVILIZATION...
THEY WERE ISOLATED, BUT VERY ADVANCED.
AFTER COLONIZING UNDERWATER THEY LOST CONTACT WITH DRY LAND, BUT BEFRIENDED OUR MER ANCESTORS.
THEY INTRODUCED TECHNOLOGY TO THE MER PEOPLE, AND THE TWO KINGDOMS FORMED...

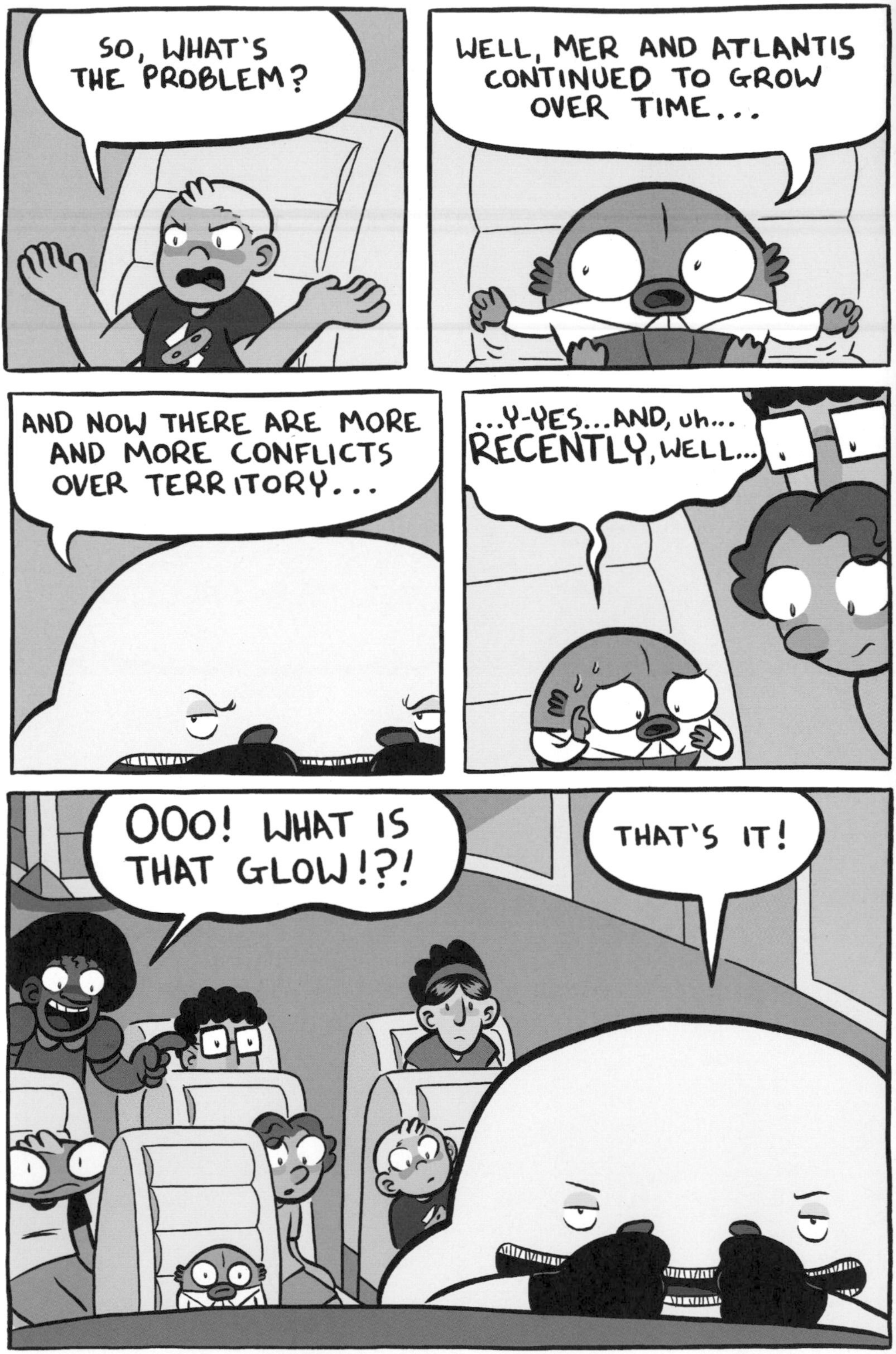
SO, WHAT'S THE PROBLEM?
WELL, MER AND ATLANTIS CONTINUED TO GROW OVER TIME...
AND NOW THERE ARE MORE AND MORE CONFLICTS OVER TERRITORY...
...Y-YES...AND, uh... RECENTLY, WELL...
OOO! WHAT IS THAT GLOW!?!
THAT'S IT!

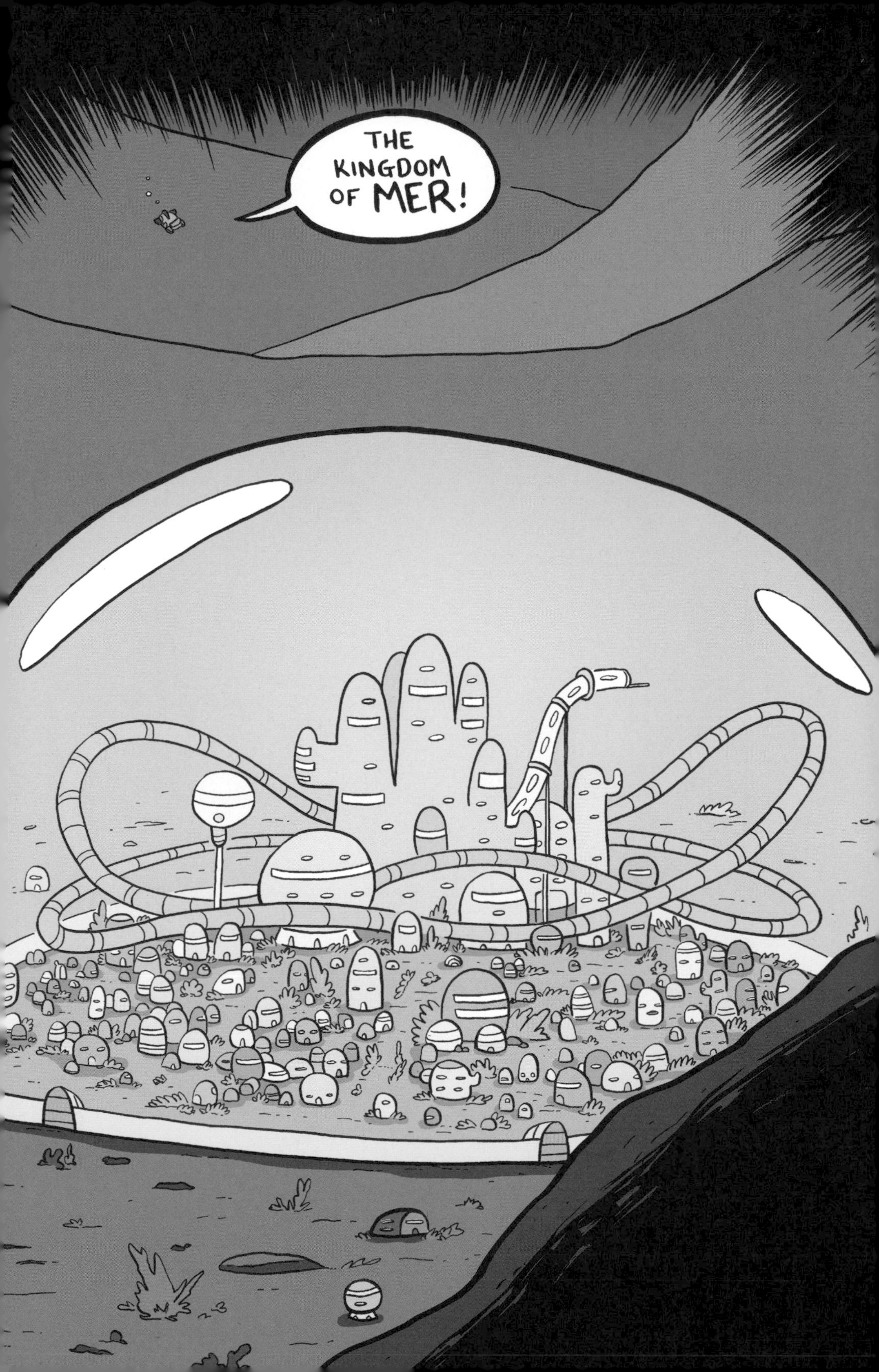
THE KINGDOM OF MER!

CHAPTER TWO

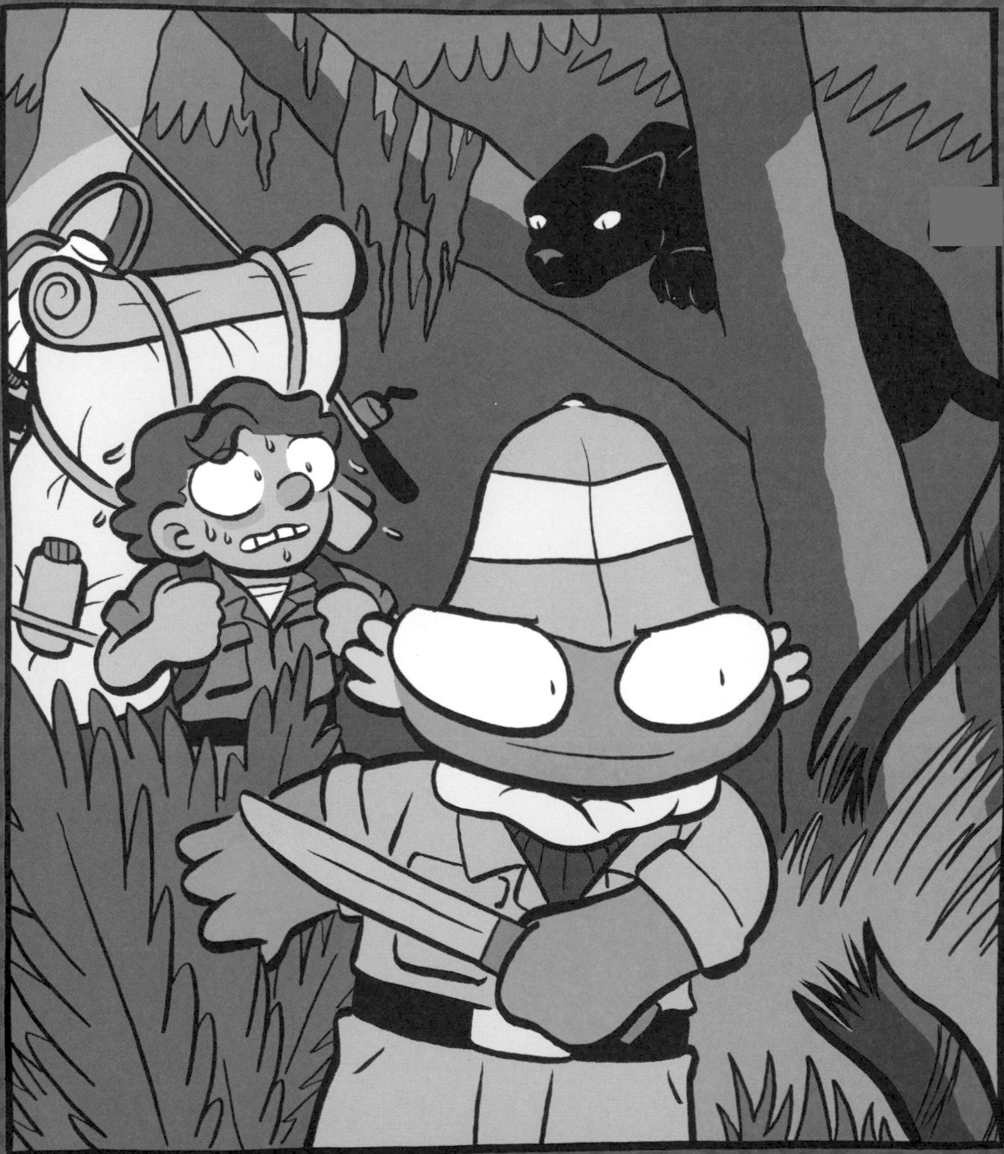

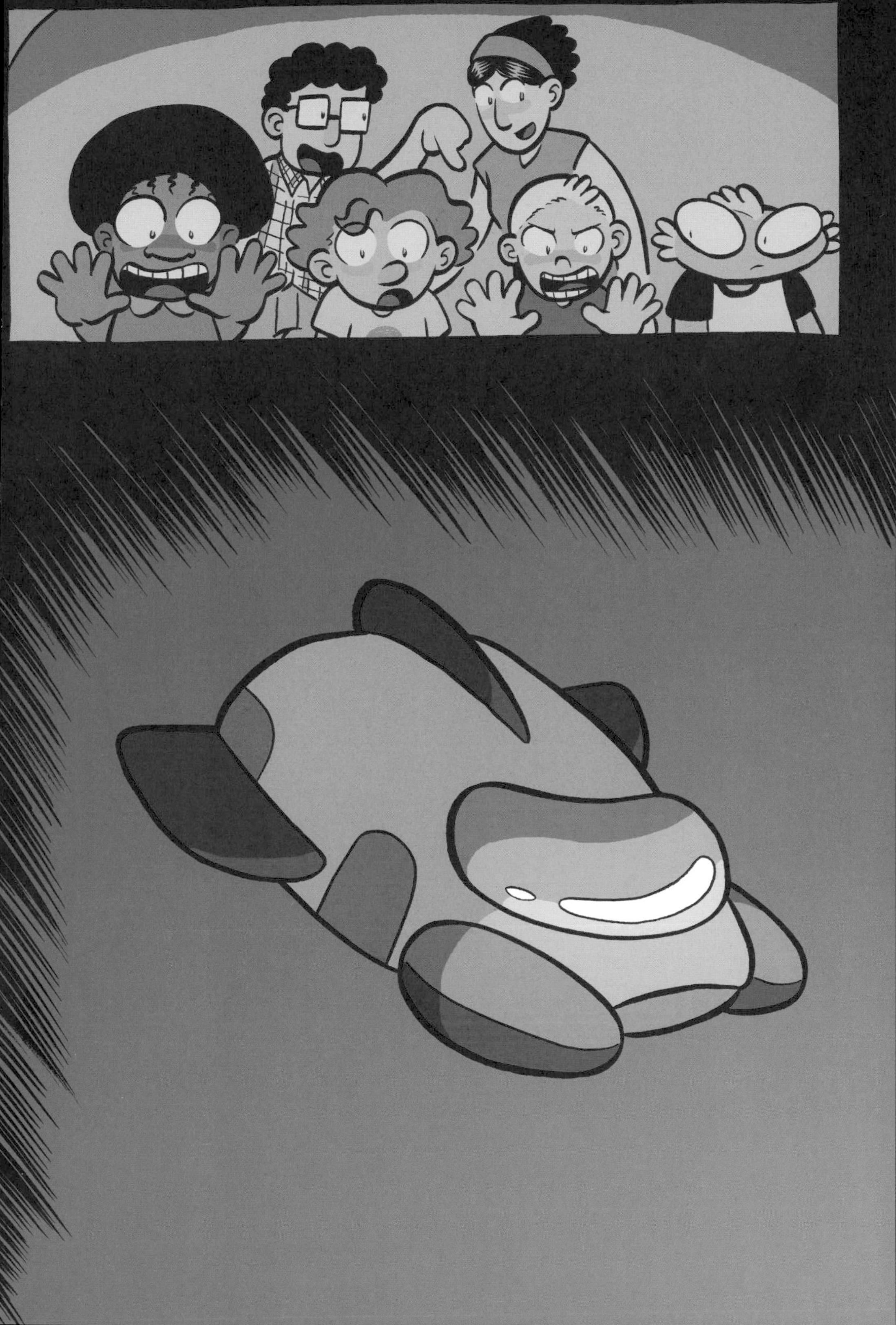

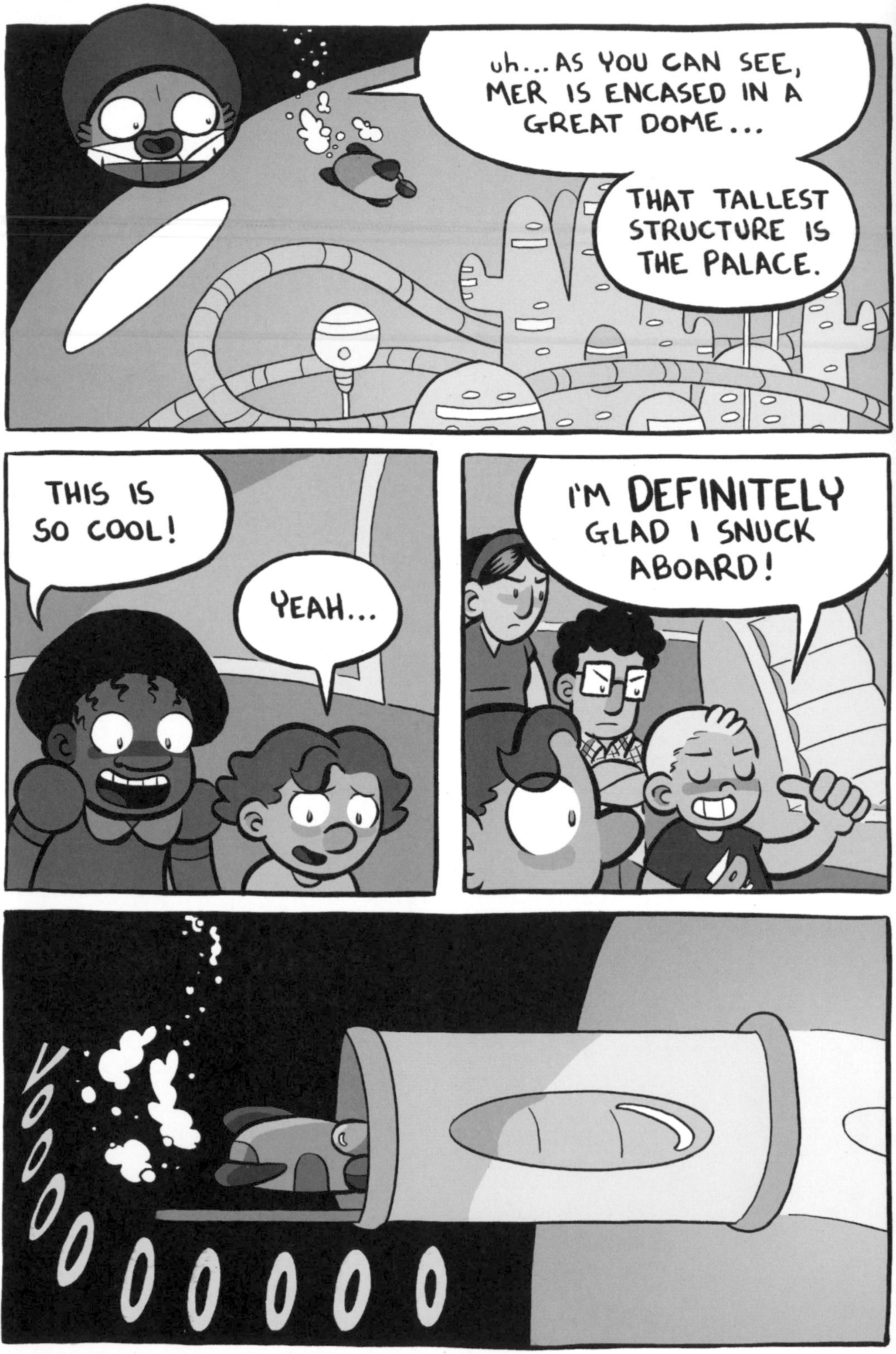
uh... AS YOU CAN SEE, MER IS ENCASED IN A GREAT DOME...
THAT TALLEST STRUCTURE IS THE PALACE.
THIS IS SO COOL!
YEAH...
I'M DEFINITELY GLAD I SNUCK ABOARD!
VOOOOOOOOOO

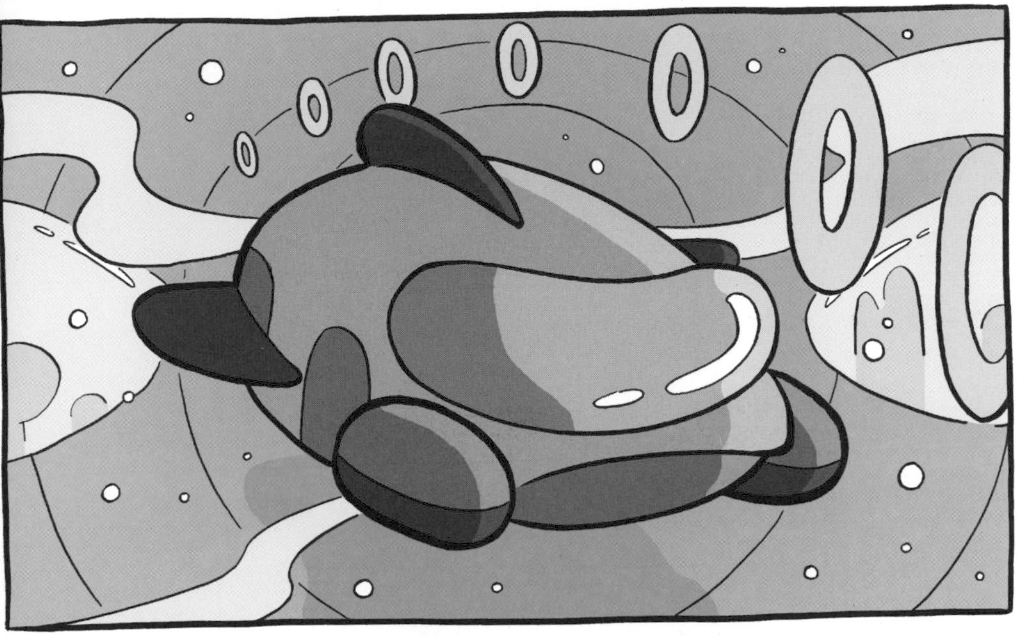

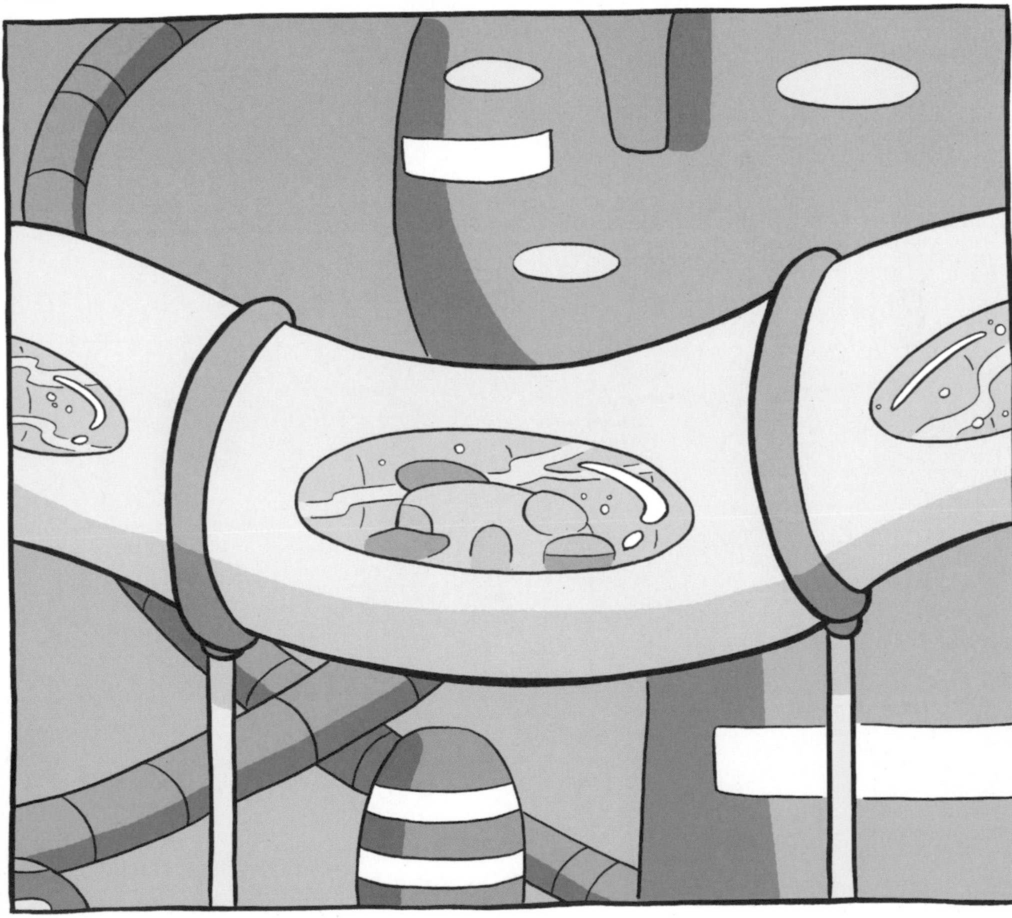

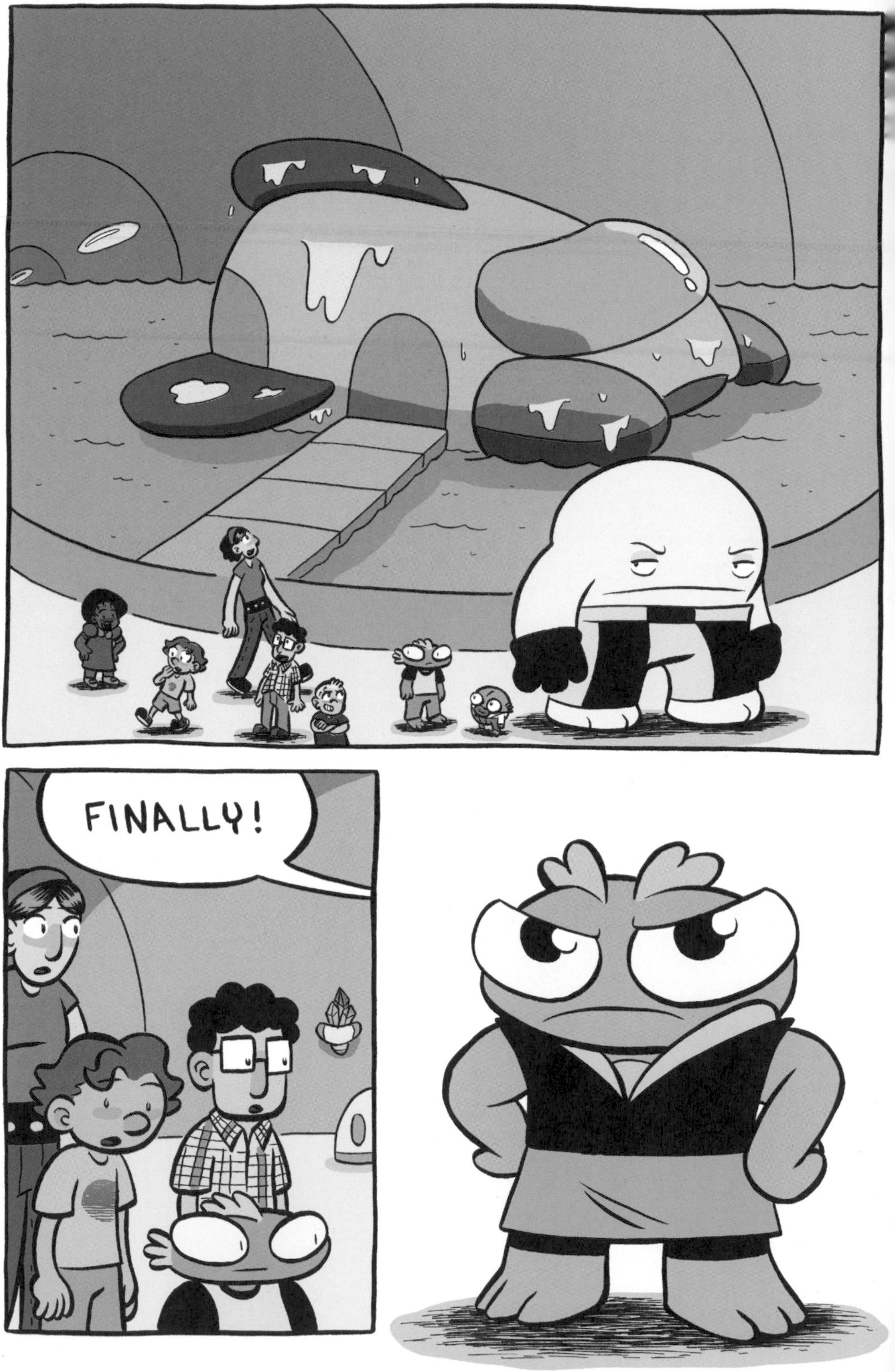
FINALLY!

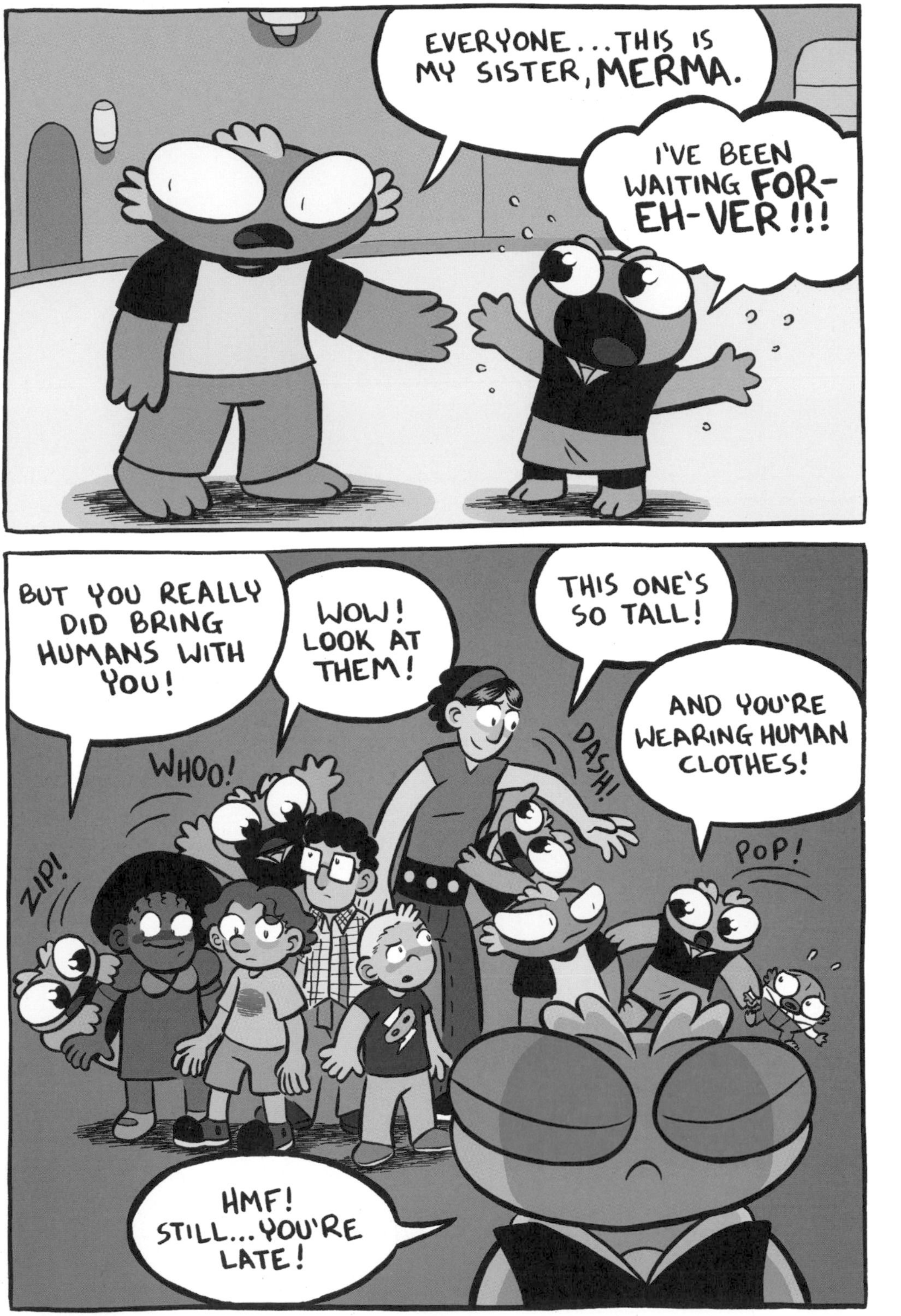
EVERYONE... THIS IS MY SISTER, MERMA.
I'VE BEEN WAITING FOR-EH-VER!!!
BUT YOU REALLY DID BRING HUMANS WITH YOU!
WOW! LOOK AT THEM!
THIS ONE'S SO TALL!
AND YOU'RE WEARING HUMAN CLOTHES!
WHOO!
DASH!
ZIP!
POP!
HMF! STILL... YOU'RE LATE!

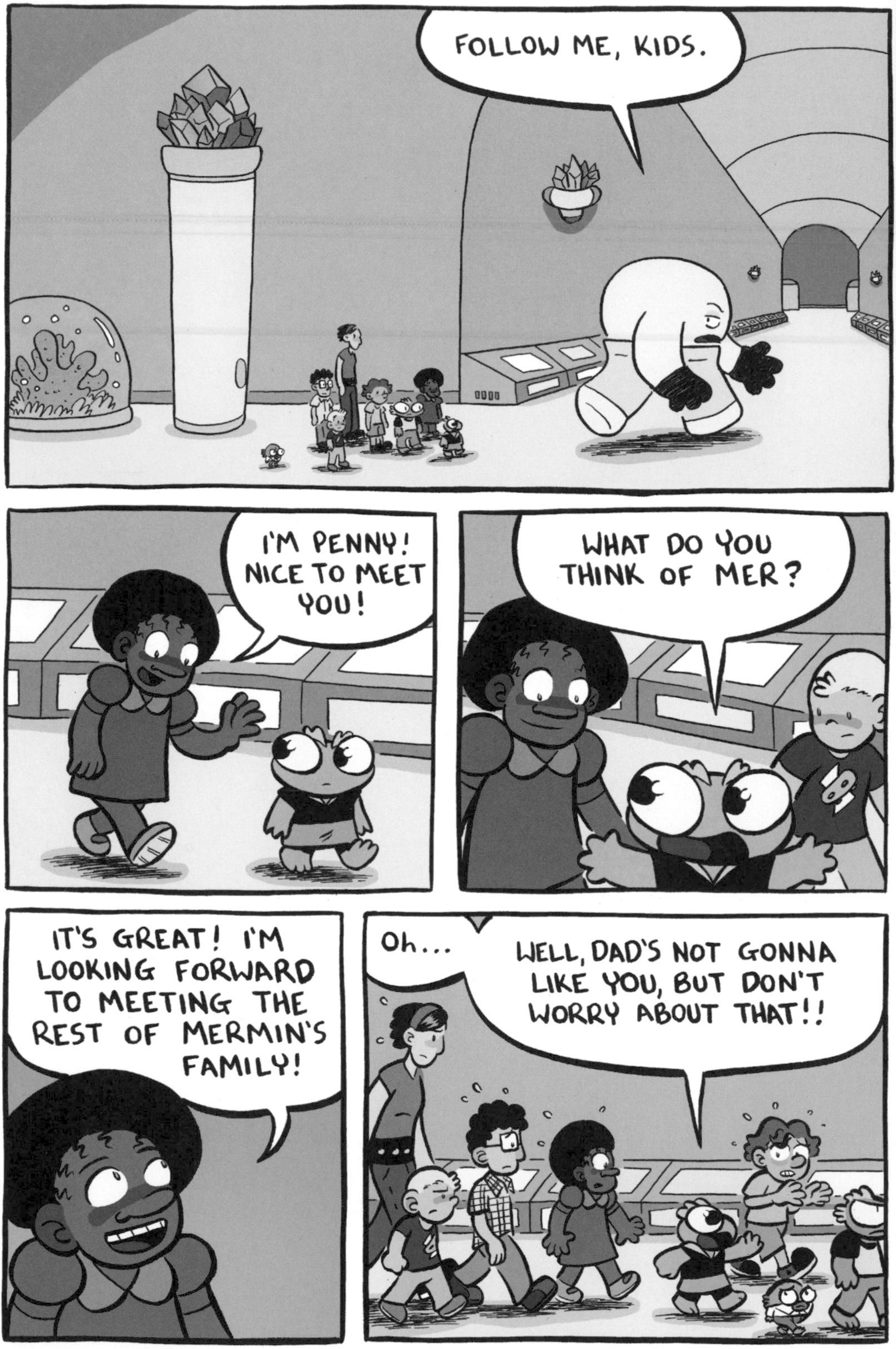
FOLLOW ME, KIDS.
I'M PENNY! NICE TO MEET YOU!
WHAT DO YOU THINK OF MER?
IT'S GREAT! I'M LOOKING FORWARD TO MEETING THE REST OF MERMIN'S FAMILY!
Oh...
WELL, DAD'S NOT GONNA LIKE YOU, BUT DON'T WORRY ABOUT THAT!!

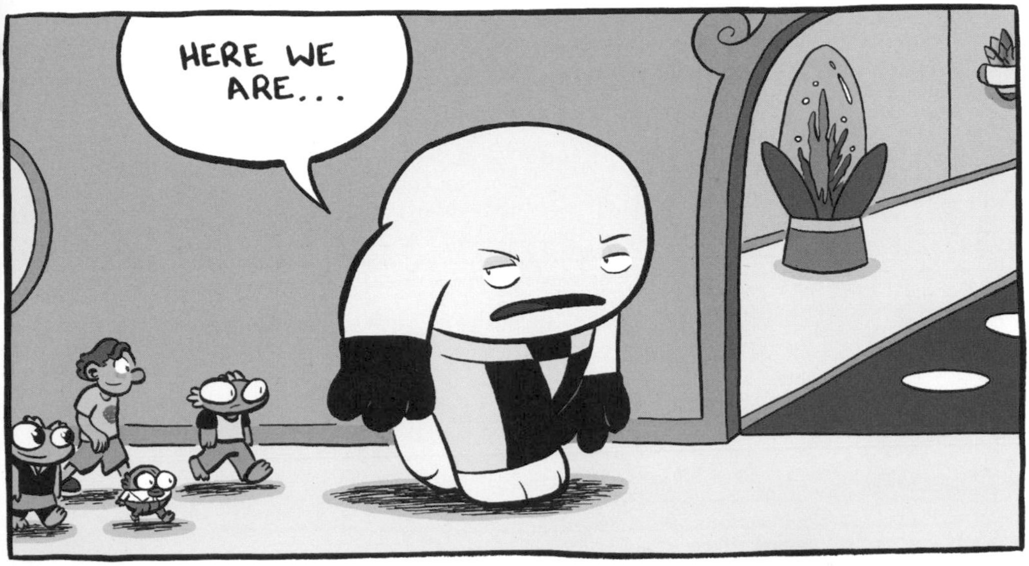
HERE WE ARE...

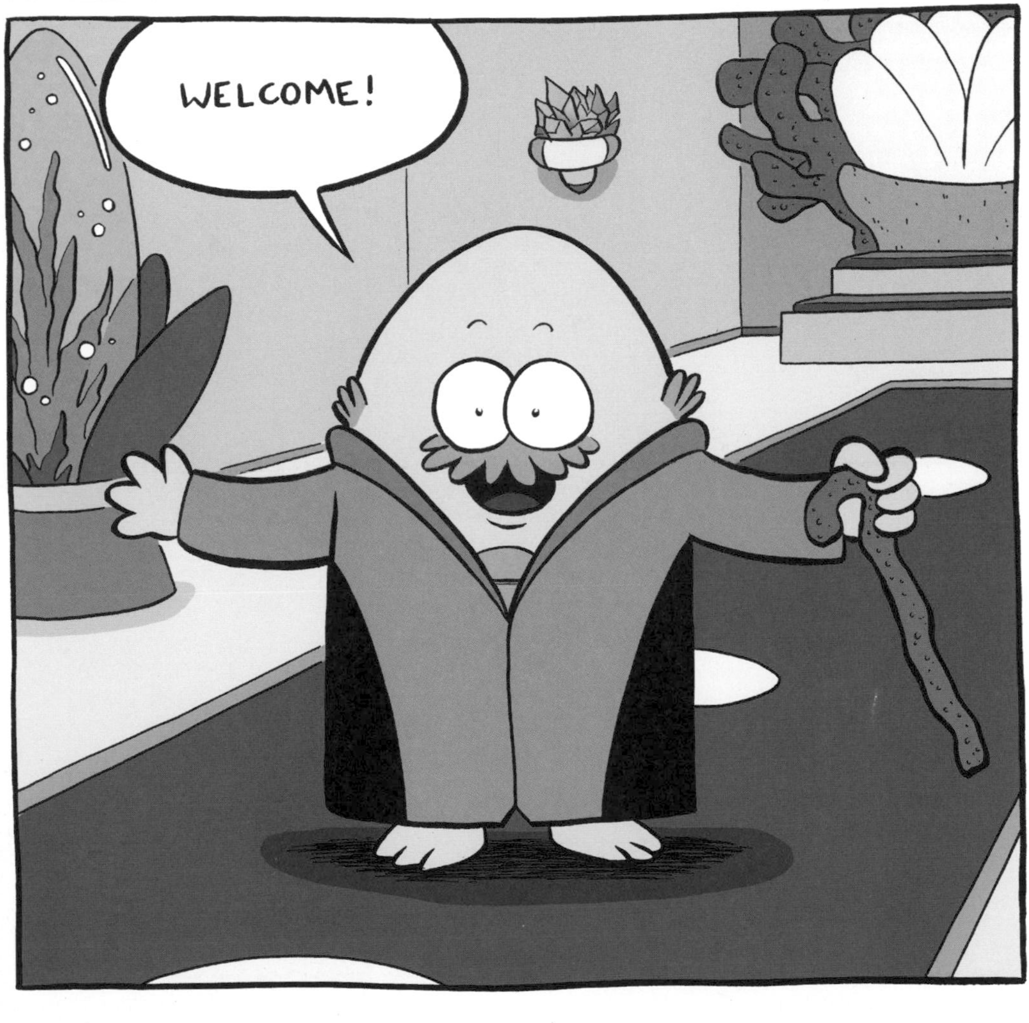
WELCOME!

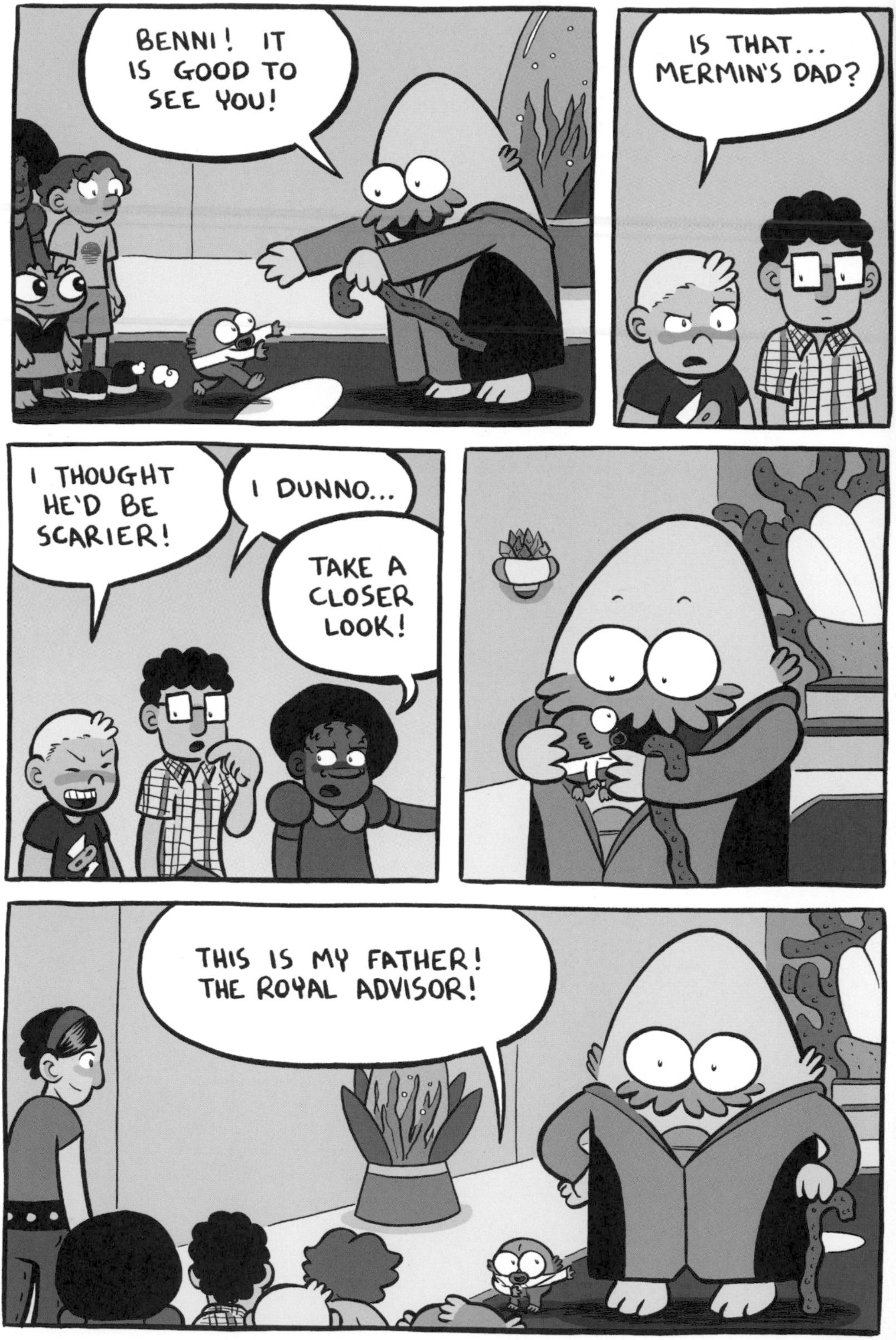
BENNI! IT IS GOOD TO SEE YOU!
IS THAT... MERMIN'S DAD?
I THOUGHT HE'D BE SCARIER!
I DUNNO...
TAKE A CLOSER LOOK!
THIS IS MY FATHER! THE ROYAL ADVISOR!

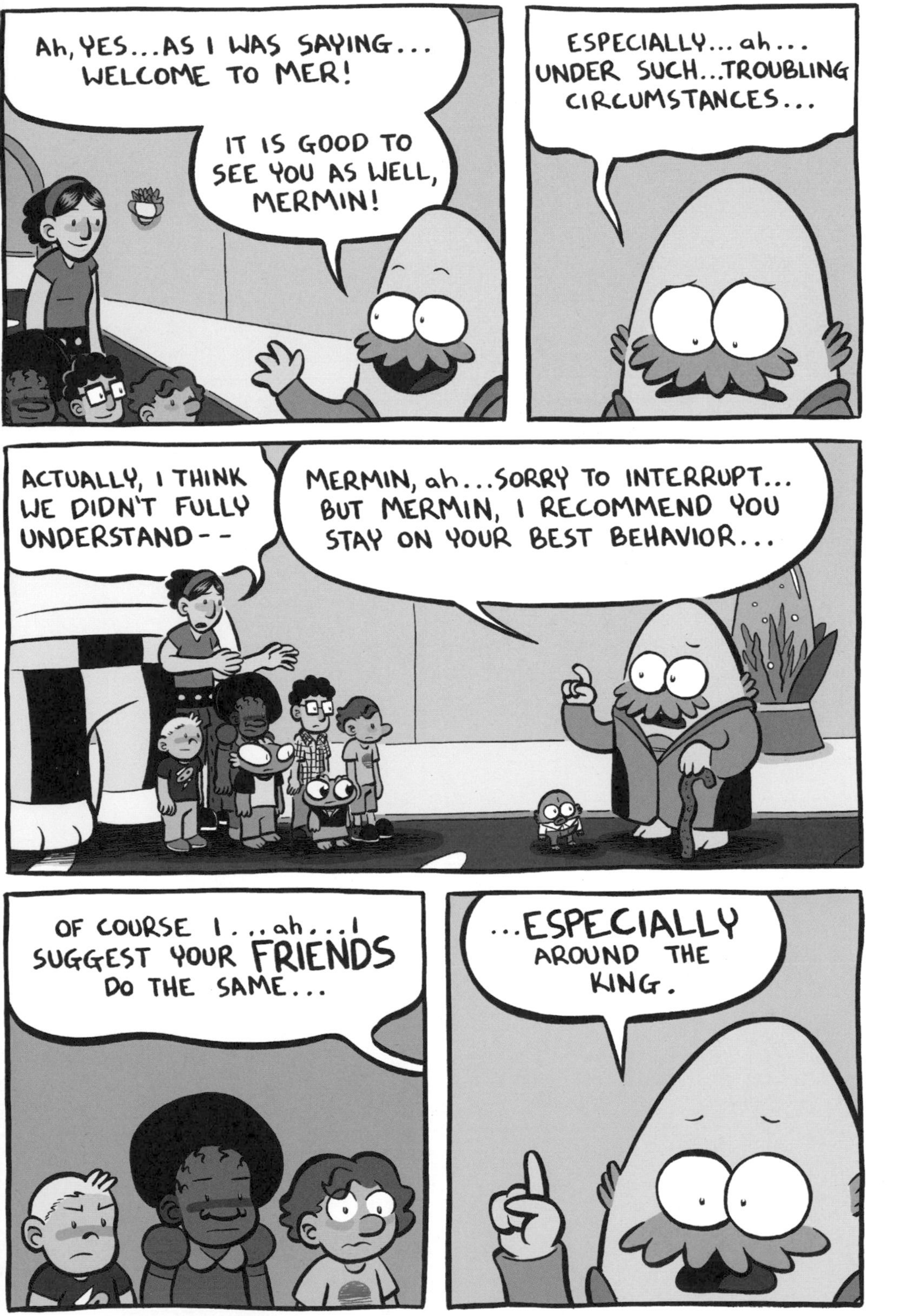
Ah, YES...AS I WAS SAYING... WELCOME TO MER!
IT IS GOOD TO SEE YOU AS WELL, MERMIN!
ESPECIALLY... ah... UNDER SUCH...TROUBLING CIRCUMSTANCES...
ACTUALLY, I THINK WE DIDN'T FULLY UNDERSTAND--
MERMIN, ah...SORRY TO INTERRUPT... BUT MERMIN, I RECOMMEND YOU STAY ON YOUR BEST BEHAVIOR...
OF COURSE I...ah...I SUGGEST YOUR FRIENDS DO THE SAME...
...ESPECIALLY AROUND THE KING.

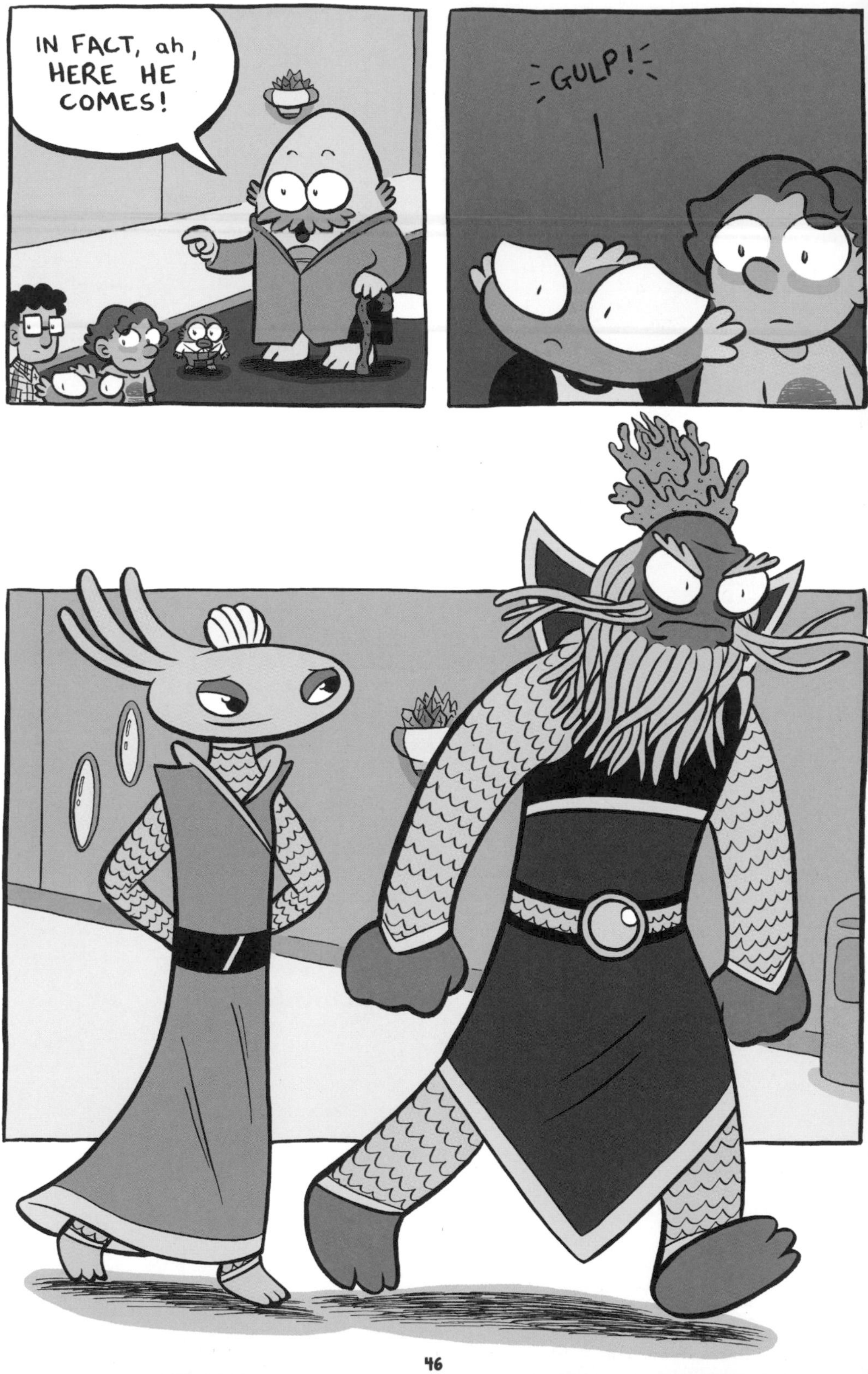
IN FACT, ah, HERE HE COMES!
GULP!

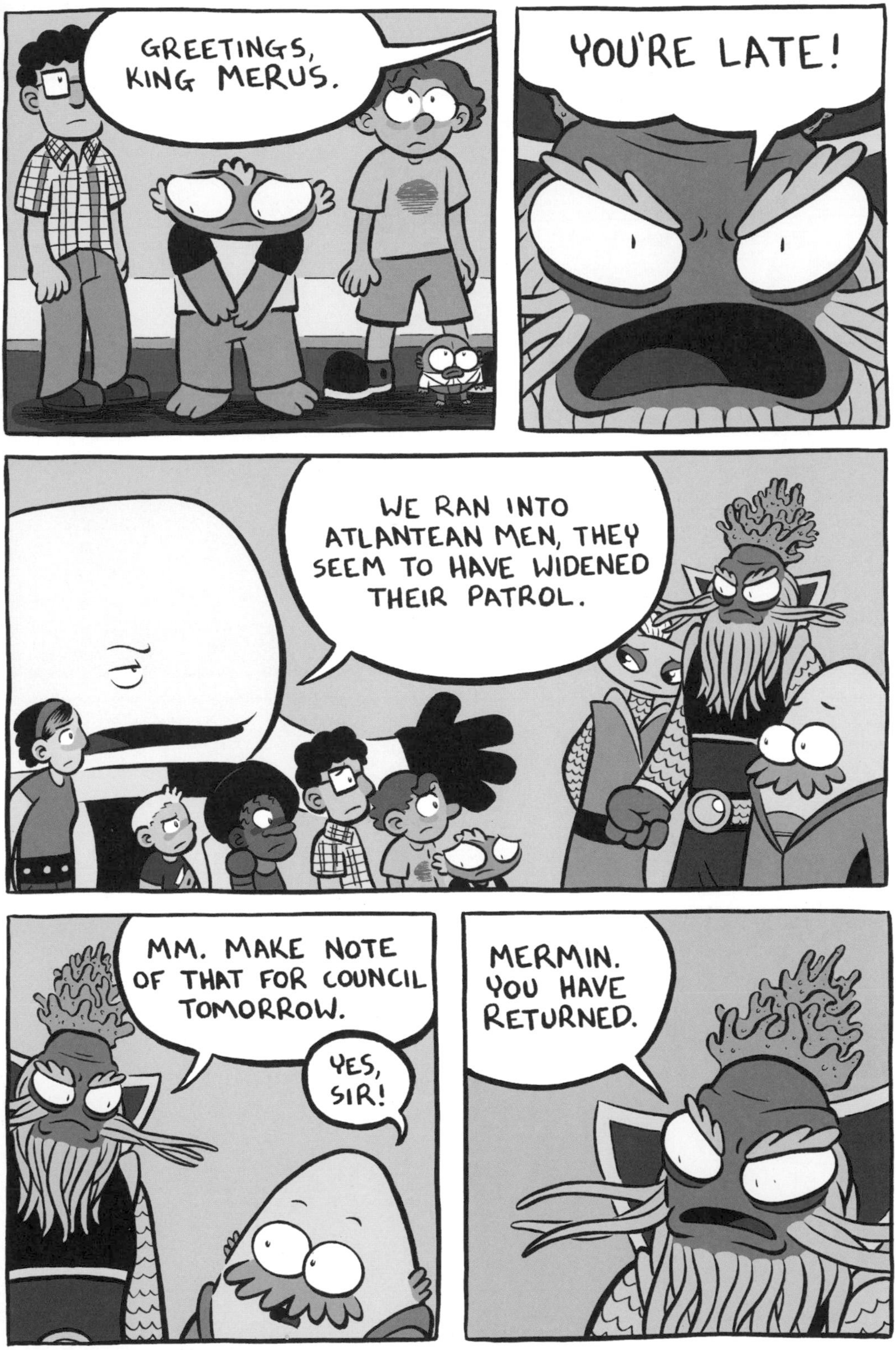
GREETINGS, KING MERUS.
YOU'RE LATE!
WE RAN INTO ATLANTEAN MEN, THEY SEEM TO HAVE WIDENED THEIR PATROL.
MM. MAKE NOTE OF THAT FOR COUNCIL TOMORROW.
YES, SIR!
MERMIN. YOU HAVE RETURNED.

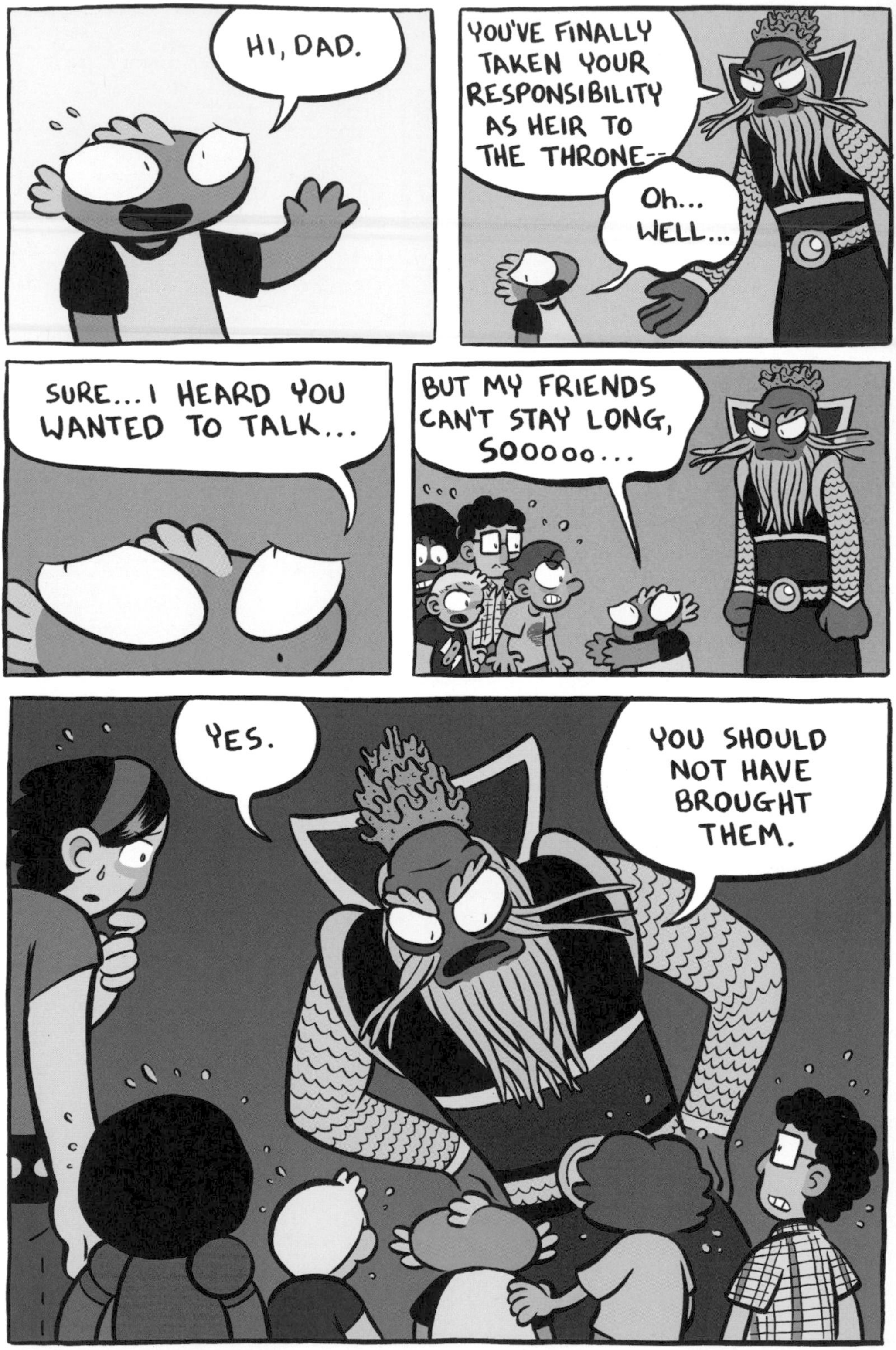
HI, DAD.
YOU'VE FINALLY TAKEN YOUR RESPONSIBILITY AS HEIR TO THE THRONE--
Oh... WELL...
SURE... I HEARD YOU WANTED TO TALK...
BUT MY FRIENDS CAN'T STAY LONG, SOOOoo...
YES.
YOU SHOULD NOT HAVE BROUGHT THEM.

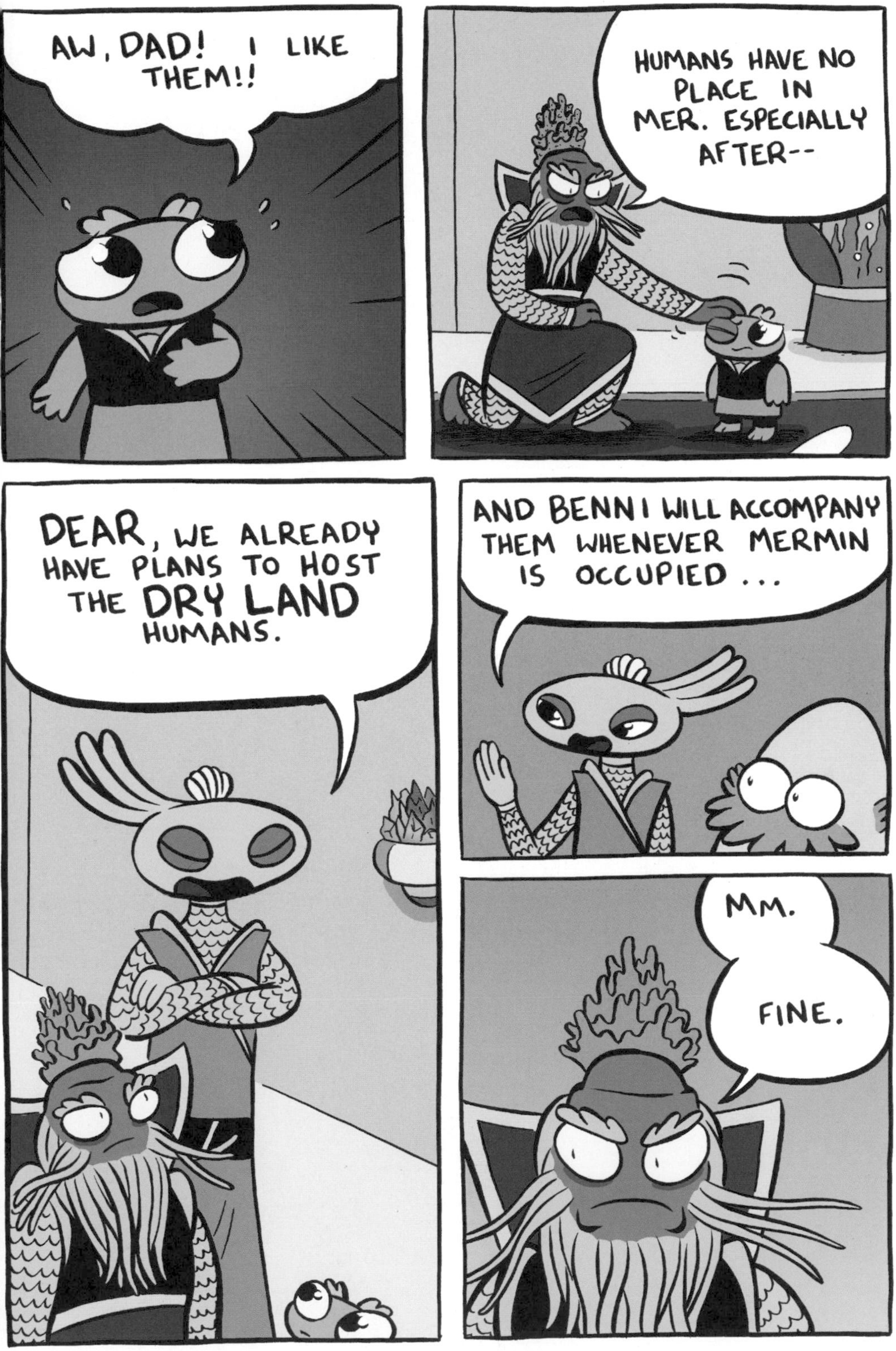
AW, DAD! I LIKE THEM!!
HUMANS HAVE NO PLACE IN MER. ESPECIALLY AFTER--
DEAR, WE ALREADY HAVE PLANS TO HOST THE DRY LAND HUMANS.
AND BENNI WILL ACCOMPANY THEM WHENEVER MERMIN IS OCCUPIED . . .
MM.
FINE.

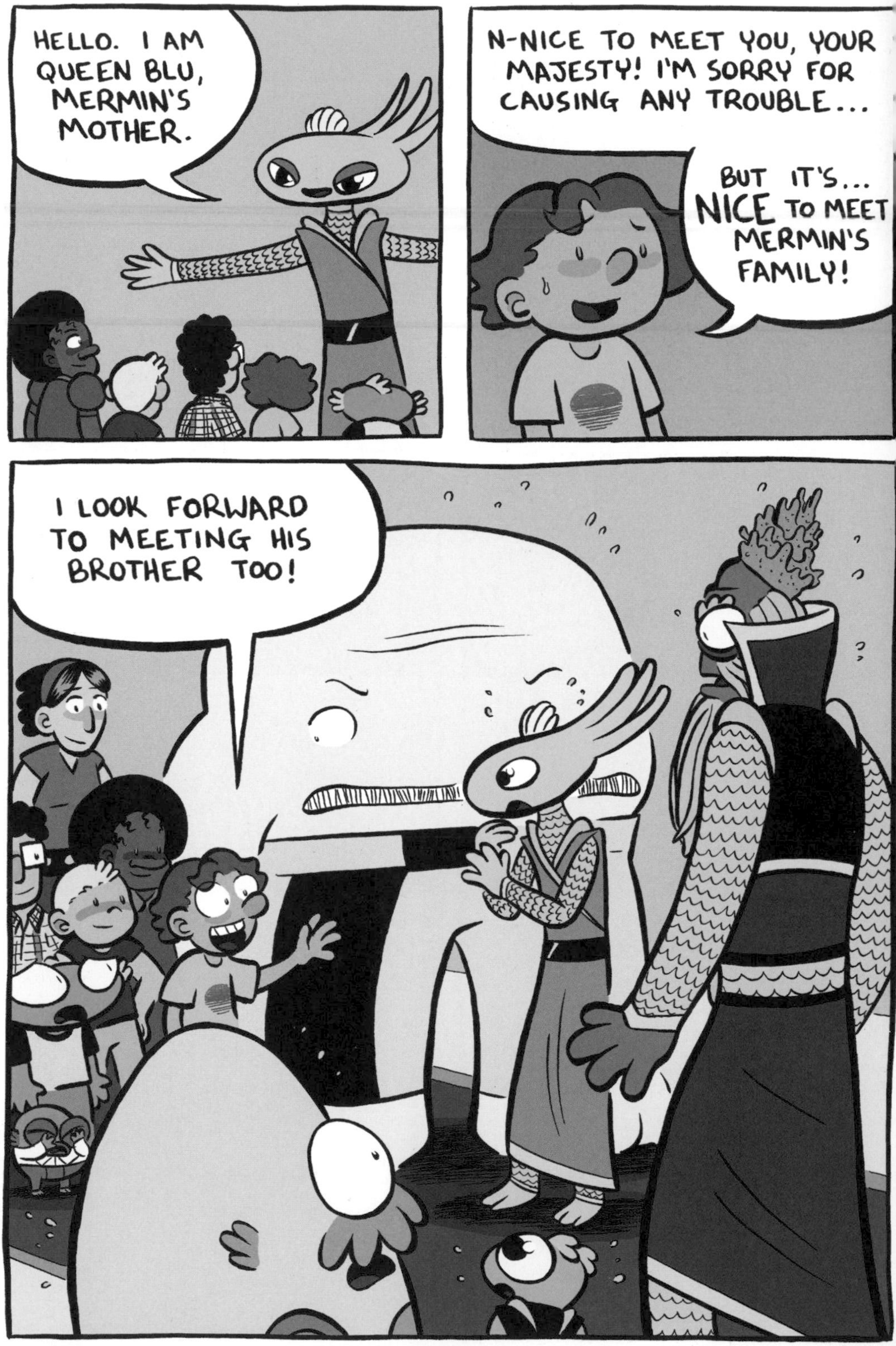
HELLO. I AM QUEEN BLU, MERMIN'S MOTHER.
N-NICE TO MEET YOU, YOUR MAJESTY! I'M SORRY FOR CAUSING ANY TROUBLE...
BUT IT'S... NICE TO MEET MERMIN'S FAMILY!
I LOOK FORWARD TO MEETING HIS BROTHER TOO!

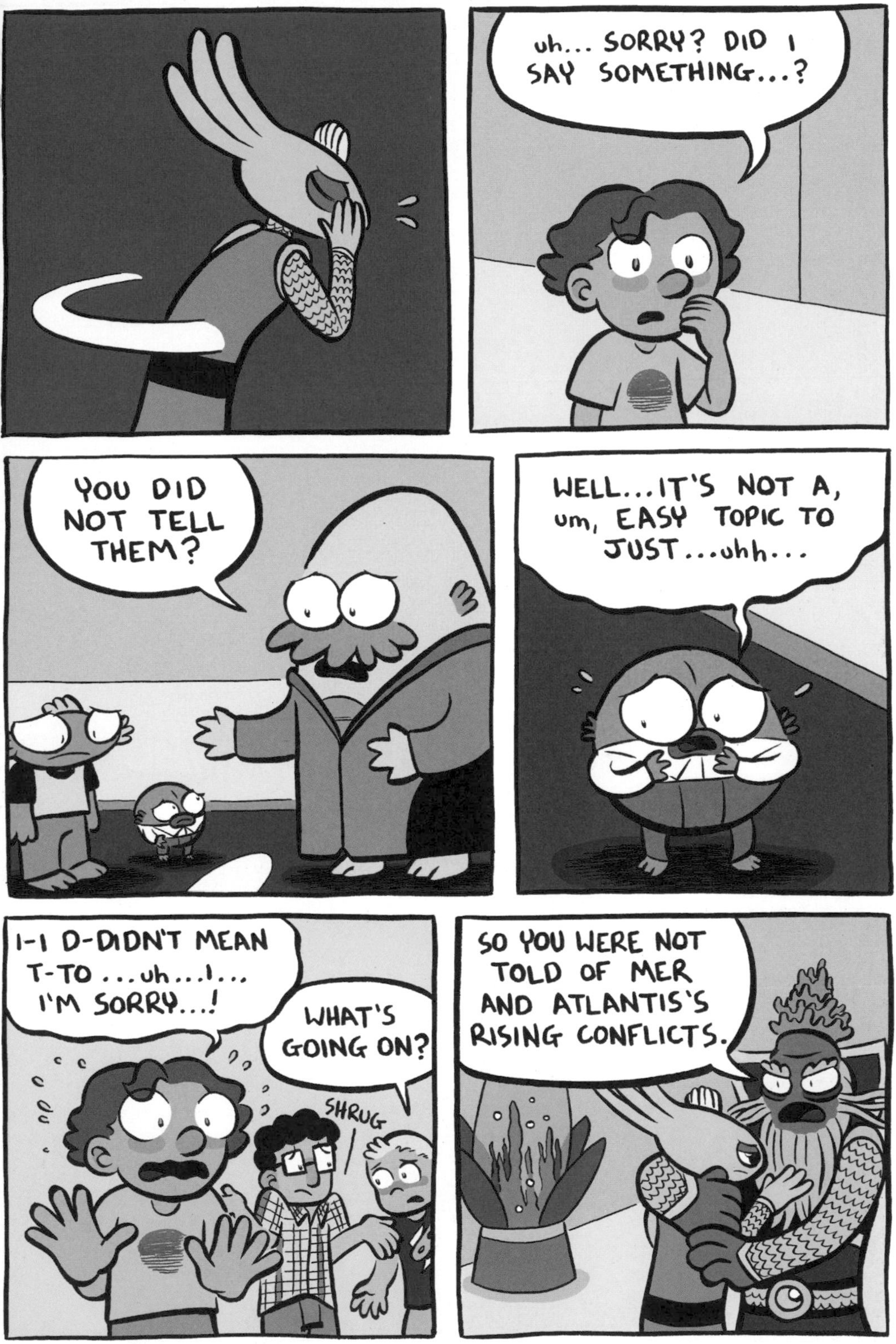
uh... SORRY? DID I SAY SOMETHING...?
YOU DID NOT TELL THEM?
WELL...IT'S NOT A, um, EASY TOPIC TO JUST...uhh...
I-I D-DIDN'T MEAN T-TO ...uh...I... I'M SORRY...!
WHAT'S GOING ON?
SHRUG
SO YOU WERE NOT TOLD OF MER AND ATLANTIS'S RISING CONFLICTS.

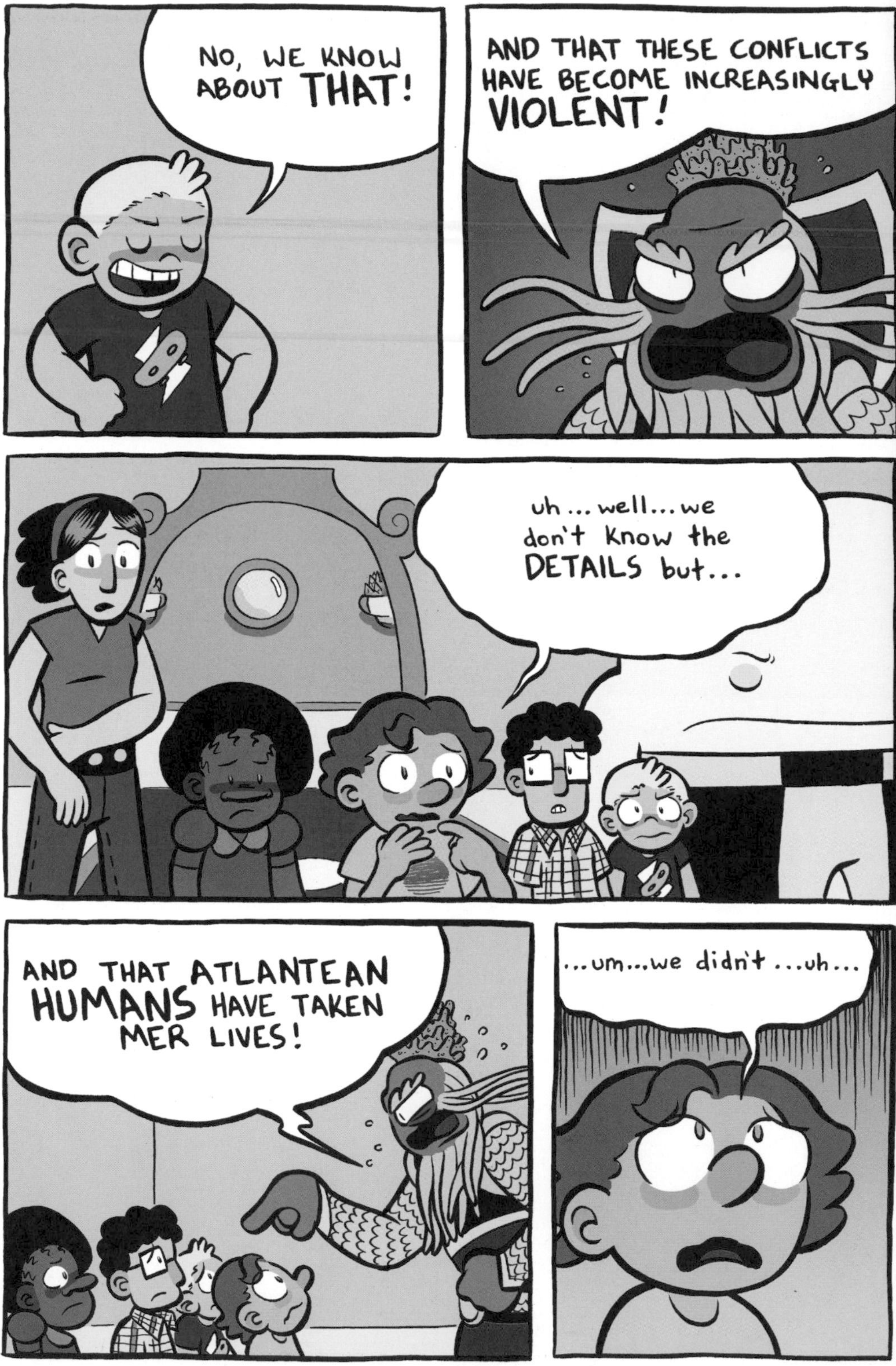
NO, WE KNOW ABOUT THAT!
AND THAT THESE CONFLICTS HAVE BECOME INCREASINGLY VIOLENT!
uh... well... we don't know the DETAILS but...
AND THAT ATLANTEAN HUMANS HAVE TAKEN MER LIVES!
...um...we didn't ...uh...

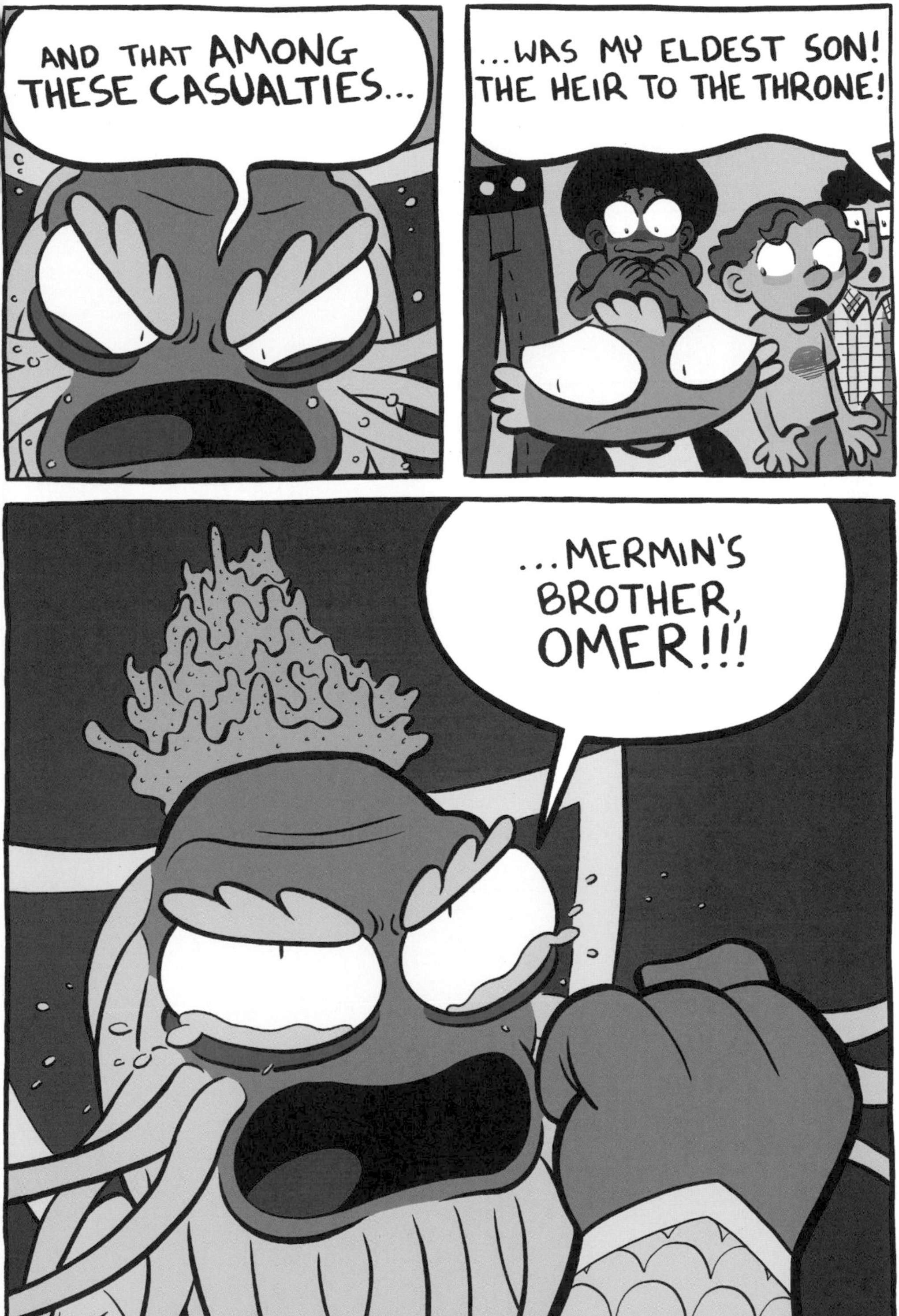
AND THAT AMONG THESE CASUALTIES...
...WAS MY ELDEST SON! THE HEIR TO THE THRONE!
...MERMIN'S BROTHER, OMER!!!

CHAPTER THREE

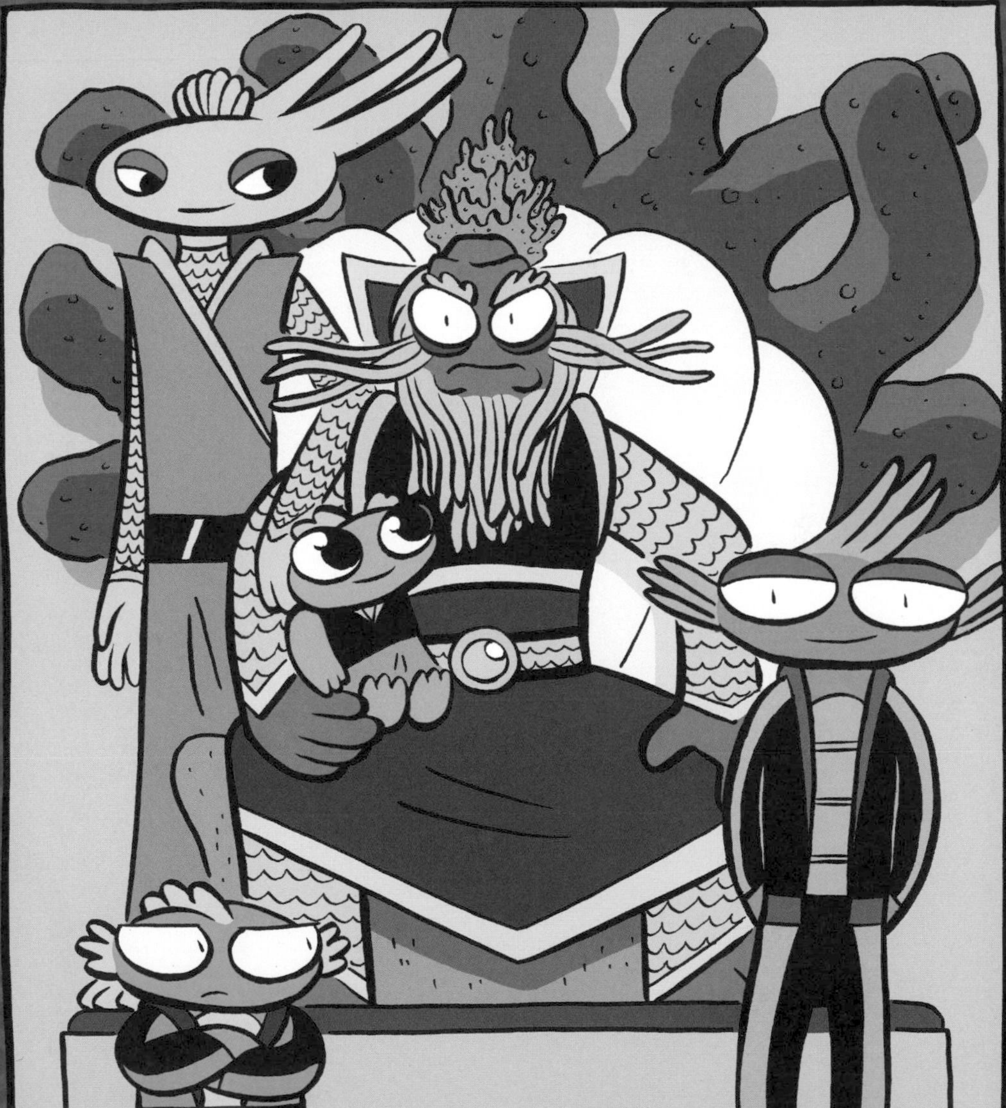

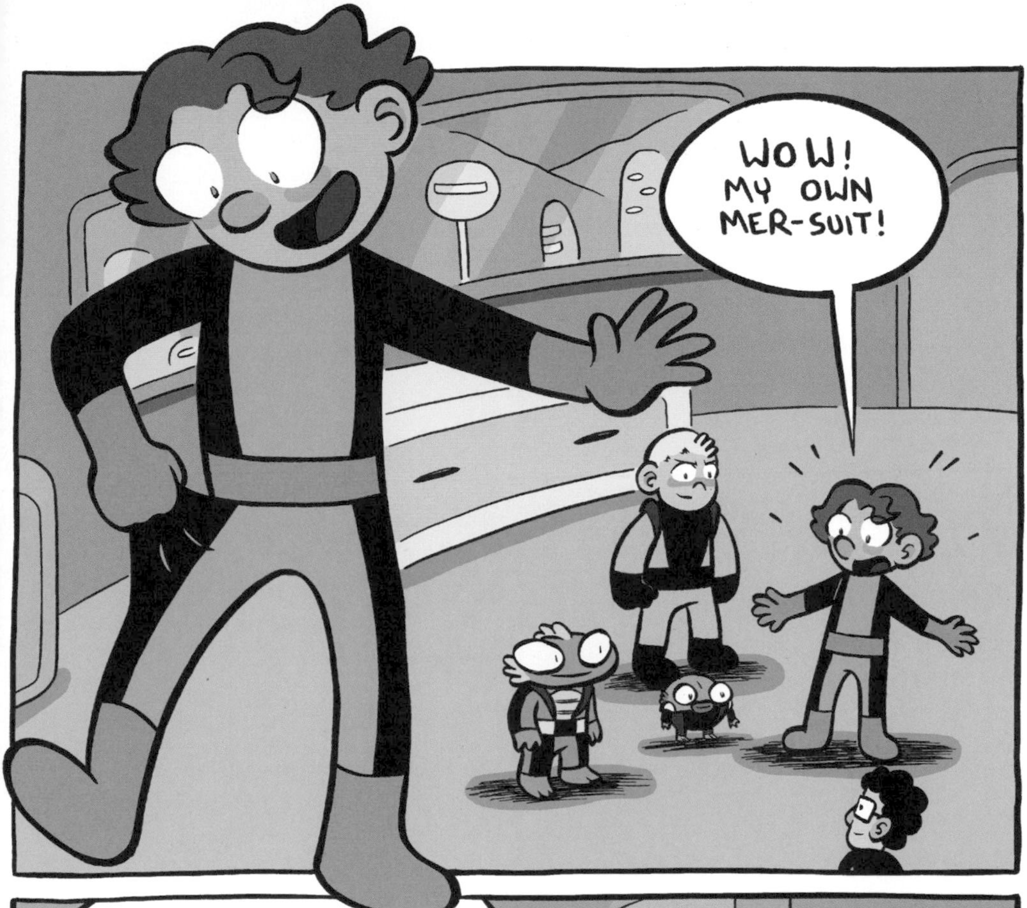
WOW! MY OWN MER-SUIT!

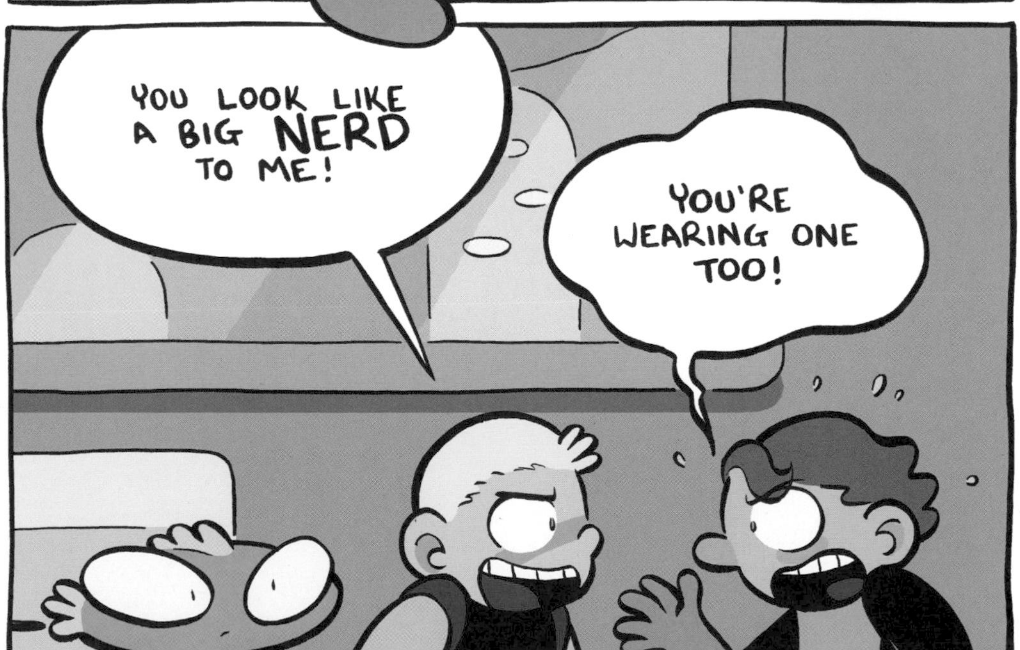
YOU LOOK LIKE A BIG NERD TO ME!
YOU'RE WEARING ONE TOO!

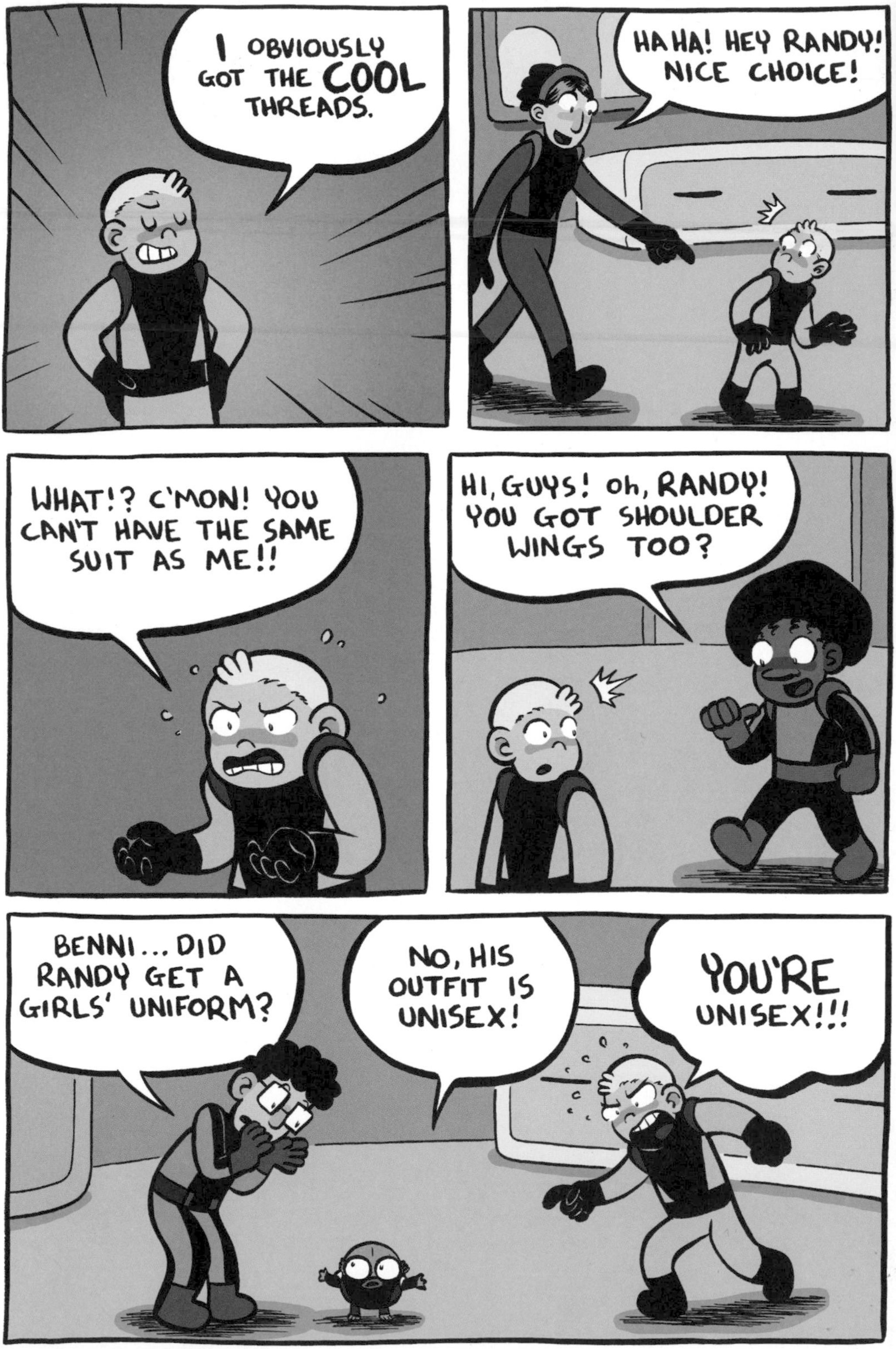
I OBVIOUSLY GOT THE COOL THREADS.
HA HA! HEY RANDY! NICE CHOICE!
WHAT!? C'MON! YOU CAN'T HAVE THE SAME SUIT AS ME!!
HI, GUYS! oh, RANDY! YOU GOT SHOULDER WINGS TOO?
BENNI... DID RANDY GET A GIRLS' UNIFORM?
NO, HIS OUTFIT IS UNISEX!
YOU'RE UNISEX!!!

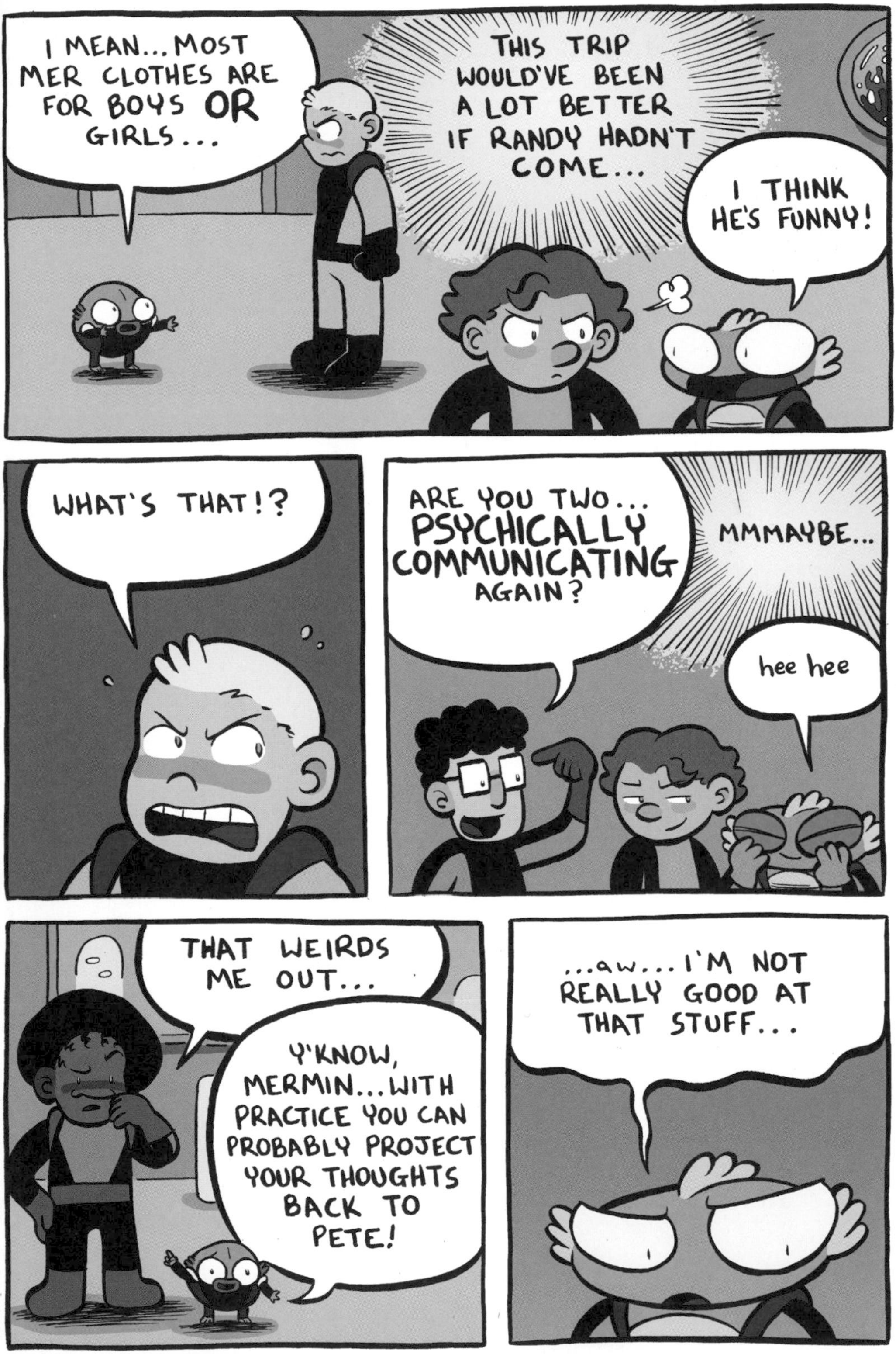
I MEAN... MOST MER CLOTHES ARE FOR BOYS OR GIRLS...
THIS TRIP WOULD'VE BEEN A LOT BETTER IF RANDY HADN'T COME...
I THINK HE'S FUNNY!
WHAT'S THAT!?
ARE YOU TWO... PSYCHICALLY COMMUNICATING AGAIN?
MMMAYBE...
hee hee
THAT WEIRDS ME OUT...
Y'KNOW, MERMIN... WITH PRACTICE YOU CAN PROBABLY PROJECT YOUR THOUGHTS BACK TO PETE!
...aw... I'M NOT REALLY GOOD AT THAT STUFF...

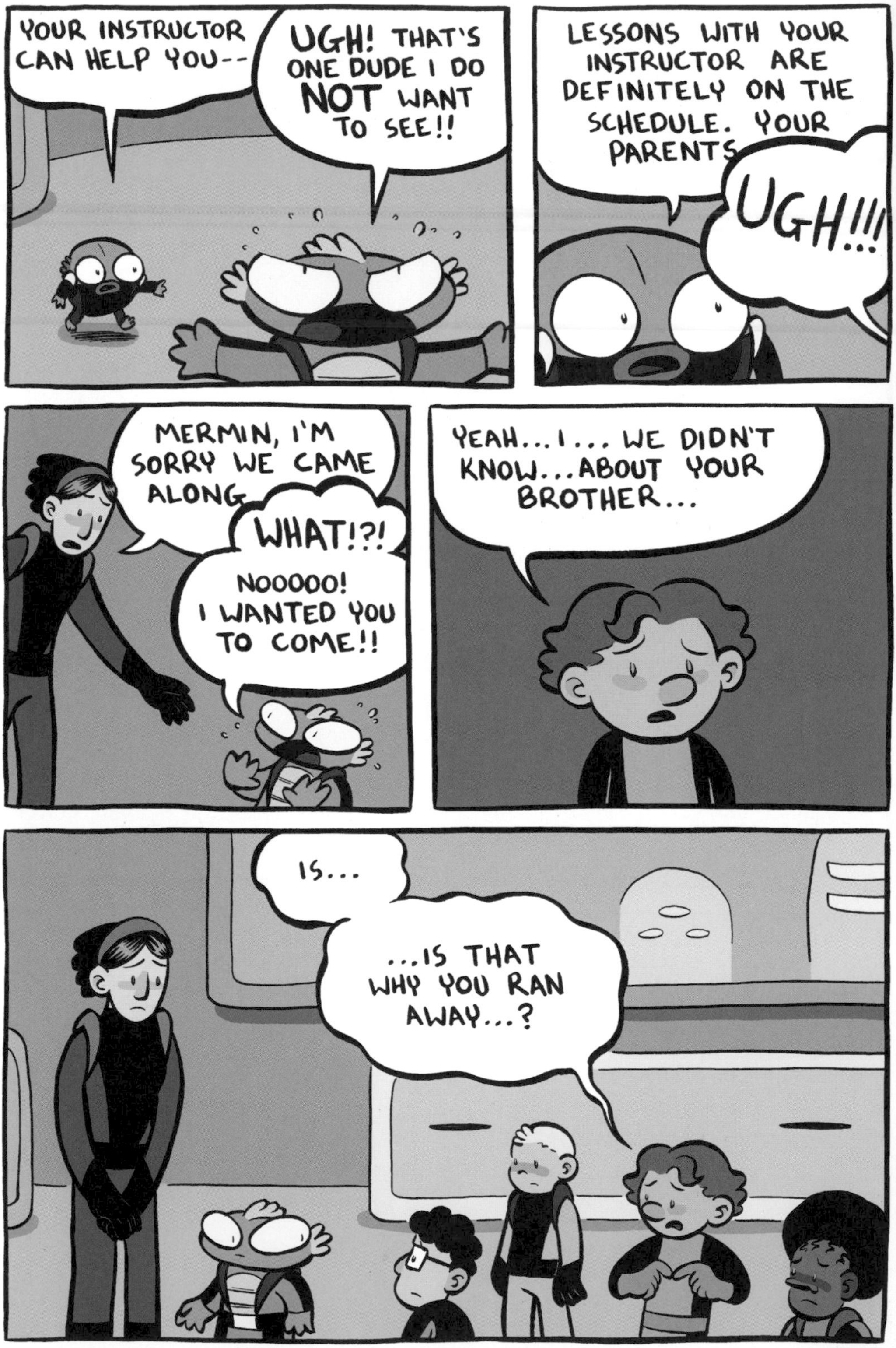
YOUR INSTRUCTOR CAN HELP YOU--
UGH! THAT'S ONE DUDE I DO NOT WANT TO SEE!!
LESSONS WITH YOUR INSTRUCTOR ARE DEFINITELY ON THE SCHEDULE. YOUR PARENTS
UGH!!!
MERMIN, I'M SORRY WE CAME ALONG
WHAT!?!
NOOOOO! I WANTED YOU TO COME!!
YEAH...I... WE DIDN'T KNOW...ABOUT YOUR BROTHER...
IS...
...IS THAT WHY YOU RAN AWAY...?

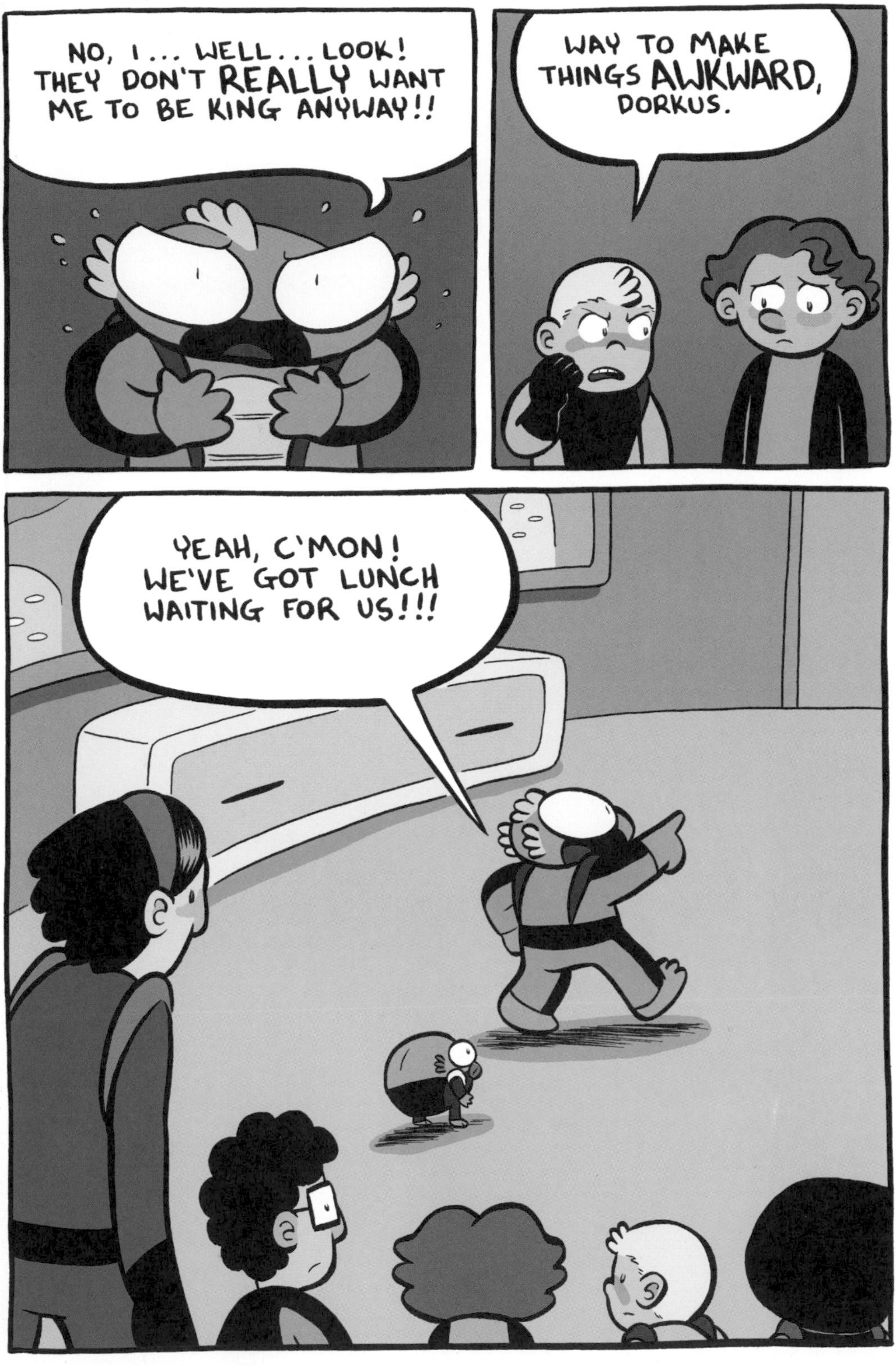
NO, I... WELL...LOOK! THEY DON'T REALLY WANT ME TO BE KING ANYWAY!!
WAY TO MAKE THINGS AWKWARD, DORKUS.
YEAH, C'MON! WE'VE GOT LUNCH WAITING FOR US!!!

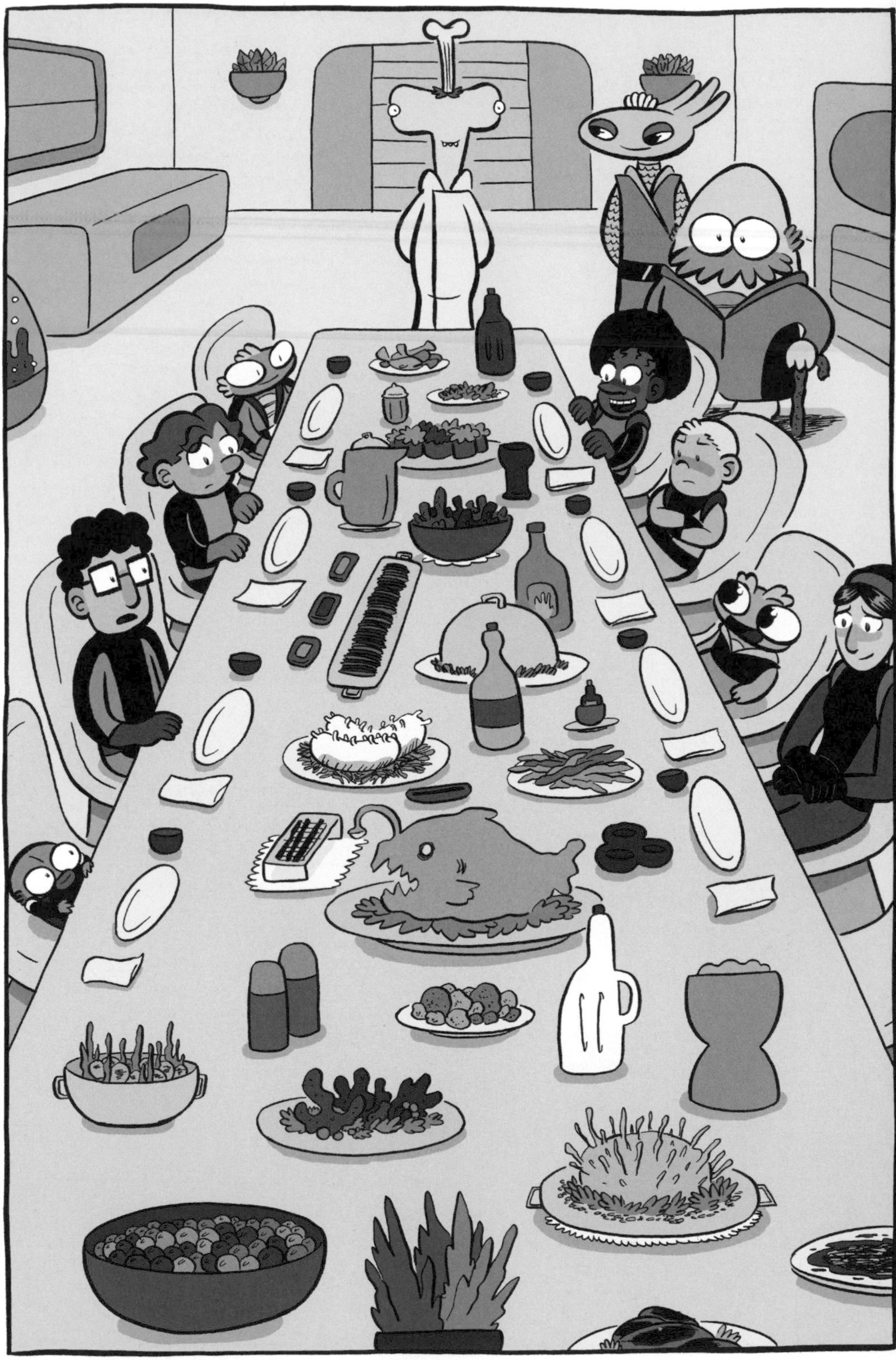

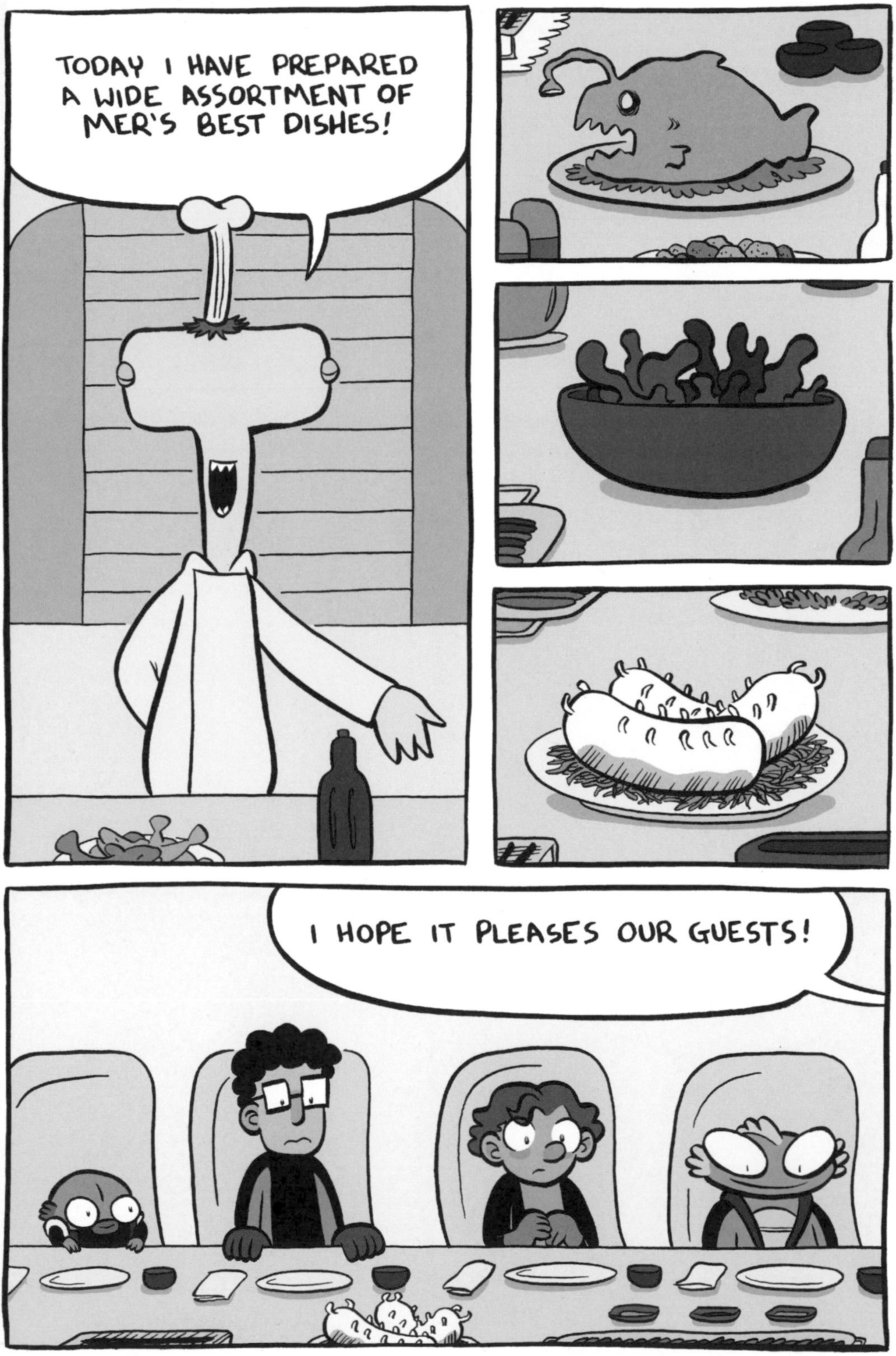
TODAY I HAVE PREPARED A WIDE ASSORTMENT OF MER'S BEST DISHES!
I HOPE IT PLEASES OUR GUESTS!

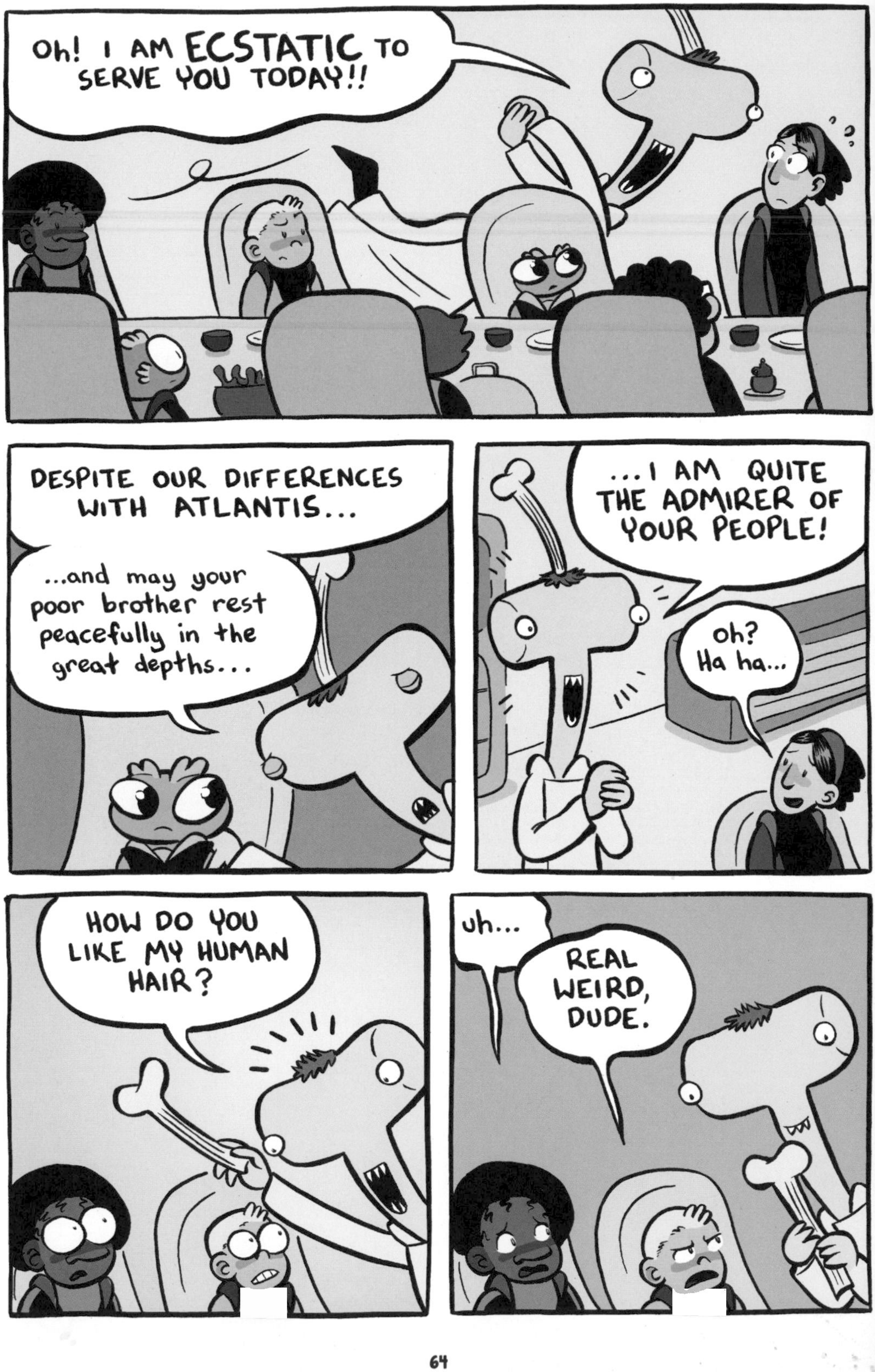

Oh! I AM ECSTATIC TO SERVE YOU TODAY!!
DESPITE OUR DIFFERENCES WITH ATLANTIS...
...and may your poor brother rest peacefully in the great depths...
...I AM QUITE THE ADMIRER OF YOUR PEOPLE!
Oh? Ha ha...
HOW DO YOU LIKE MY HUMAN HAIR?
uh...
REAL WEIRD, DUDE.

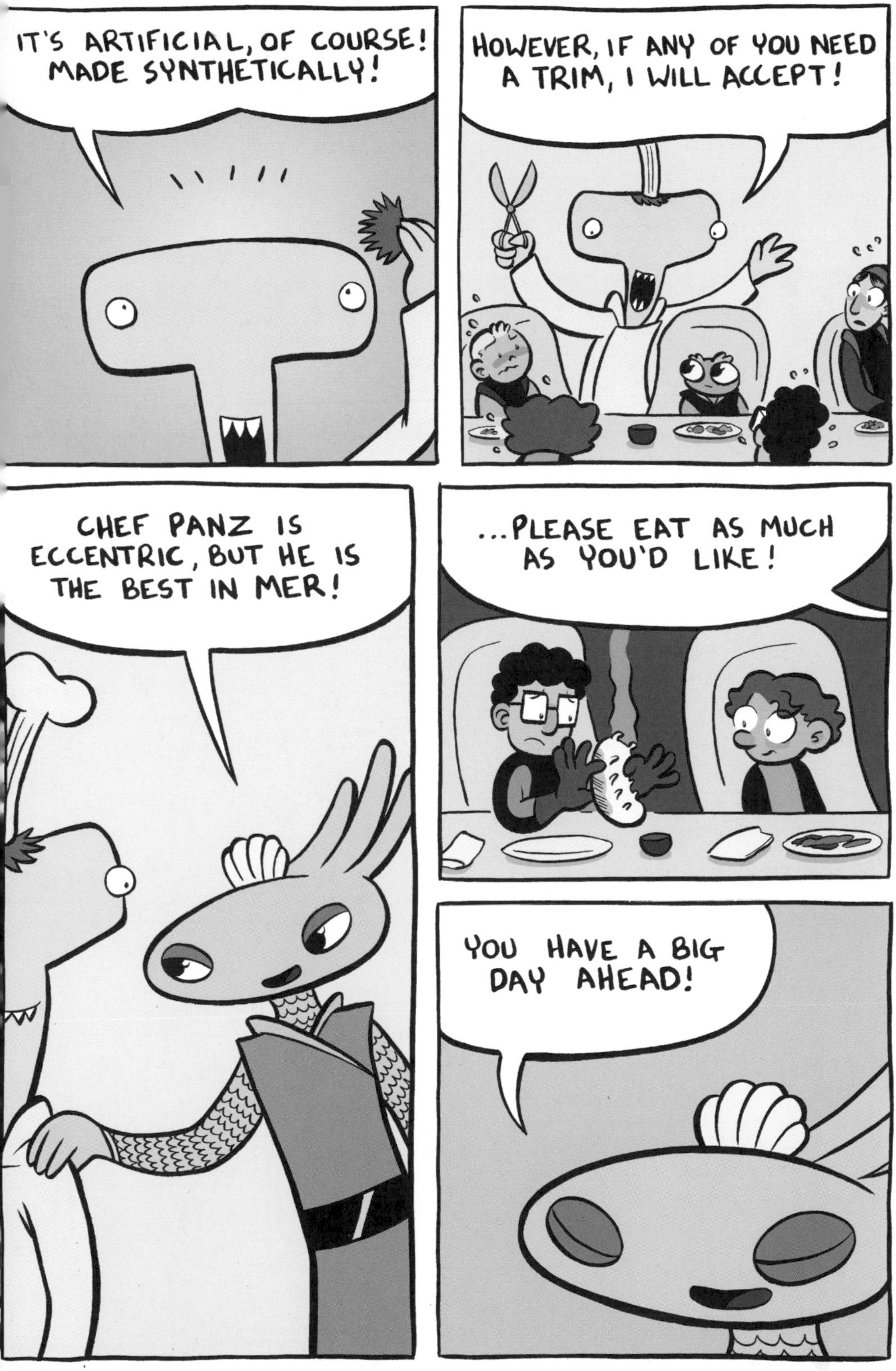
IT'S ARTIFICIAL, OF COURSE! MADE SYNTHETICALLY!
HOWEVER, IF ANY OF YOU NEED A TRIM, I WILL ACCEPT!
CHEF PANZ IS ECCENTRIC, BUT HE IS THE BEST IN MER!
...PLEASE EAT AS MUCH AS YOU'D LIKE!
YOU HAVE A BIG DAY AHEAD!

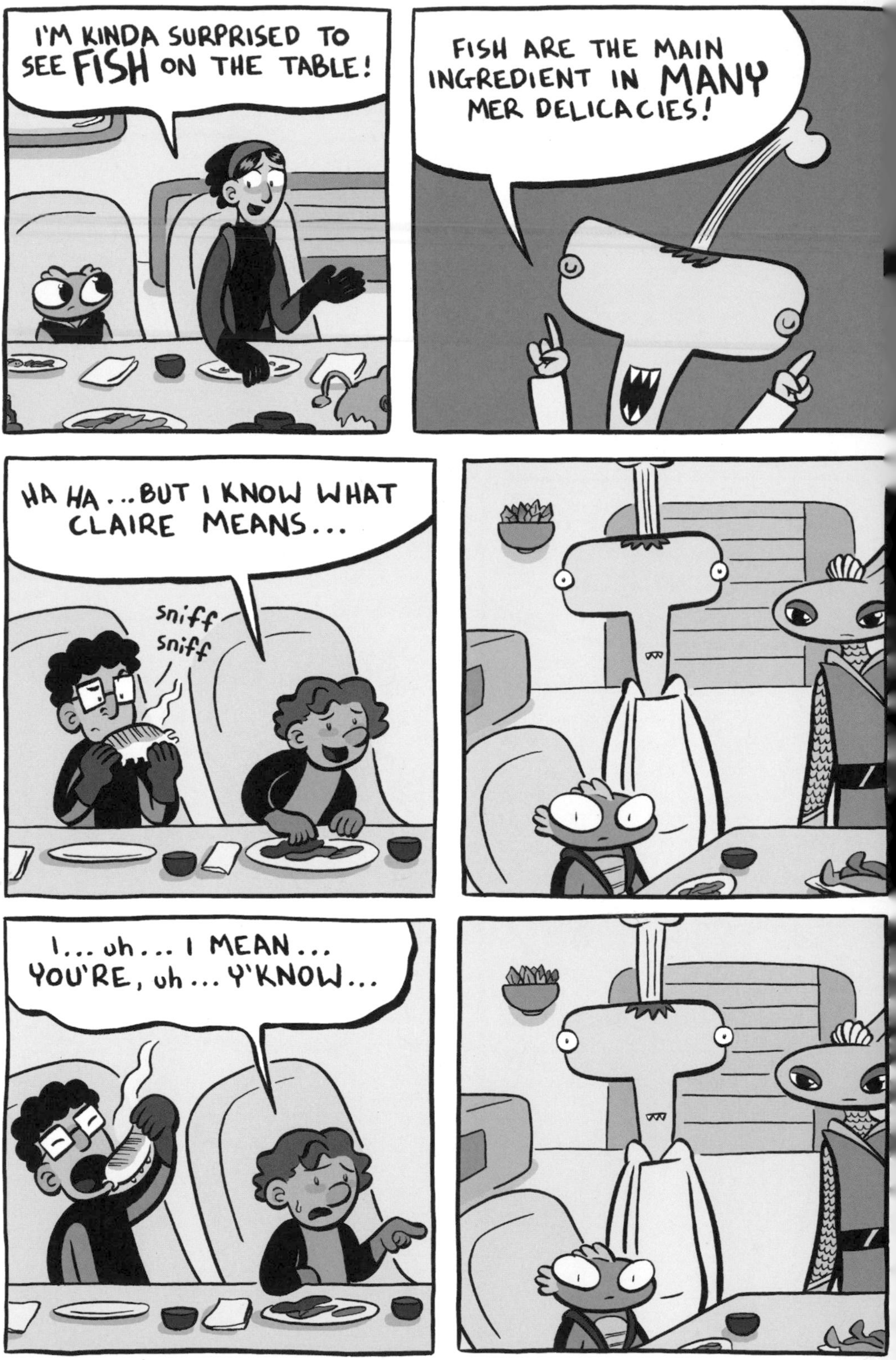
I'M KINDA SURPRISED TO SEE FISH ON THE TABLE!
FISH ARE THE MAIN INGREDIENT IN MANY MER DELICACIES!
HA HA ... BUT I KNOW WHAT CLAIRE MEANS ...
sniff sniff
I ... uh ... I MEAN ... YOU'RE, uh ... Y'KNOW ...

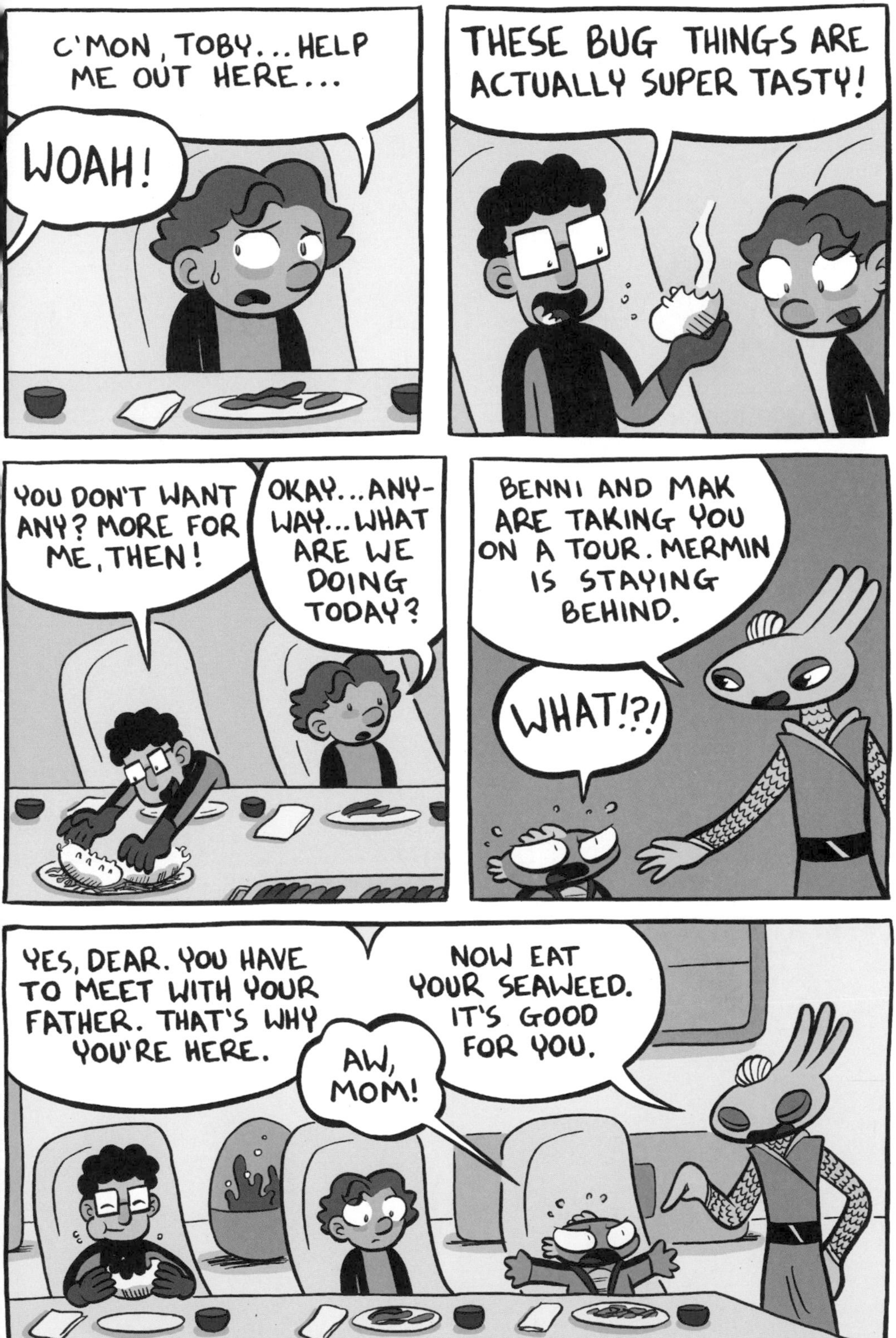
C'MON, TOBY... HELP ME OUT HERE...
WOAH!
THESE BUG THINGS ARE ACTUALLY SUPER TASTY!
YOU DON'T WANT ANY? MORE FOR ME, THEN!
OKAY... ANY-WAY... WHAT ARE WE DOING TODAY?
BENNI AND MAK ARE TAKING YOU ON A TOUR. MERMIN IS STAYING BEHIND.
WHAT!?!
YES, DEAR. YOU HAVE TO MEET WITH YOUR FATHER. THAT'S WHY YOU'RE HERE.
AW, MOM!
NOW EAT YOUR SEAWEED. IT'S GOOD FOR YOU.

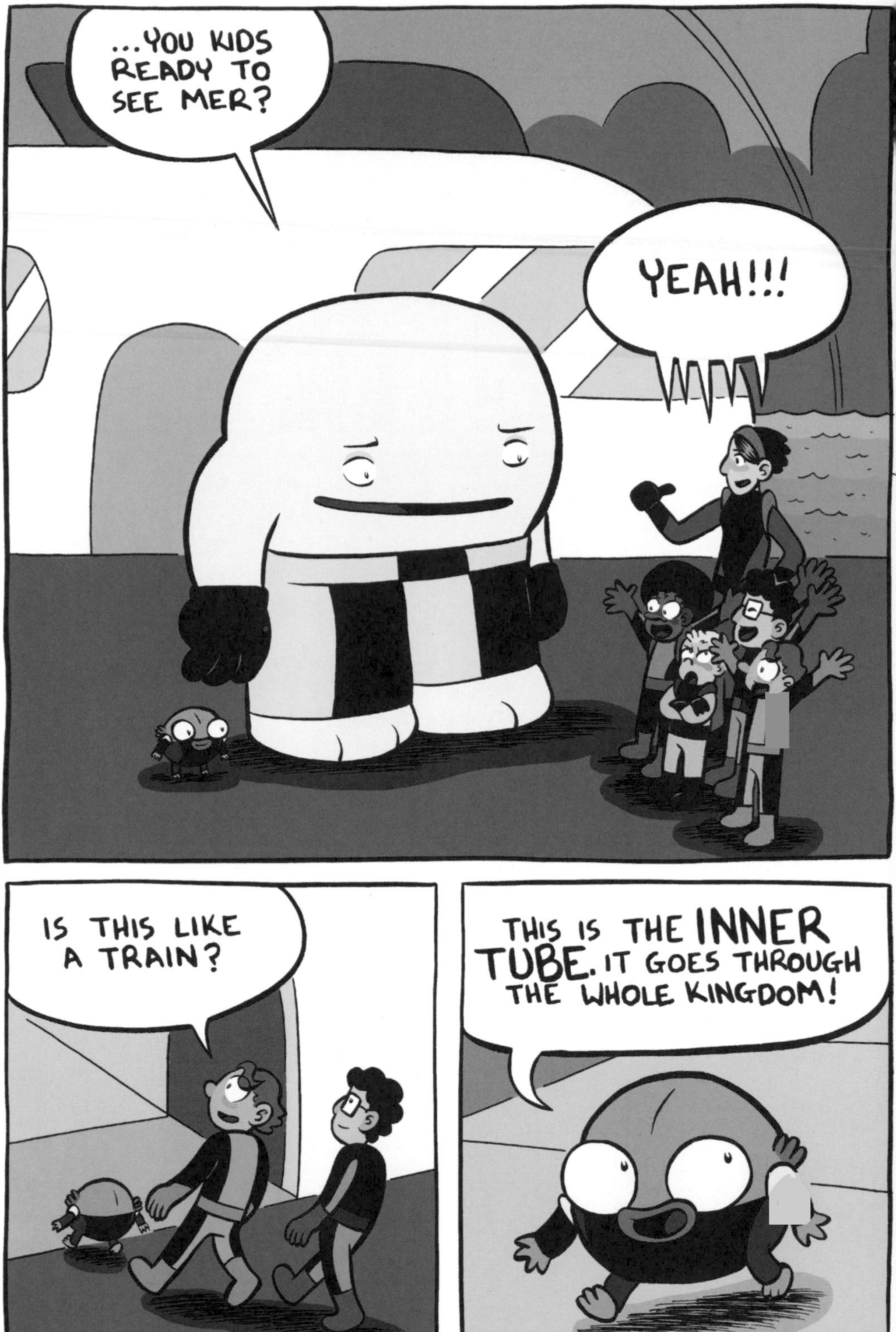
...YOU KIDS READY TO SEE MER?
YEAH!!!
IS THIS LIKE A TRAIN?
THIS IS THE INNER TUBE. IT GOES THROUGH THE WHOLE KINGDOM!

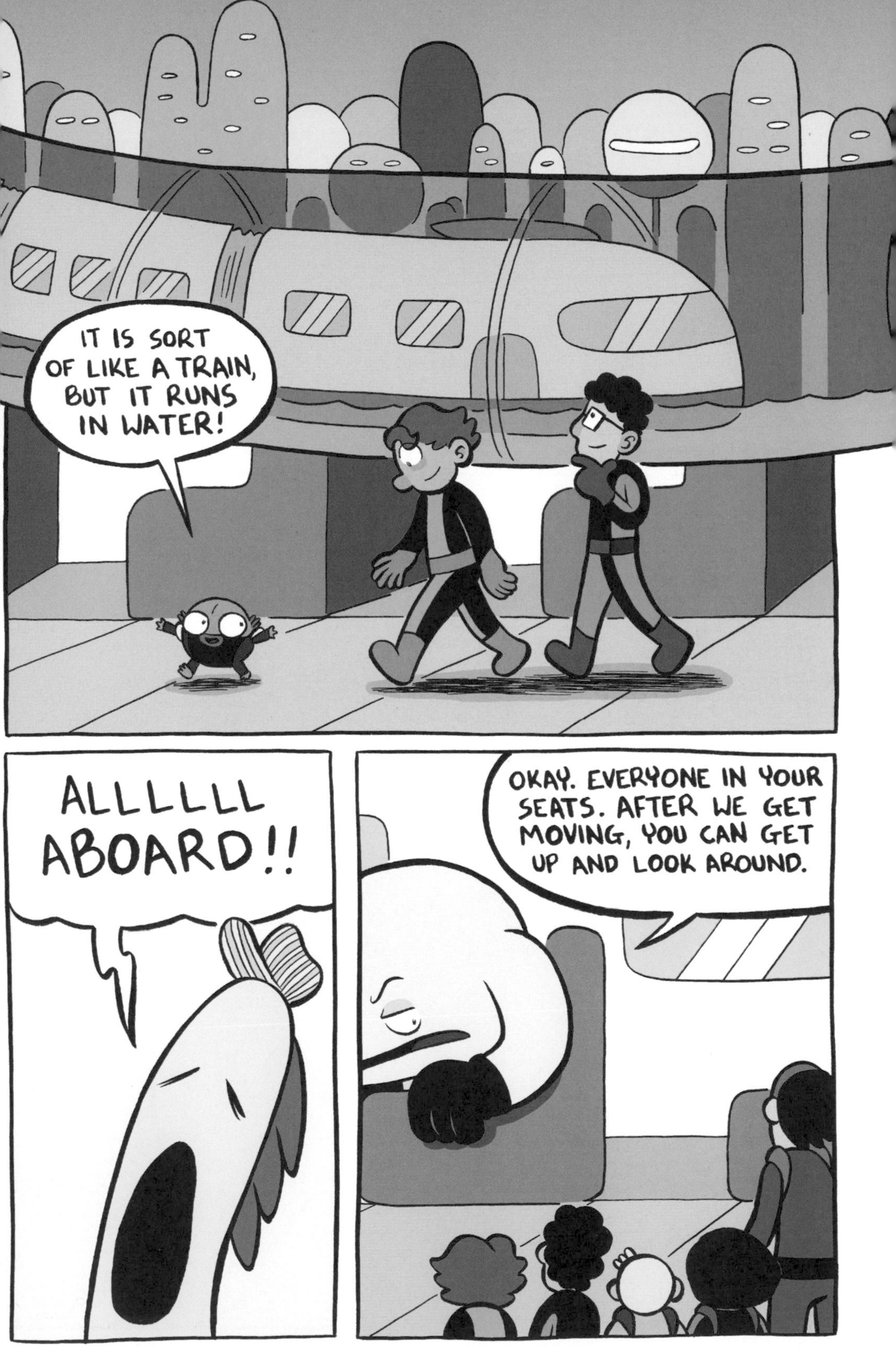
IT IS SORT OF LIKE A TRAIN, BUT IT RUNS IN WATER!
ALLLLLL ABOARD!!
OKAY. EVERYONE IN YOUR SEATS. AFTER WE GET MOVING, YOU CAN GET UP AND LOOK AROUND.

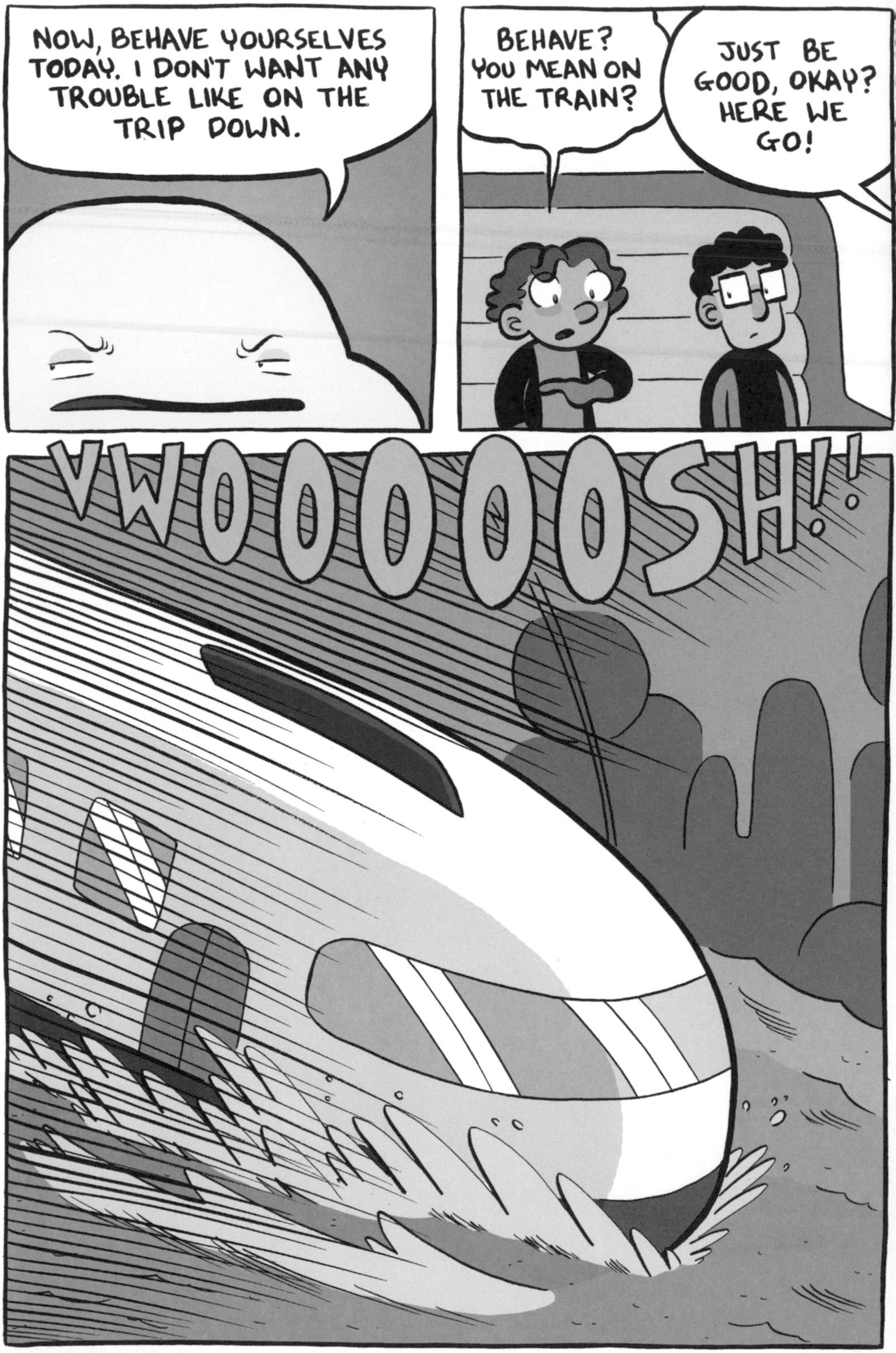
NOW, BEHAVE YOURSELVES TODAY. I DON'T WANT ANY TROUBLE LIKE ON THE TRIP DOWN.
BEHAVE? YOU MEAN ON THE TRAIN?
JUST BE GOOD, OKAY? HERE WE GO!
VWOOOOOSH!!

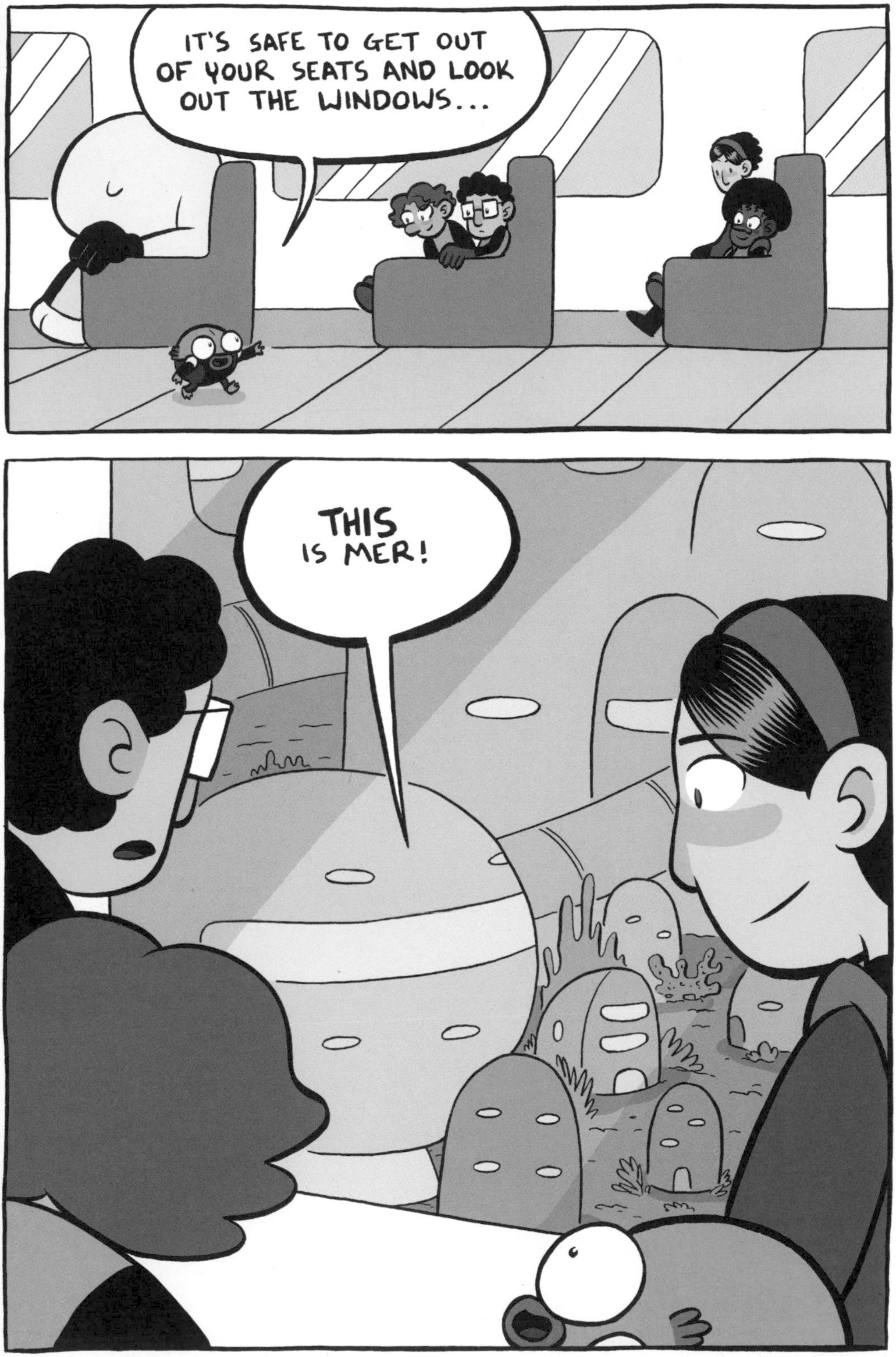
IT'S SAFE TO GET OUT OF YOUR SEATS AND LOOK OUT THE WINDOWS...
THIS IS MER!

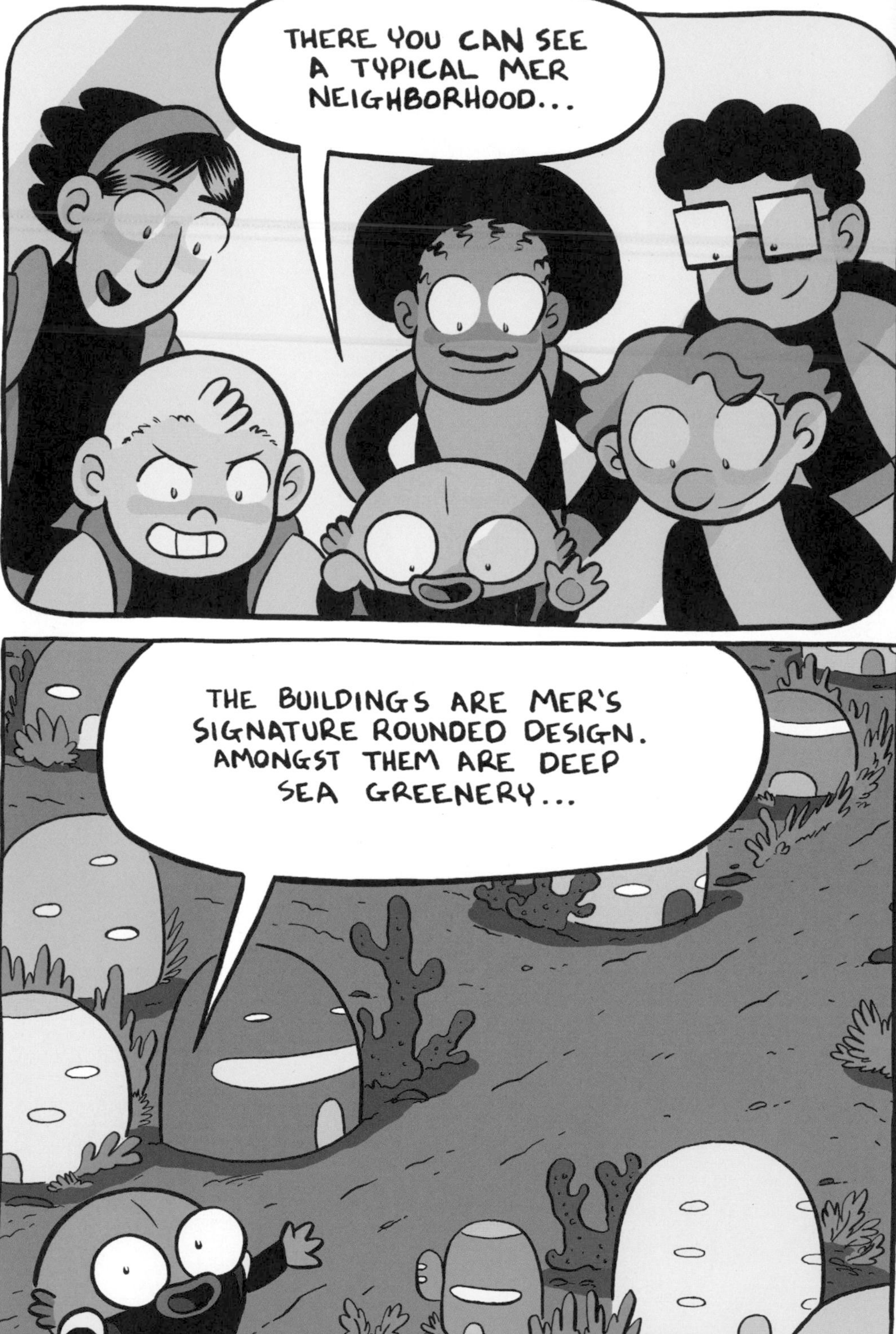
THERE YOU CAN SEE A TYPICAL MER NEIGHBORHOOD...
THE BUILDINGS ARE MER'S SIGNATURE ROUNDED DESIGN. AMONGST THEM ARE DEEP SEA GREENERY...

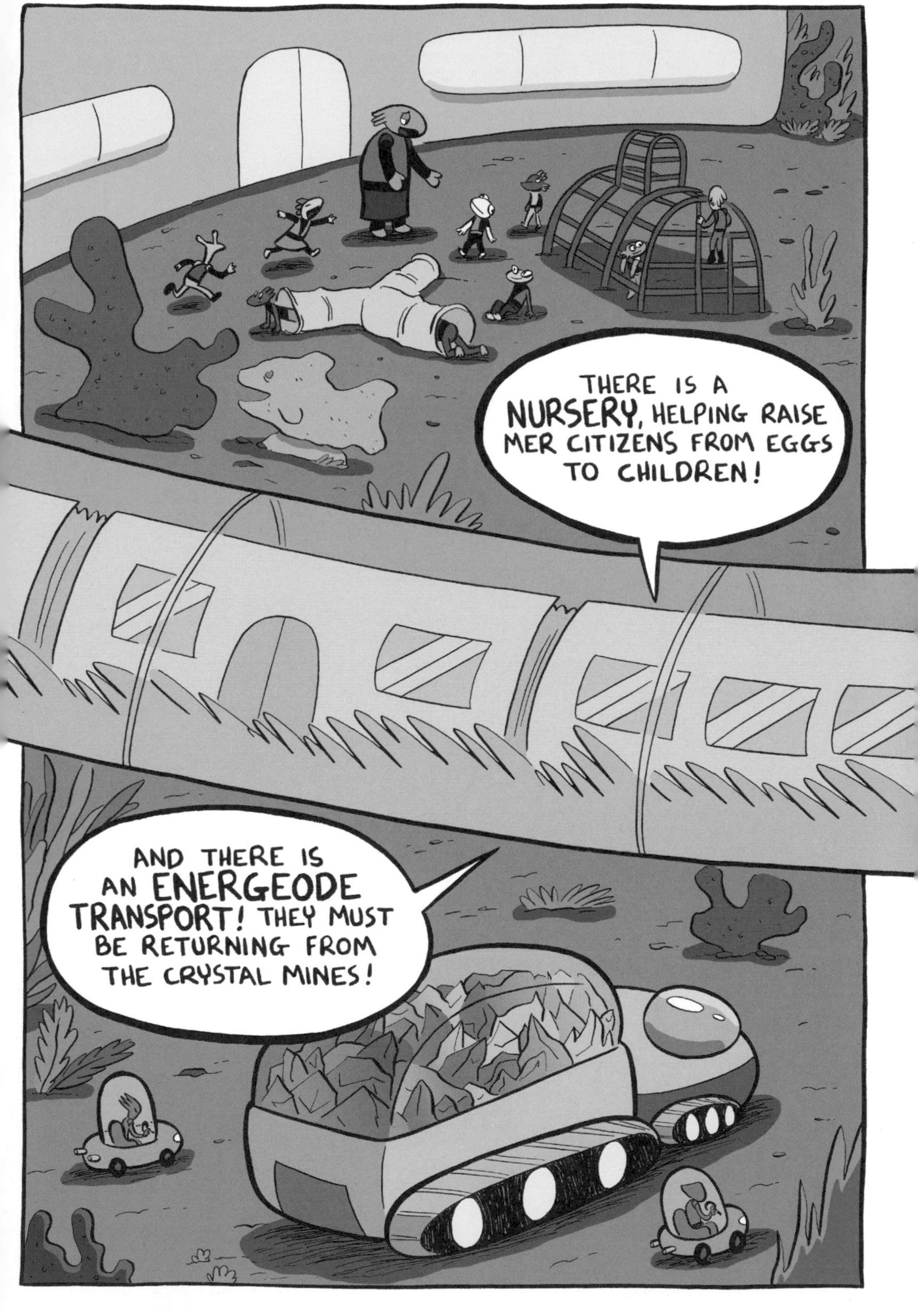
THERE IS A NURSERY, HELPING RAISE MER CITIZENS FROM EGGS TO CHILDREN!
AND THERE IS AN ENERGEODE TRANSPORT! THEY MUST BE RETURNING FROM THE CRYSTAL MINES!

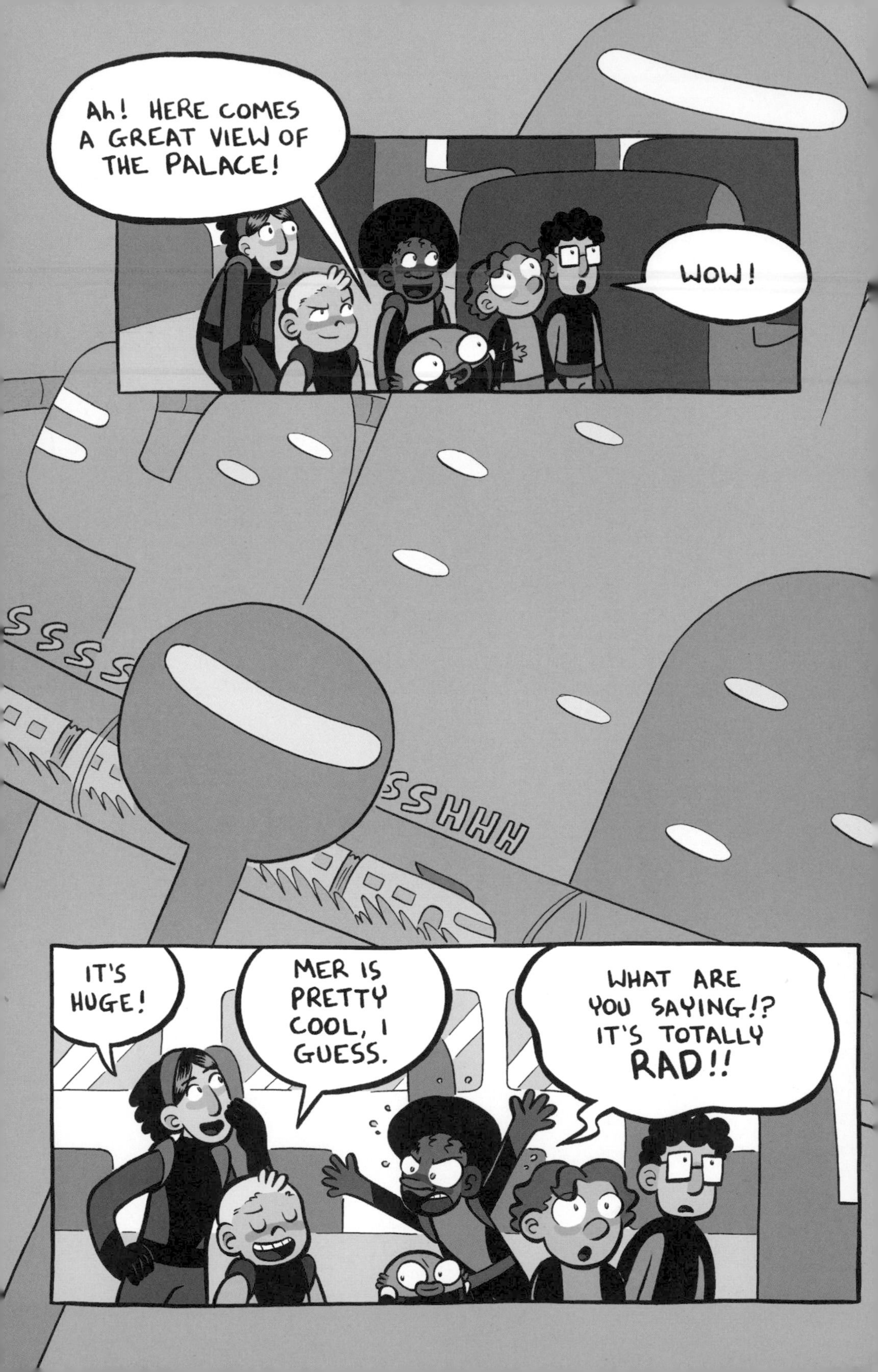

AH! HERE COMES A GREAT VIEW OF THE PALACE!
WOW!
SSSS
SSHHH
IT'S HUGE!
MER IS PRETTY COOL, I GUESS.
WHAT ARE YOU SAYING!? IT'S TOTALLY RAD!!

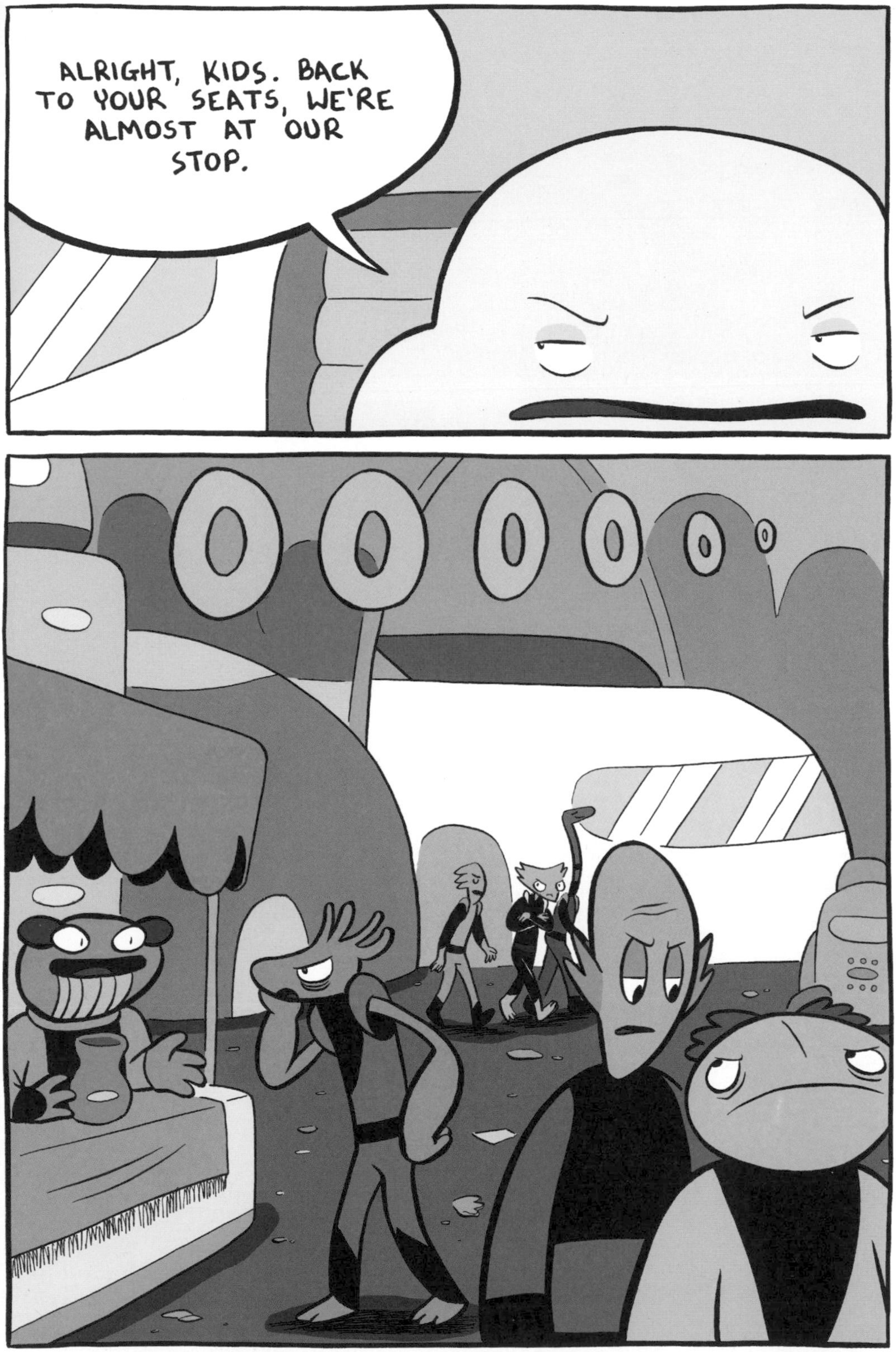
ALRIGHT, KIDS. BACK TO YOUR SEATS, WE'RE ALMOST AT OUR STOP.

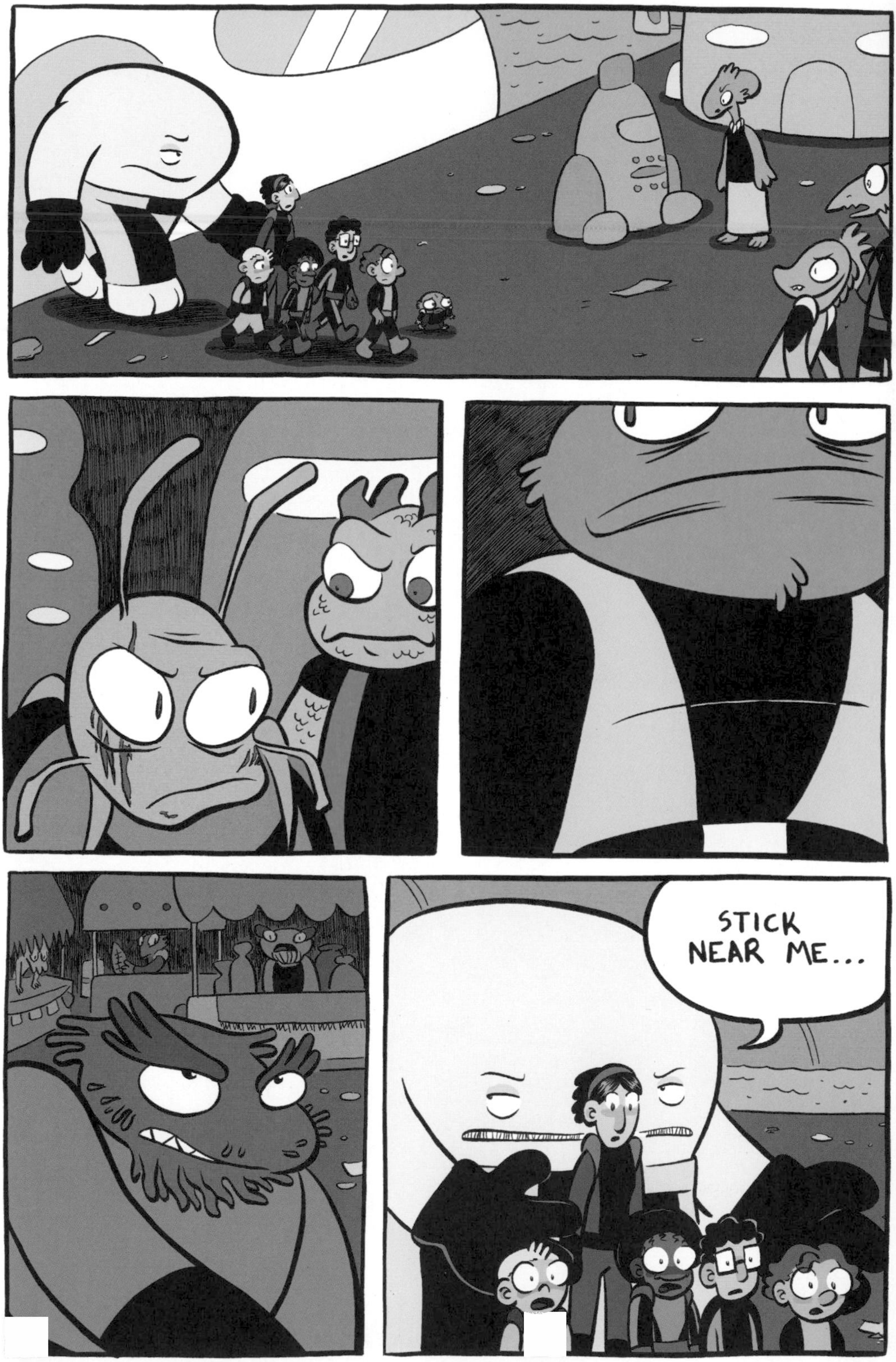
STICK NEAR ME...

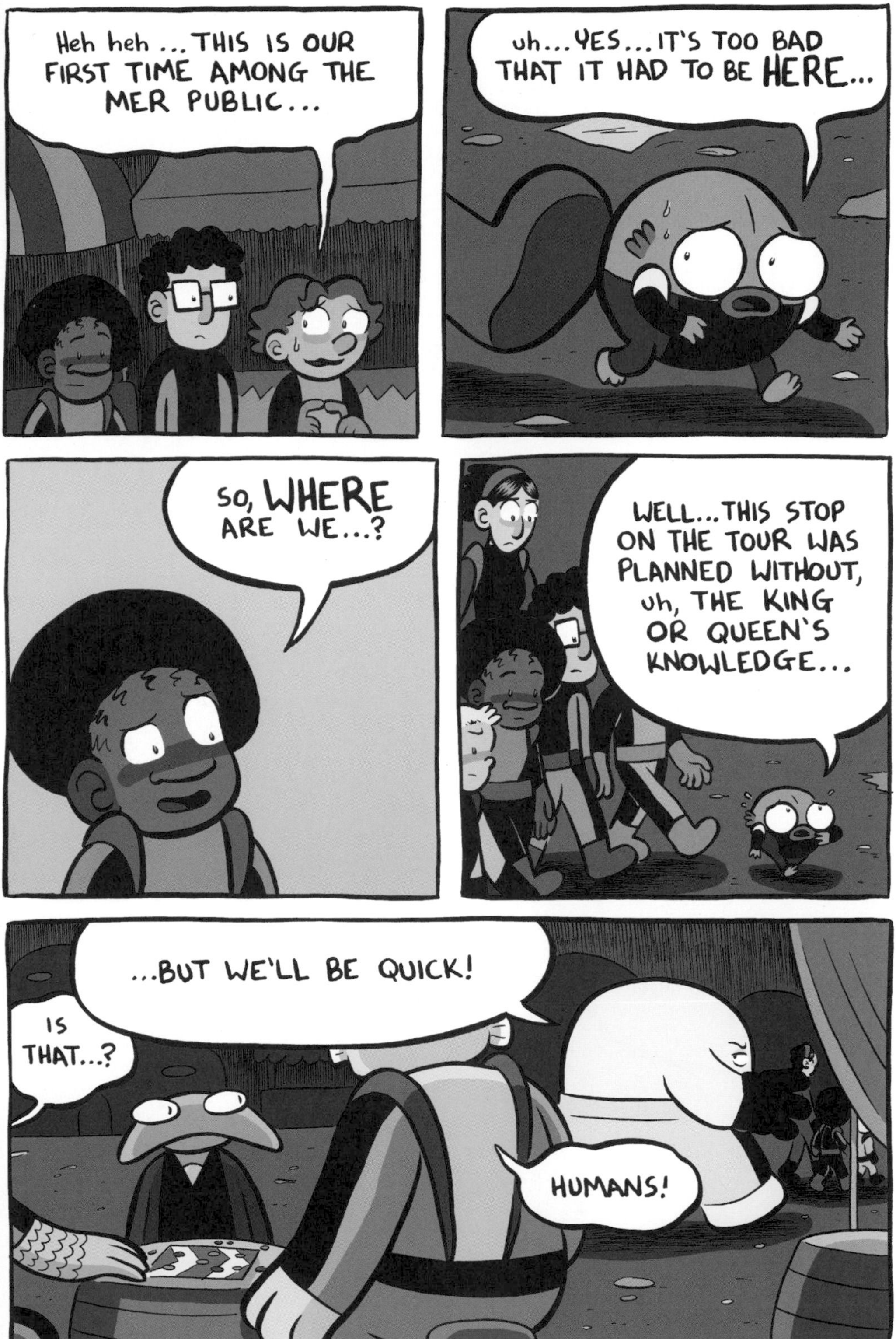

Heh heh ... THIS IS OUR FIRST TIME AMONG THE MER PUBLIC...
uh... YES... IT'S TOO BAD THAT IT HAD TO BE HERE...
SO, WHERE ARE WE...?
WELL... THIS STOP ON THE TOUR WAS PLANNED WITHOUT, uh, THE KING OR QUEEN'S KNOWLEDGE...
...BUT WE'LL BE QUICK!
IS THAT...?
HUMANS!

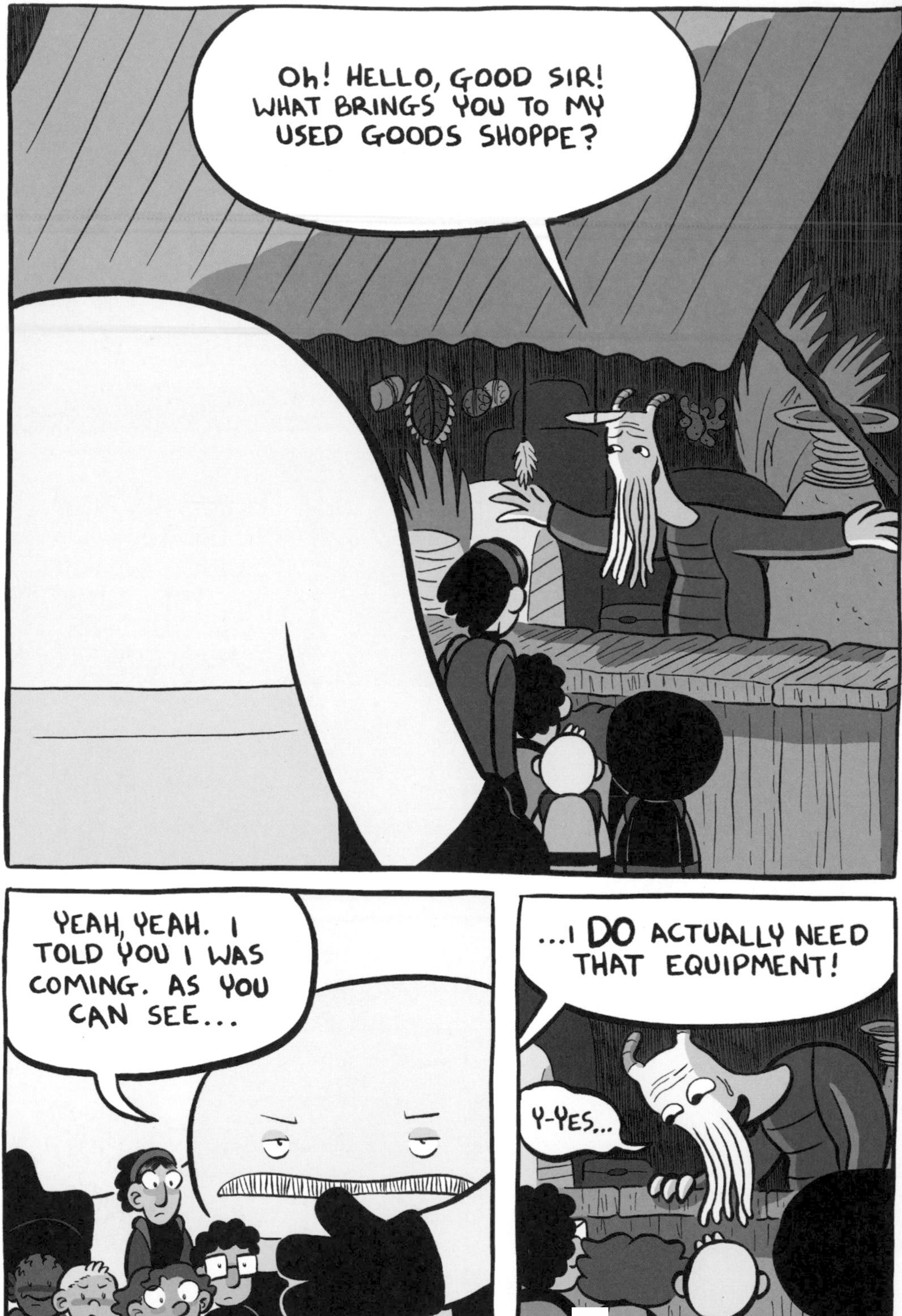
OH! HELLO, GOOD SIR! WHAT BRINGS YOU TO MY USED GOODS SHOPPE?
YEAH, YEAH. I TOLD YOU I WAS COMING. AS YOU CAN SEE...
...I DO ACTUALLY NEED THAT EQUIPMENT!
Y-YES...

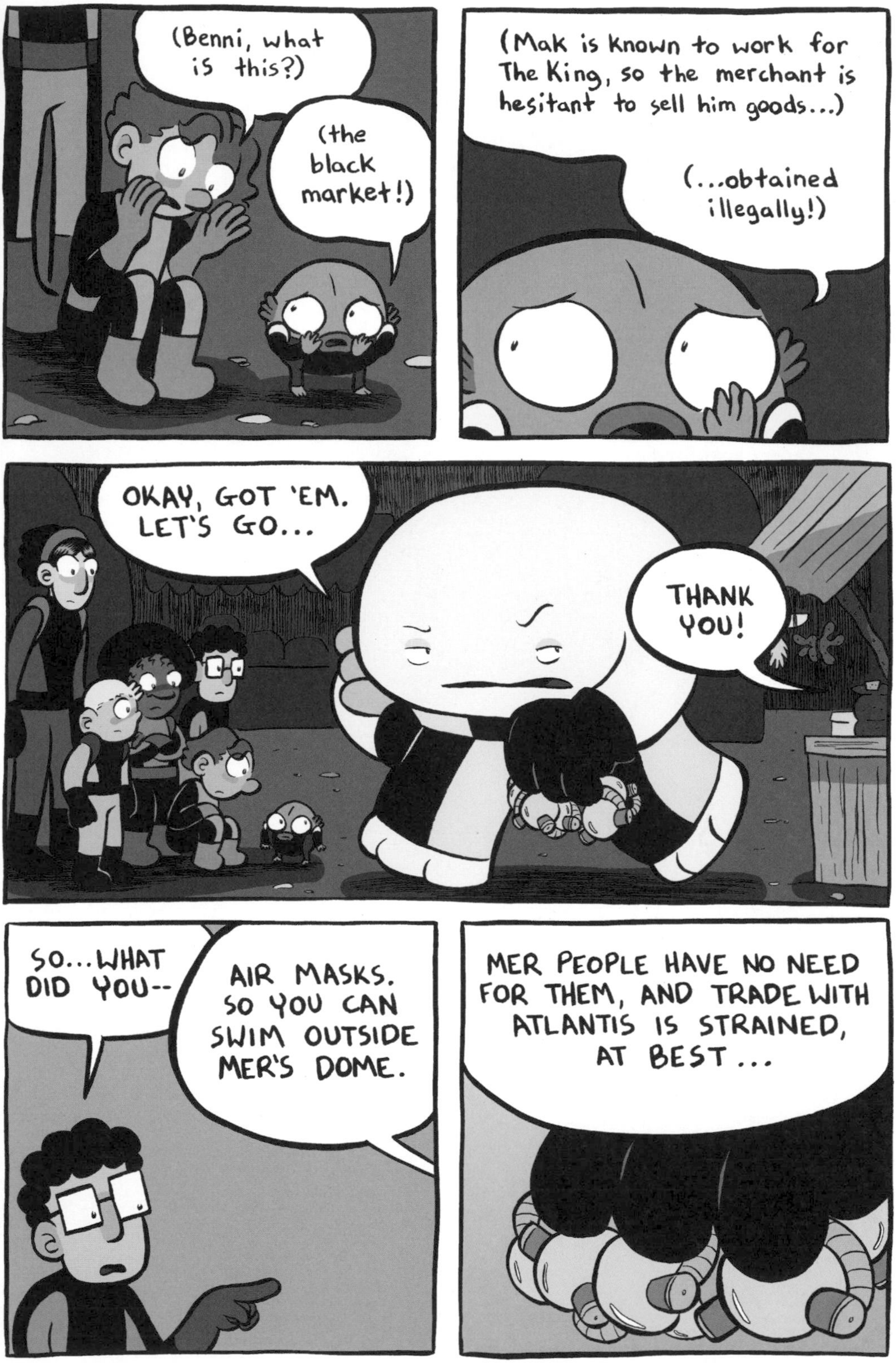
(Benni, what is this?)
(the black market!)
(Mak is known to work for The King, so the merchant is hesitant to sell him goods...)
(...obtained illegally!)
OKAY, GOT 'EM. LET'S GO...
THANK YOU!
SO...WHAT DID YOU--
AIR MASKS. SO YOU CAN SWIM OUTSIDE MER'S DOME.
MER PEOPLE HAVE NO NEED FOR THEM, AND TRADE WITH ATLANTIS IS STRAINED, AT BEST...

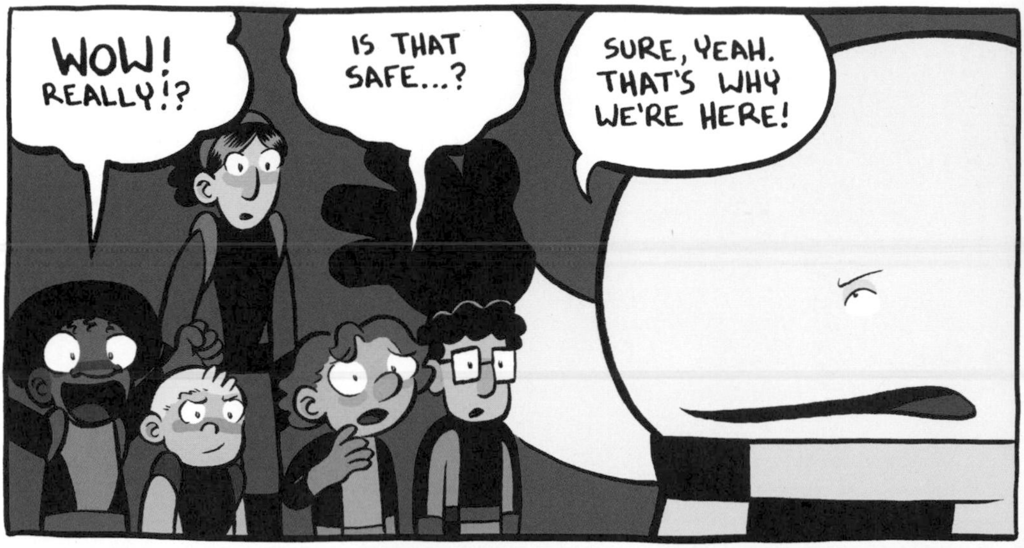
WOW! REALLY!?
IS THAT SAFE...?
SURE, YEAH. THAT'S WHY WE'RE HERE!

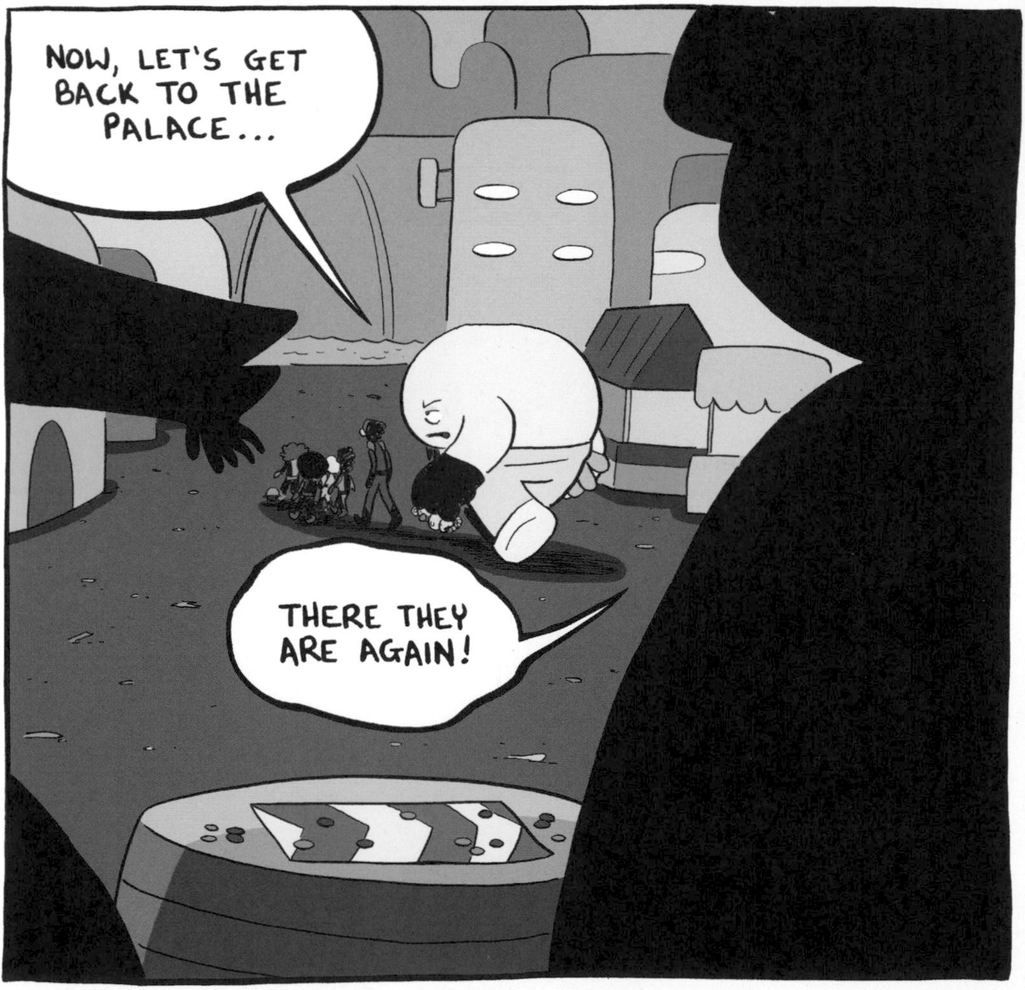
NOW, LET'S GET BACK TO THE PALACE...
THERE THEY ARE AGAIN!

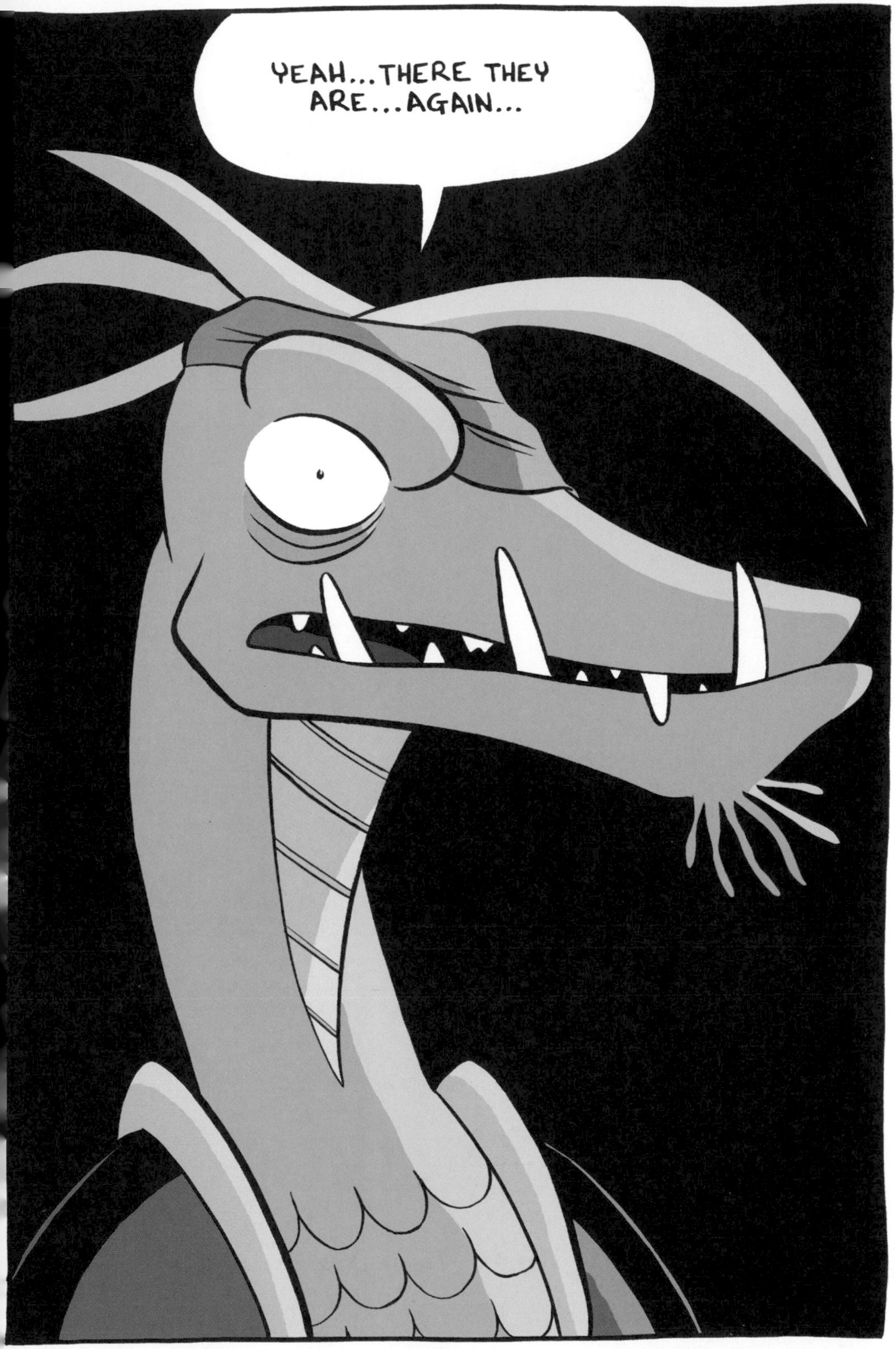
YEAH...THERE THEY ARE...AGAIN...

CHAPTER FOUR

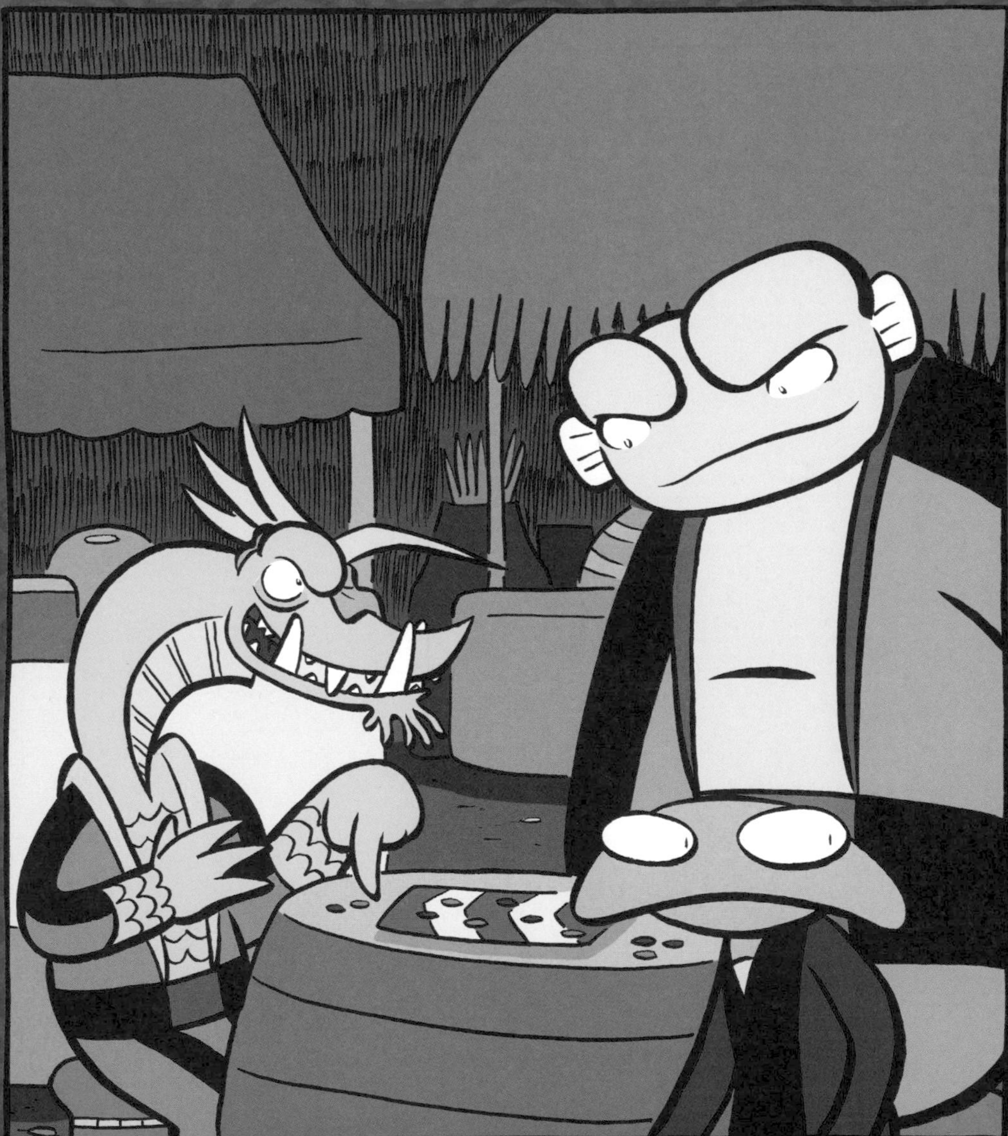

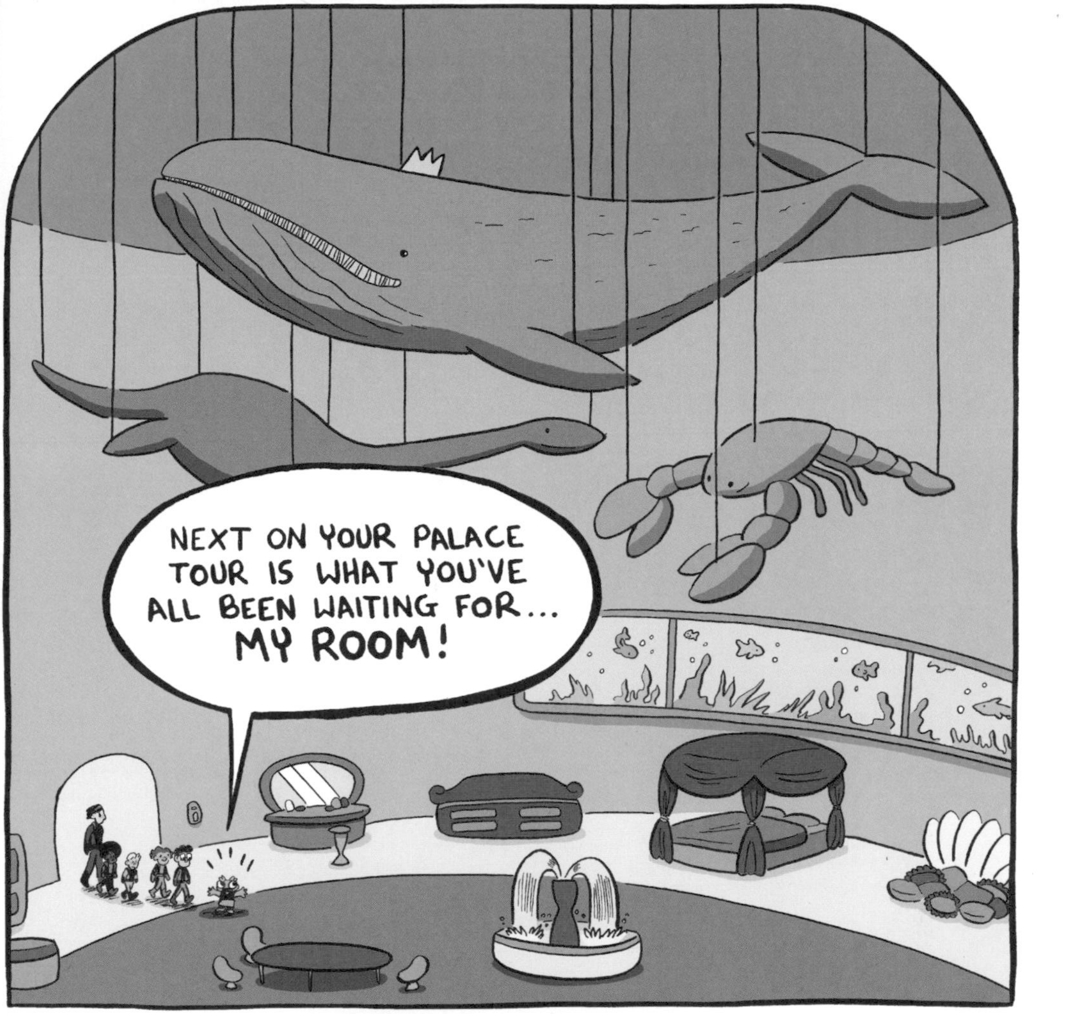
NEXT ON YOUR PALACE TOUR IS WHAT YOU'VE ALL BEEN WAITING FOR... MY ROOM!

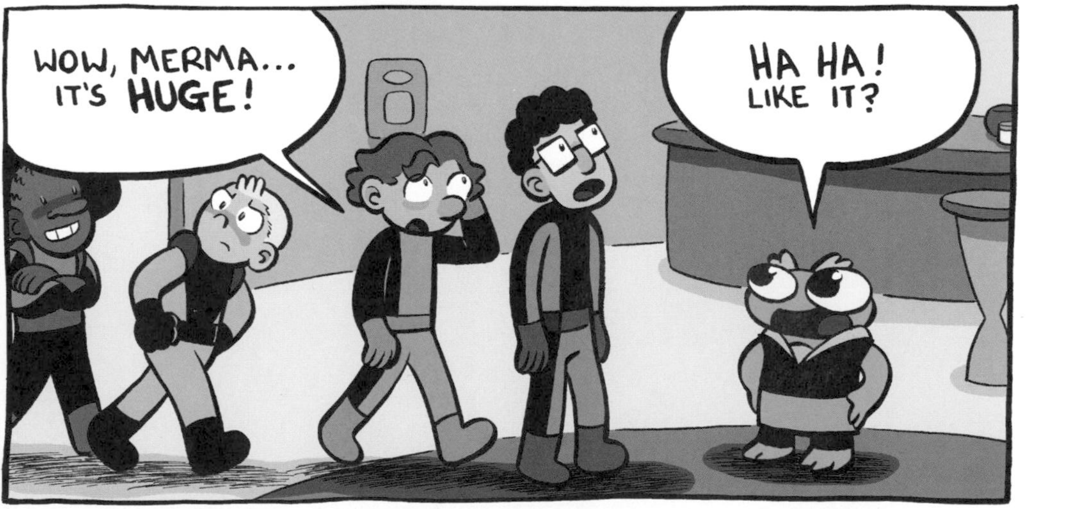
WOW, MERMA... IT'S HUGE!
HA HA! LIKE IT?

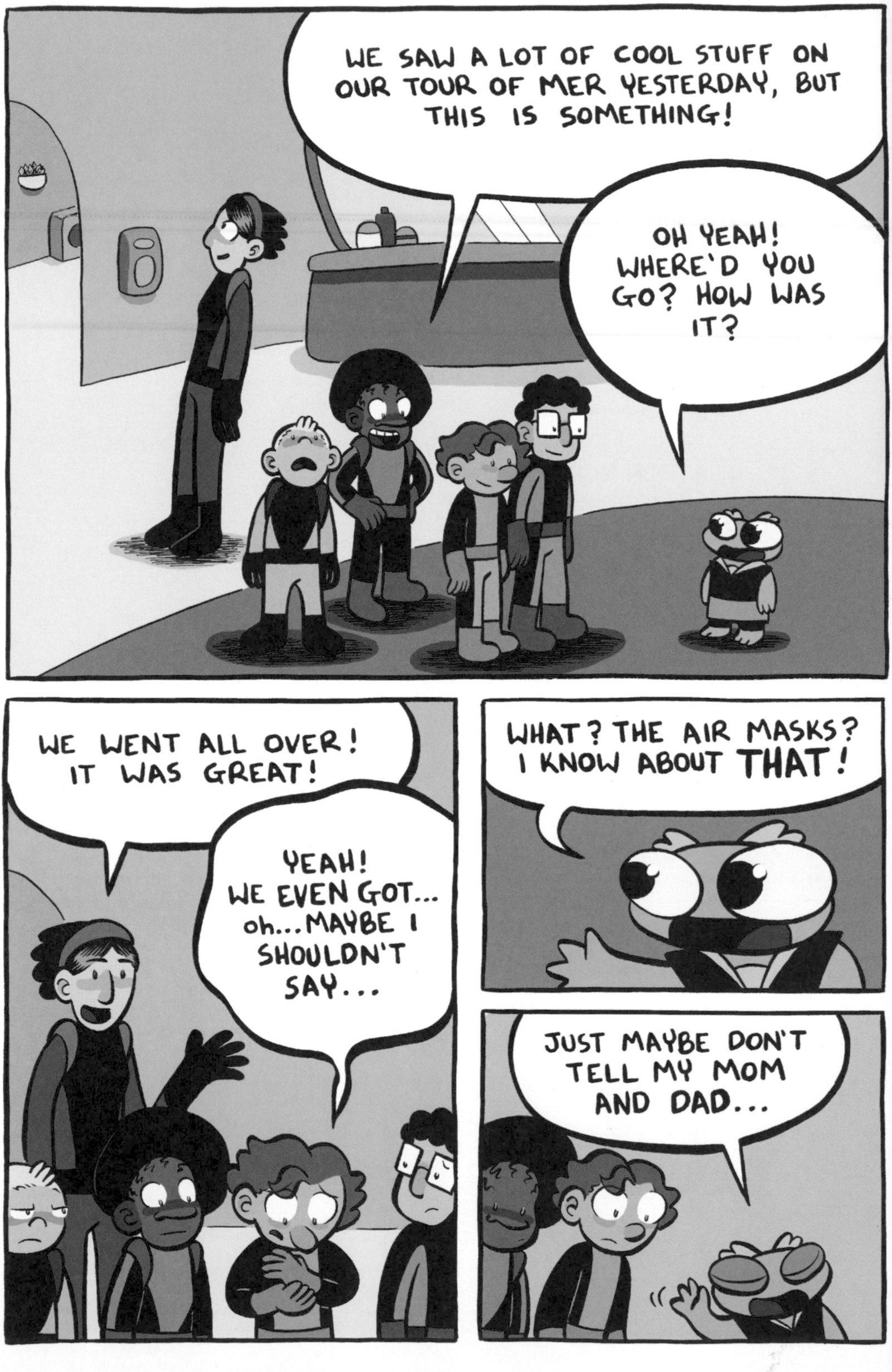
WE SAW A LOT OF COOL STUFF ON OUR TOUR OF MER YESTERDAY, BUT THIS IS SOMETHING!
OH YEAH! WHERE'D YOU GO? HOW WAS IT?
WE WENT ALL OVER! IT WAS GREAT!
YEAH! WE EVEN GOT... oh...MAYBE I SHOULDN'T SAY...
WHAT? THE AIR MASKS? I KNOW ABOUT THAT!
JUST MAYBE DON'T TELL MY MOM AND DAD...

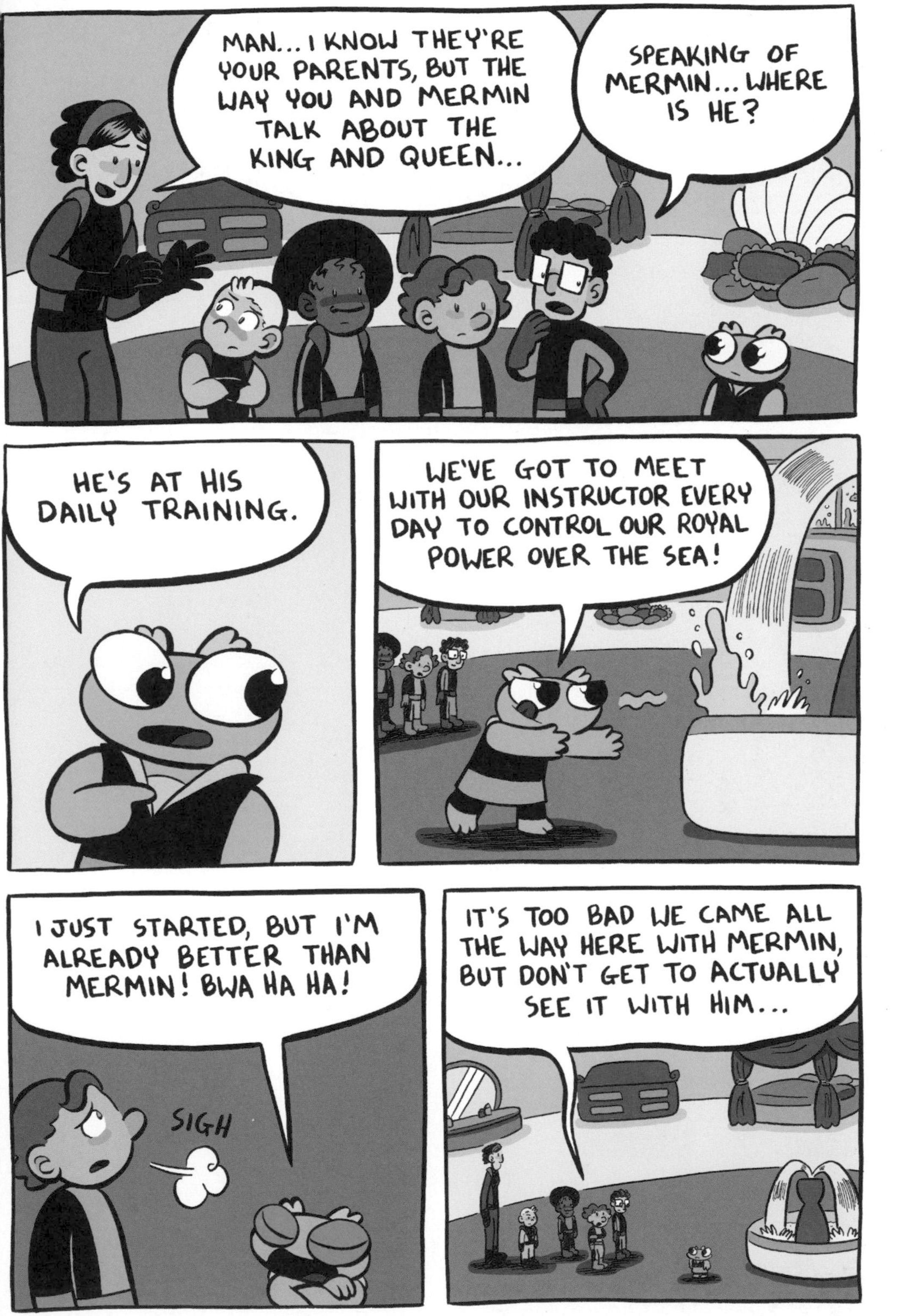
MAN... I KNOW THEY'RE YOUR PARENTS, BUT THE WAY YOU AND MERMIN TALK ABOUT THE KING AND QUEEN...
SPEAKING OF MERMIN... WHERE IS HE?
HE'S AT HIS DAILY TRAINING.
WE'VE GOT TO MEET WITH OUR INSTRUCTOR EVERY DAY TO CONTROL OUR ROYAL POWER OVER THE SEA!
I JUST STARTED, BUT I'M ALREADY BETTER THAN MERMIN! BWA HA HA!
SIGH
IT'S TOO BAD WE CAME ALL THE WAY HERE WITH MERMIN, BUT DON'T GET TO ACTUALLY SEE IT WITH HIM...

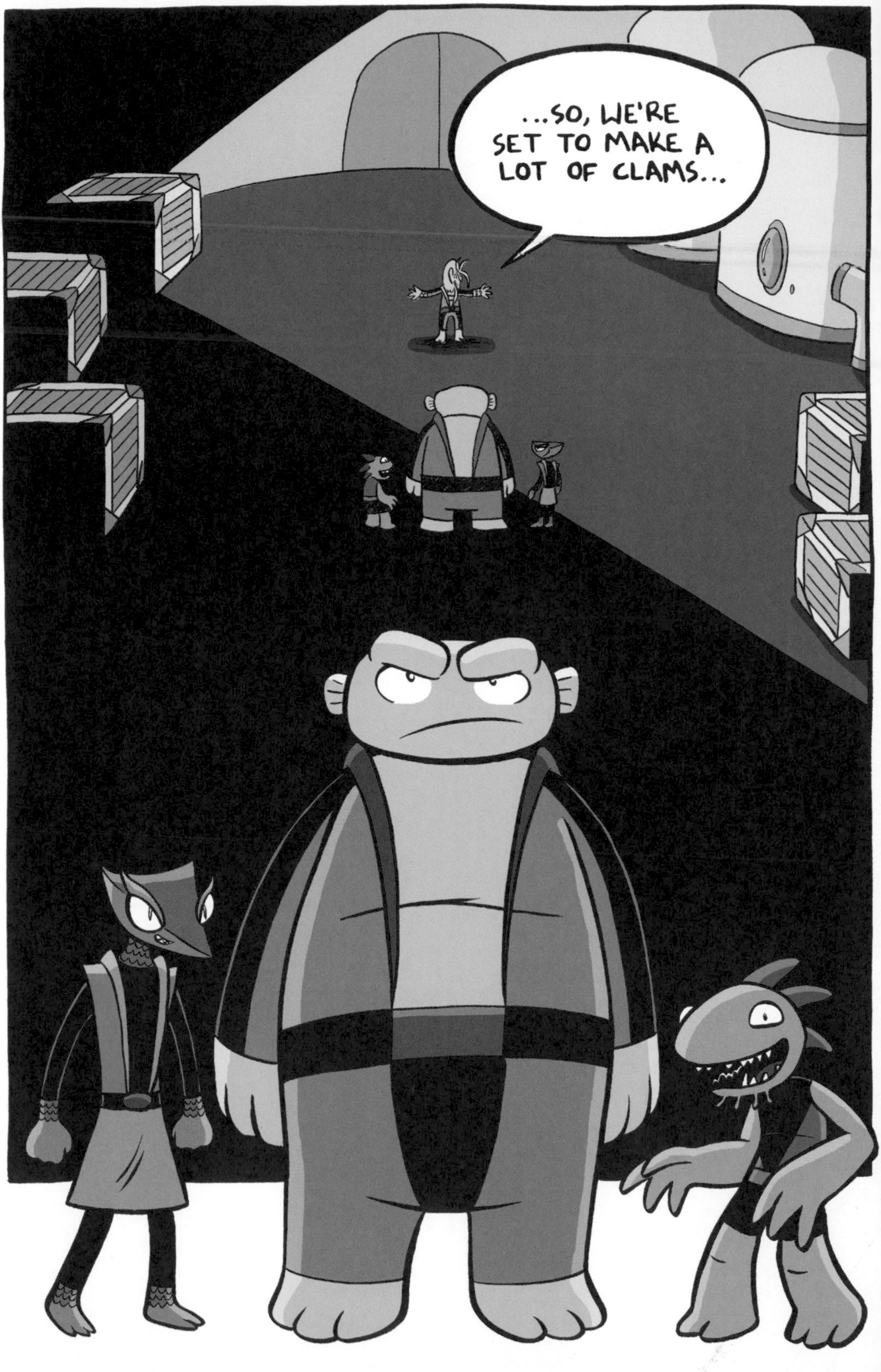
...SO, WE'RE SET TO MAKE A LOT OF CLAMS...

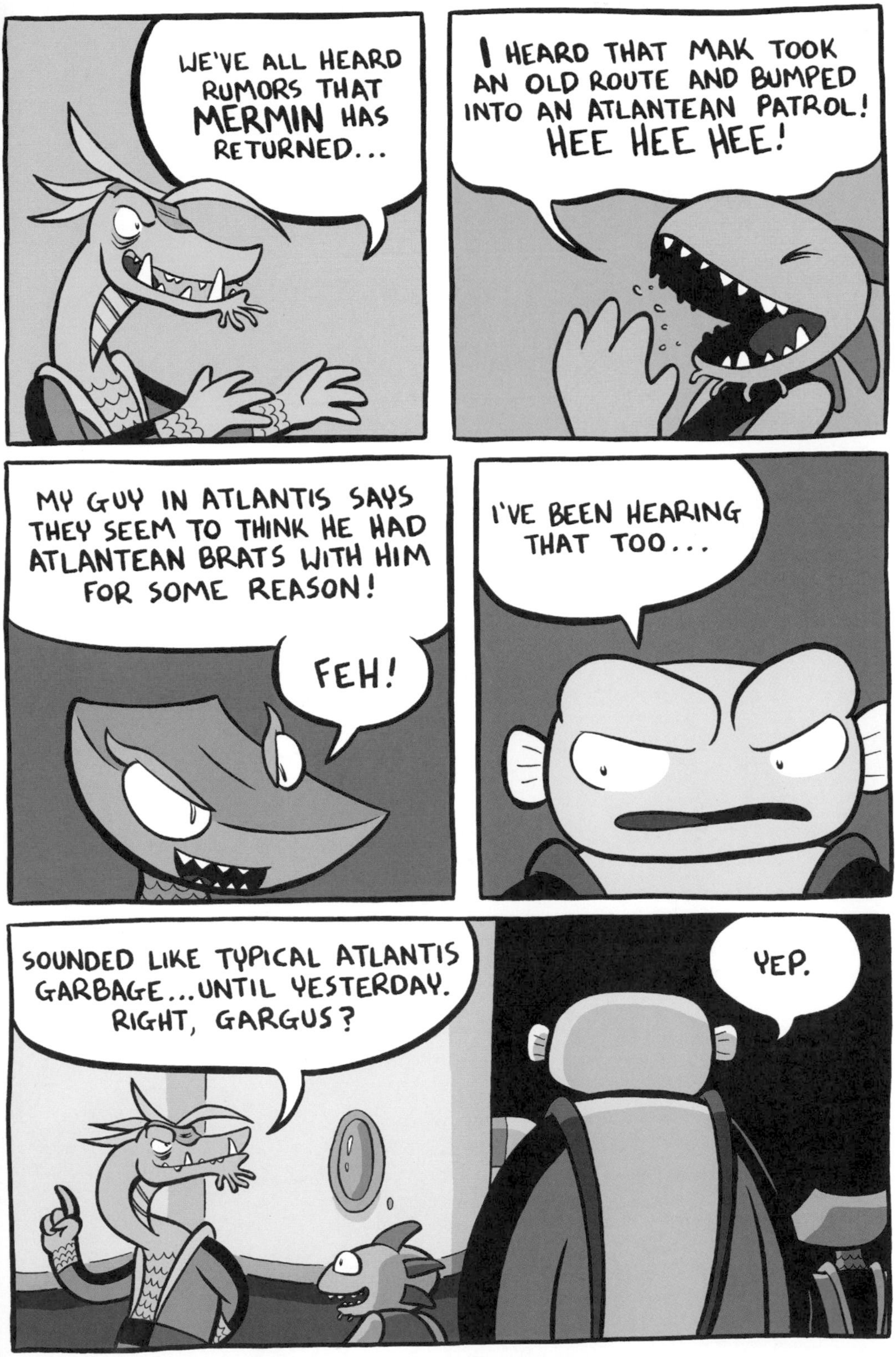
WE'VE ALL HEARD RUMORS THAT MERMIN HAS RETURNED...
I HEARD THAT MAK TOOK AN OLD ROUTE AND BUMPED INTO AN ATLANTEAN PATROL! HEE HEE HEE!
MY GUY IN ATLANTIS SAYS THEY SEEM TO THINK HE HAD ATLANTEAN BRATS WITH HIM FOR SOME REASON!
FEH!
I'VE BEEN HEARING THAT TOO...
SOUNDED LIKE TYPICAL ATLANTIS GARBAGE...UNTIL YESTERDAY. RIGHT, GARGUS?
YEP.

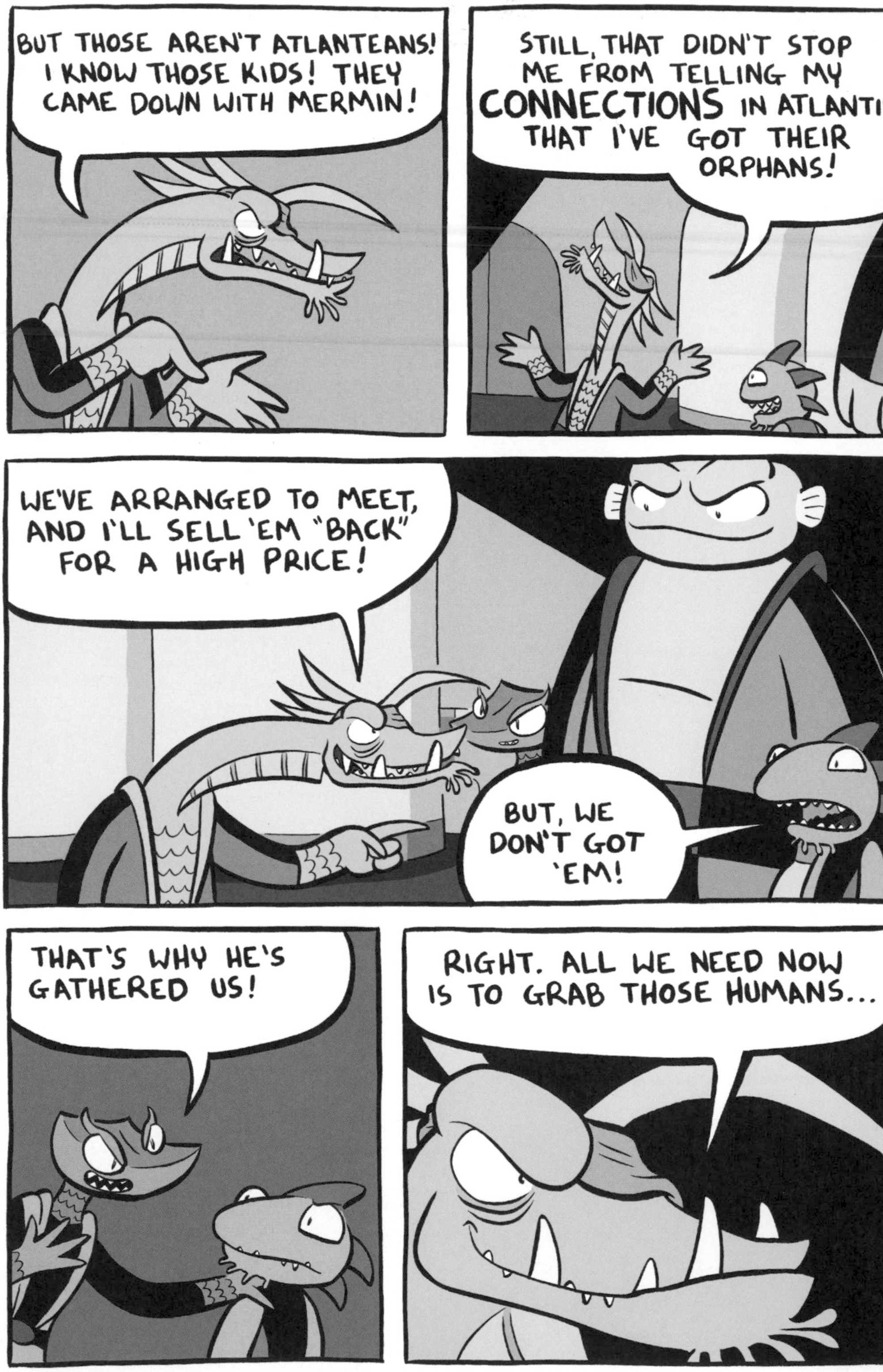
BUT THOSE AREN'T ATLANTEANS! I KNOW THOSE KIDS! THEY CAME DOWN WITH MERMIN!
STILL, THAT DIDN'T STOP ME FROM TELLING MY CONNECTIONS IN ATLANTIS THAT I'VE GOT THEIR ORPHANS!
WE'VE ARRANGED TO MEET, AND I'LL SELL 'EM "BACK" FOR A HIGH PRICE!
BUT, WE DON'T GOT 'EM!
THAT'S WHY HE'S GATHERED US!
RIGHT. ALL WE NEED NOW IS TO GRAB THOSE HUMANS...

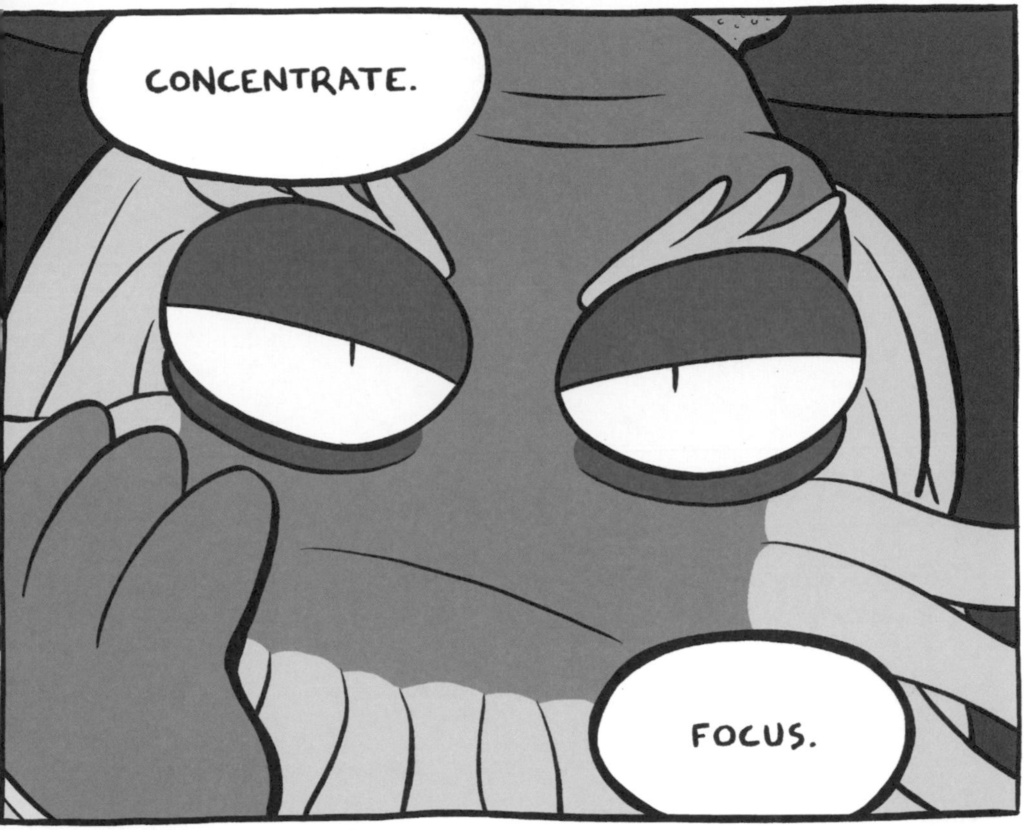
CONCENTRATE.
FOCUS.

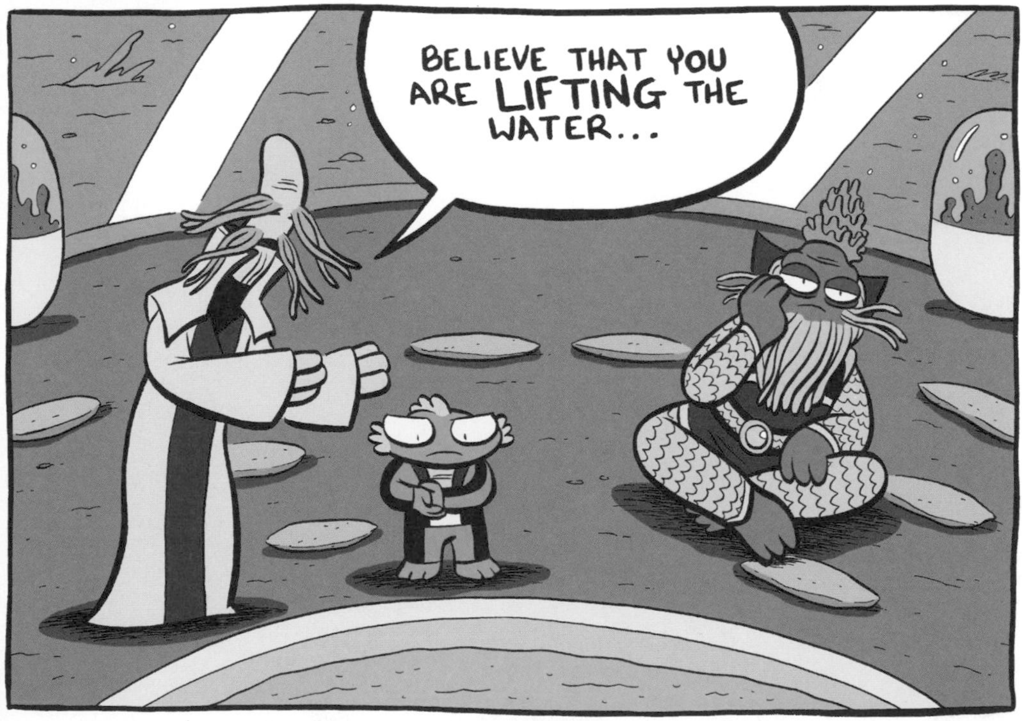
BELIEVE THAT YOU ARE LIFTING THE WATER...

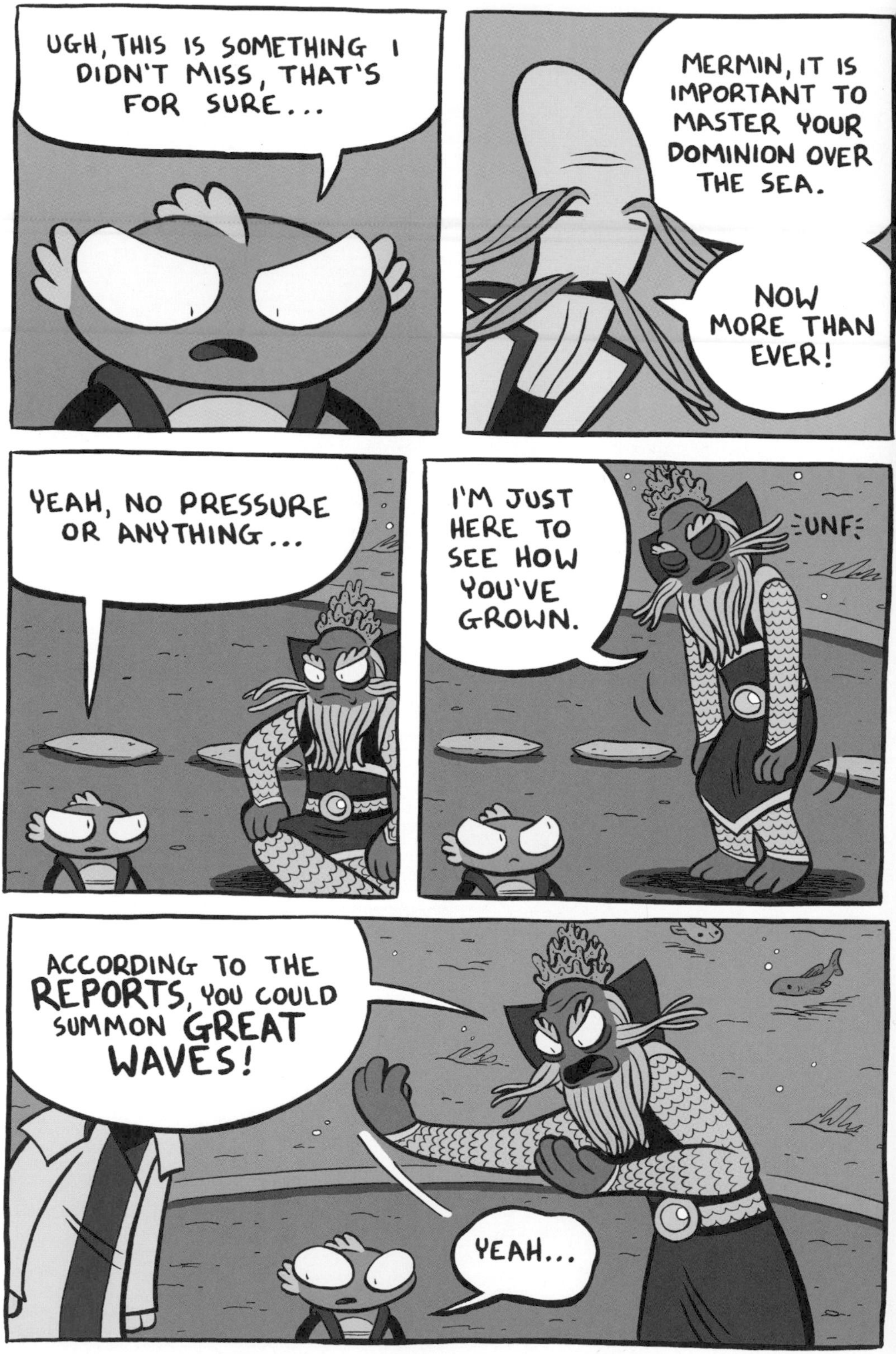
UGH, THIS IS SOMETHING I DIDN'T MISS, THAT'S FOR SURE...
MERMIN, IT IS IMPORTANT TO MASTER YOUR DOMINION OVER THE SEA.
NOW MORE THAN EVER!
YEAH, NO PRESSURE OR ANYTHING...
I'M JUST HERE TO SEE HOW YOU'VE GROWN.
UNF
ACCORDING TO THE REPORTS, YOU COULD SUMMON GREAT WAVES!
YEAH...

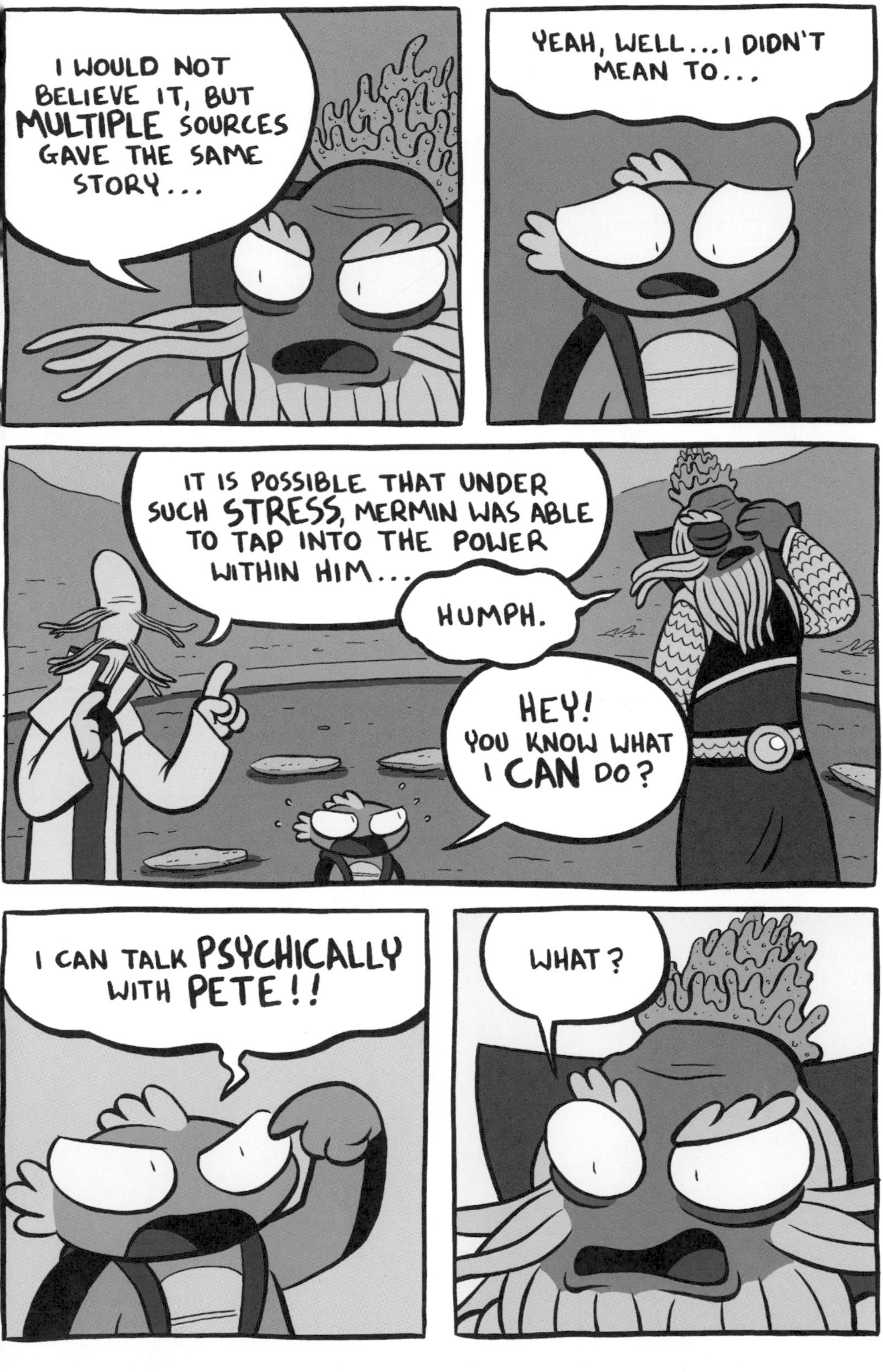
I WOULD NOT BELIEVE IT, BUT MULTIPLE SOURCES GAVE THE SAME STORY...
YEAH, WELL...I DIDN'T MEAN TO...
IT IS POSSIBLE THAT UNDER SUCH STRESS, MERMIN WAS ABLE TO TAP INTO THE POWER WITHIN HIM...
HUMPH.
HEY! YOU KNOW WHAT I CAN DO?
I CAN TALK PSYCHICALLY WITH PETE!!
WHAT?

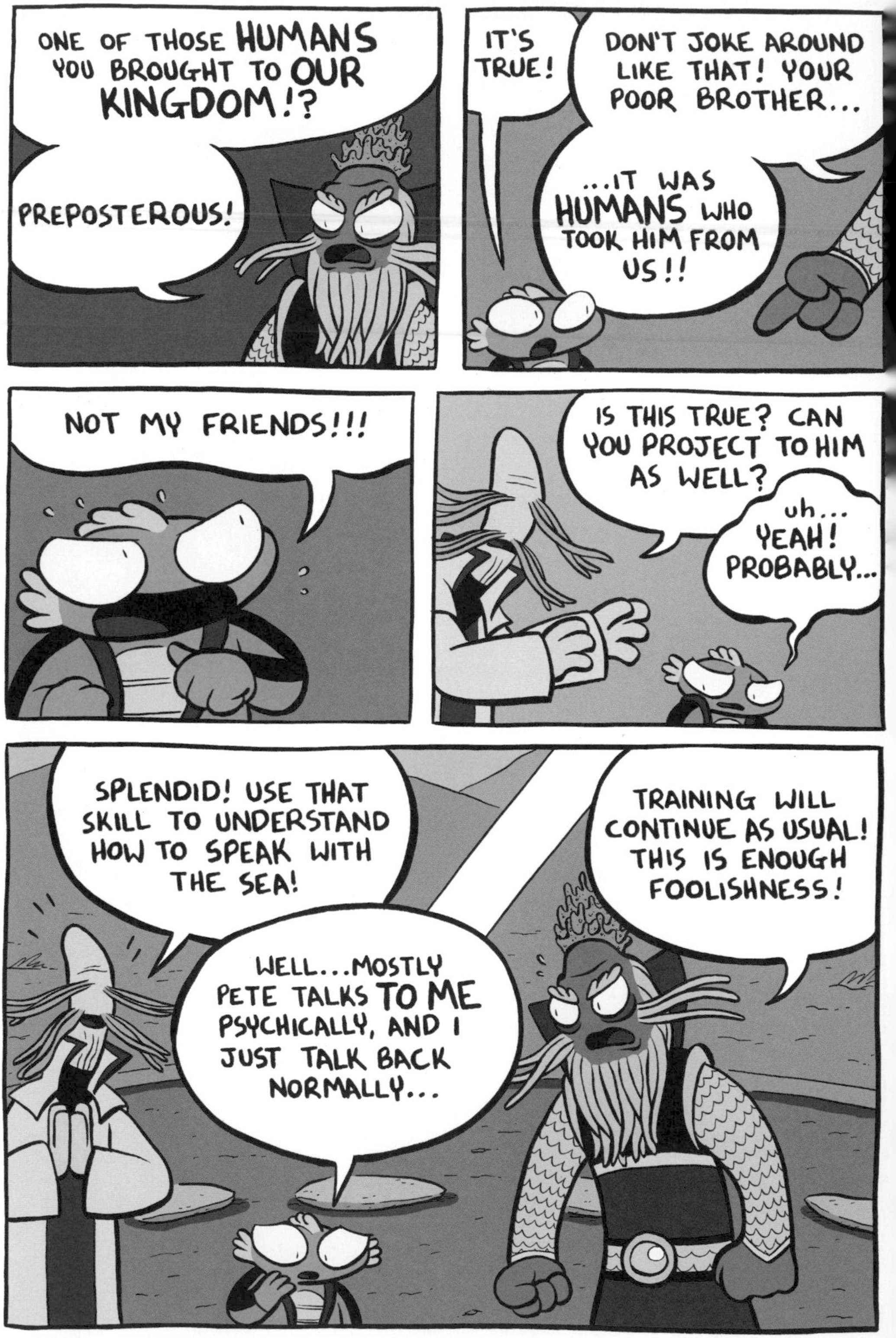
ONE OF THOSE HUMANS YOU BROUGHT TO OUR KINGDOM!?
PREPOSTEROUS!
IT'S TRUE!
DON'T JOKE AROUND LIKE THAT! YOUR POOR BROTHER...
...IT WAS HUMANS WHO TOOK HIM FROM US!!
NOT MY FRIENDS!!!
IS THIS TRUE? CAN YOU PROJECT TO HIM AS WELL?
uh... YEAH! PROBABLY...
SPLENDID! USE THAT SKILL TO UNDERSTAND HOW TO SPEAK WITH THE SEA!
TRAINING WILL CONTINUE AS USUAL! THIS IS ENOUGH FOOLISHNESS!
WELL...MOSTLY PETE TALKS TO ME PSYCHICALLY, AND I JUST TALK BACK NORMALLY...

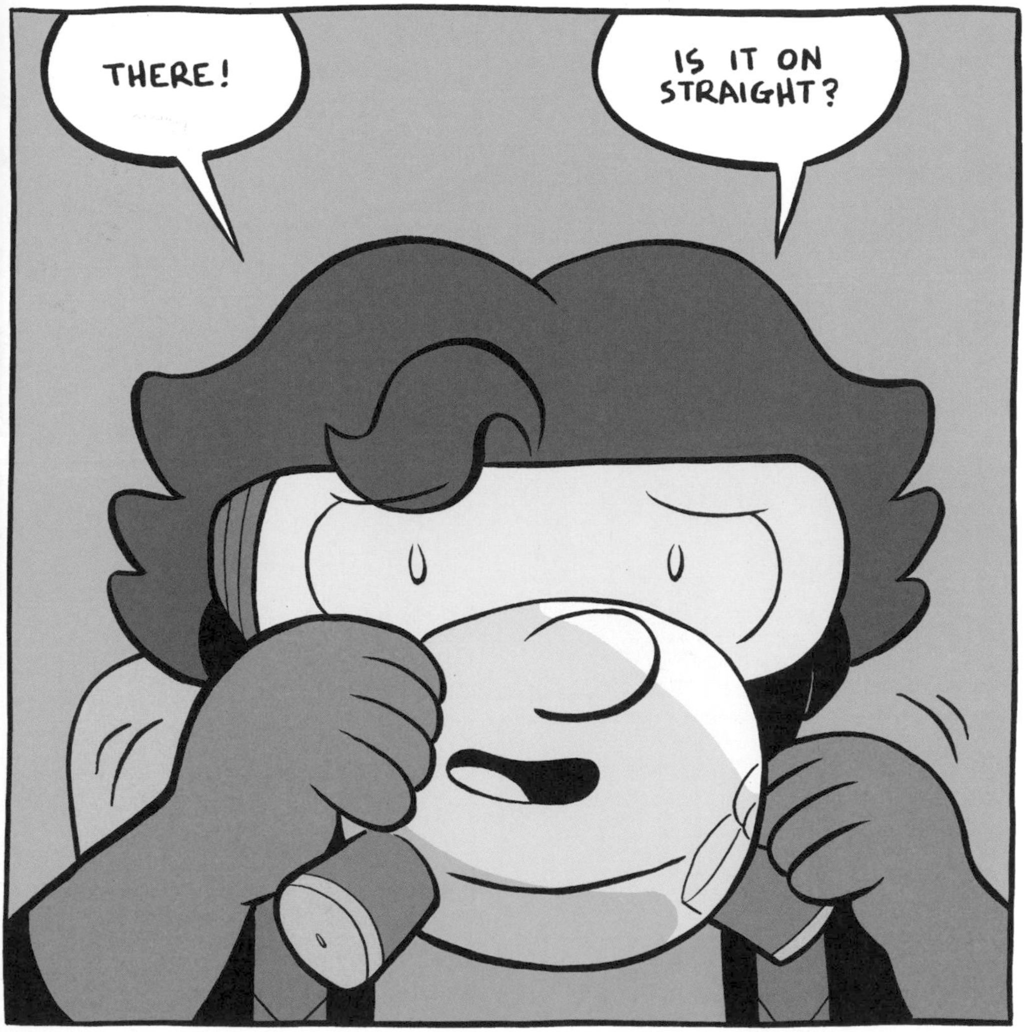
THERE!
IS IT ON STRAIGHT?

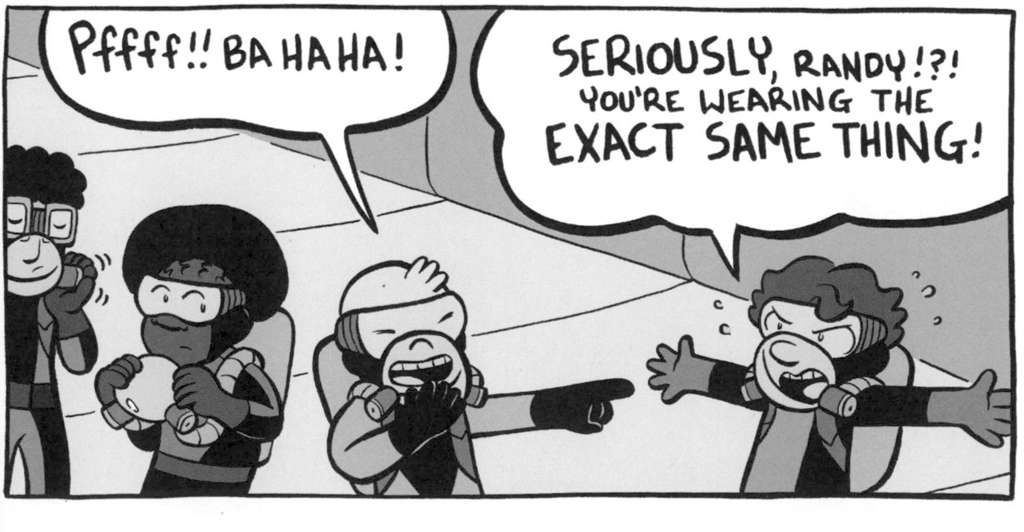
Pffff!! BA HA HA!
SERIOUSLY, RANDY!?! YOU'RE WEARING THE EXACT SAME THING!

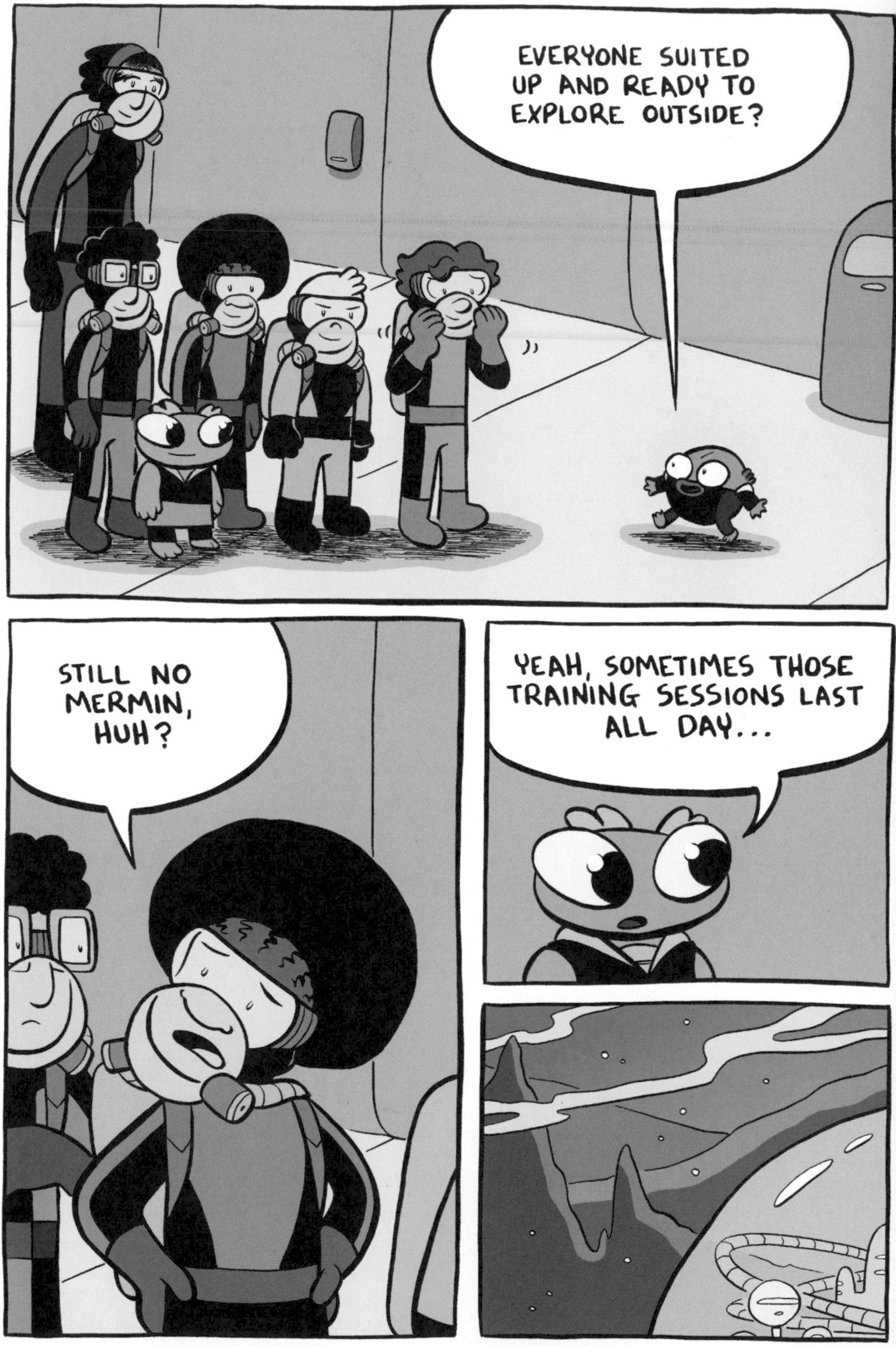
EVERYONE SUITED UP AND READY TO EXPLORE OUTSIDE?
STILL NO MERMIN, HUH?
YEAH, SOMETIMES THOSE TRAINING SESSIONS LAST ALL DAY...

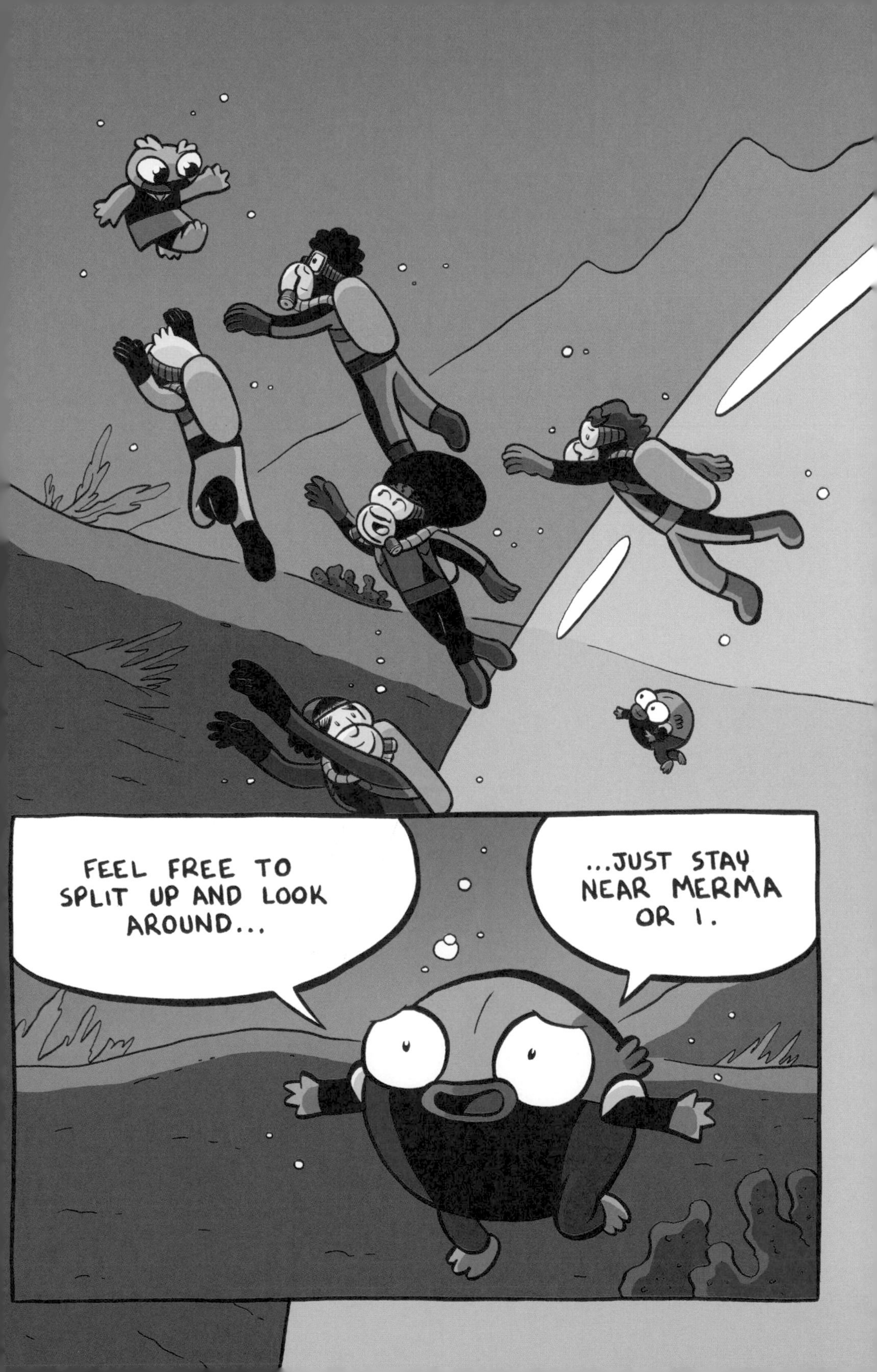

FEEL FREE TO SPLIT UP AND LOOK AROUND...
...JUST STAY NEAR MERMA OR I.

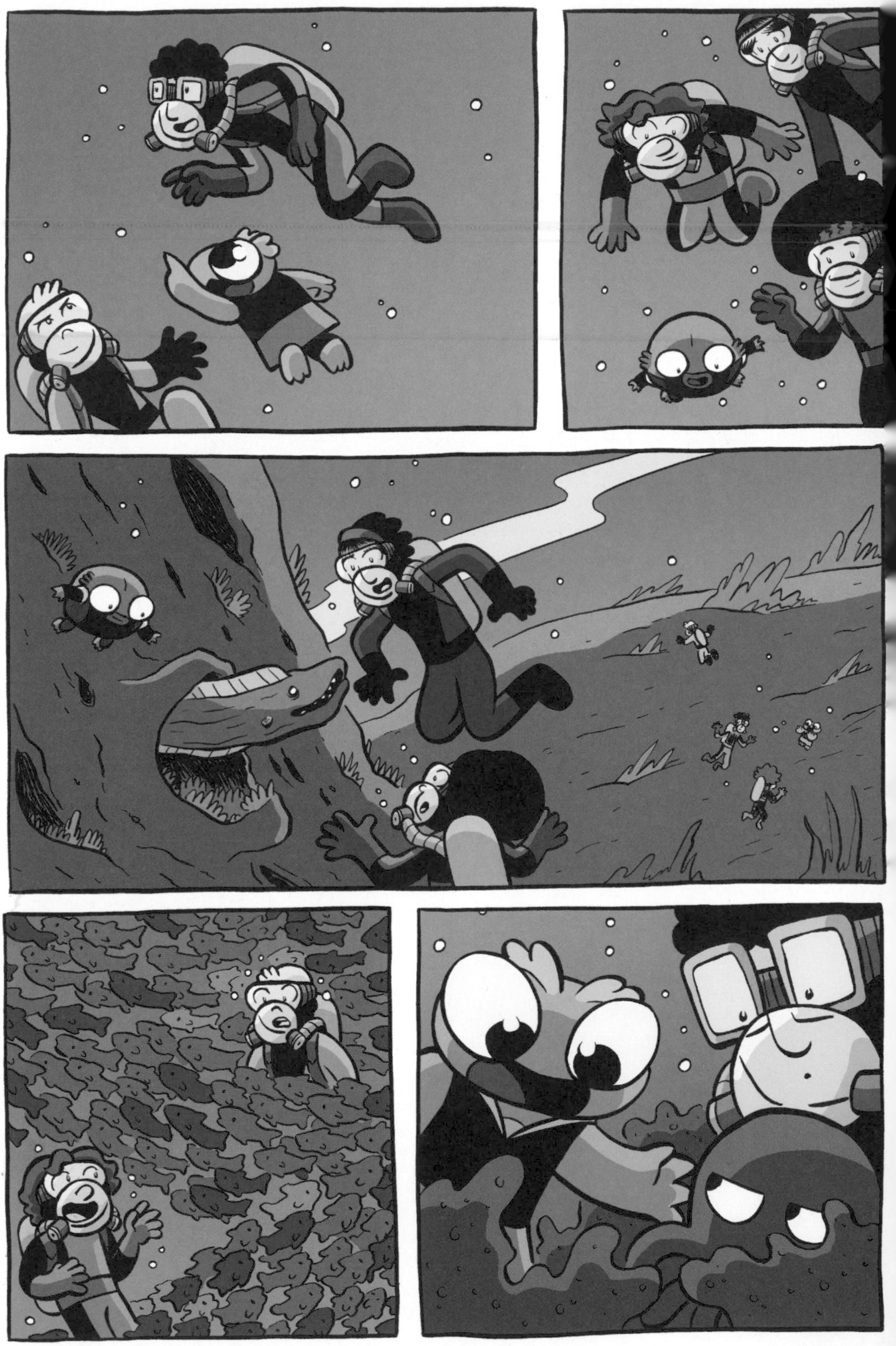

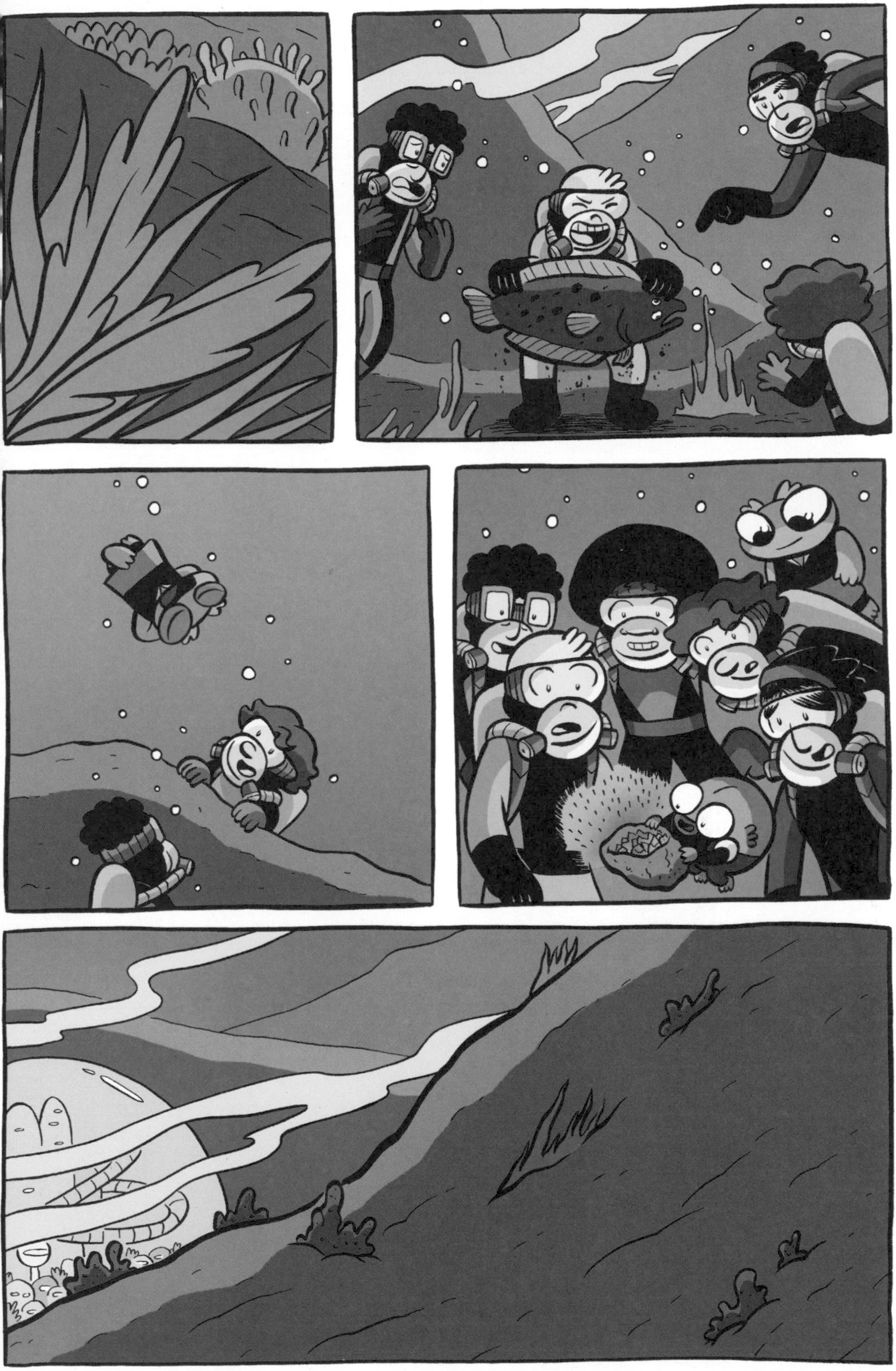

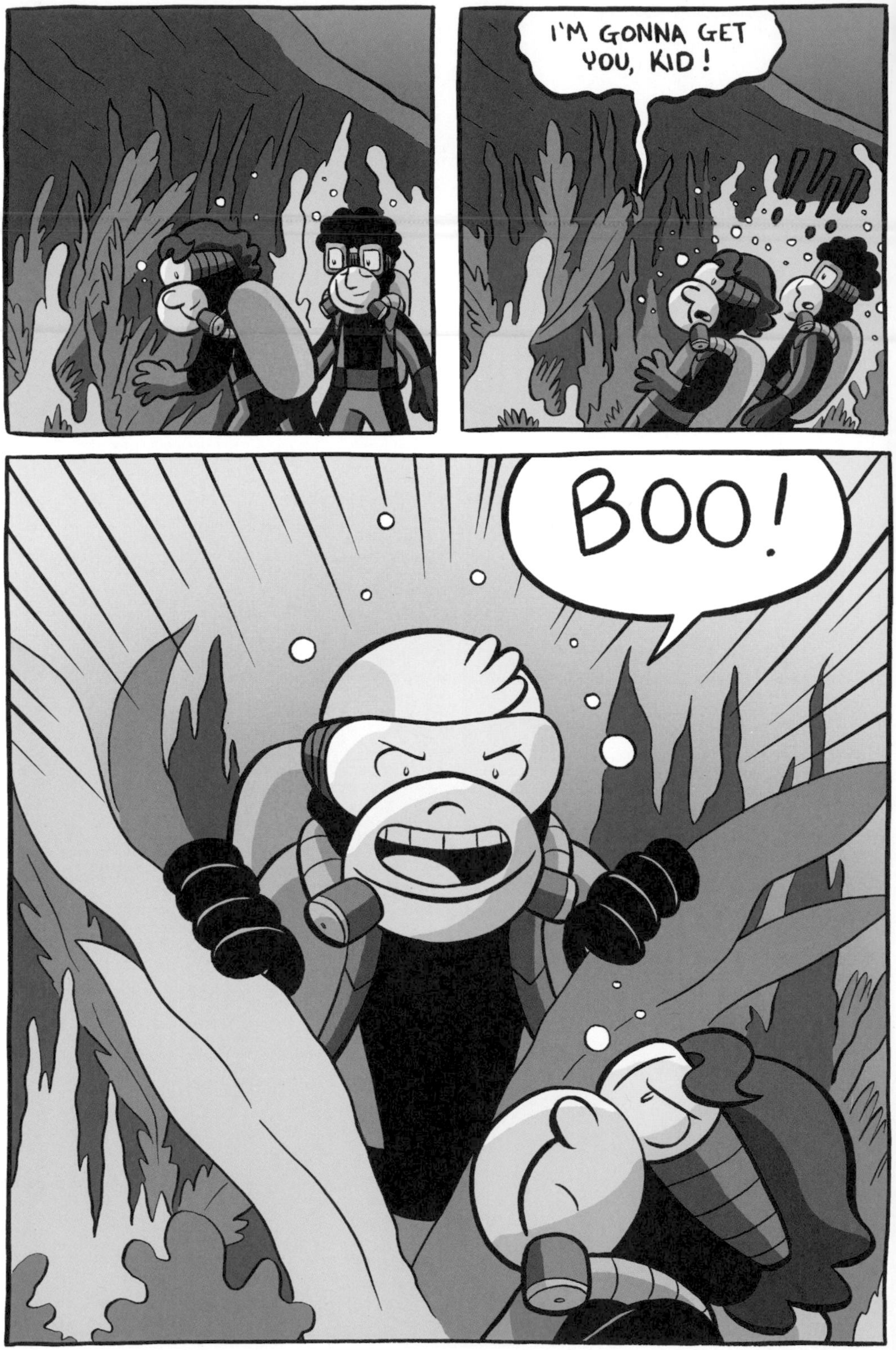
I'M GONNA GET YOU, KID!
BOO!

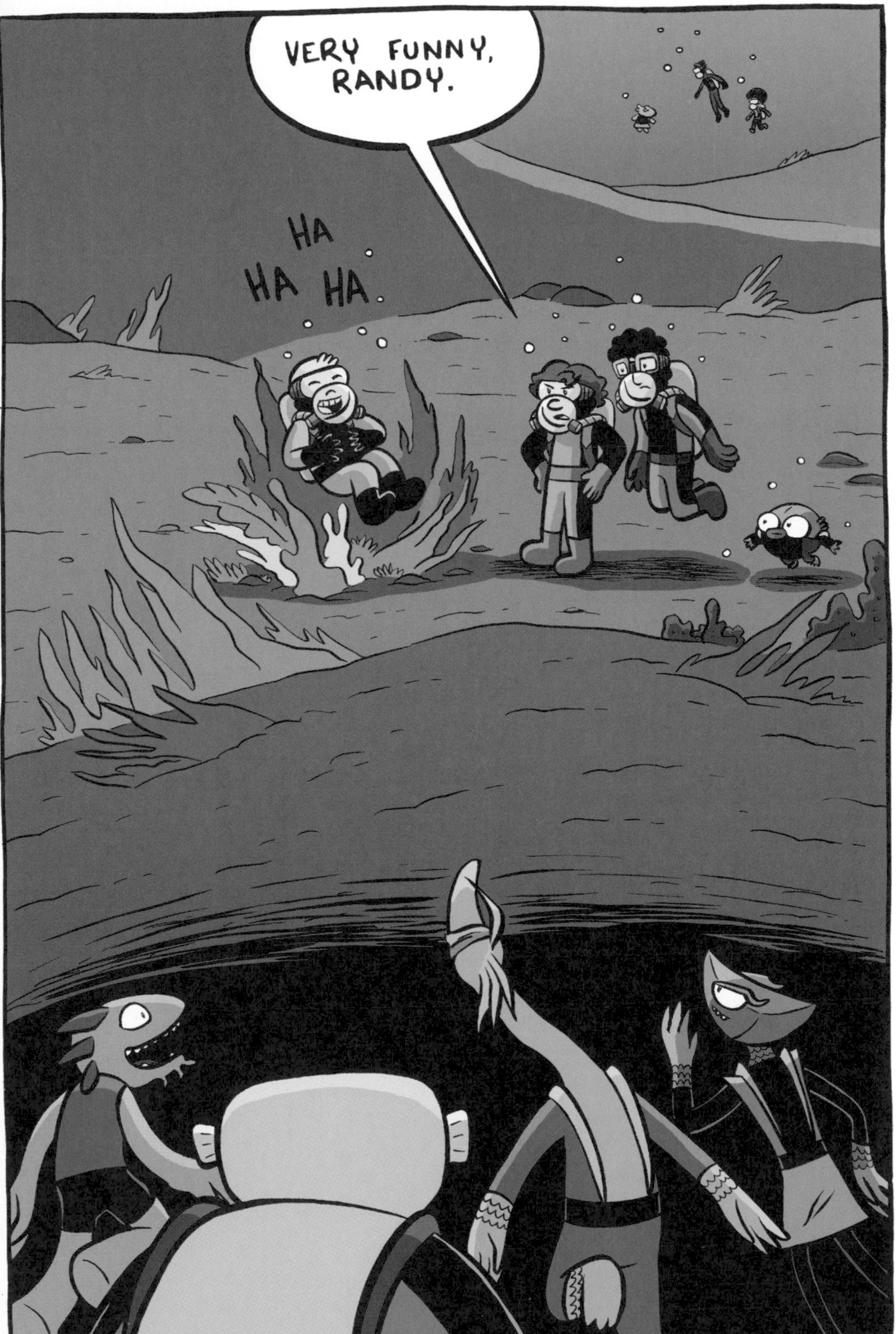
VERY FUNNY, RANDY.
HA HA HA.

CHAPTER FIVE

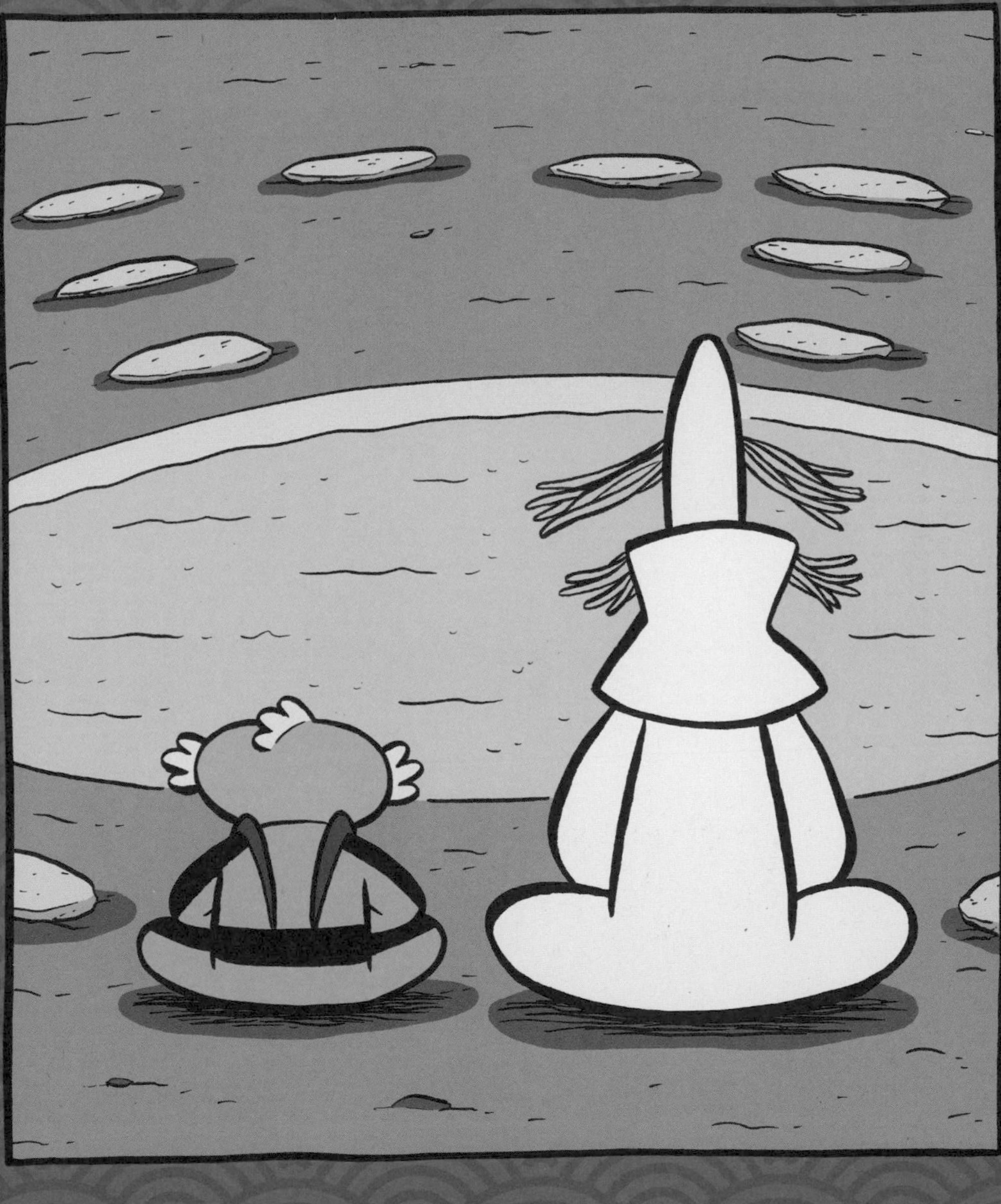

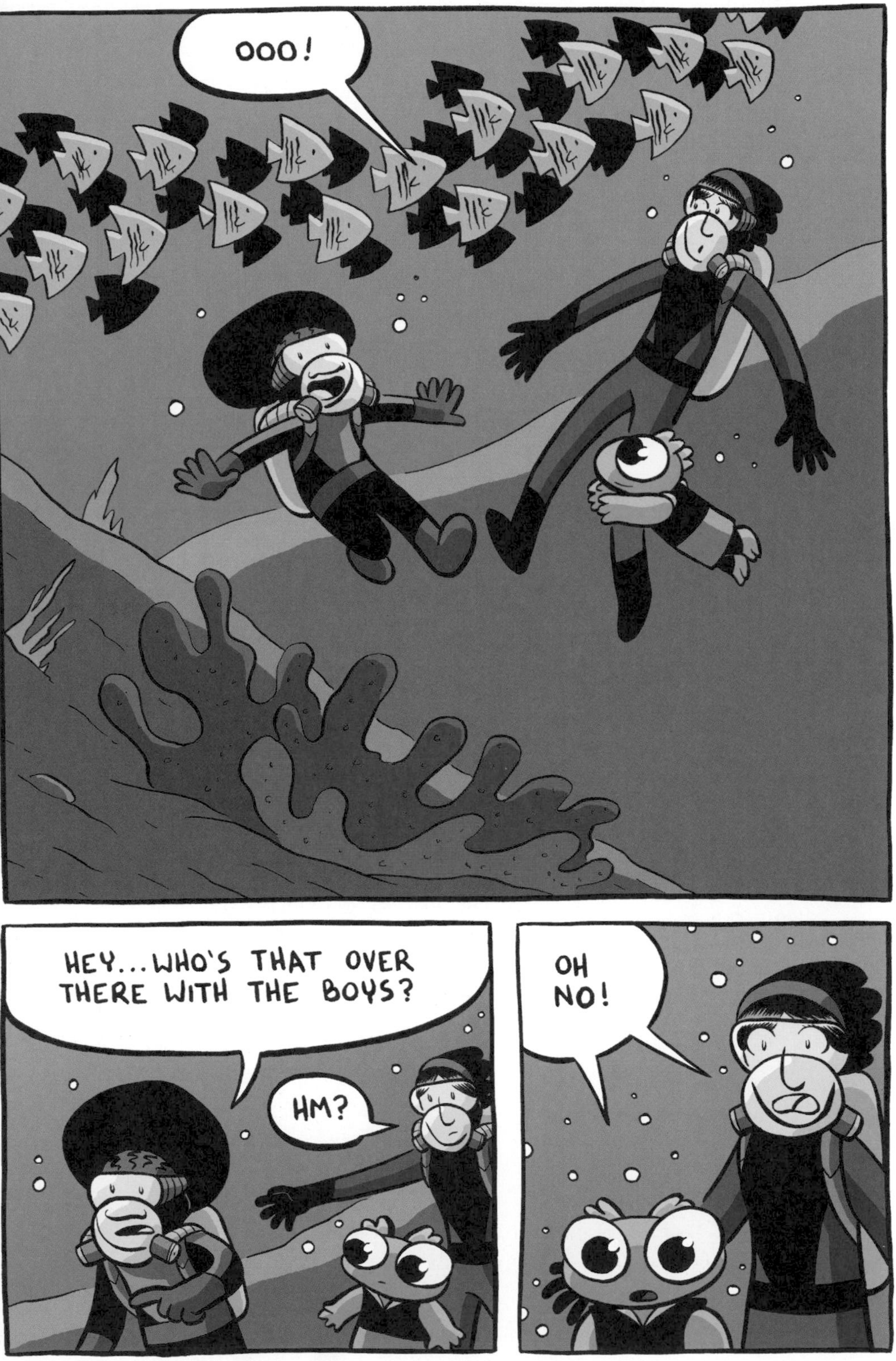
OOO!
HEY...WHO'S THAT OVER THERE WITH THE BOYS?
HM?
OH NO!

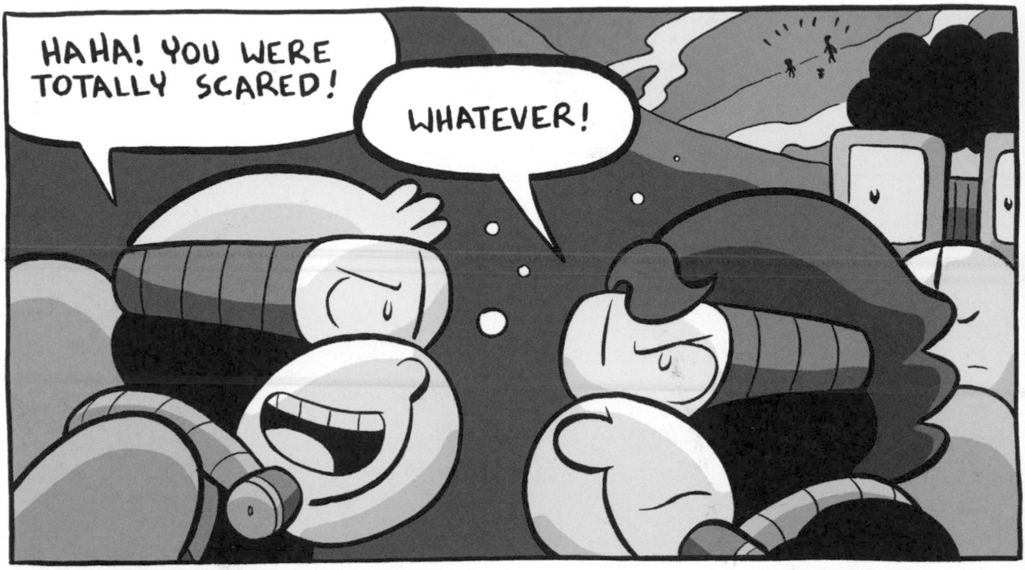
HAHA! YOU WERE TOTALLY SCARED!
WHATEVER!

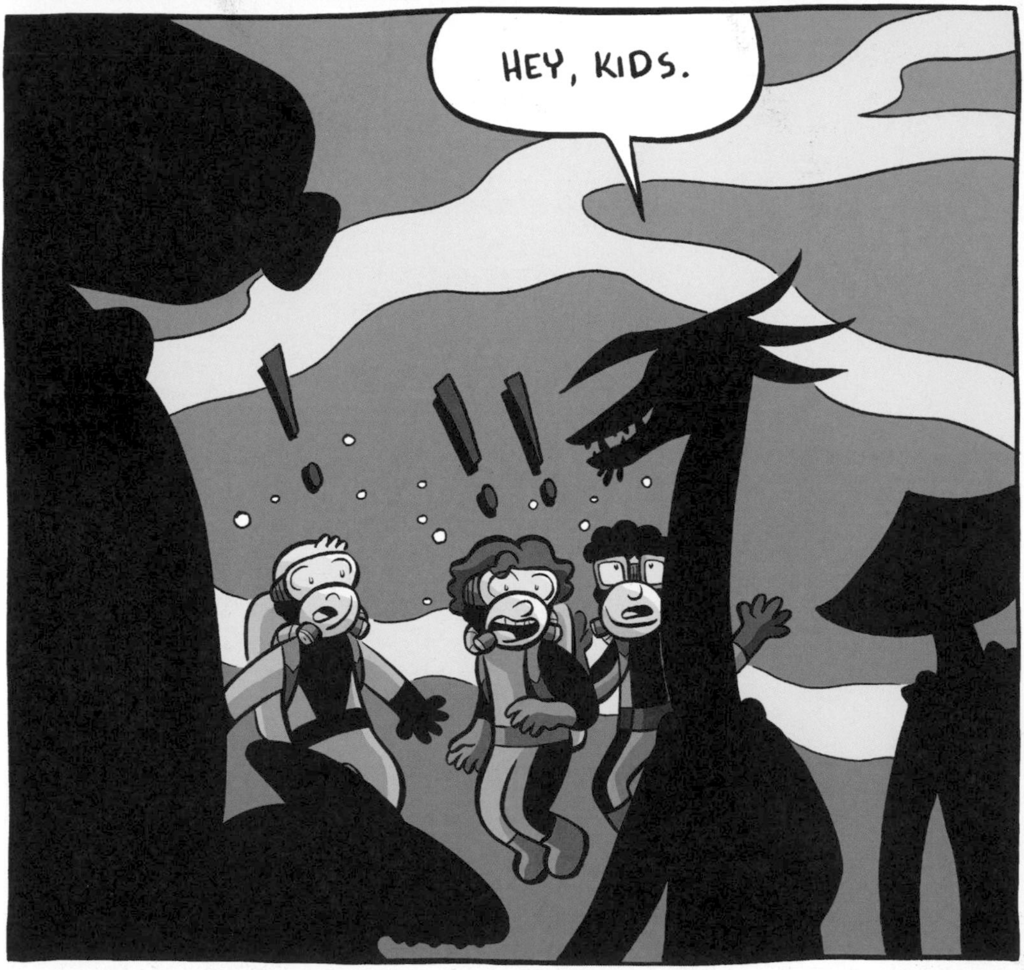
HEY, KIDS.

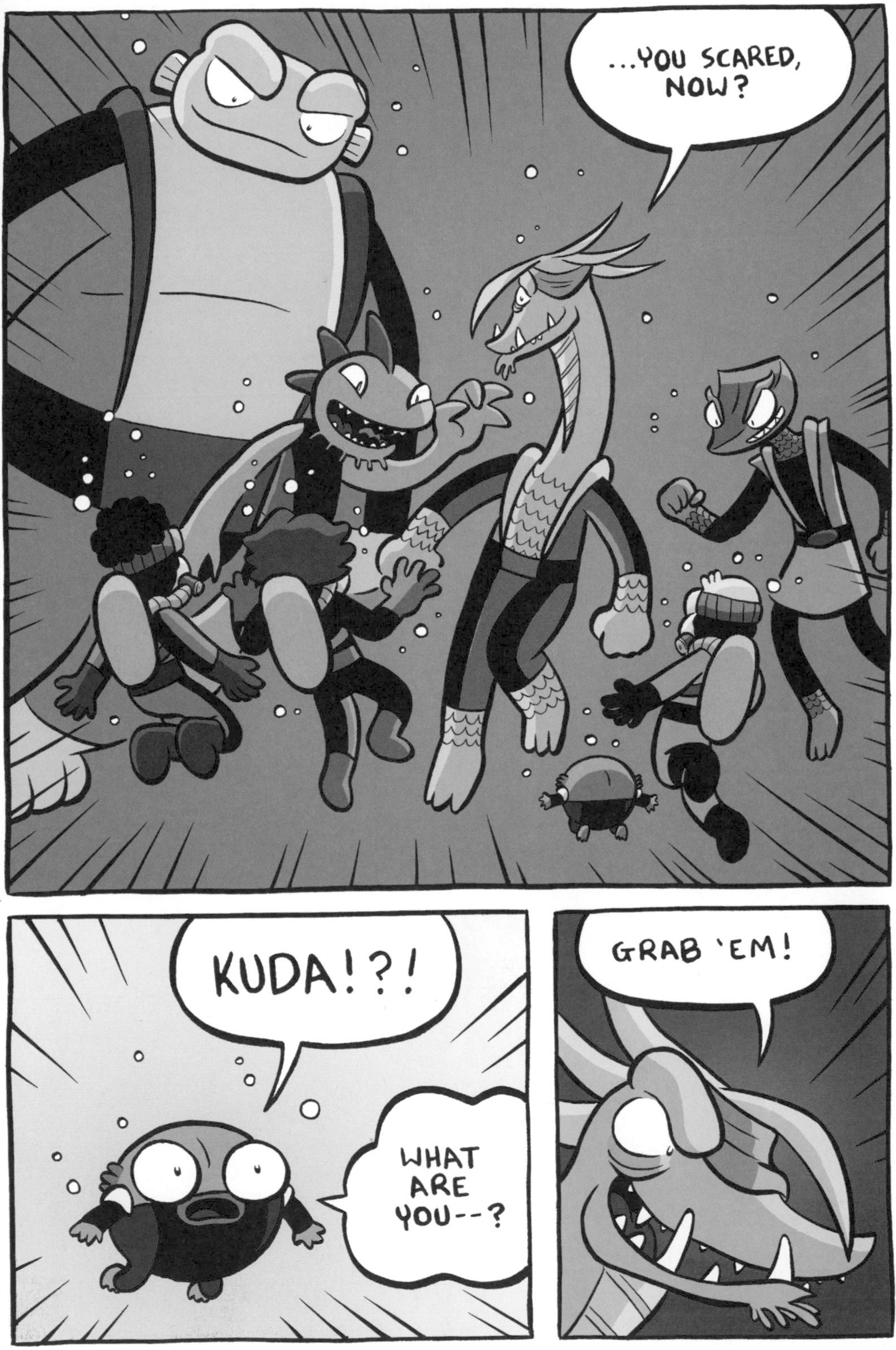

...YOU SCARED, NOW?
KUDA!?!
WHAT ARE YOU--?
GRAB 'EM!

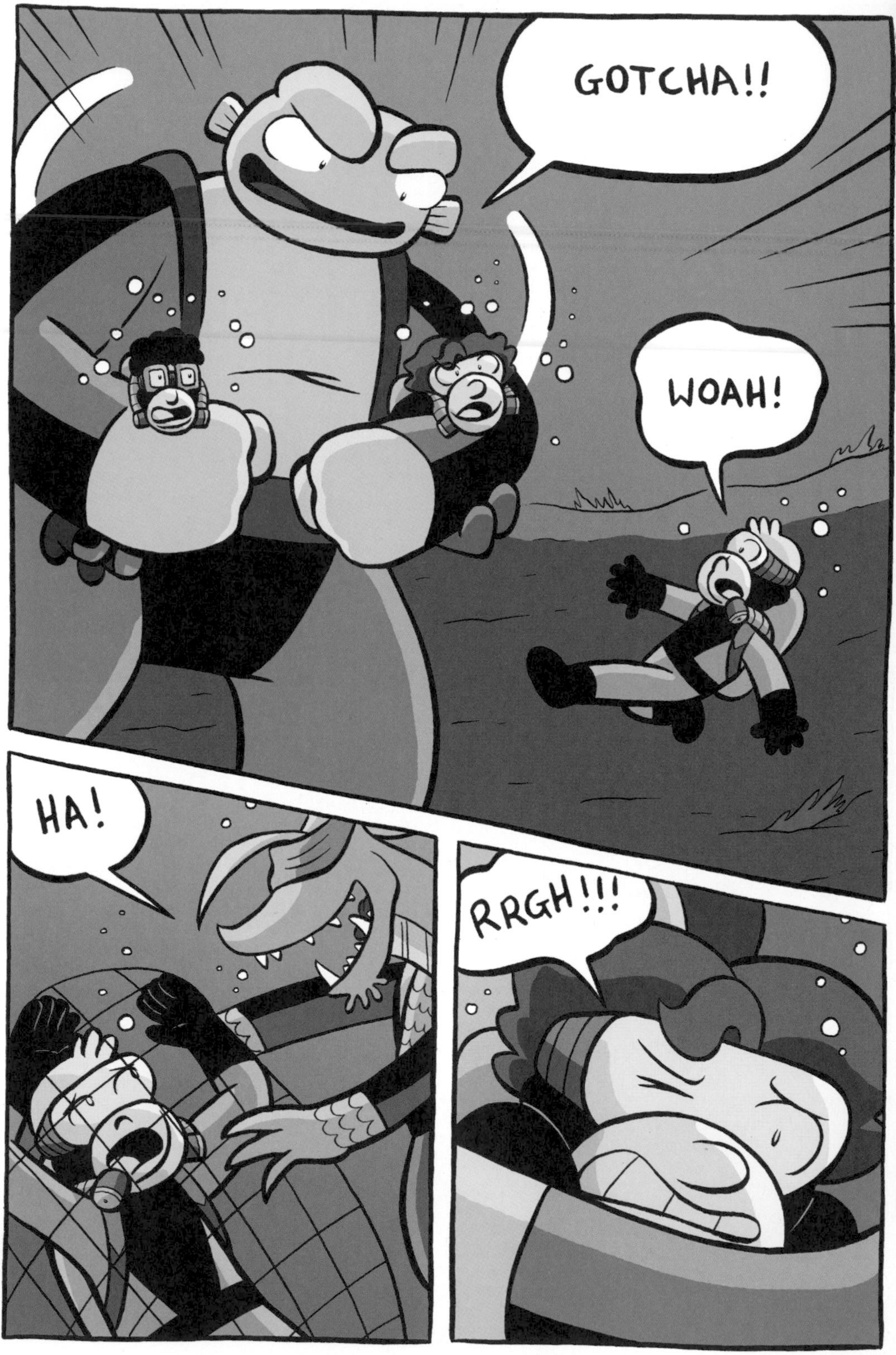
GOTCHA!!
WOAH!
HA!
RRGH!!!

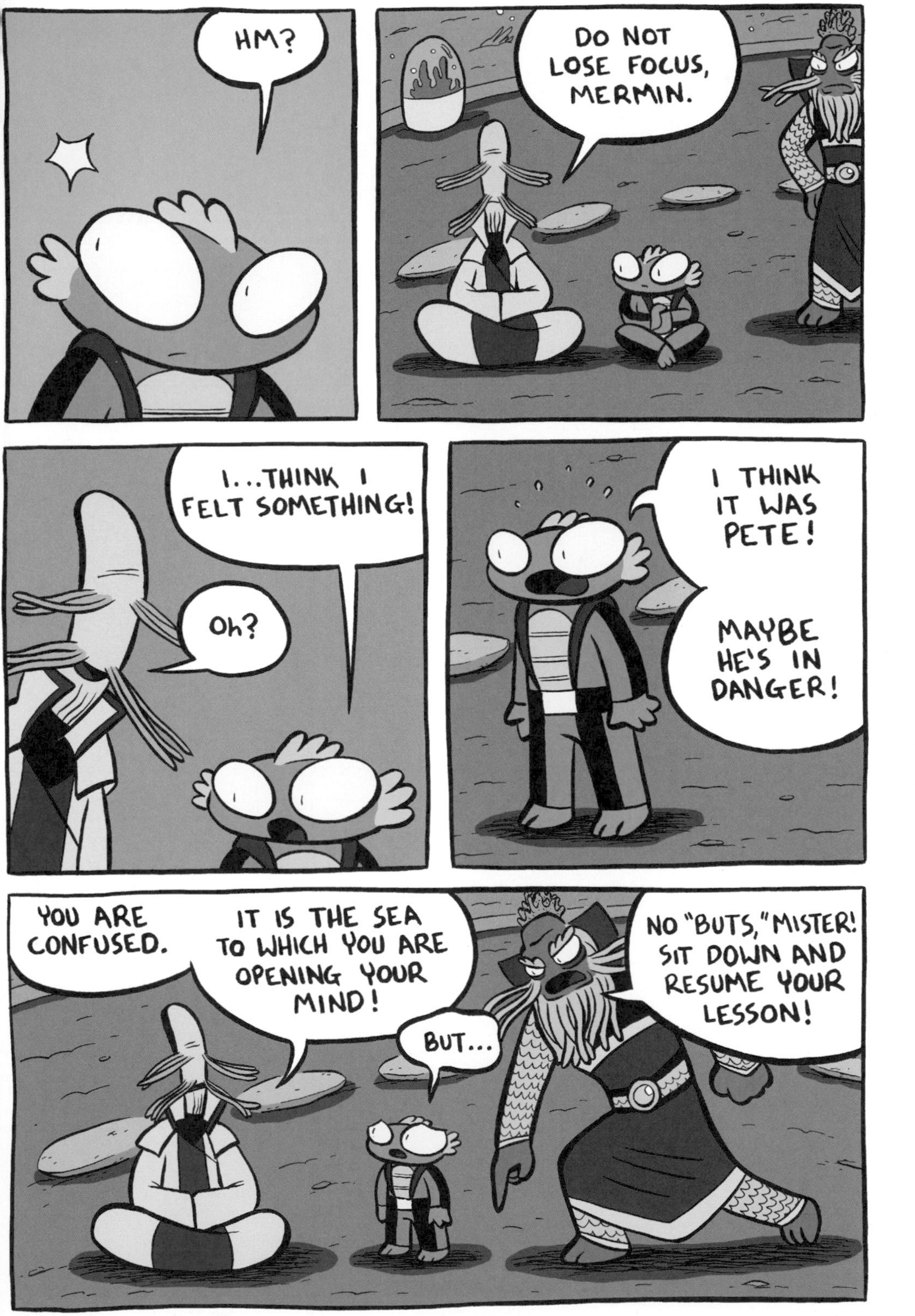
HM?
DO NOT LOSE FOCUS, MERMIN.
I...THINK I FELT SOMETHING!
Oh?
I THINK IT WAS PETE!
MAYBE HE'S IN DANGER!
YOU ARE CONFUSED.
IT IS THE SEA TO WHICH YOU ARE OPENING YOUR MIND!
BUT...
NO "BUTS," MISTER! SIT DOWN AND RESUME YOUR LESSON!

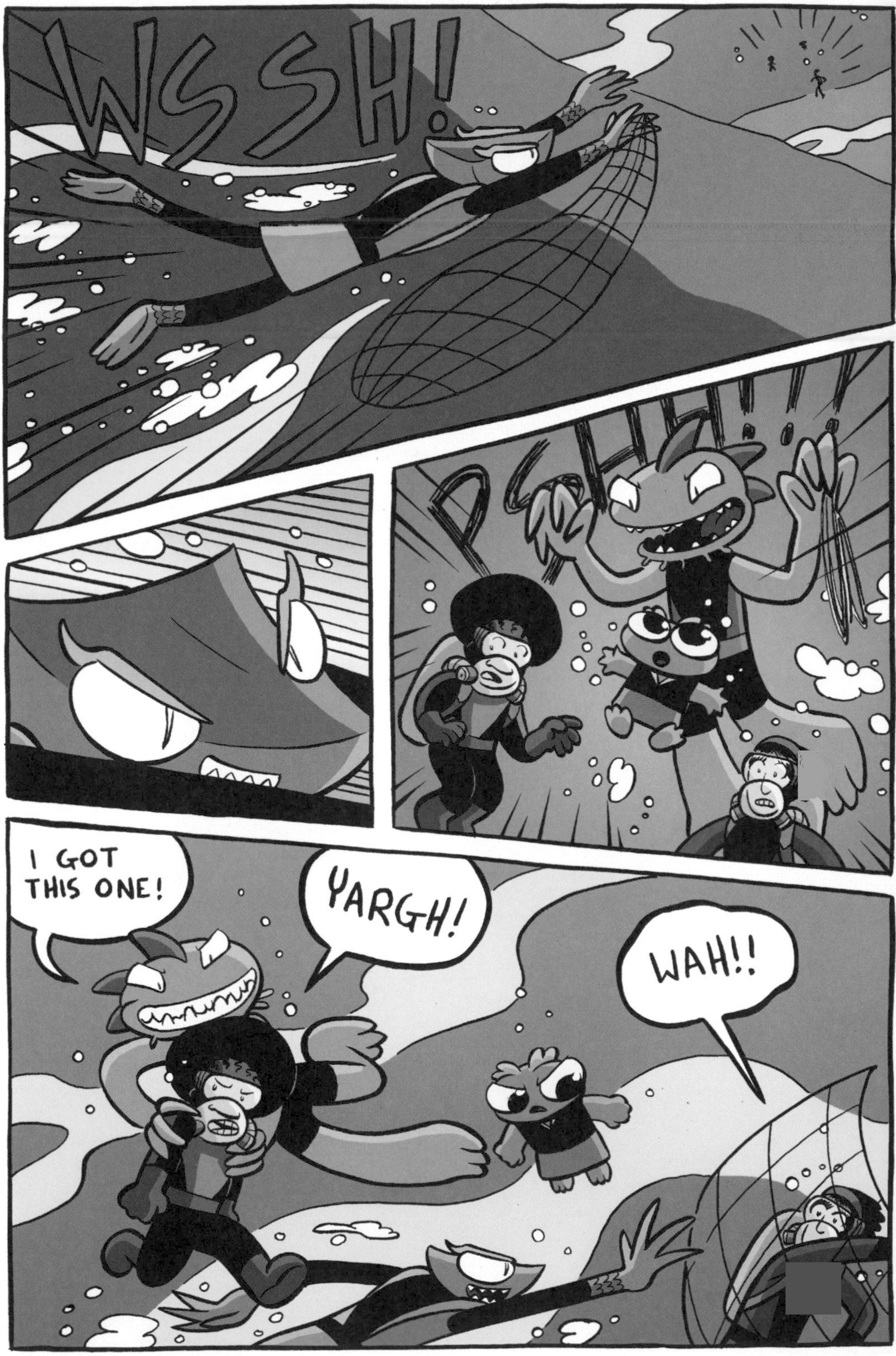
WSSH!
PSCHHH!!
I GOT THIS ONE!
YARGH!
WAH!!

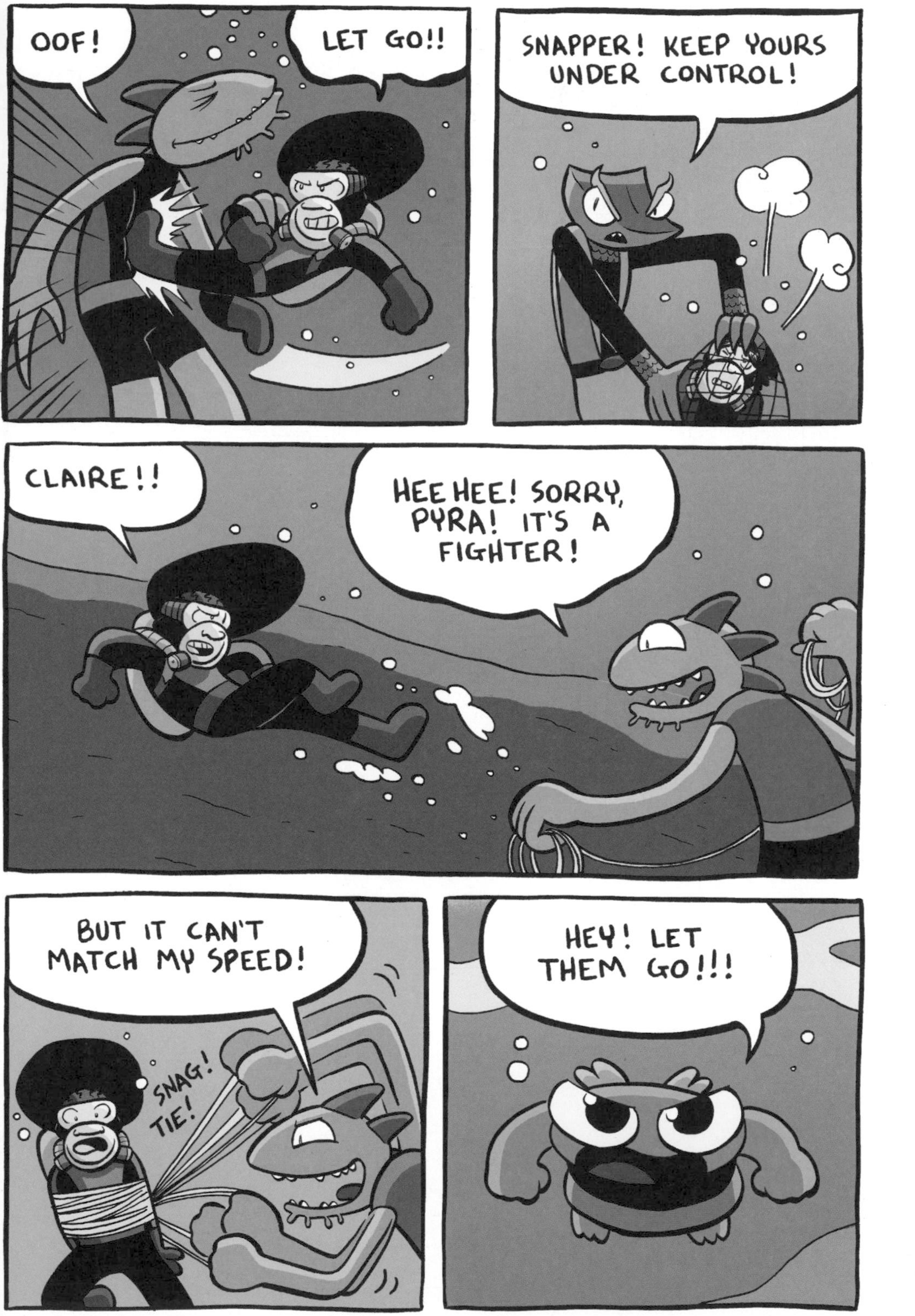
OOF!
LET GO!!
SNAPPER! KEEP YOURS UNDER CONTROL!
CLAIRE!!
HEE HEE! SORRY, PYRA! IT'S A FIGHTER!
BUT IT CAN'T MATCH MY SPEED!
SNAG! TIE!
HEY! LET THEM GO!!!

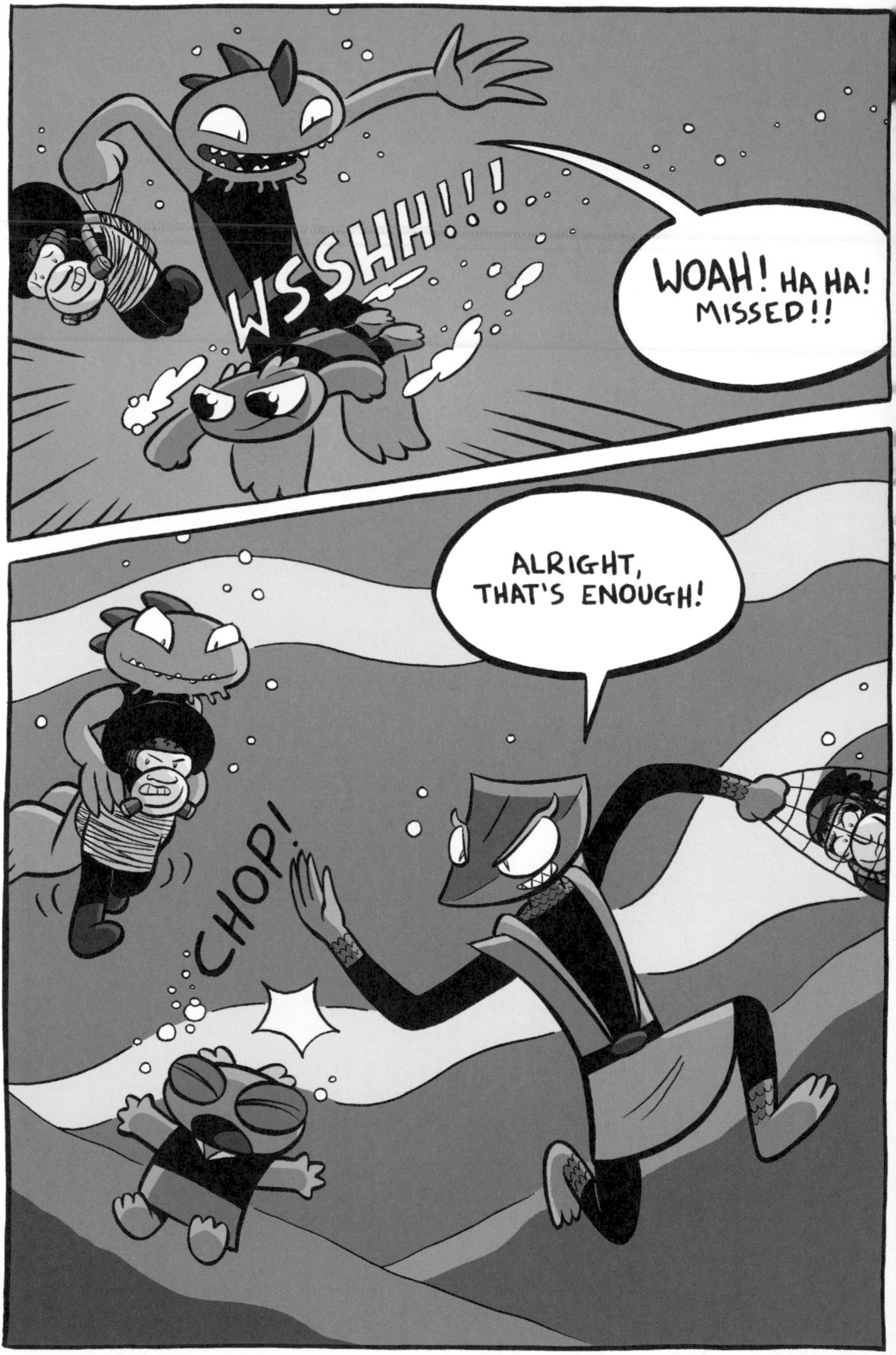
WSSHH!!!
WOAH! HA HA! MISSED!!
ALRIGHT, THAT'S ENOUGH!
CHOP!

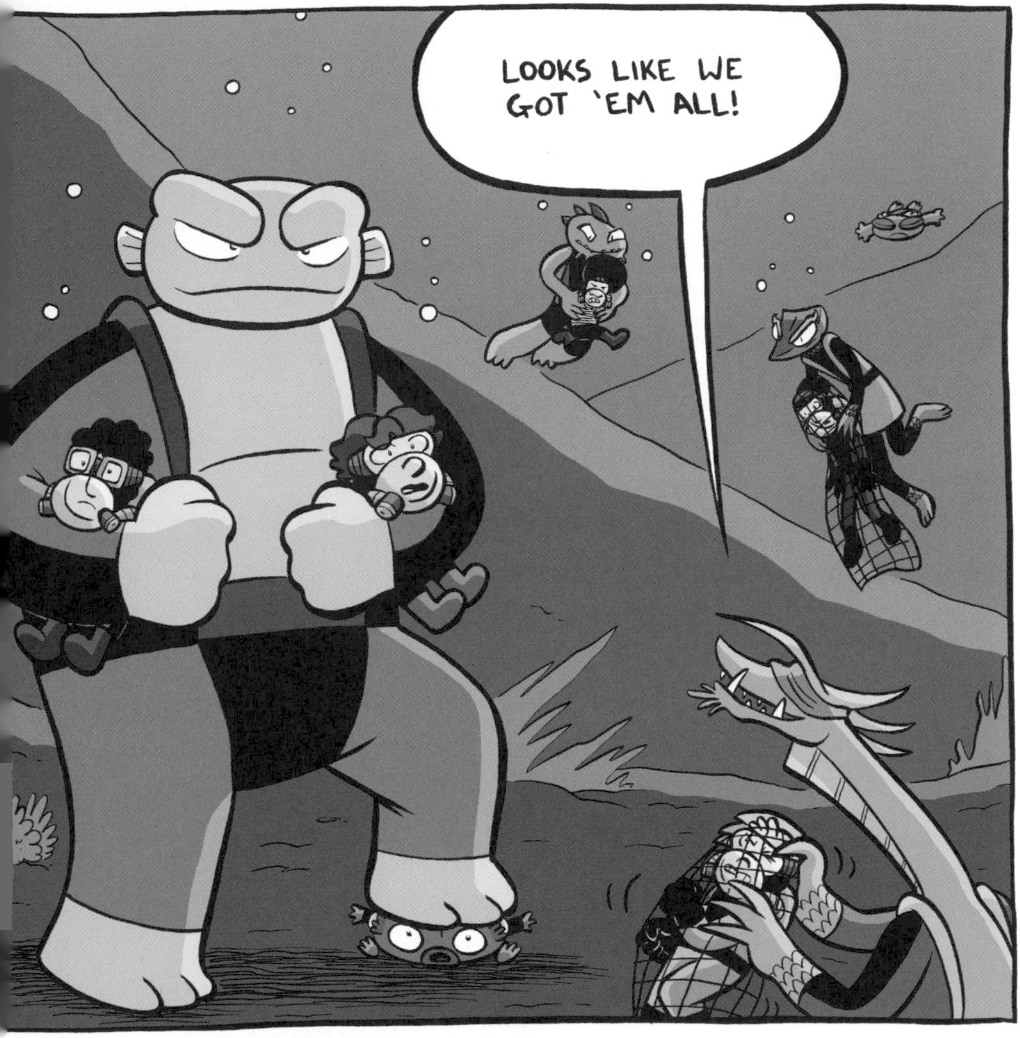
LOOKS LIKE WE GOT 'EM ALL!

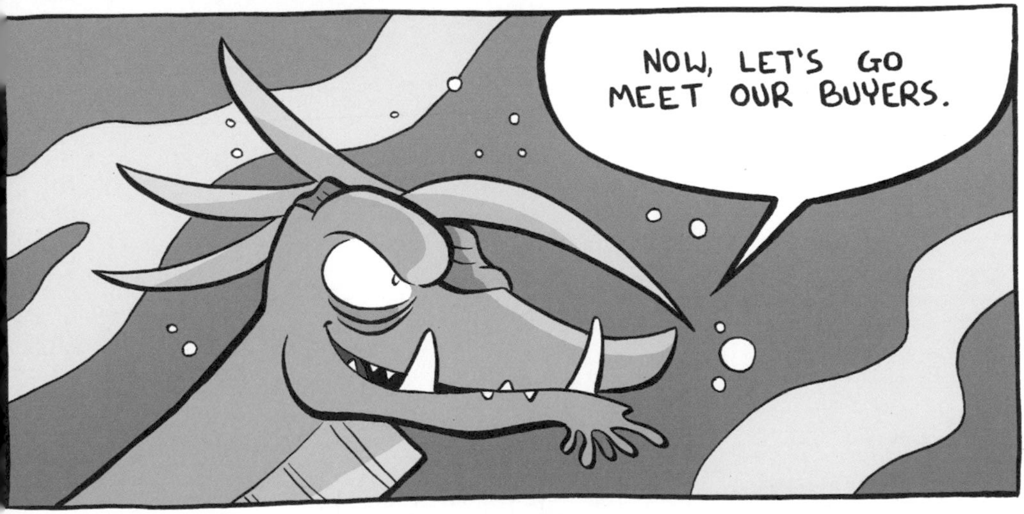
NOW, LET'S GO MEET OUR BUYERS.

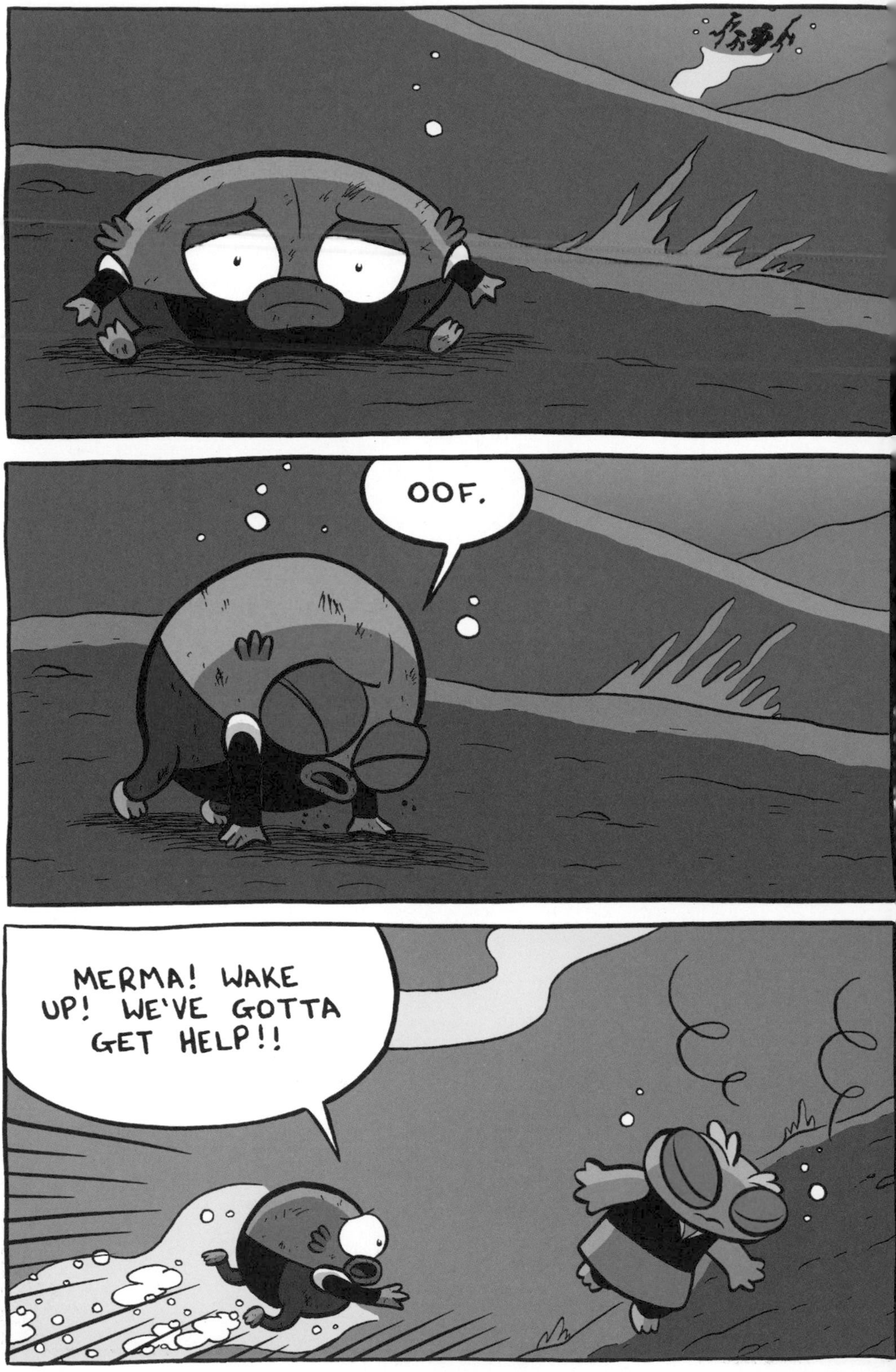
OOF.
MERMA! WAKE UP! WE'VE GOTTA GET HELP!!

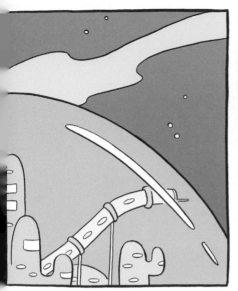

. . . I STILL SENSE TENSION. YOU REALLY MUST RELAX.

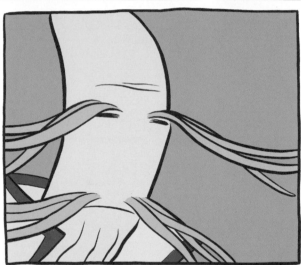

HOO! OKAY...

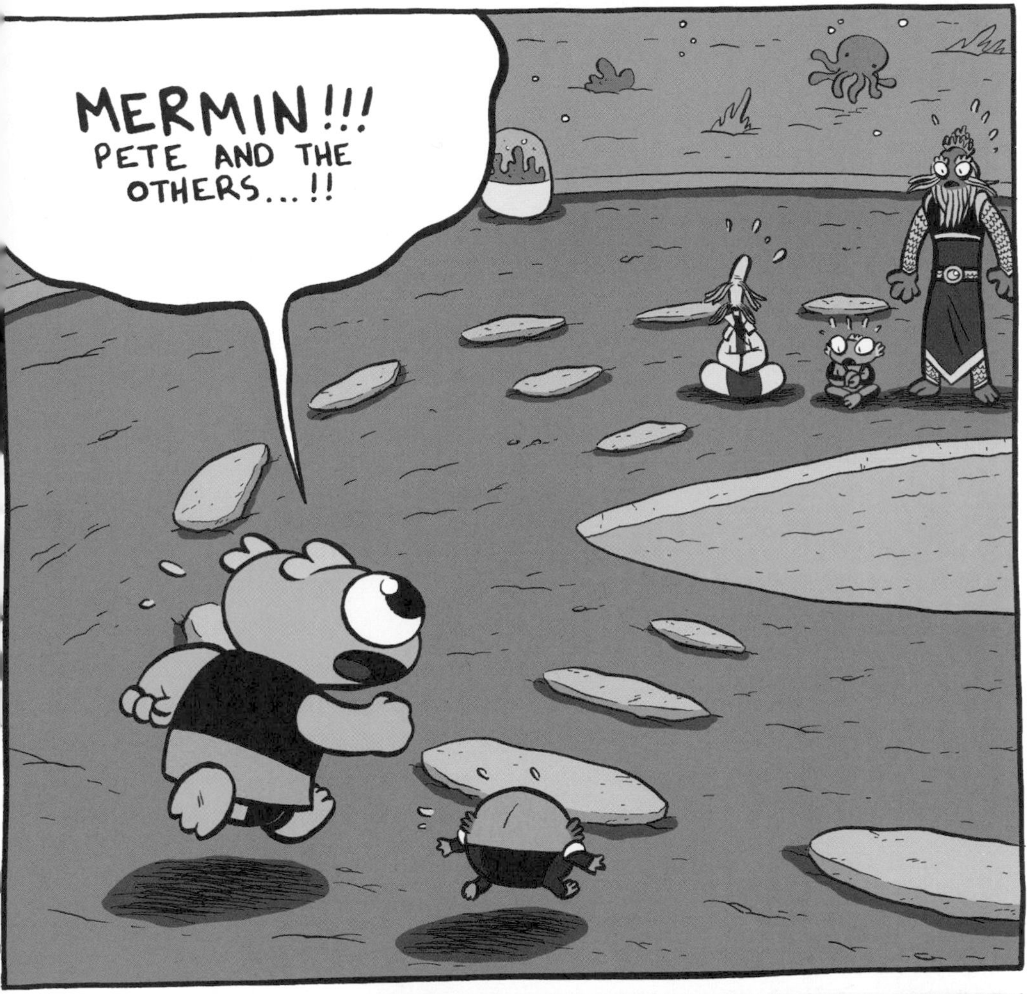
MERMIN!!!
PETE AND THE OTHERS...!!

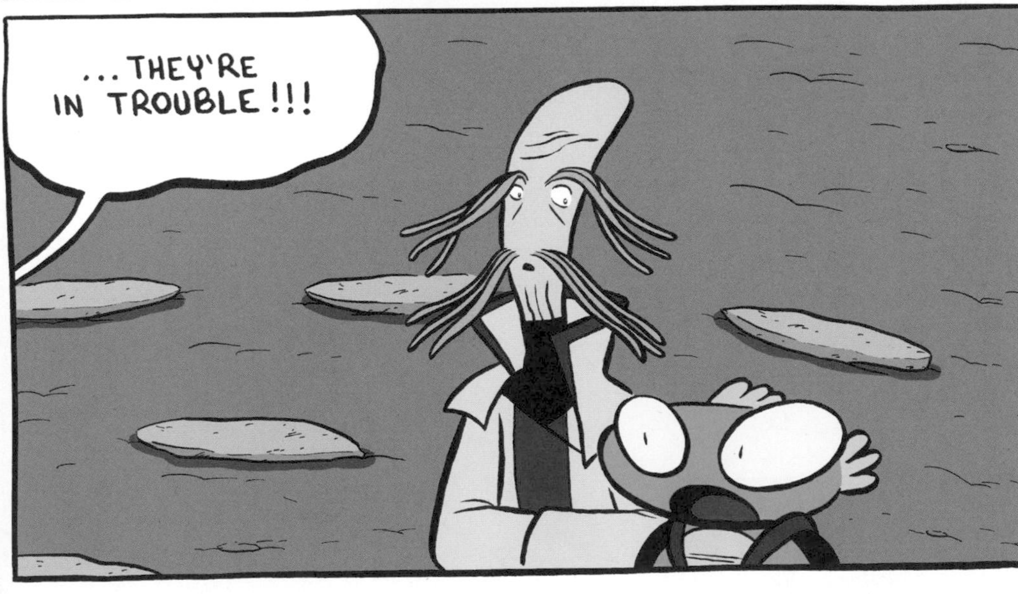
...THEY'RE IN TROUBLE!!!

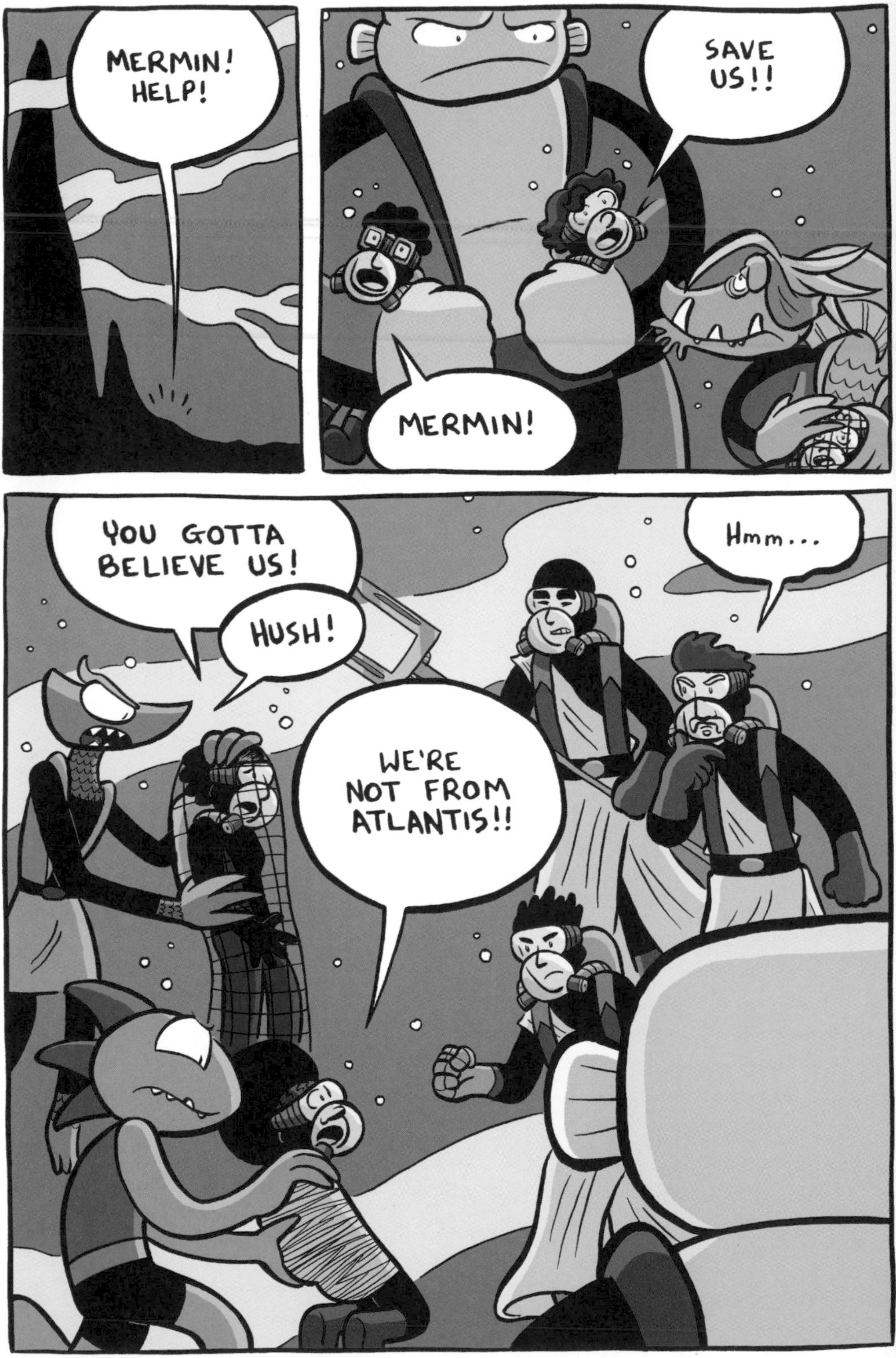
MERMIN! HELP!
SAVE US!!
MERMIN!
YOU GOTTA BELIEVE US!
HUSH!
Hmm...
WE'RE NOT FROM ATLANTIS!!

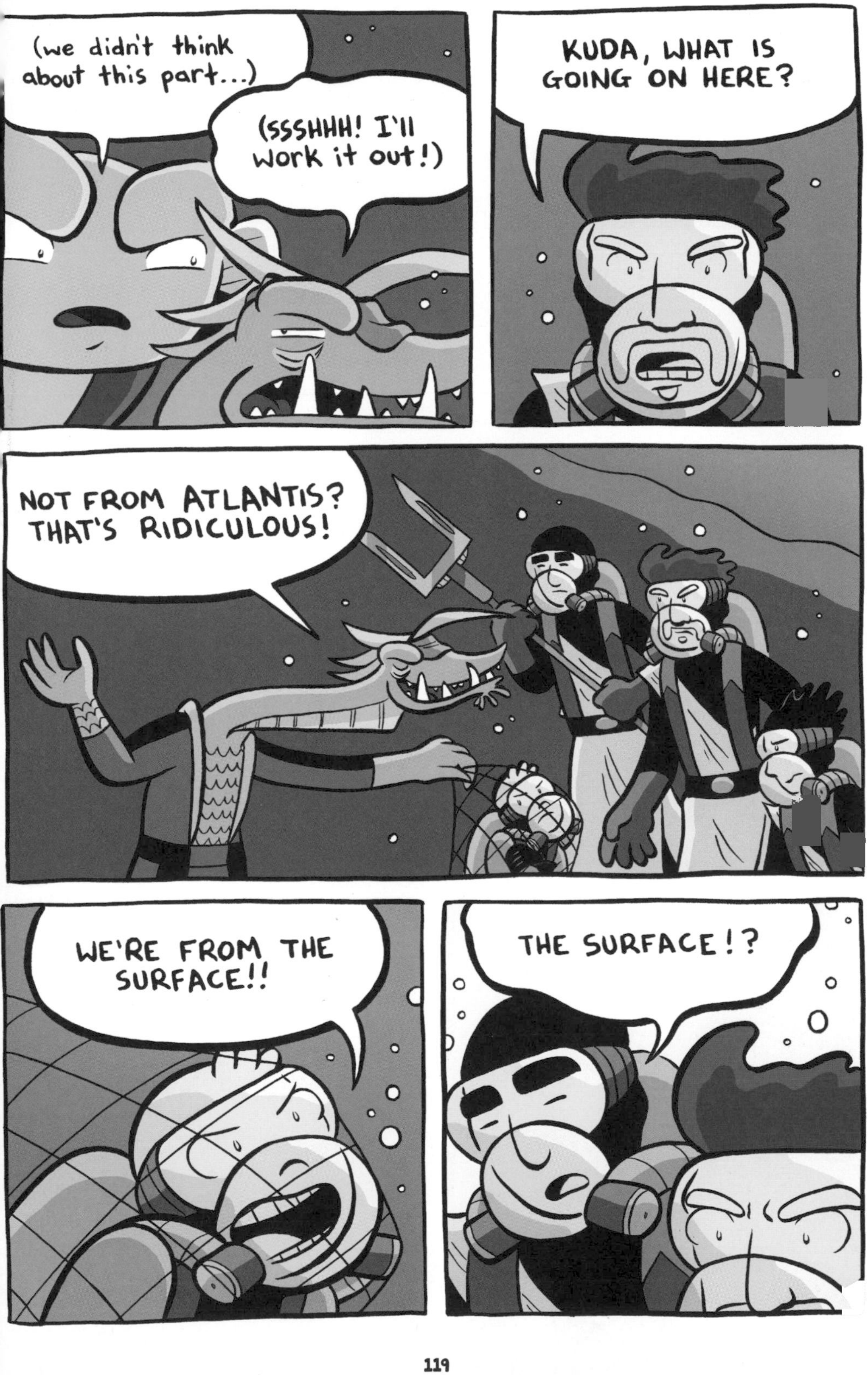
(we didn't think about this part...)
(SSSHHH! I'll work it out!)
KUDA, WHAT IS GOING ON HERE?
NOT FROM ATLANTIS? THAT'S RIDICULOUS!
WE'RE FROM THE SURFACE!!
THE SURFACE!?

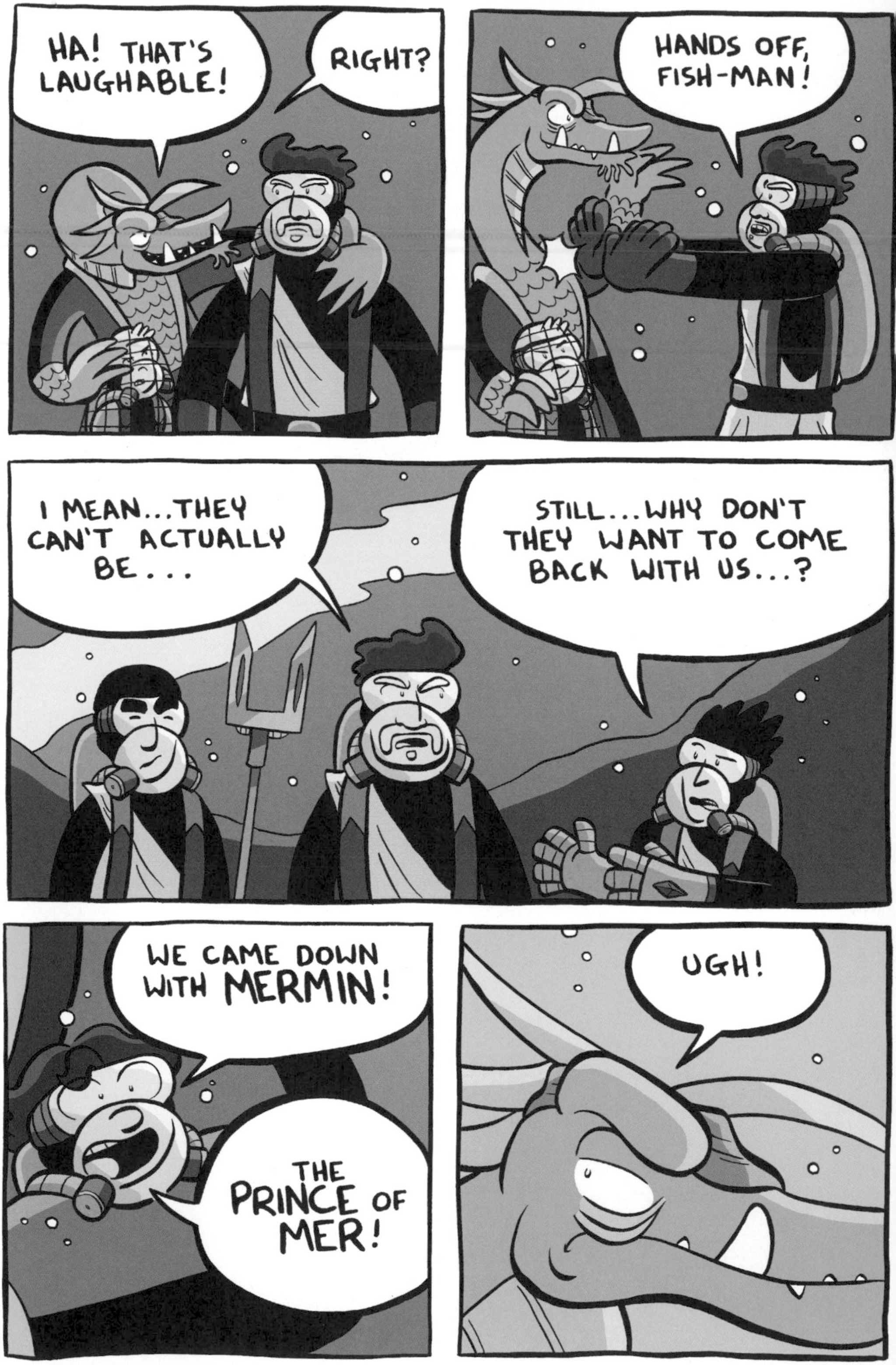
HA! THAT'S LAUGHABLE!
RIGHT?
HANDS OFF, FISH-MAN!
I MEAN...THEY CAN'T ACTUALLY BE...
STILL...WHY DON'T THEY WANT TO COME BACK WITH US...?
WE CAME DOWN WITH MERMIN!
THE PRINCE OF MER!
UGH!

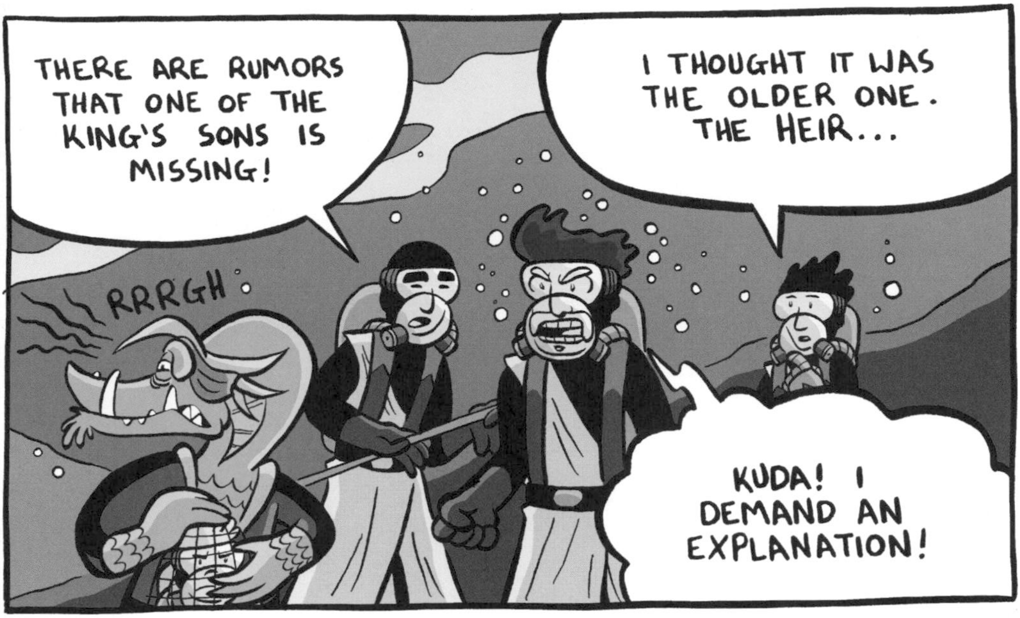
THERE ARE RUMORS THAT ONE OF THE KING'S SONS IS MISSING!
I THOUGHT IT WAS THE OLDER ONE. THE HEIR...
RRRGH
KUDA! I DEMAND AN EXPLANATION!

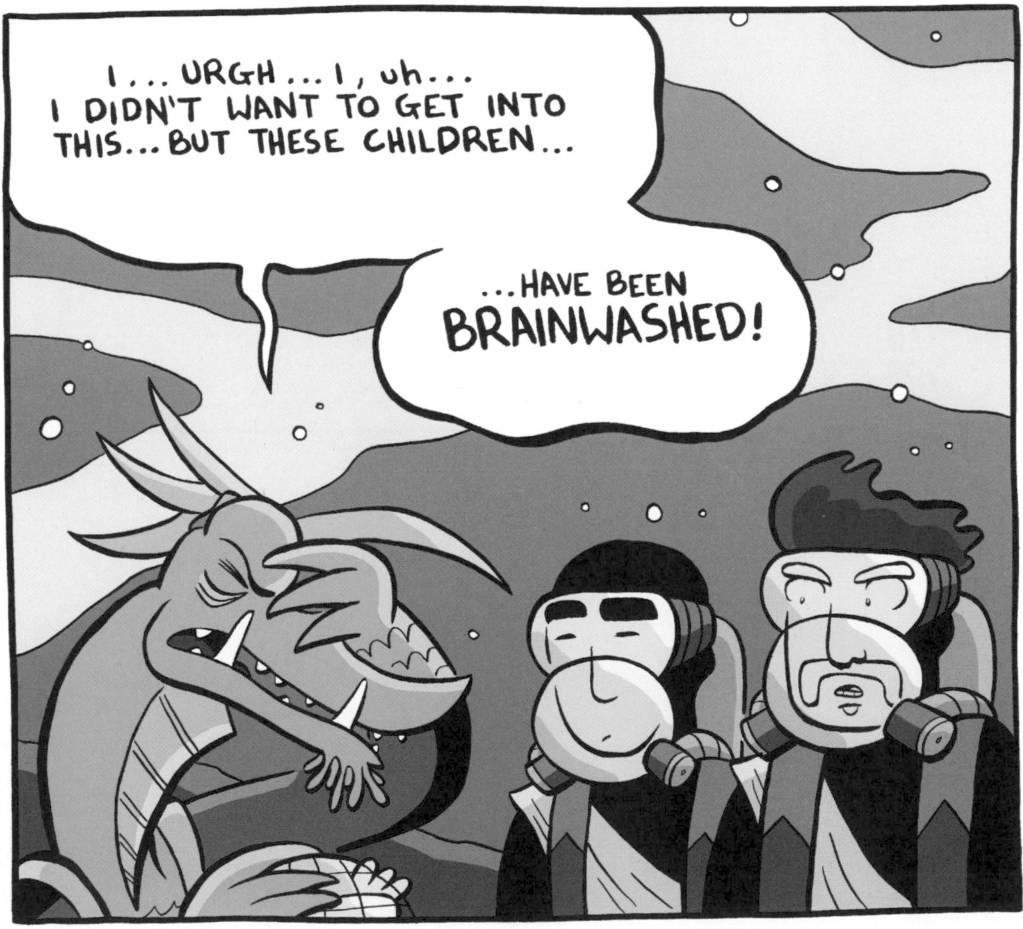
I... URGH... I, uh... I DIDN'T WANT TO GET INTO THIS... BUT THESE CHILDREN...
...HAVE BEEN BRAINWASHED!

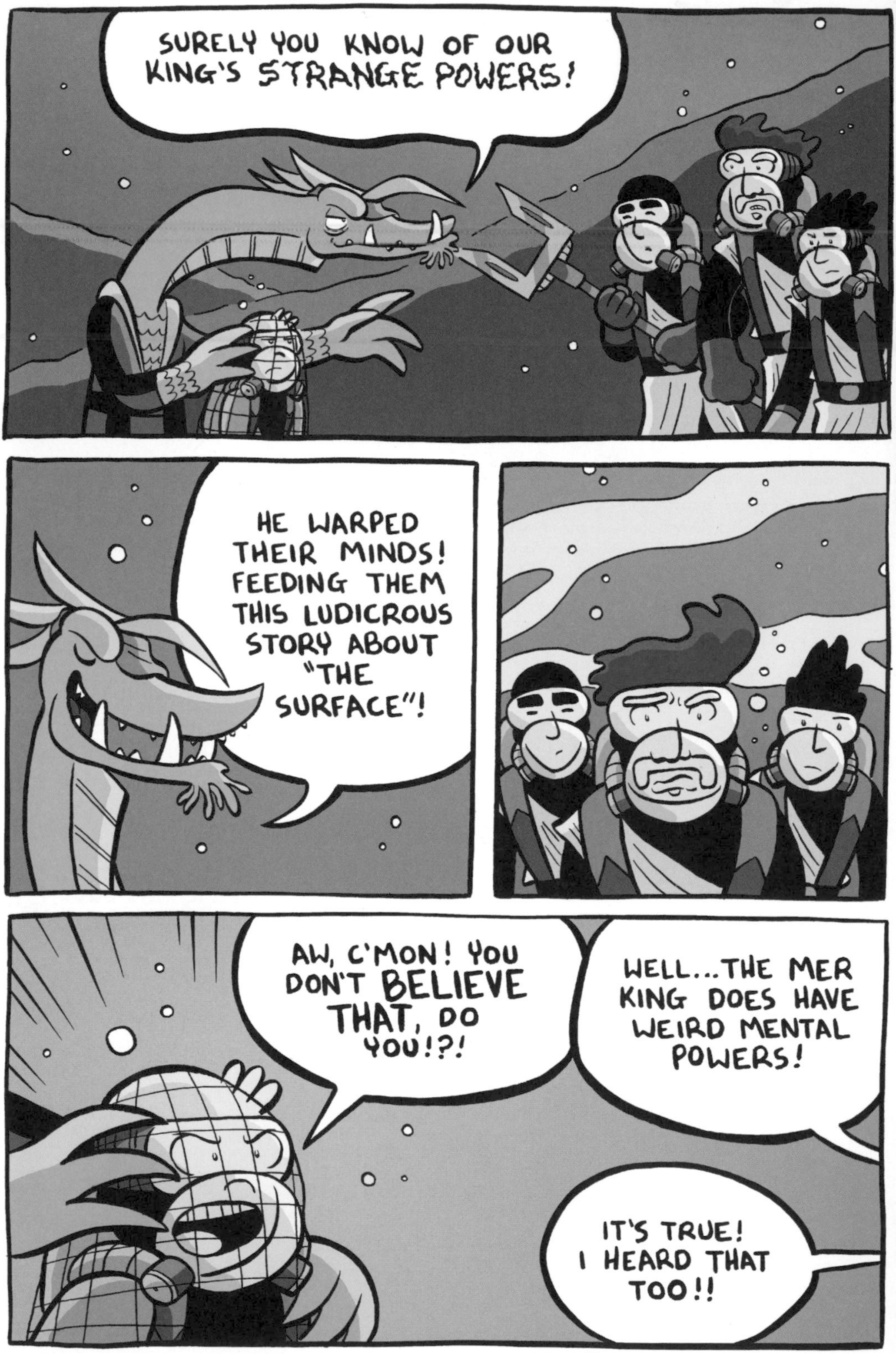
SURELY YOU KNOW OF OUR KING'S STRANGE POWERS!
HE WARPED THEIR MINDS! FEEDING THEM THIS LUDICROUS STORY ABOUT "THE SURFACE"!
AW, C'MON! YOU DON'T BELIEVE THAT, DO YOU!?!
WELL...THE MER KING DOES HAVE WEIRD MENTAL POWERS!
IT'S TRUE! I HEARD THAT TOO!!

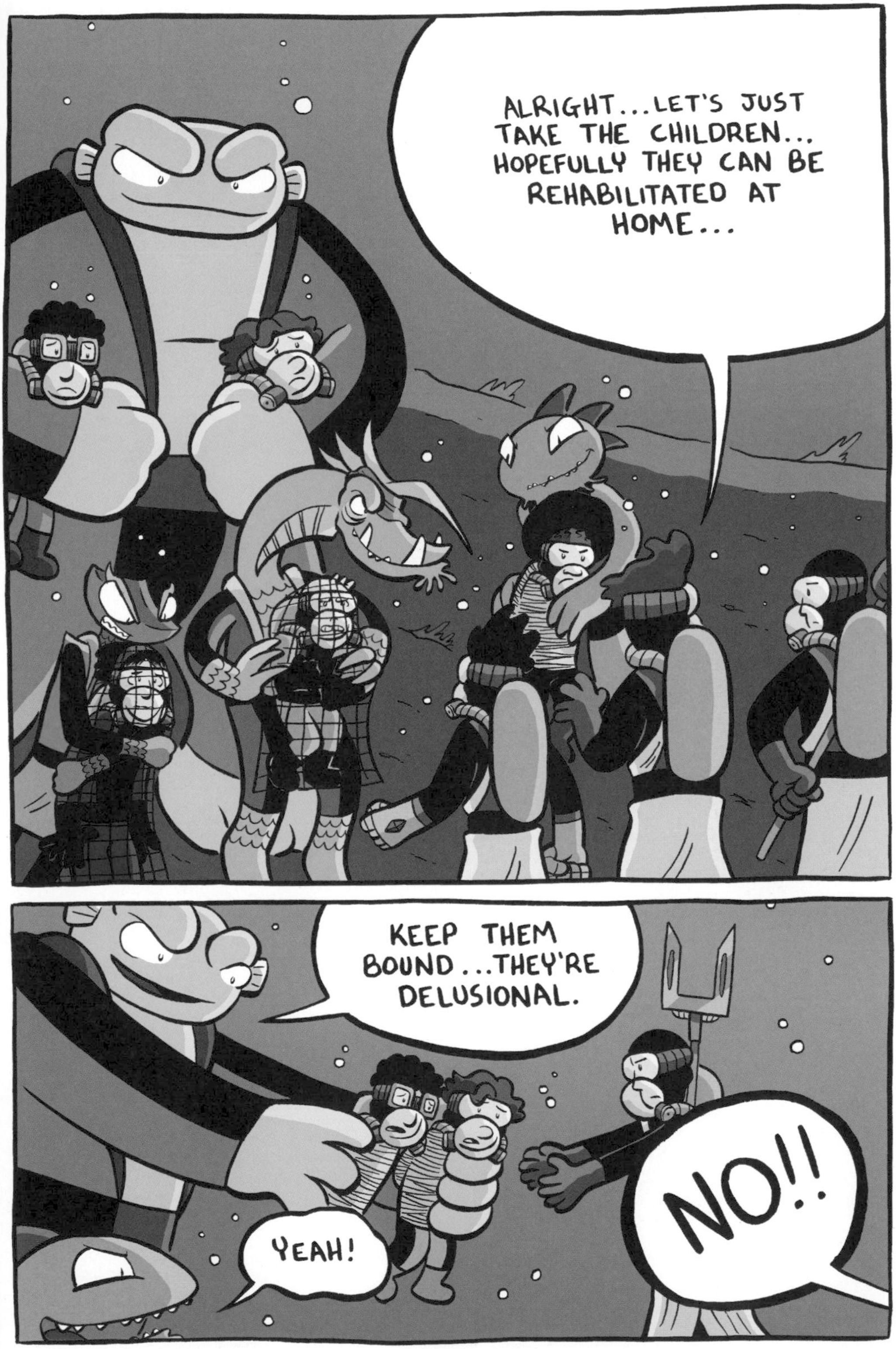
ALRIGHT...LET'S JUST TAKE THE CHILDREN... HOPEFULLY THEY CAN BE REHABILITATED AT HOME...
KEEP THEM BOUND...THEY'RE DELUSIONAL.
YEAH!
NO!!

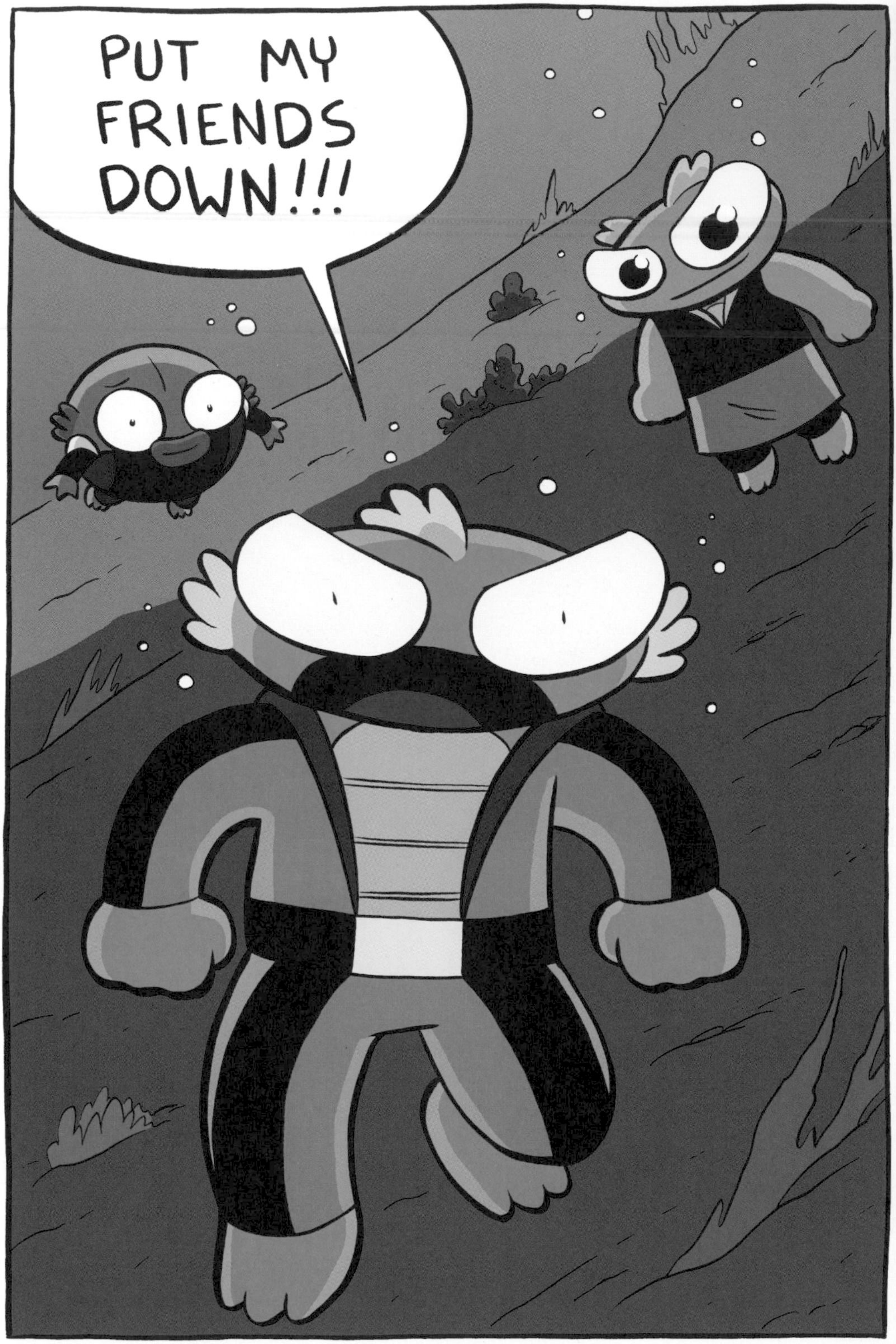
PUT MY FRIENDS DOWN!!!

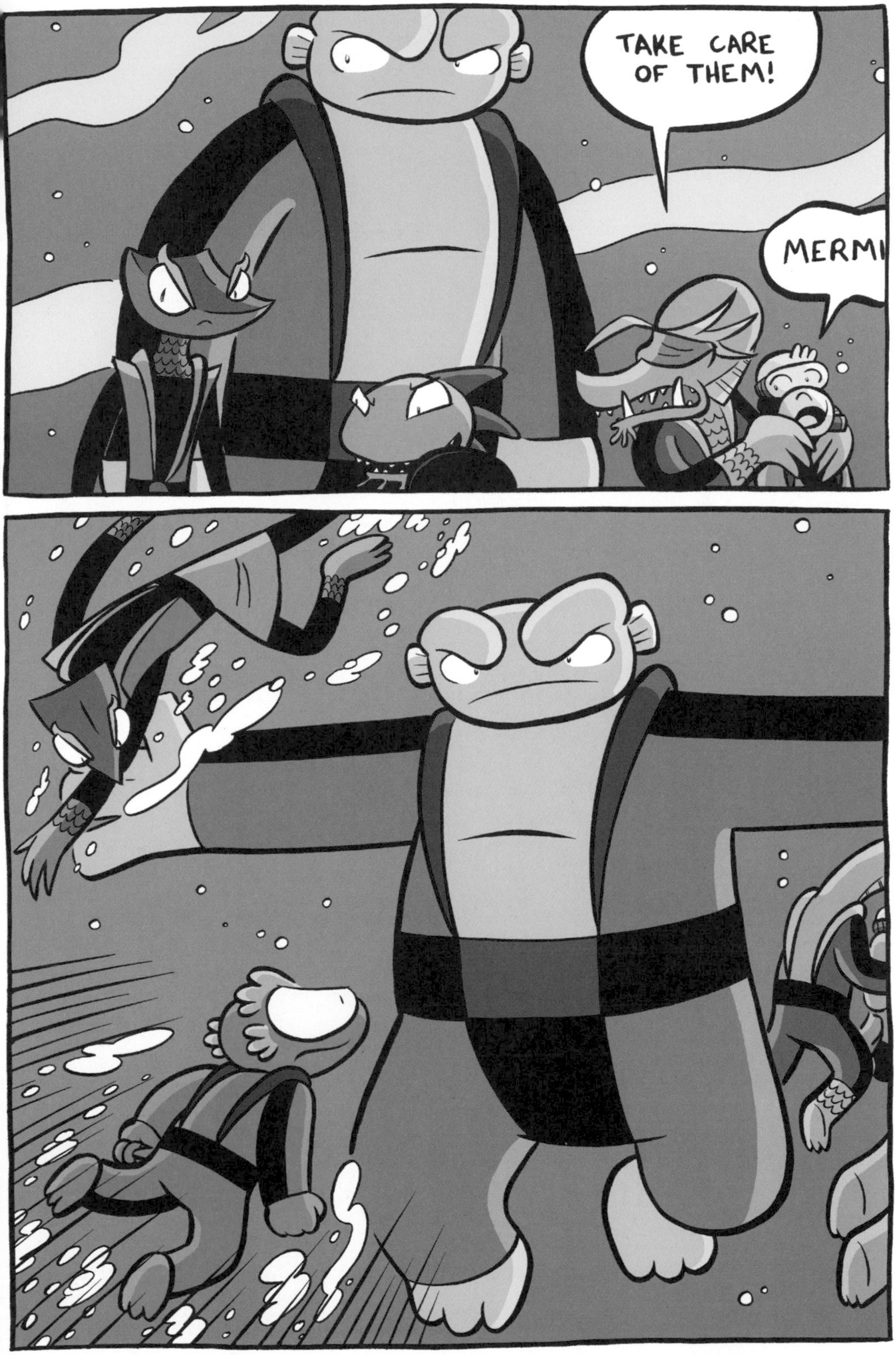
TAKE CARE OF THEM!
MERMI

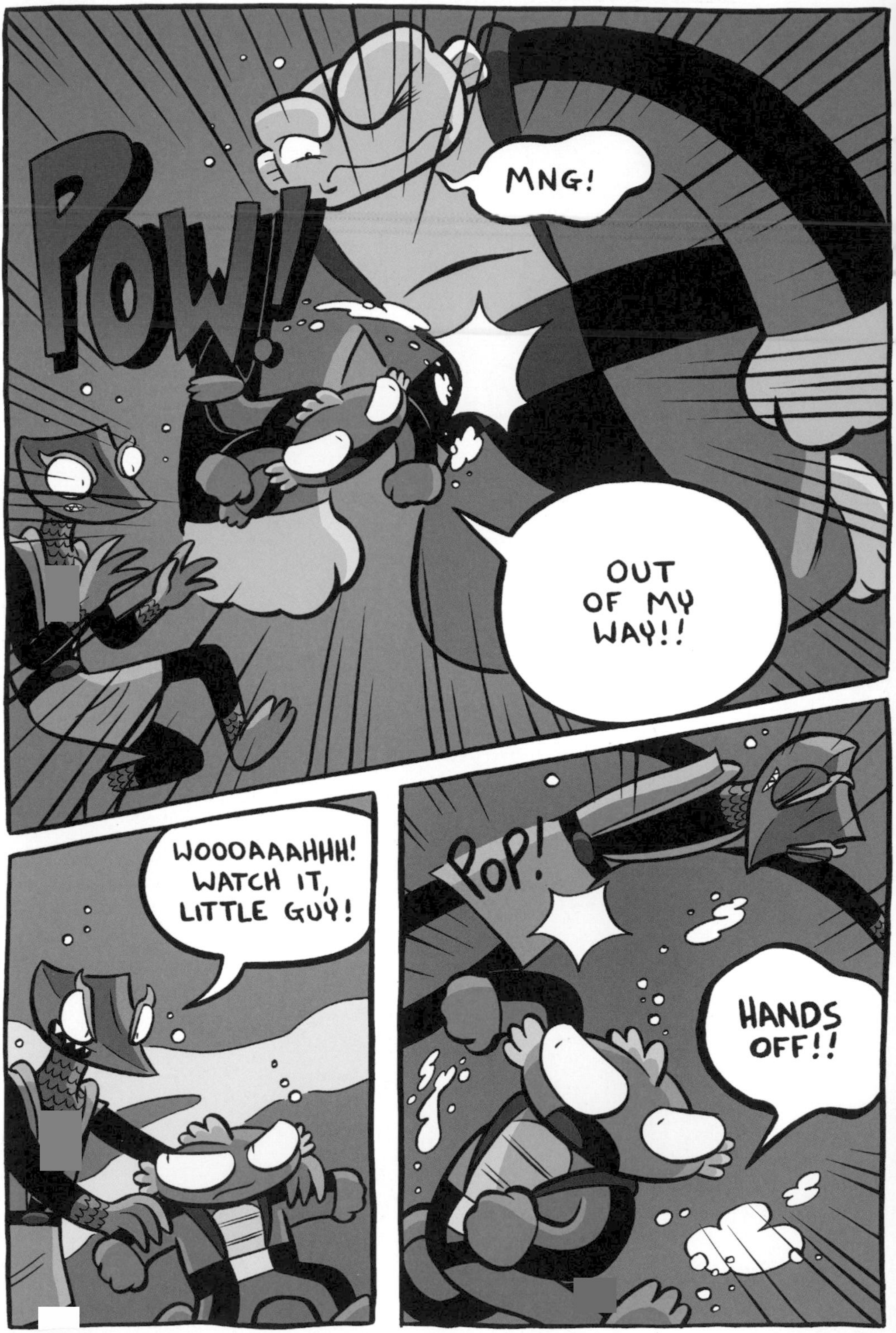
POW!!
MNG!
OUT OF MY WAY!!
WOOOAAAHHH! WATCH IT, LITTLE GUY!
POP!
HANDS OFF!!

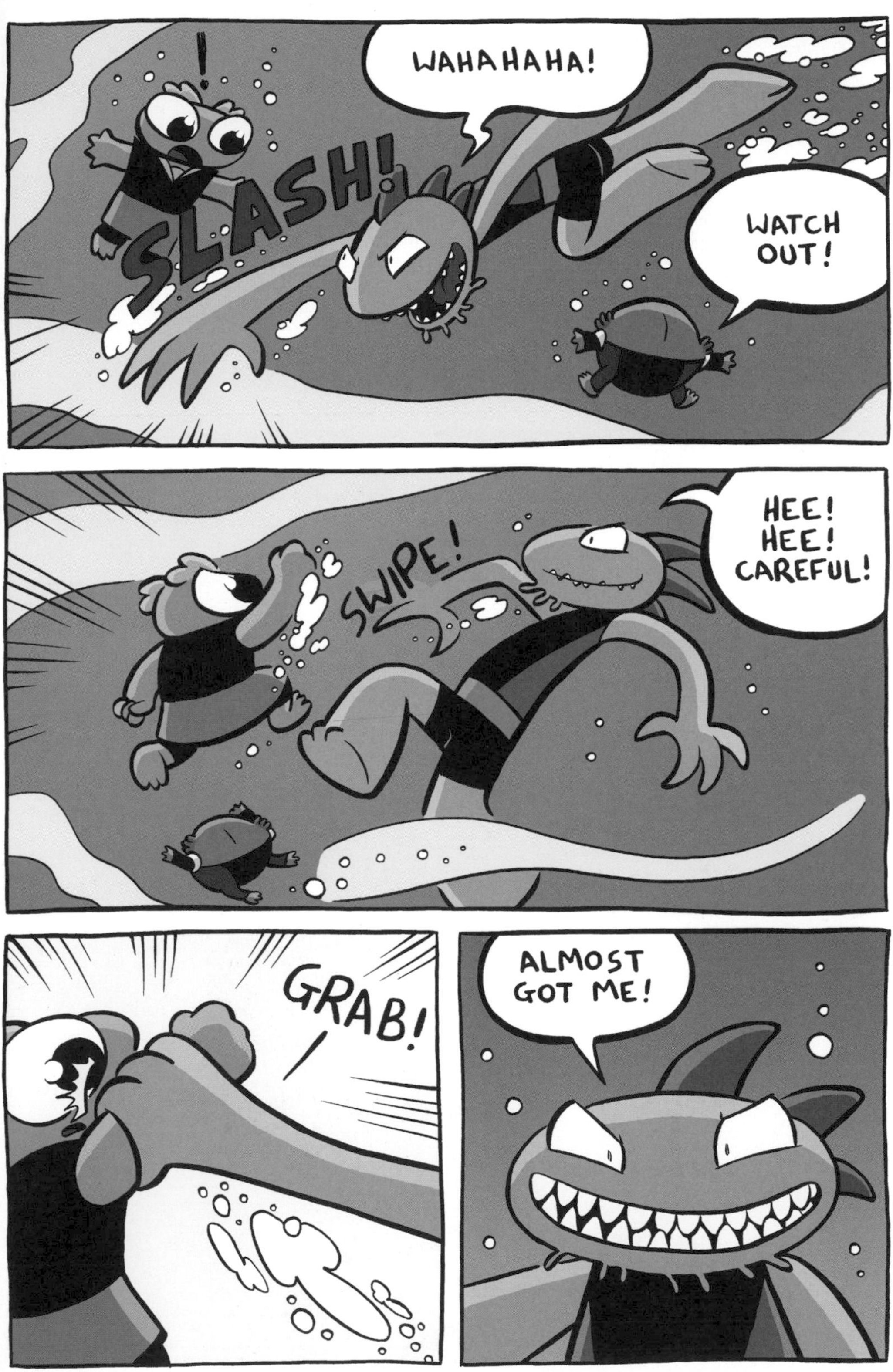
!
WAHAHAHAHA!
SLASH!
WATCH OUT!
SWIPE!
HEE! HEE! CAREFUL!
GRAB!
ALMOST GOT ME!

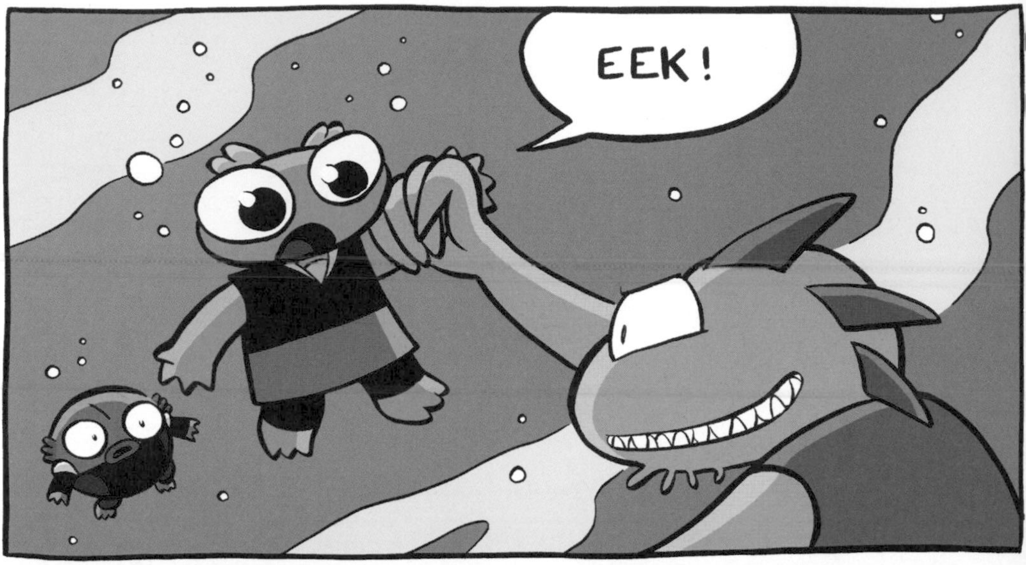
EEK!

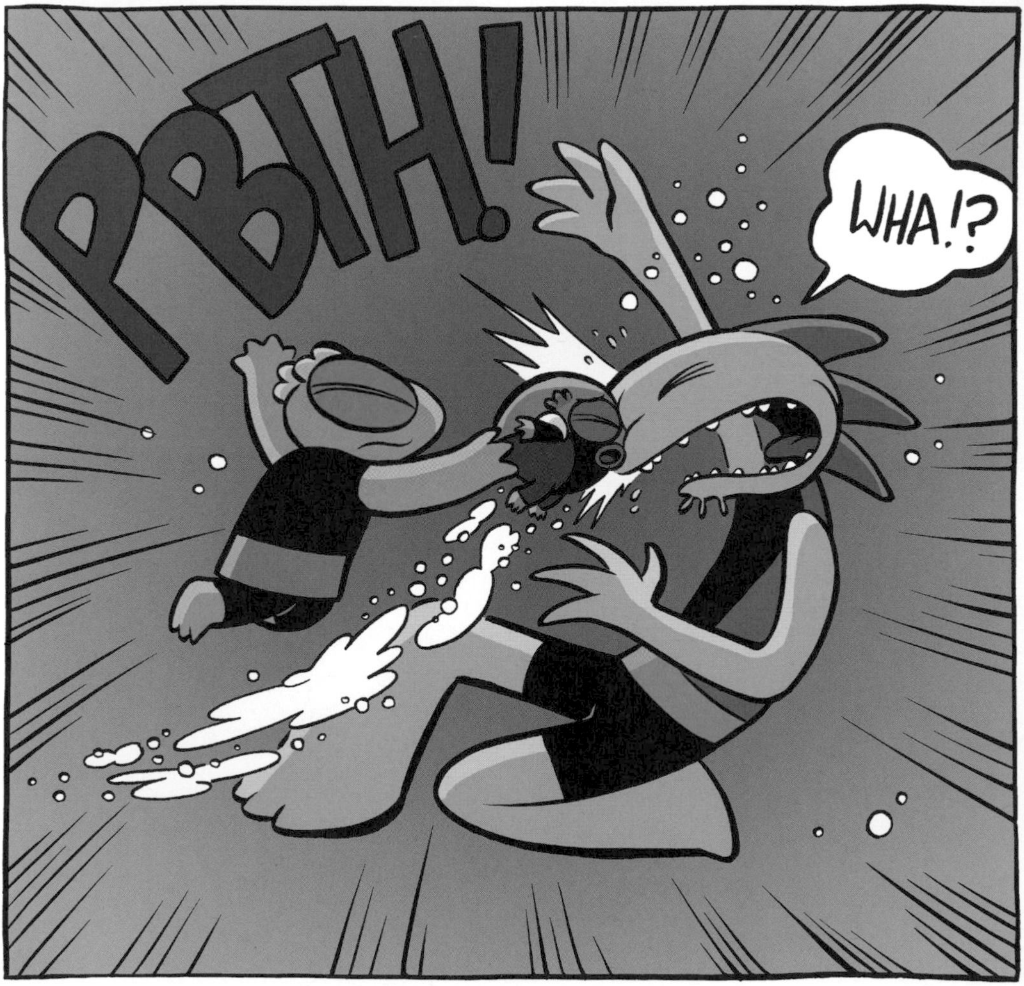
PBTTH!
WHA!?

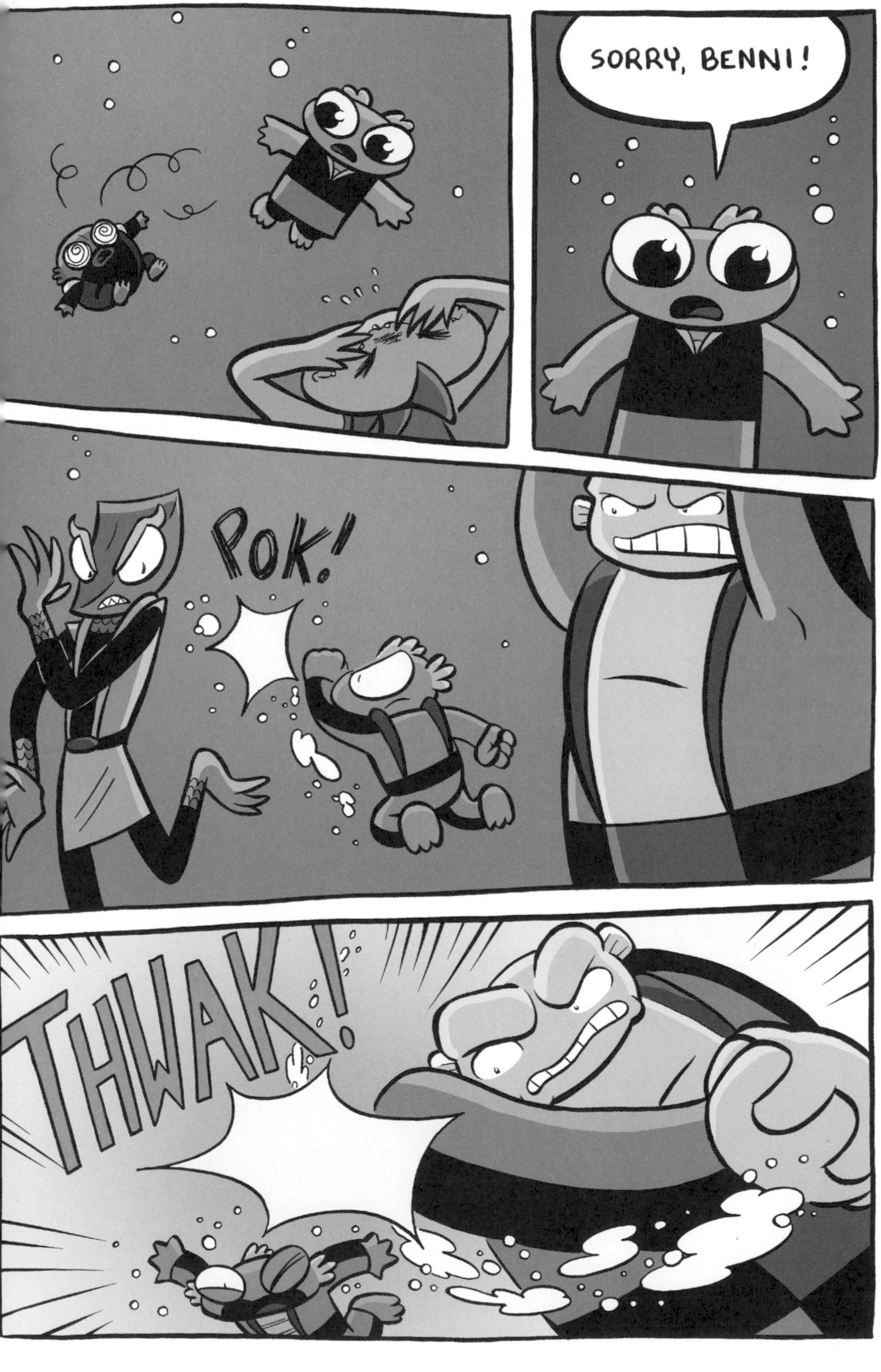
SORRY, BENNI!
POK!
THWAK!

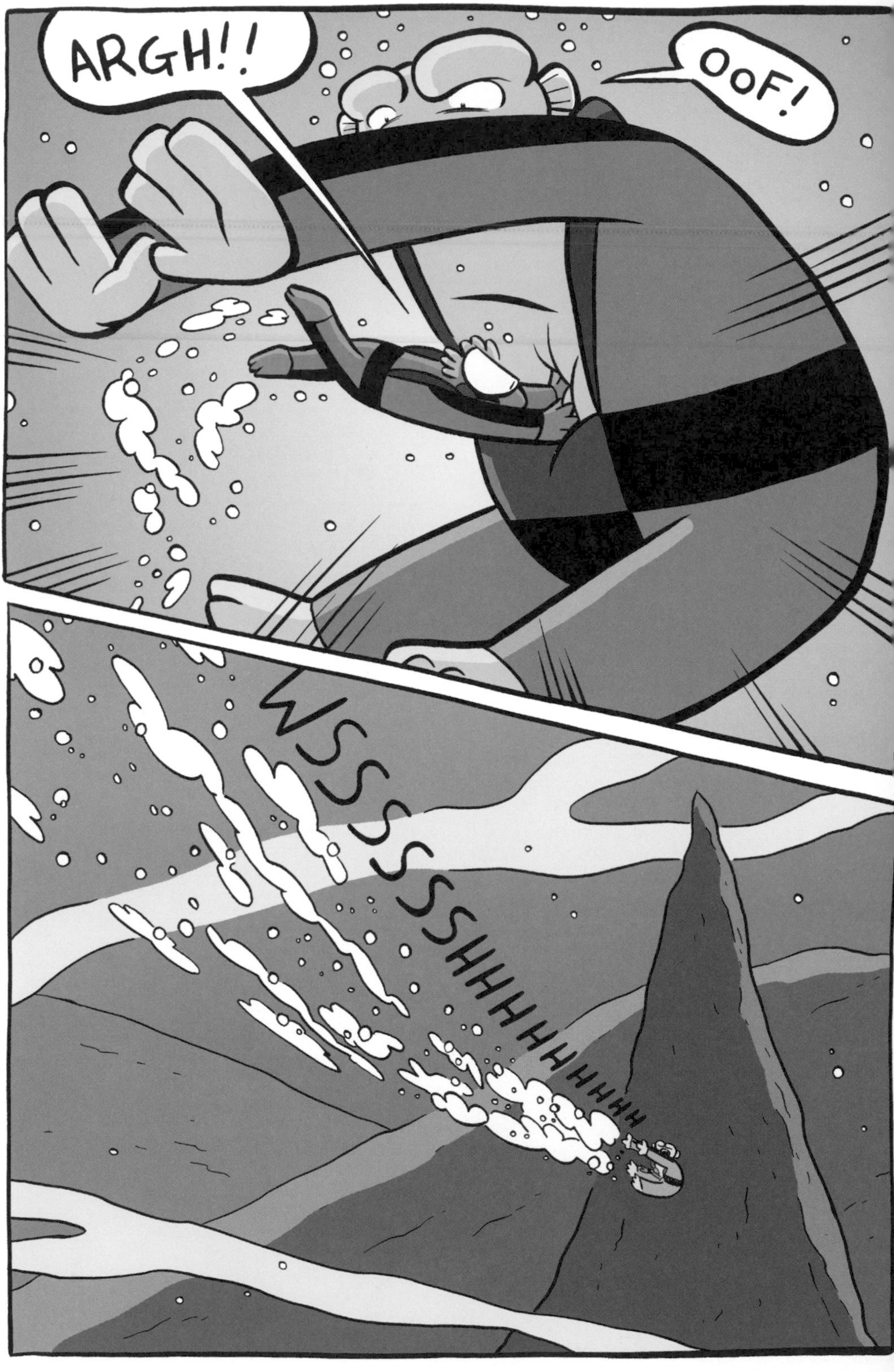
ARGH!!
OOF!
WSSSSSSHHHHHHHHHHH

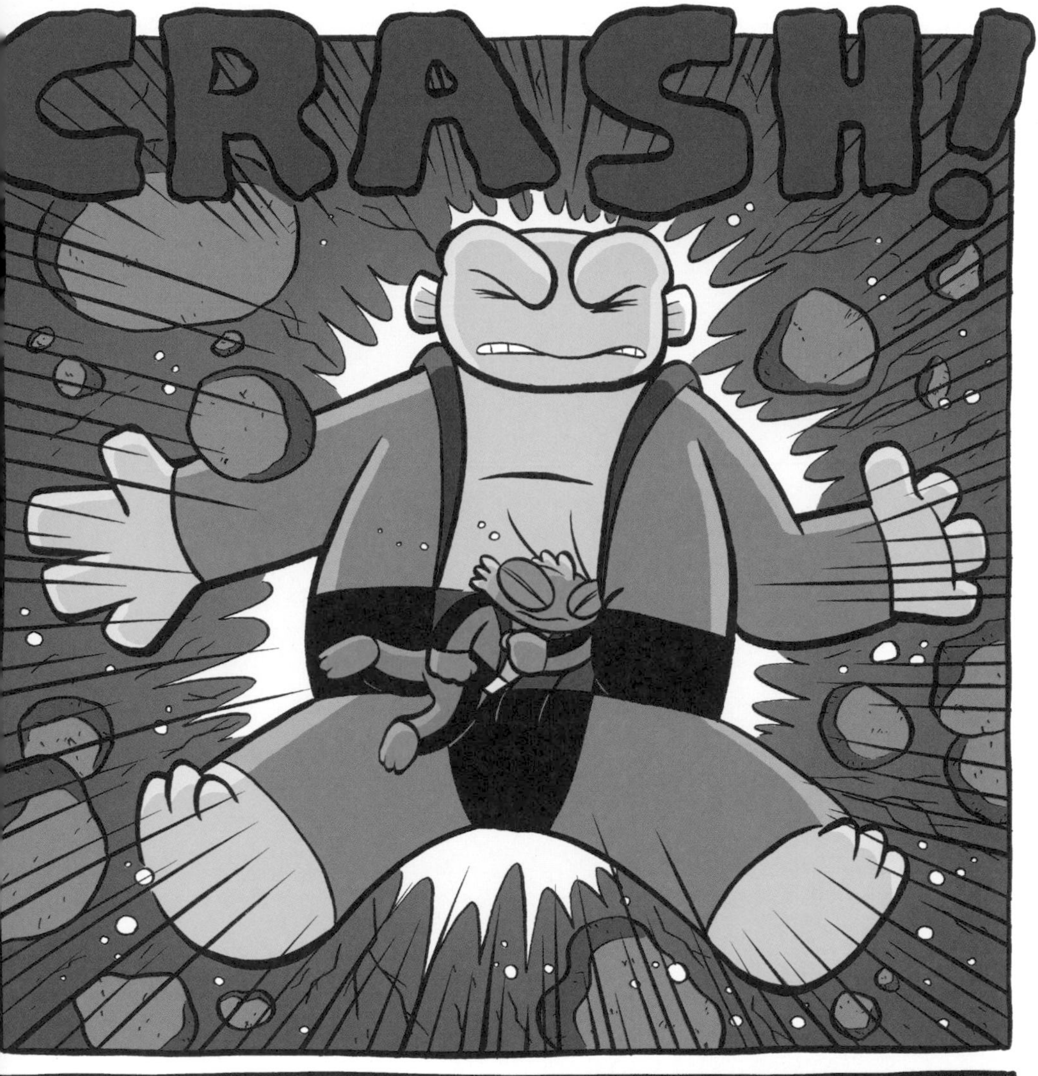
CRASH!

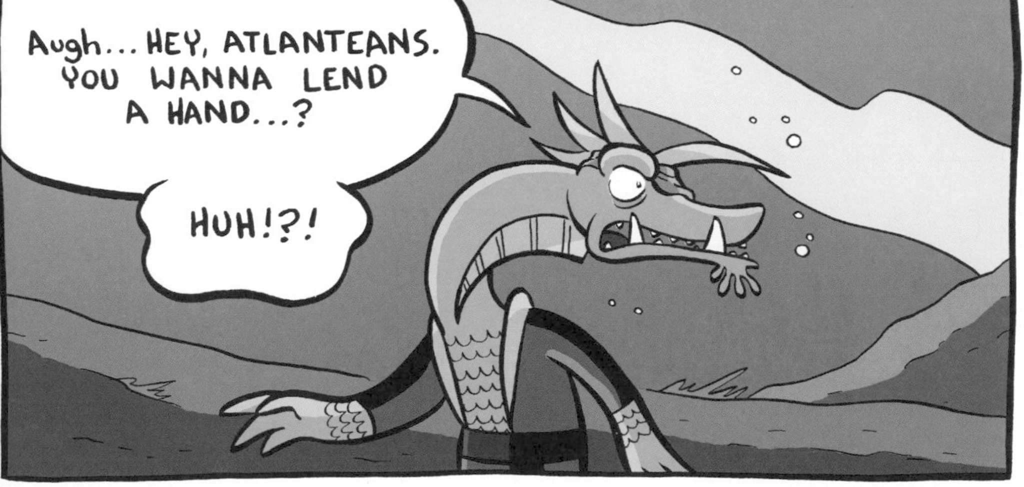
Augh... HEY, ATLANTEANS. YOU WANNA LEND A HAND...?
HUH!?!

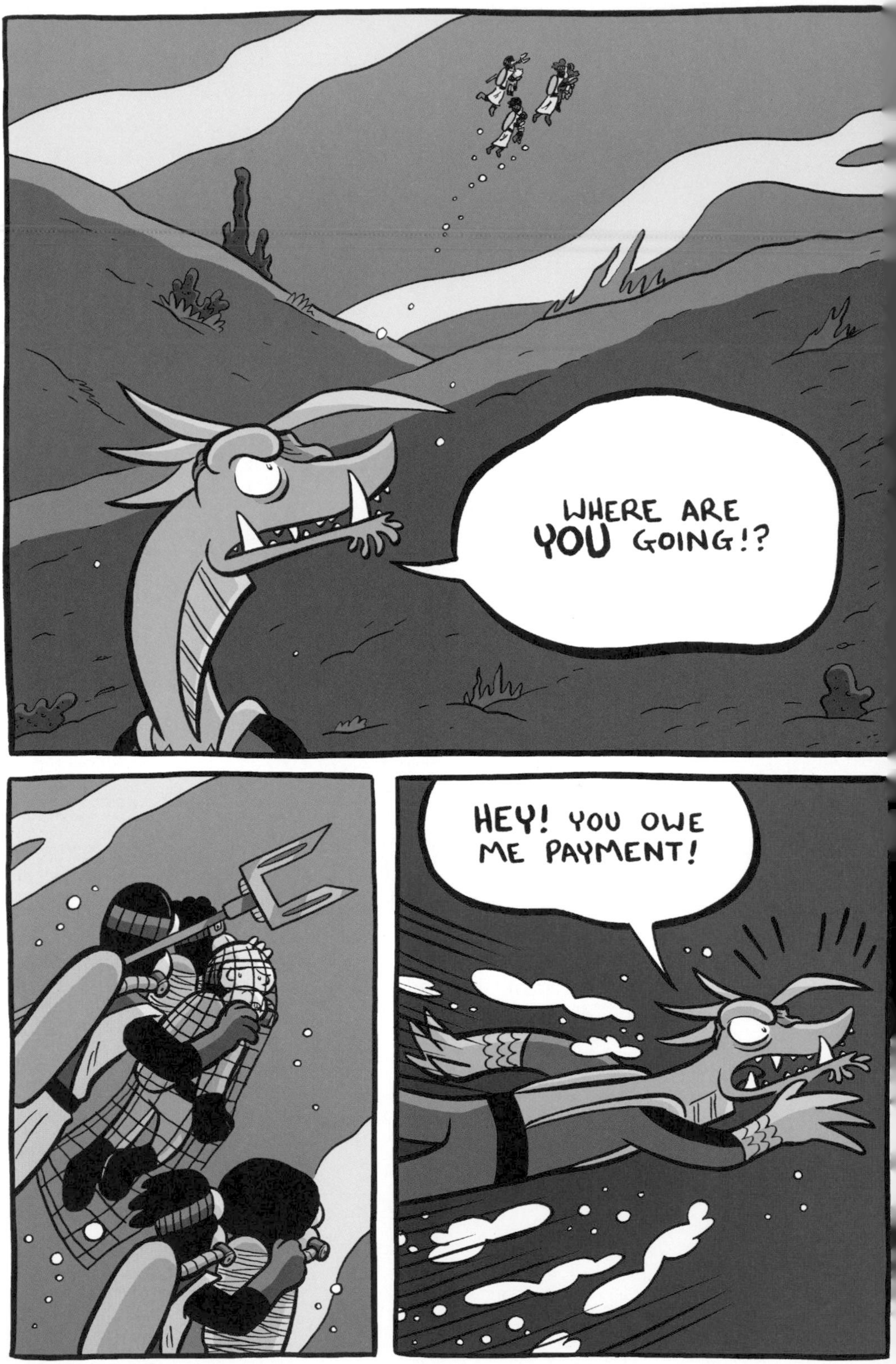
WHERE ARE YOU GOING!?
HEY! YOU OWE ME PAYMENT!

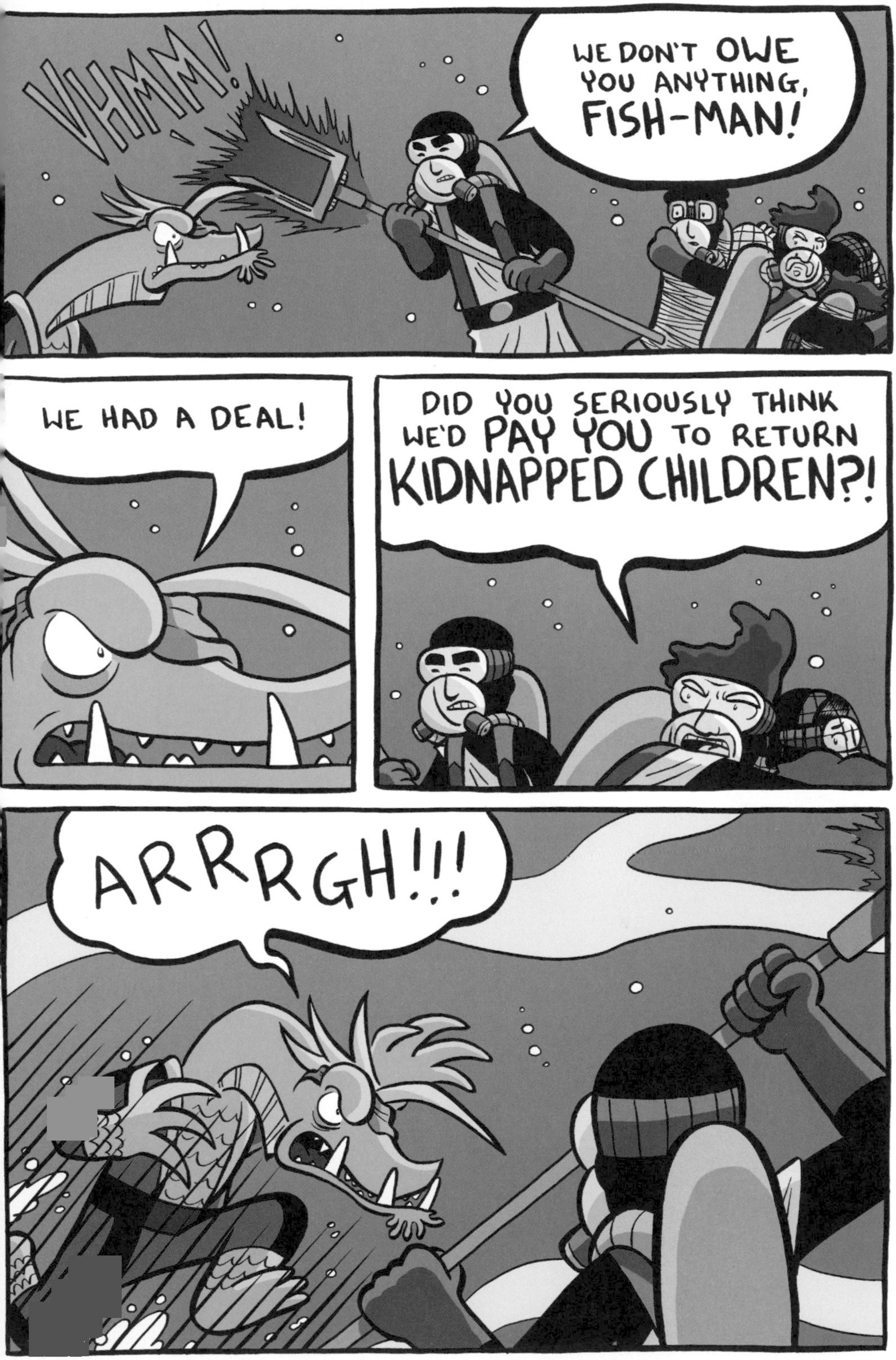
VHMM!
WE DON'T OWE YOU ANYTHING, FISH-MAN!
WE HAD A DEAL!
DID YOU SERIOUSLY THINK WE'D PAY YOU TO RETURN KIDNAPPED CHILDREN?!
ARRRGH!!!

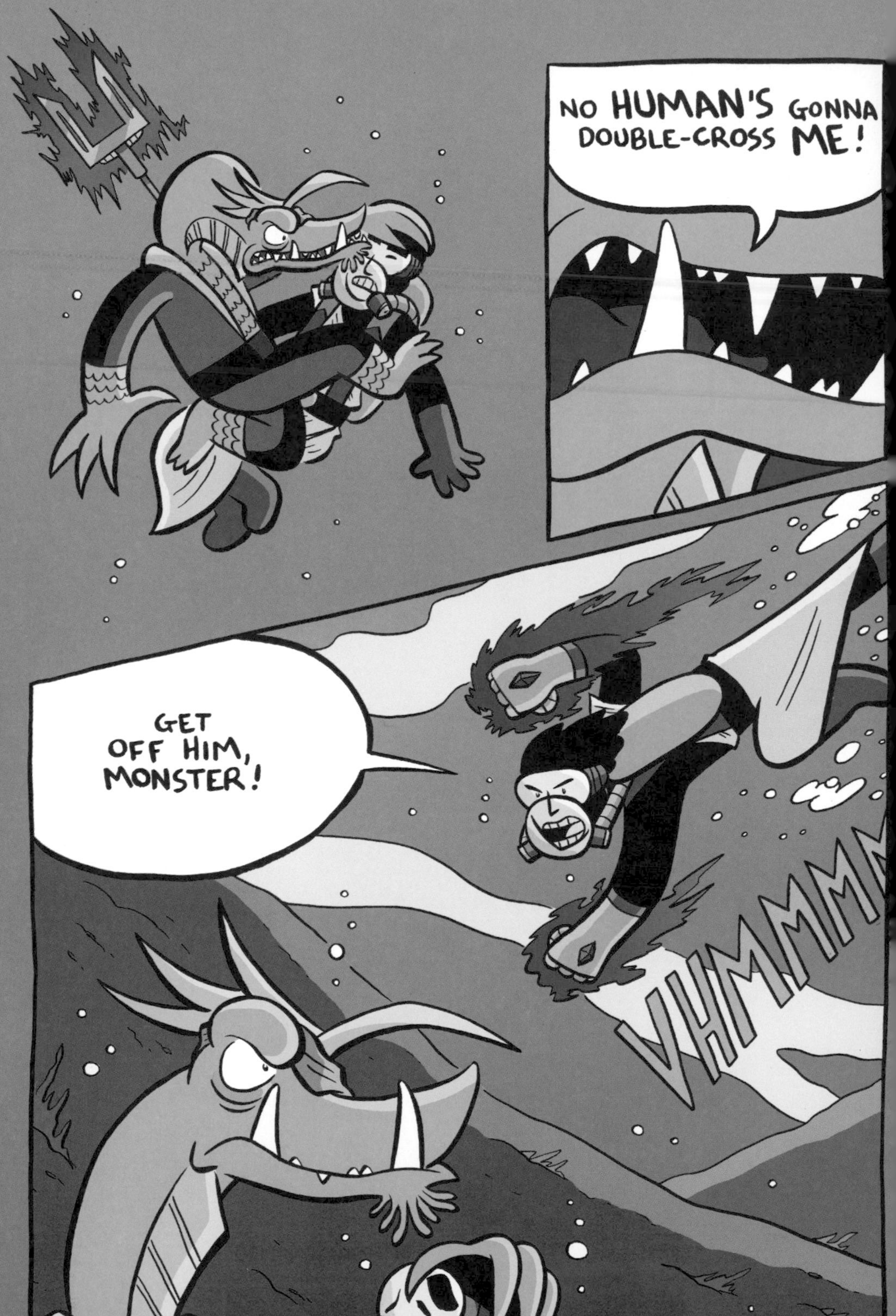
NO HUMAN'S GONNA DOUBLE-CROSS ME!
GET OFF HIM, MONSTER!
VHMMMM

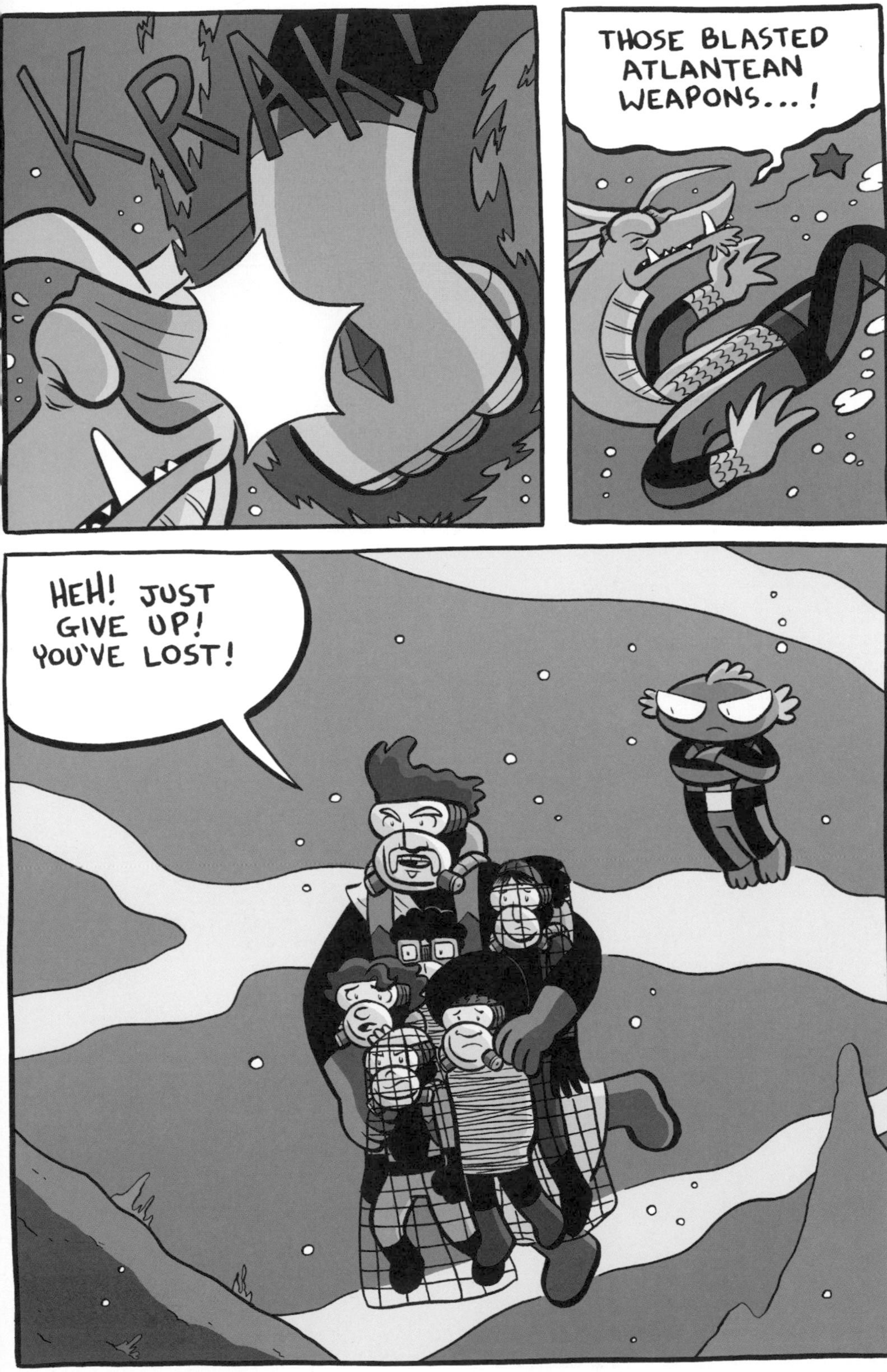
KRAK!
THOSE BLASTED ATLANTEAN WEAPONS...!
HEH! JUST GIVE UP! YOU'VE LOST!

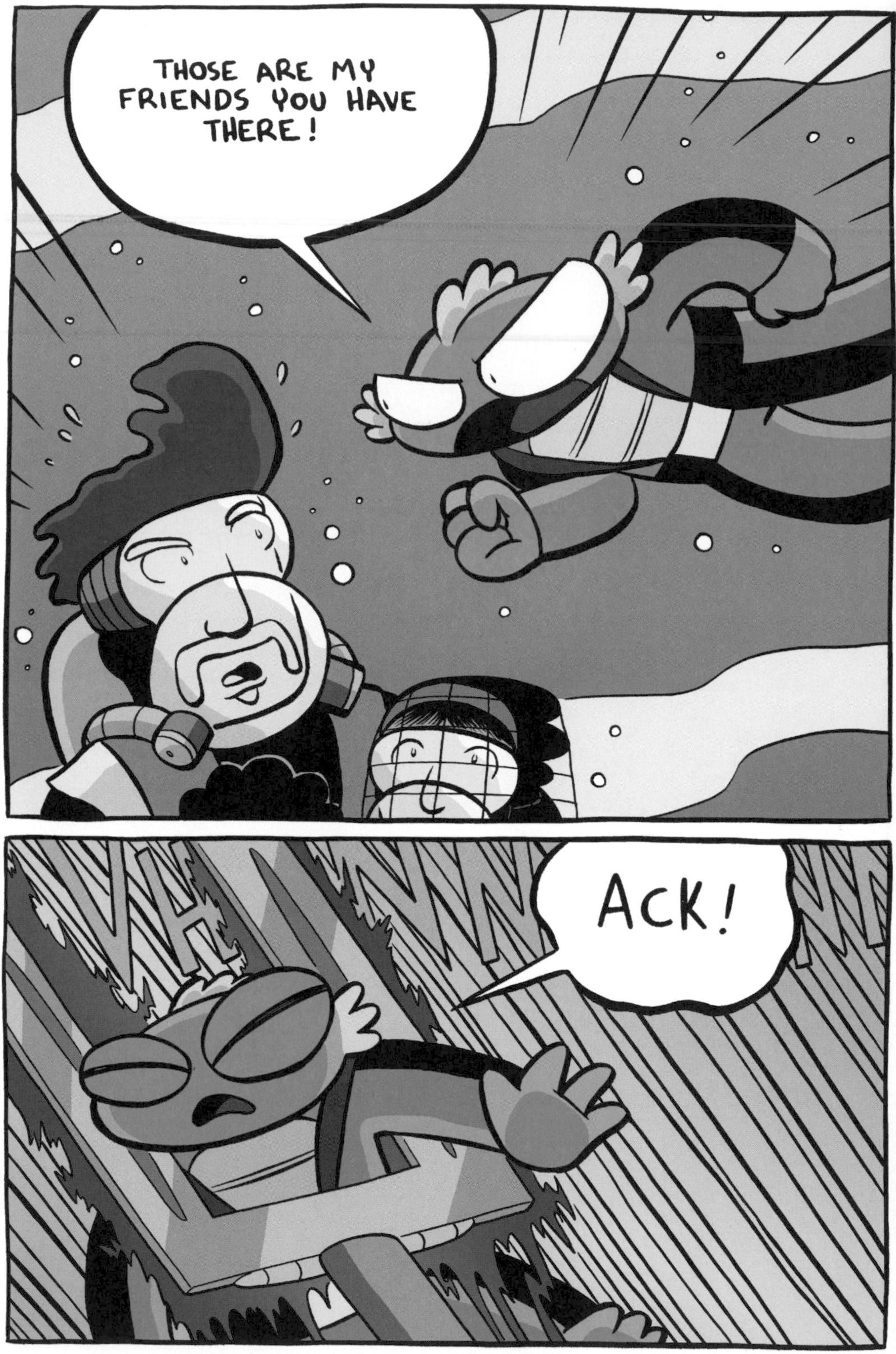
THOSE ARE MY FRIENDS YOU HAVE THERE!
ACK!

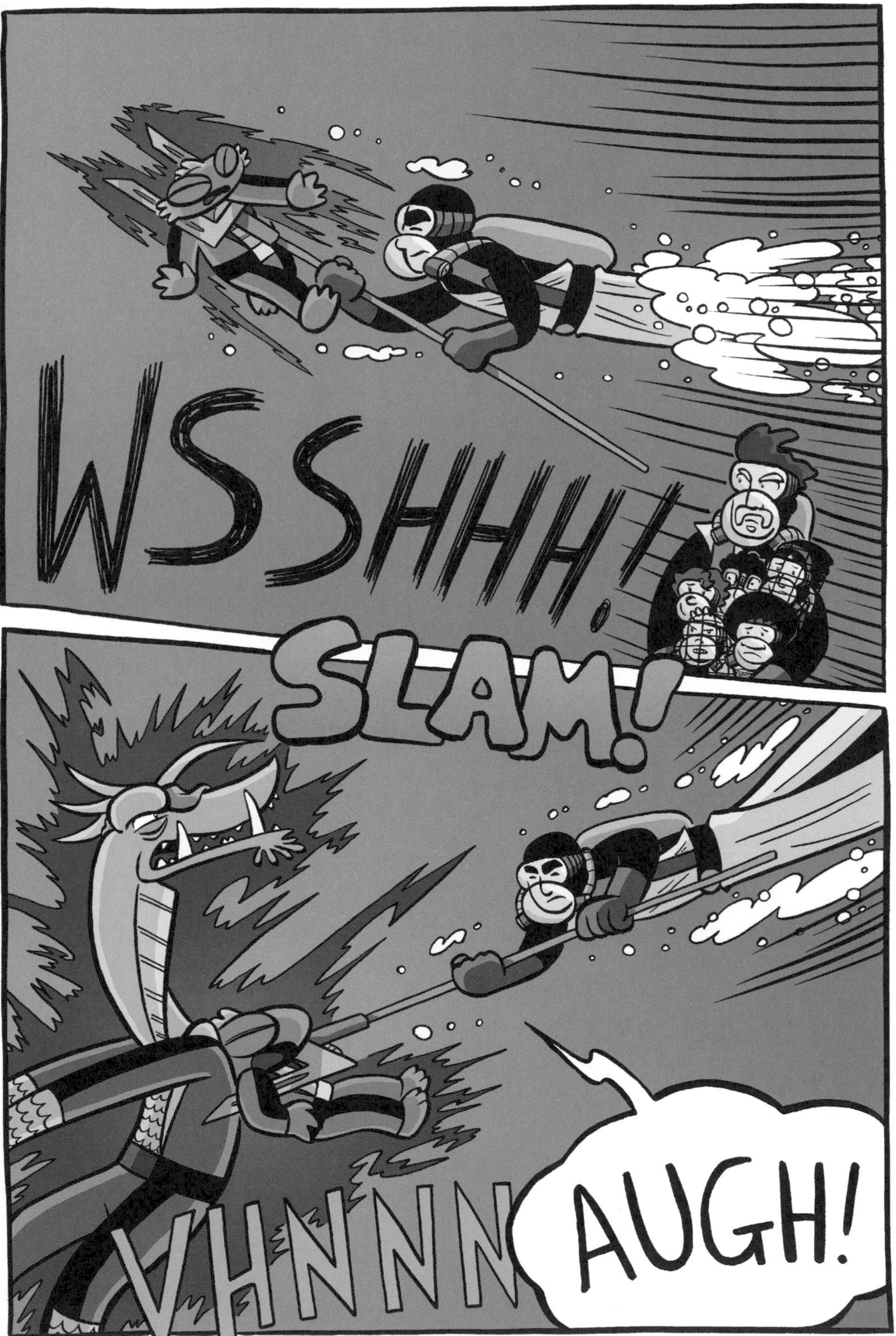
WSSHHH!
SLAM!
VHNNN
AUGH!

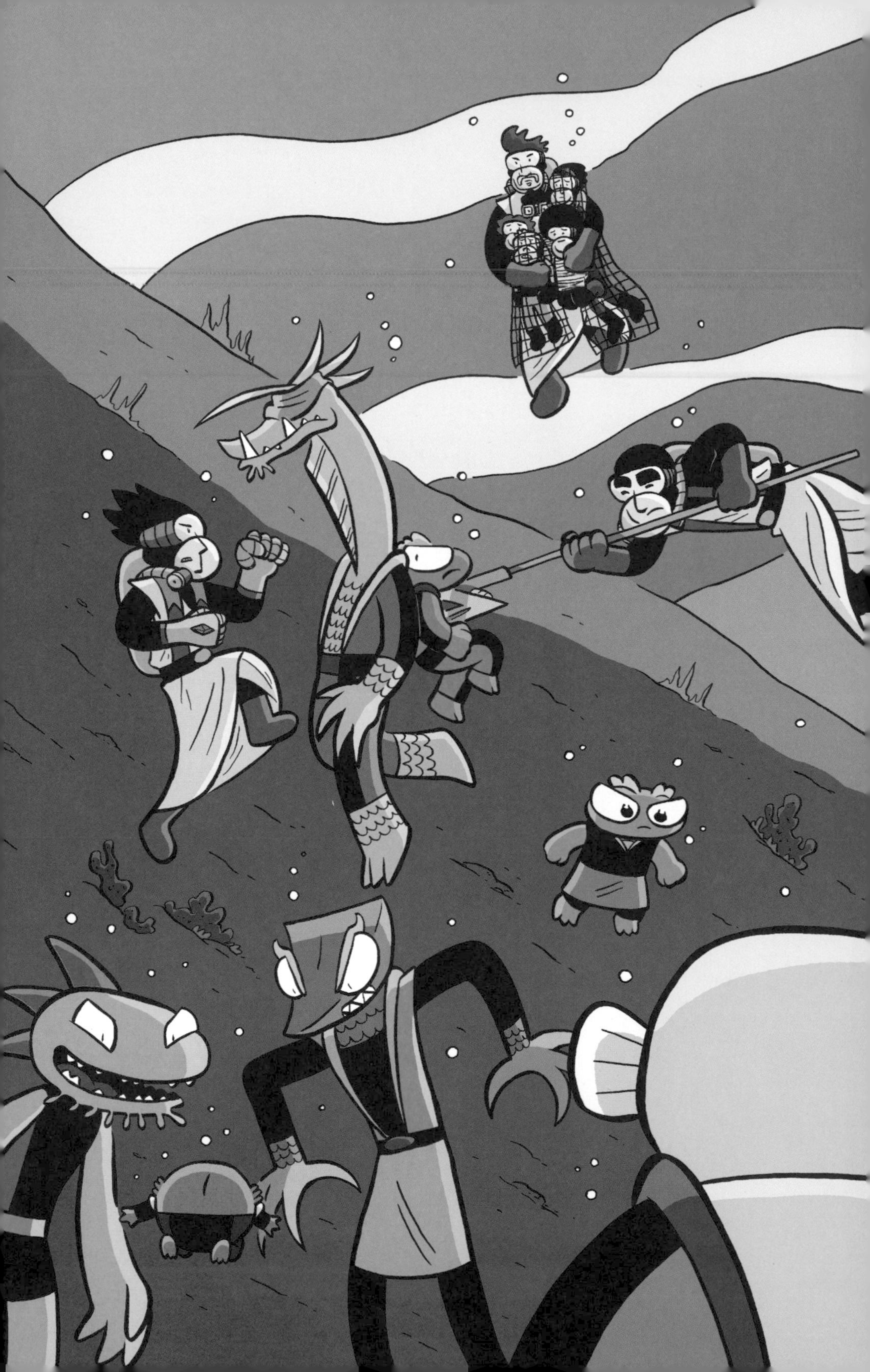

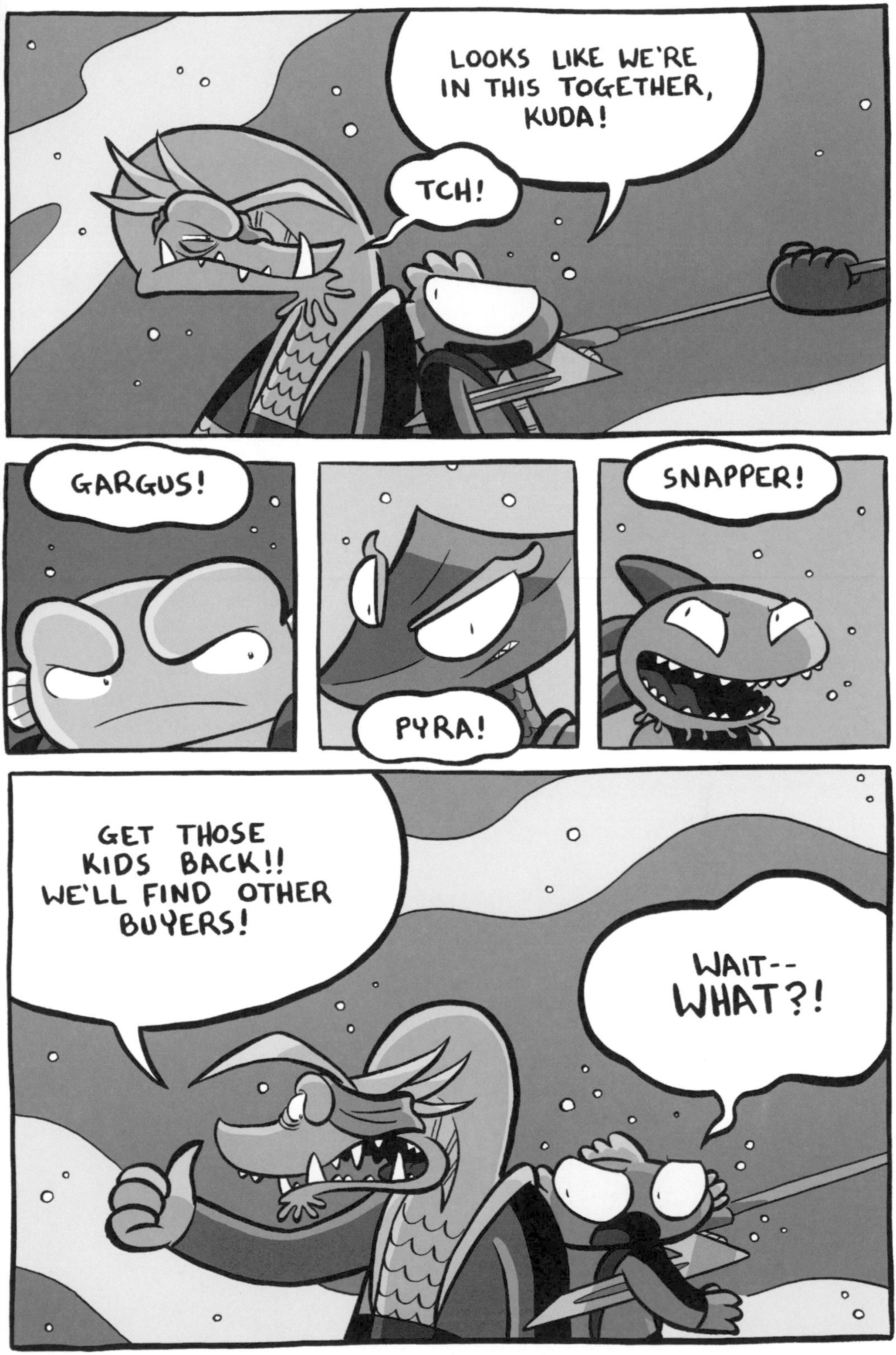
LOOKS LIKE WE'RE IN THIS TOGETHER, KUDA!
TCH!
GARGUS!
PYRA!
SNAPPER!
GET THOSE KIDS BACK!! WE'LL FIND OTHER BUYERS!
WAIT-- WHAT?!

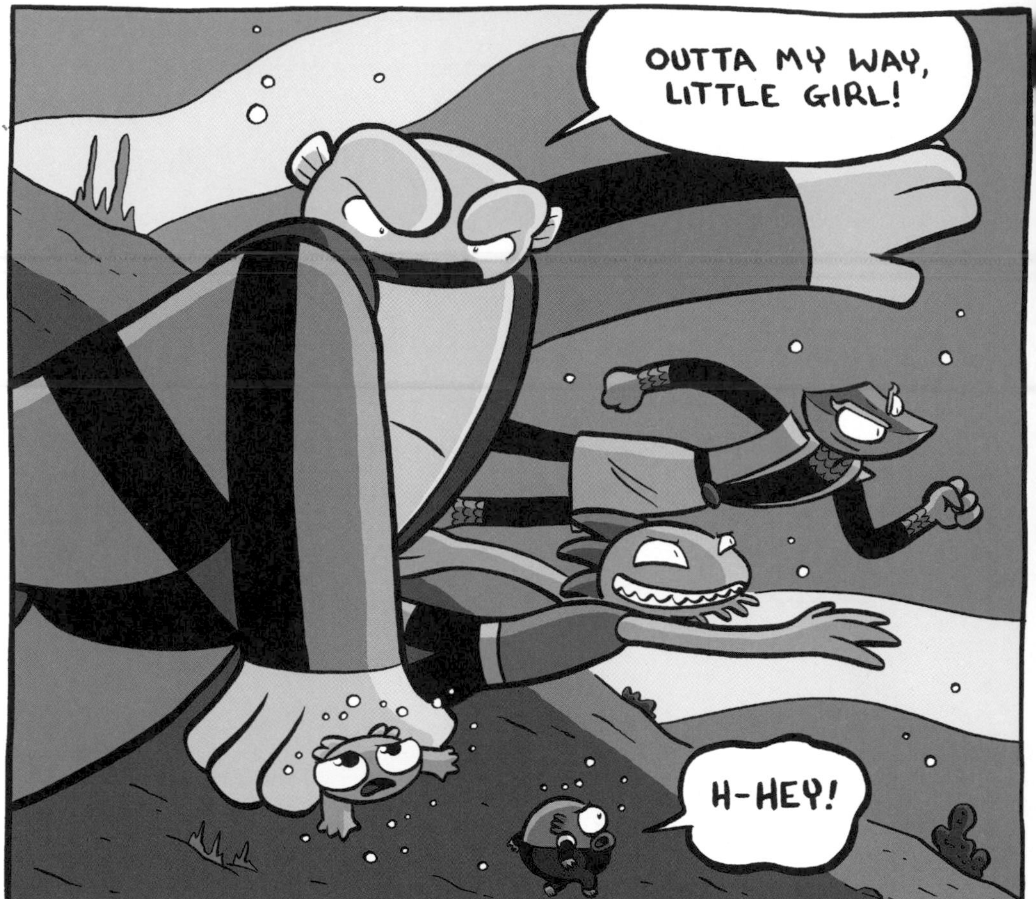
OUTTA MY WAY, LITTLE GIRL!
H-HEY!

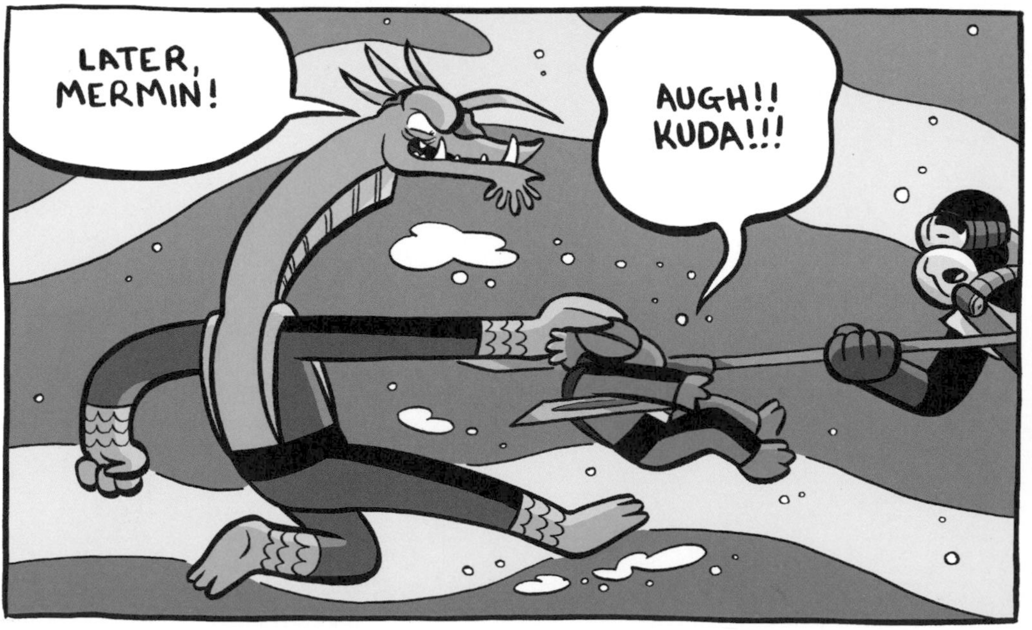
LATER, MERMIN!
AUGH!! KUDA!!!

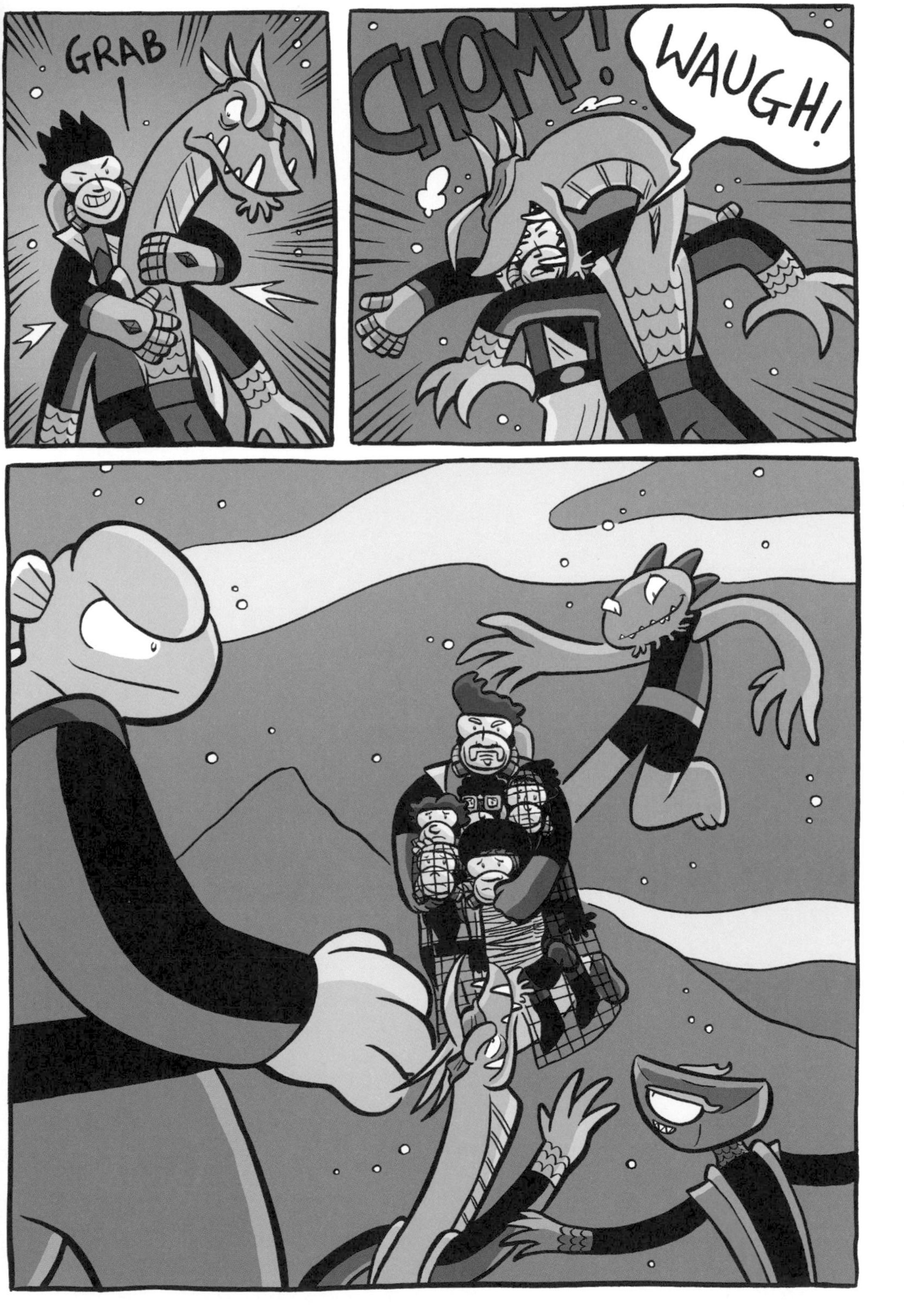
GRAB
CHOMP!
WAUGH!

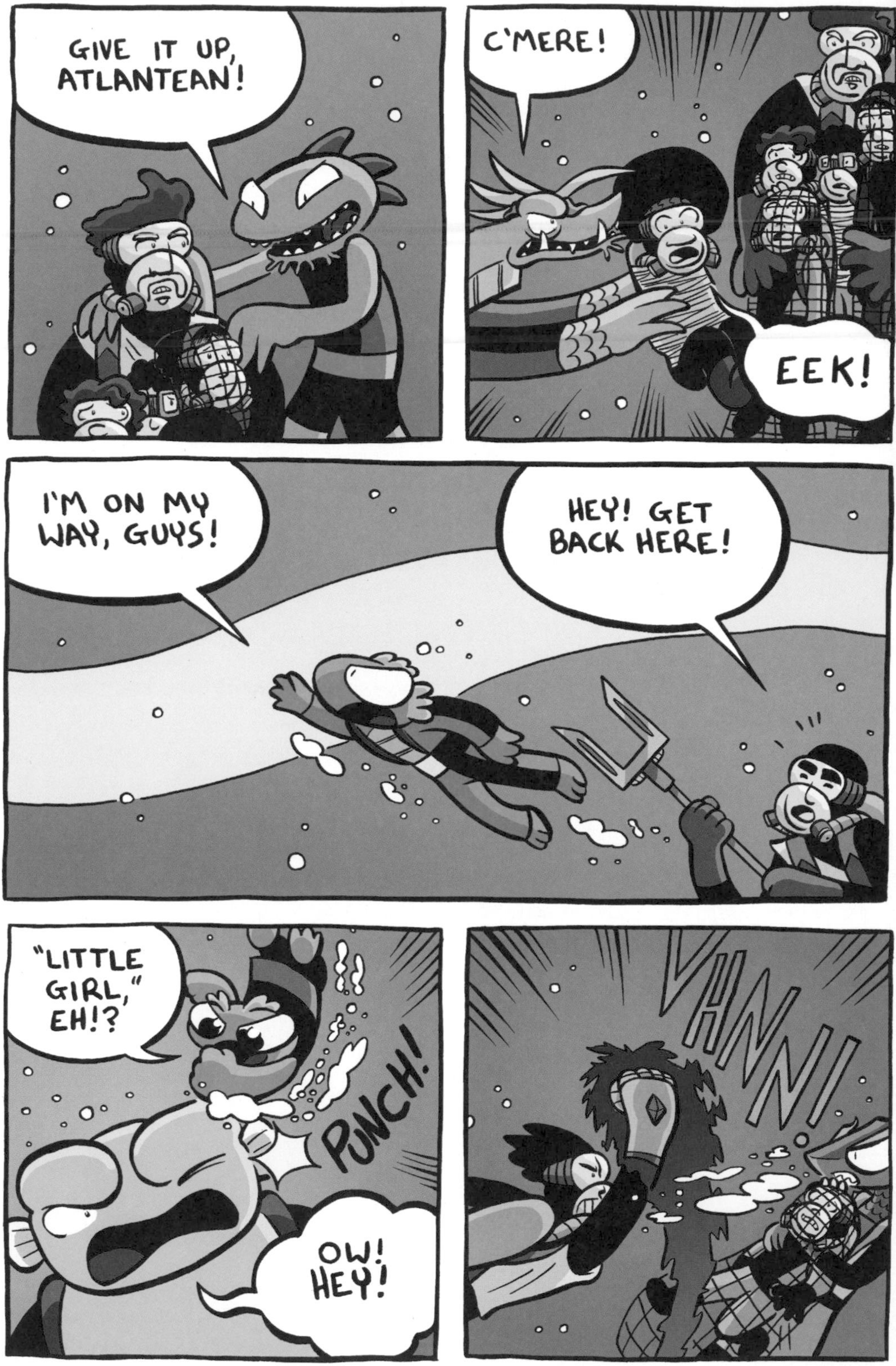
GIVE IT UP, ATLANTEAN!
C'MERE!
EEK!
I'M ON MY WAY, GUYS!
HEY! GET BACK HERE!
"LITTLE GIRL," EH!?
PUNCH!
OW! HEY!
VHNN!

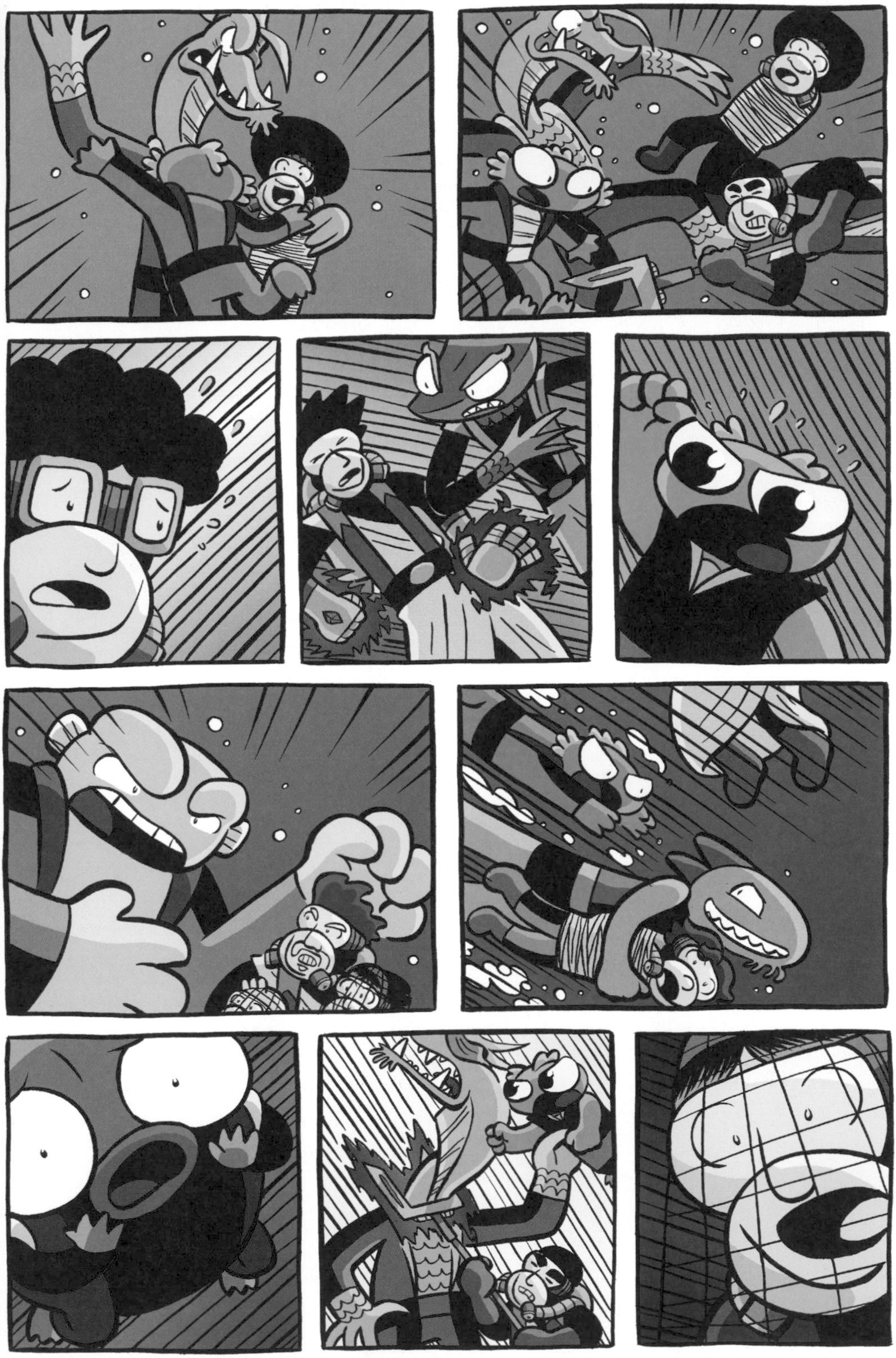

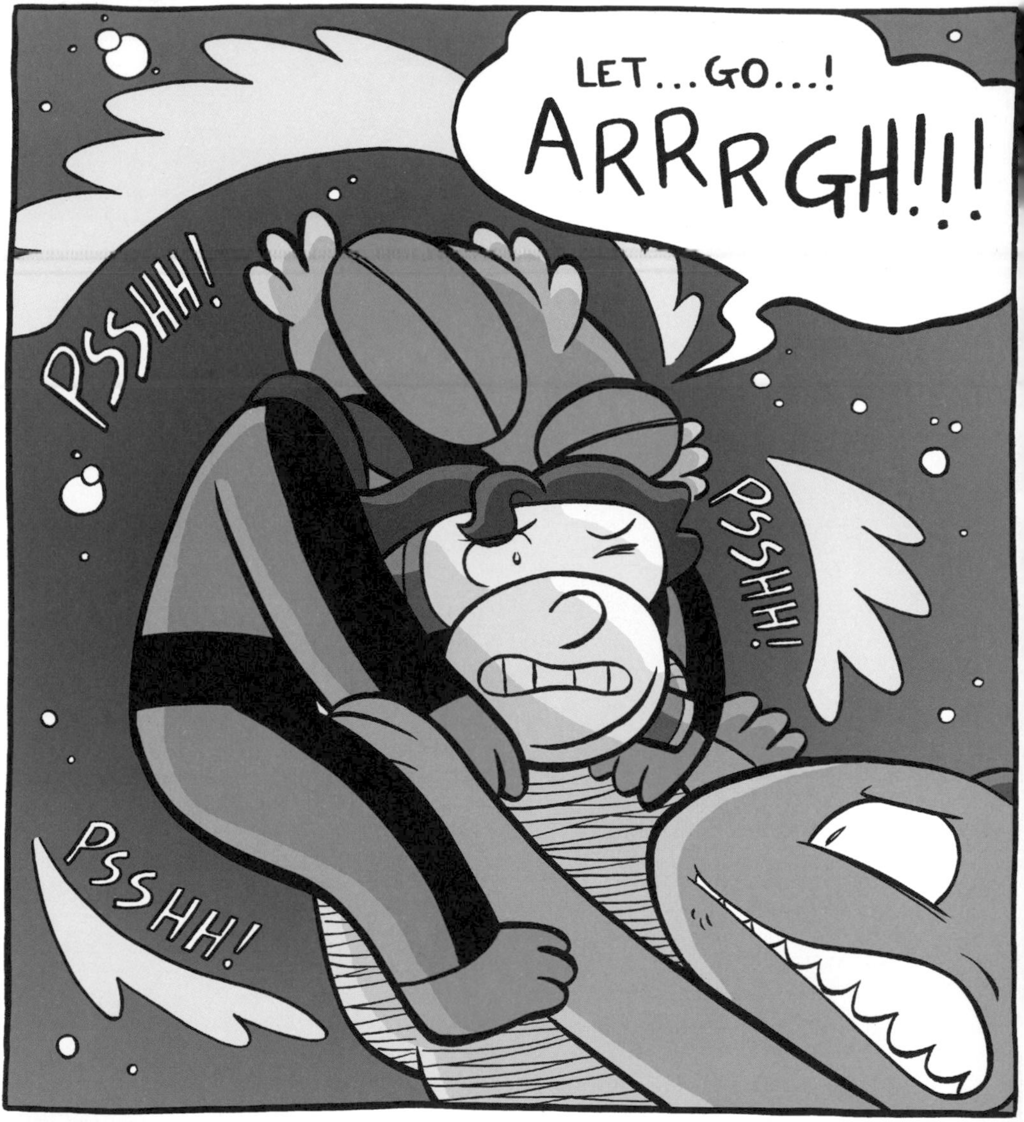
LET...GO...!
ARRRGH!!!
PSSHH!
PSSHH!
PSSHH!

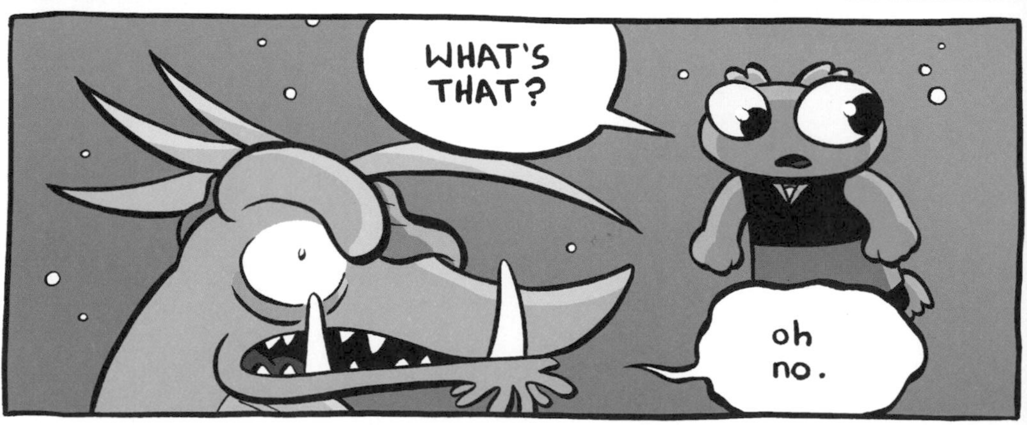
WHAT'S THAT?
oh no.

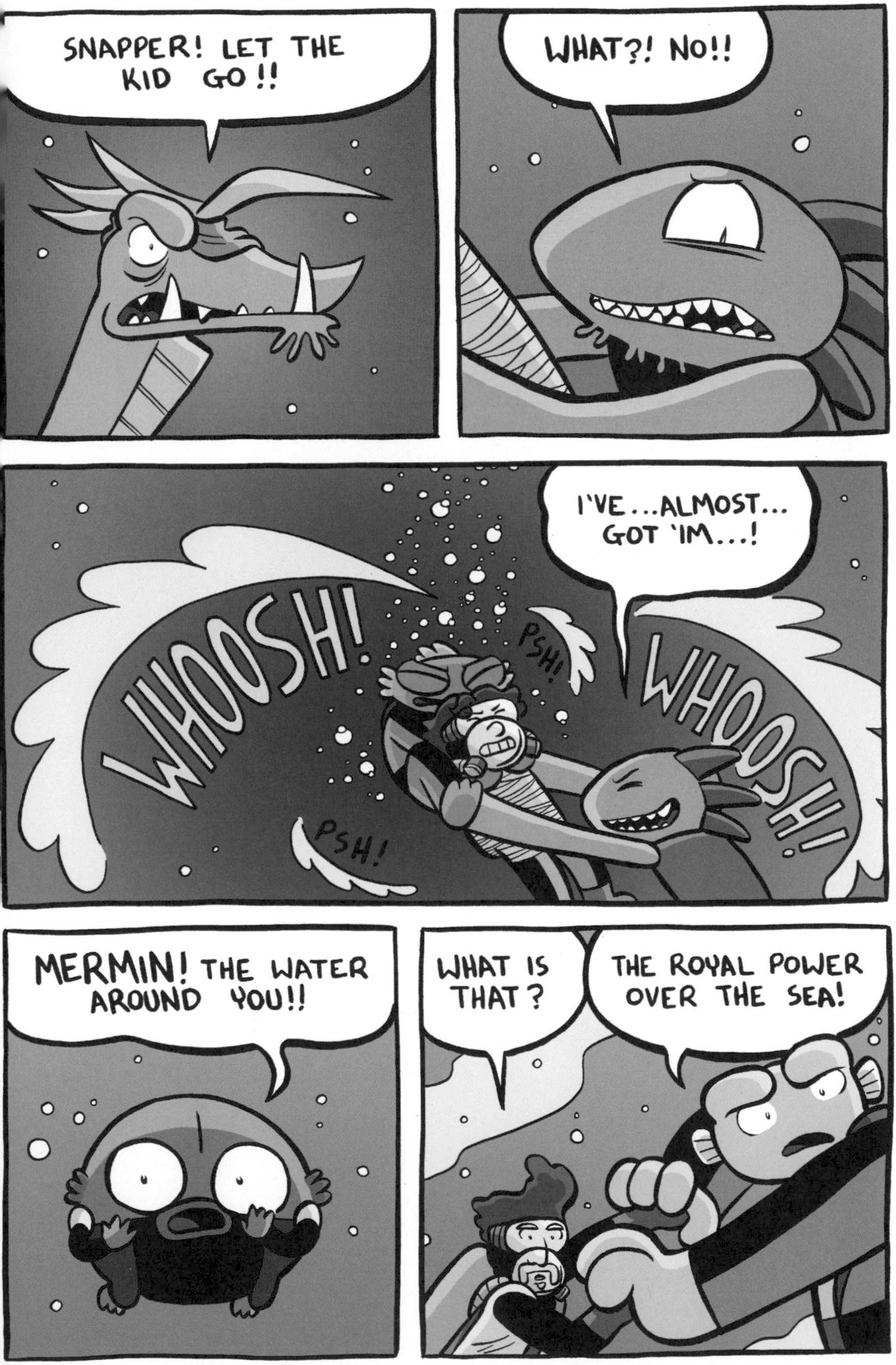
SNAPPER! LET THE KID GO!!
WHAT?! NO!!
I'VE...ALMOST... GOT 'IM...!
WHOOSH!
PSH!
WHOOSH!
PSH!
MERMIN! THE WATER AROUND YOU!!
WHAT IS THAT?
THE ROYAL POWER OVER THE SEA!

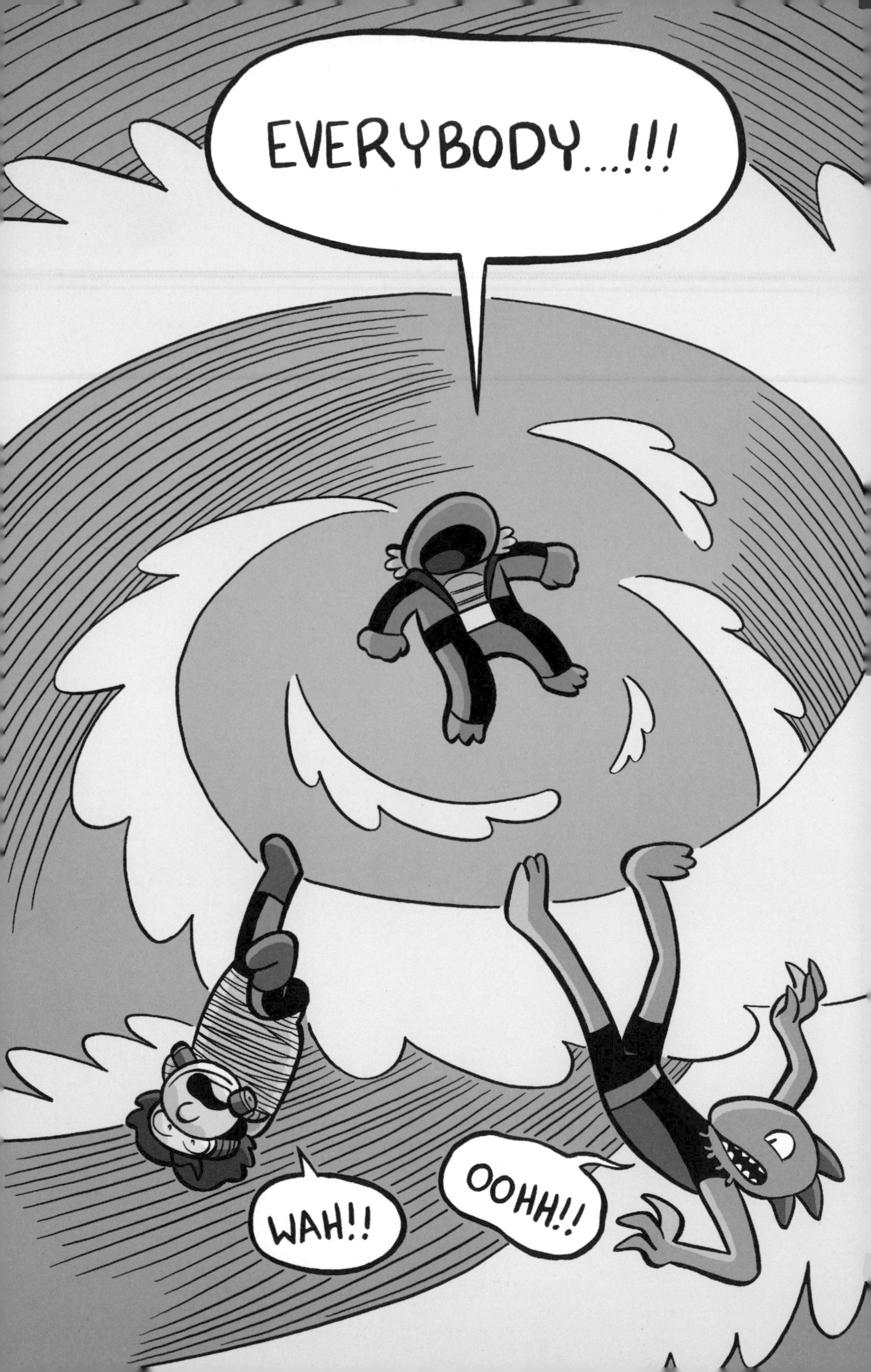
EVERYBODY...!!!
WAH!!
OOHH!!

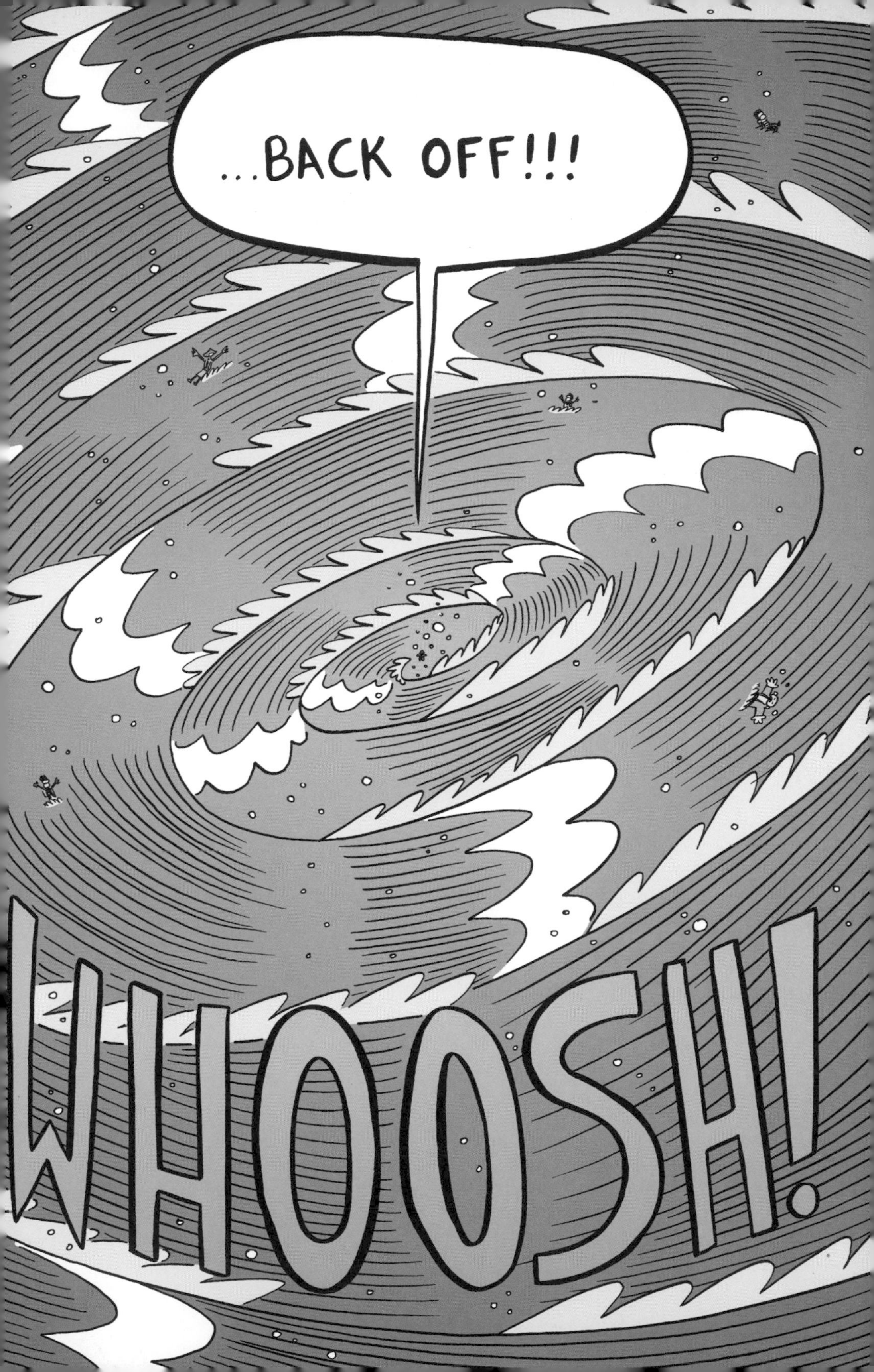
...BACK OFF!!!
WHOOSH!

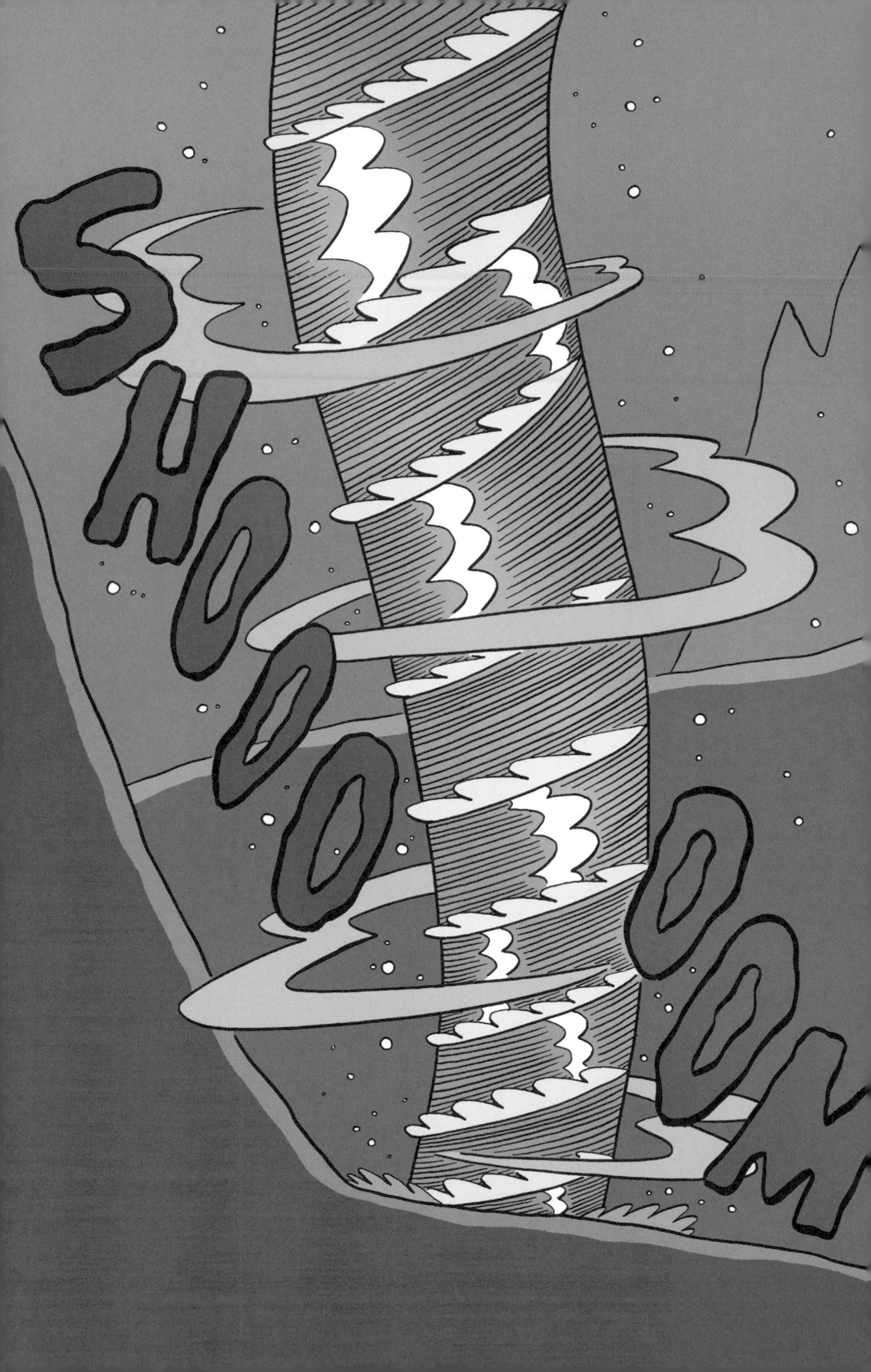
SHOOOOOOM

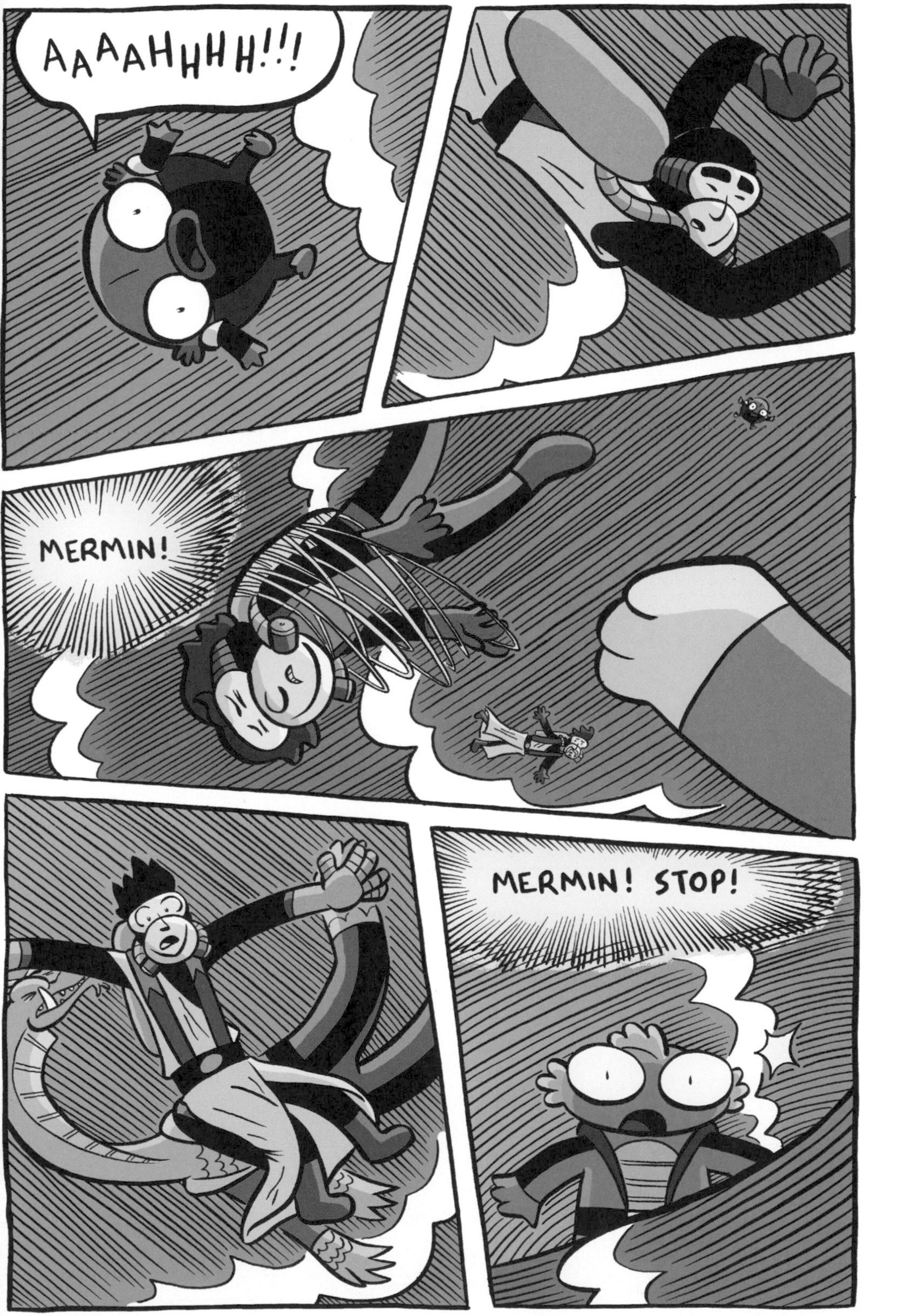
AAAAHHHH!!!
MERMIN!
MERMIN! STOP!

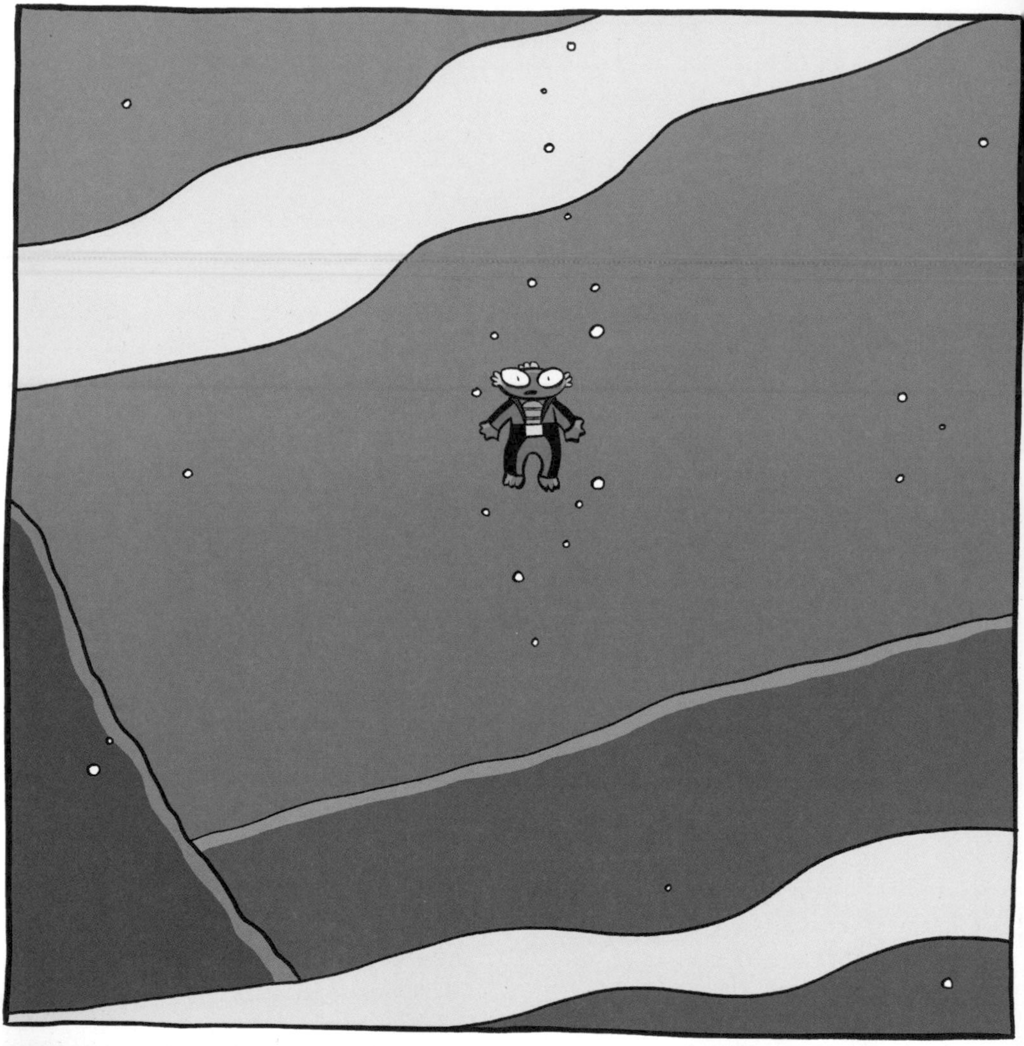

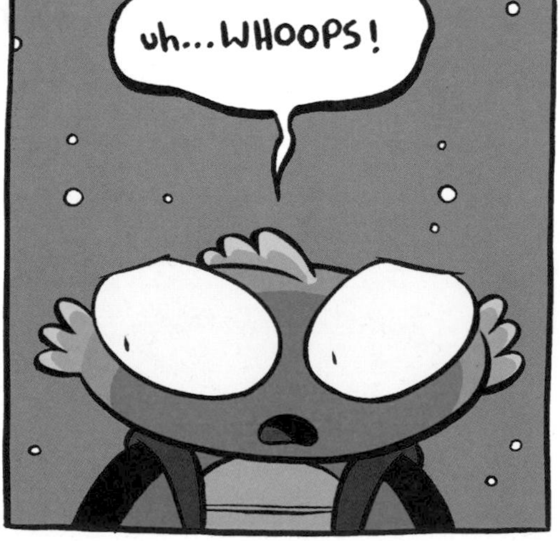
uh...WHOOPS!

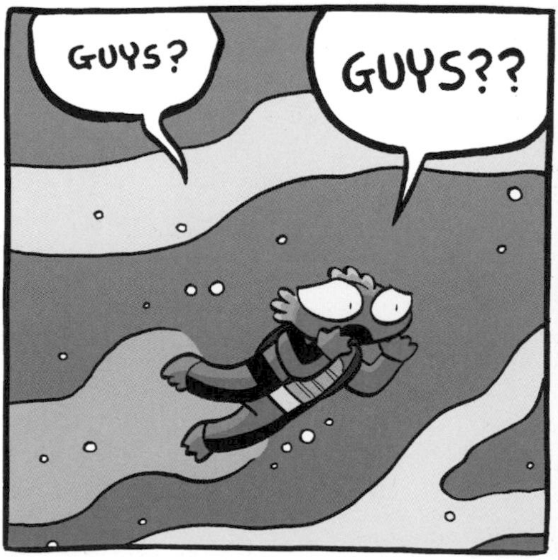
GUYS?
GUYS??

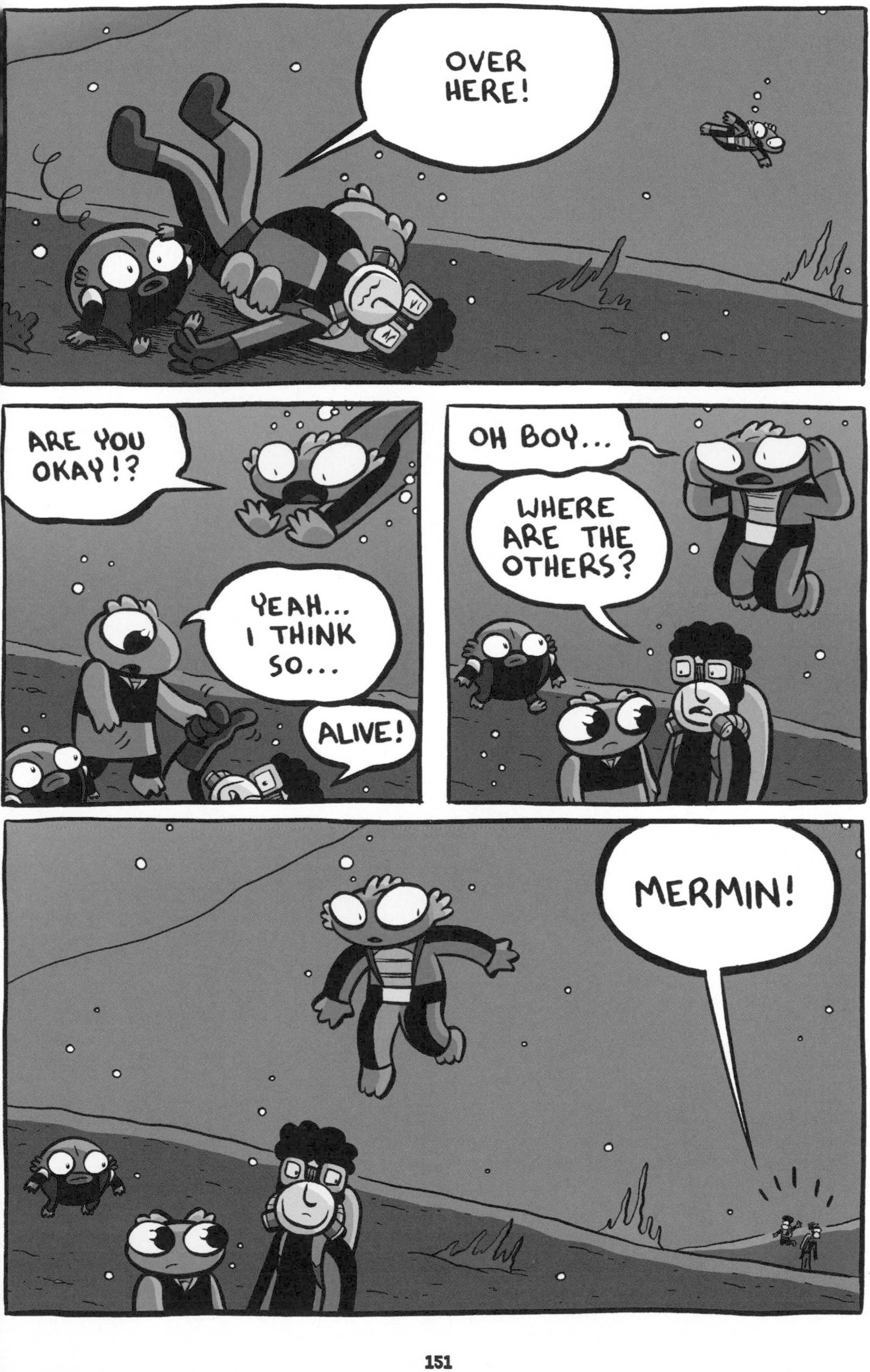
OVER HERE!
ARE YOU OKAY!?
YEAH... I THINK SO...
ALIVE!
OH BOY...
WHERE ARE THE OTHERS?
MERMIN!

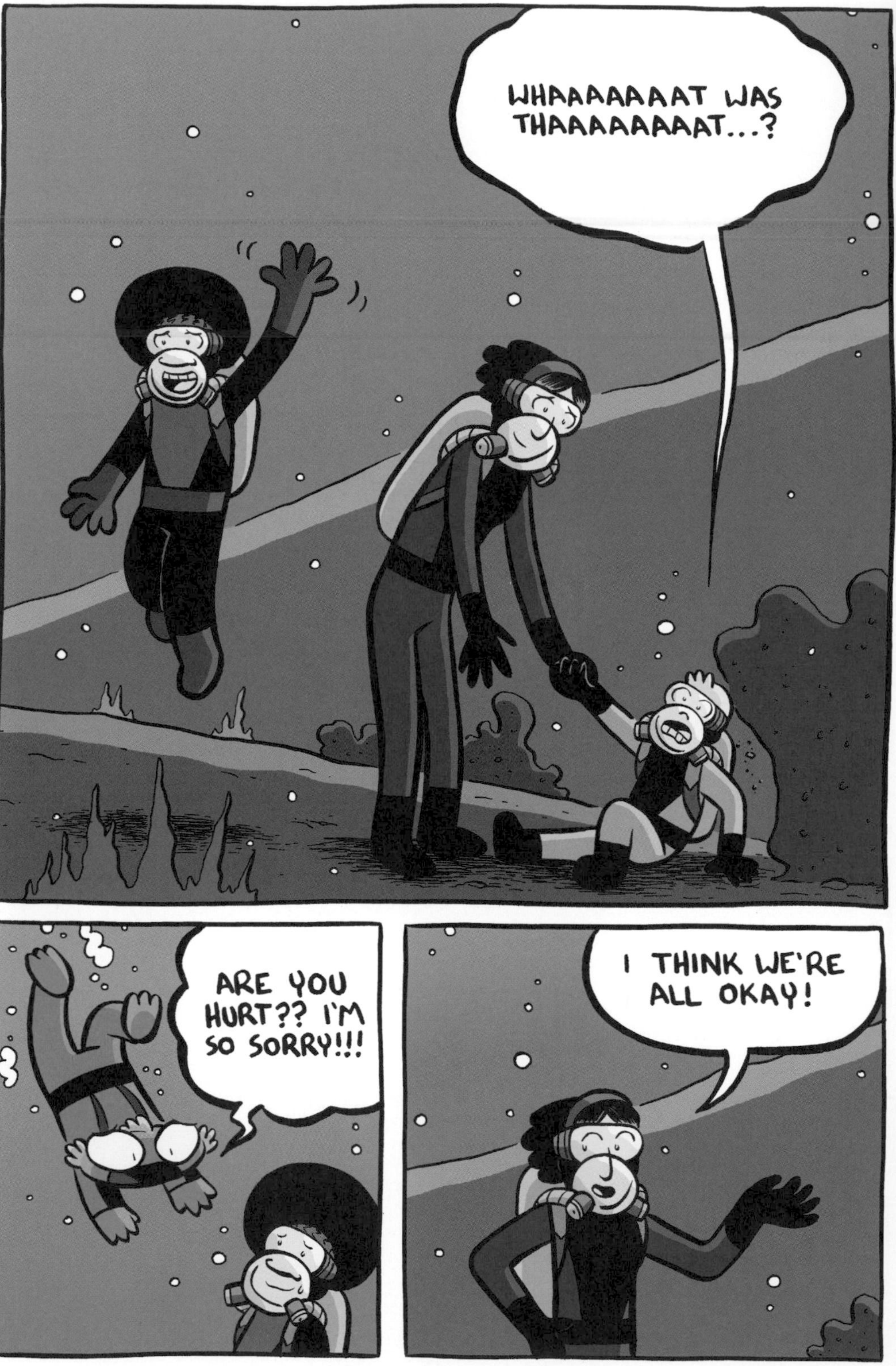
WHAAAAAAAT WAS THAAAAAAAAT...?
ARE YOU HURT?? I'M SO SORRY!!!
I THINK WE'RE ALL OKAY!

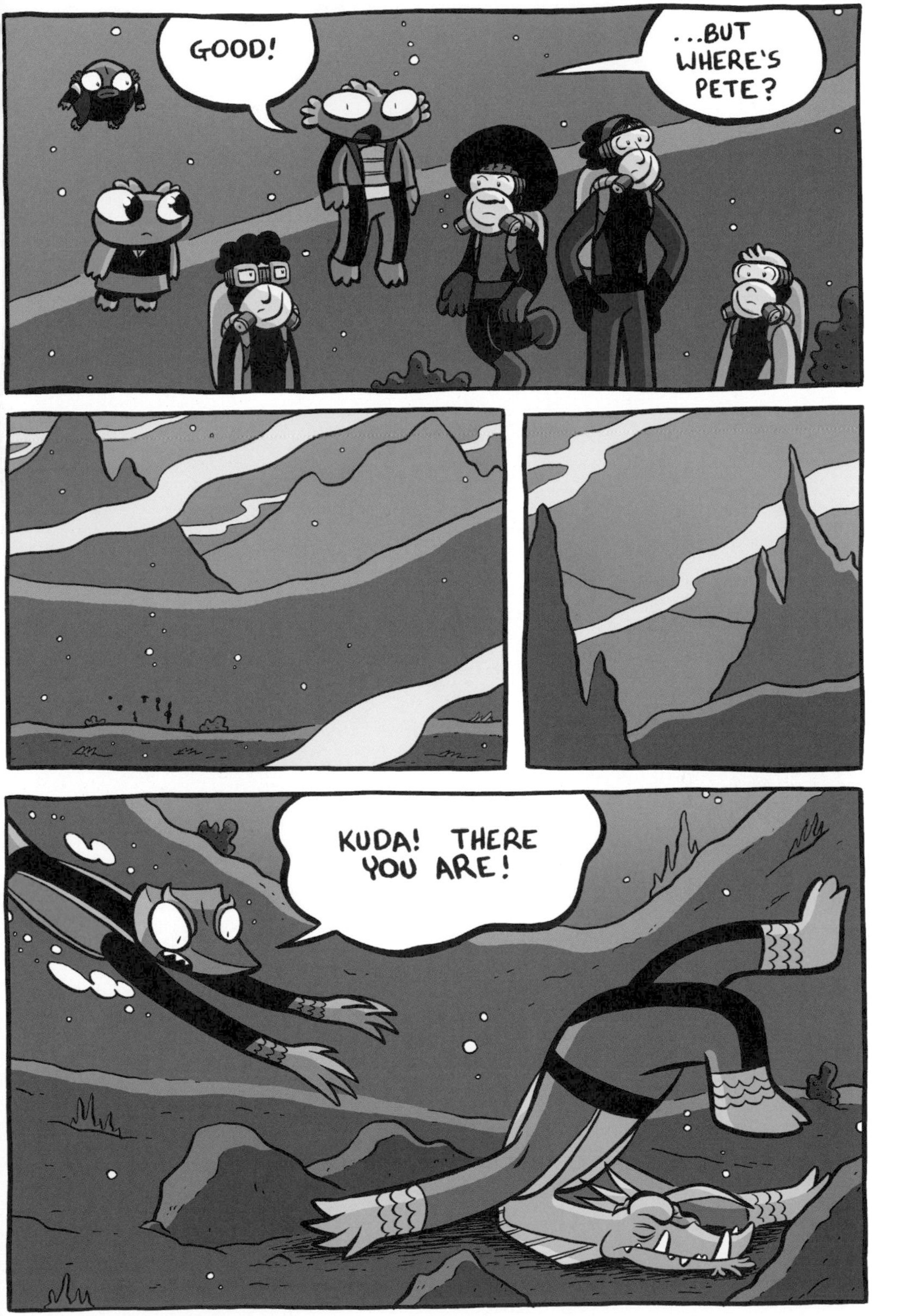
GOOD!
...BUT WHERE'S PETE?
KUDA! THERE YOU ARE!

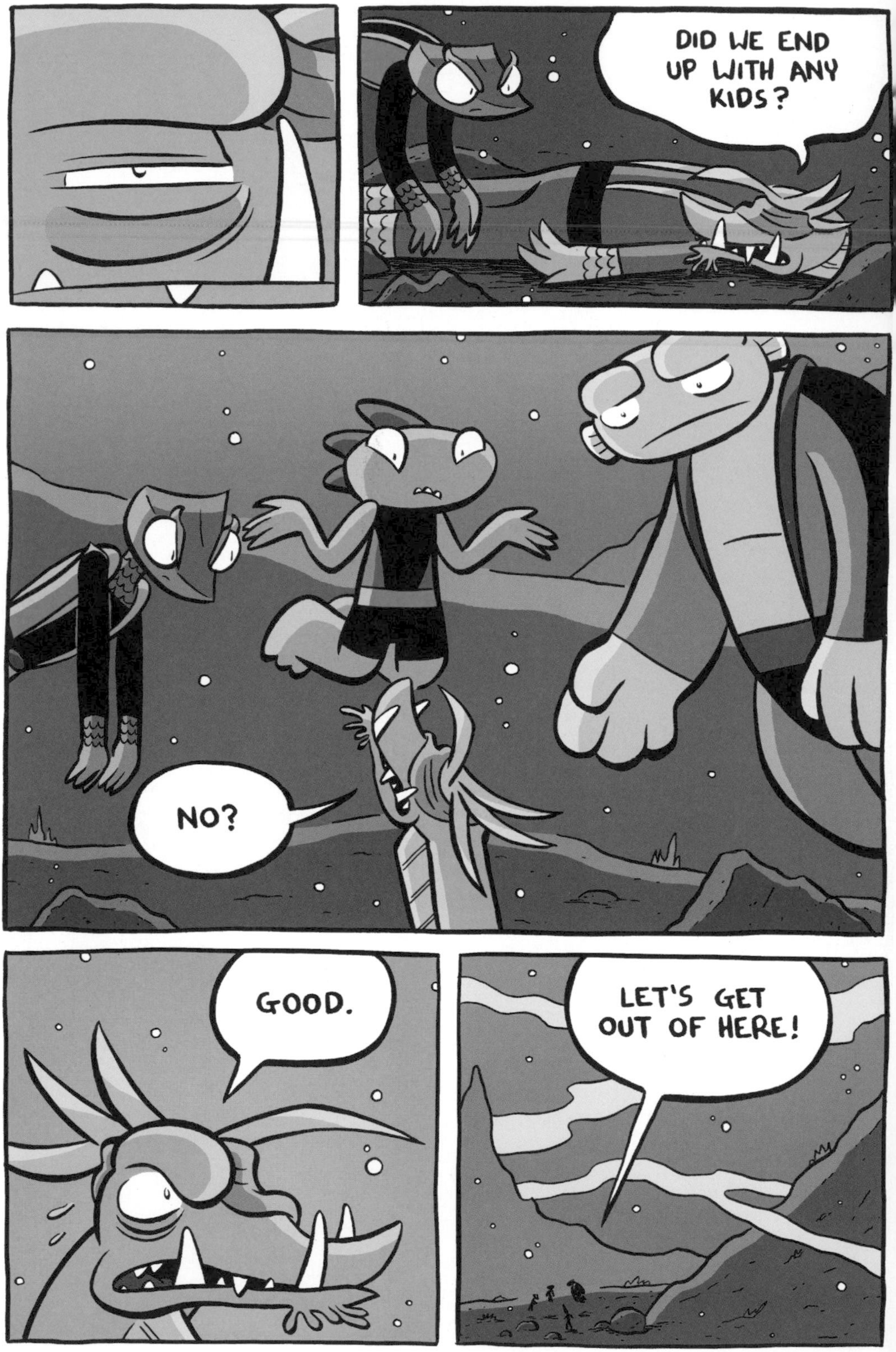
DID WE END UP WITH ANY KIDS?
NO?
GOOD.
LET'S GET OUT OF HERE!

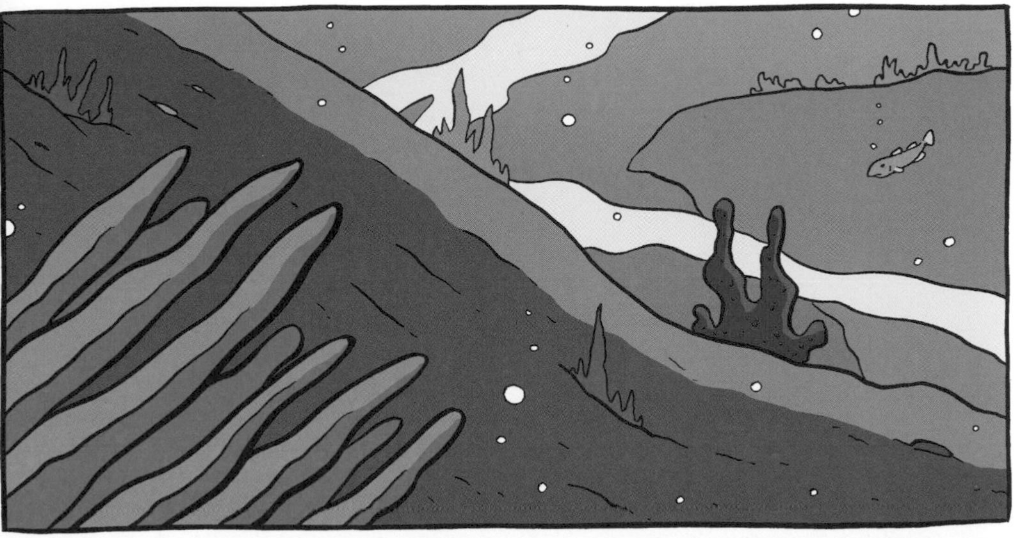

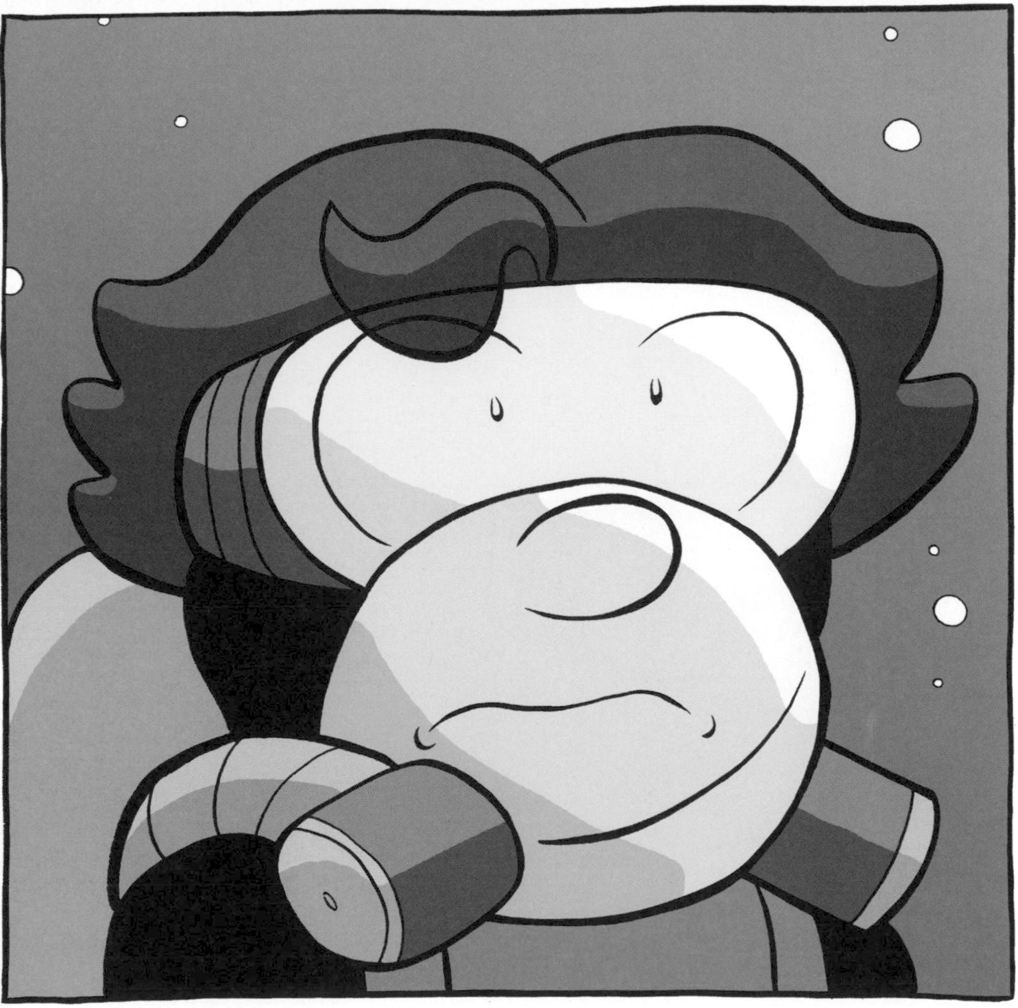

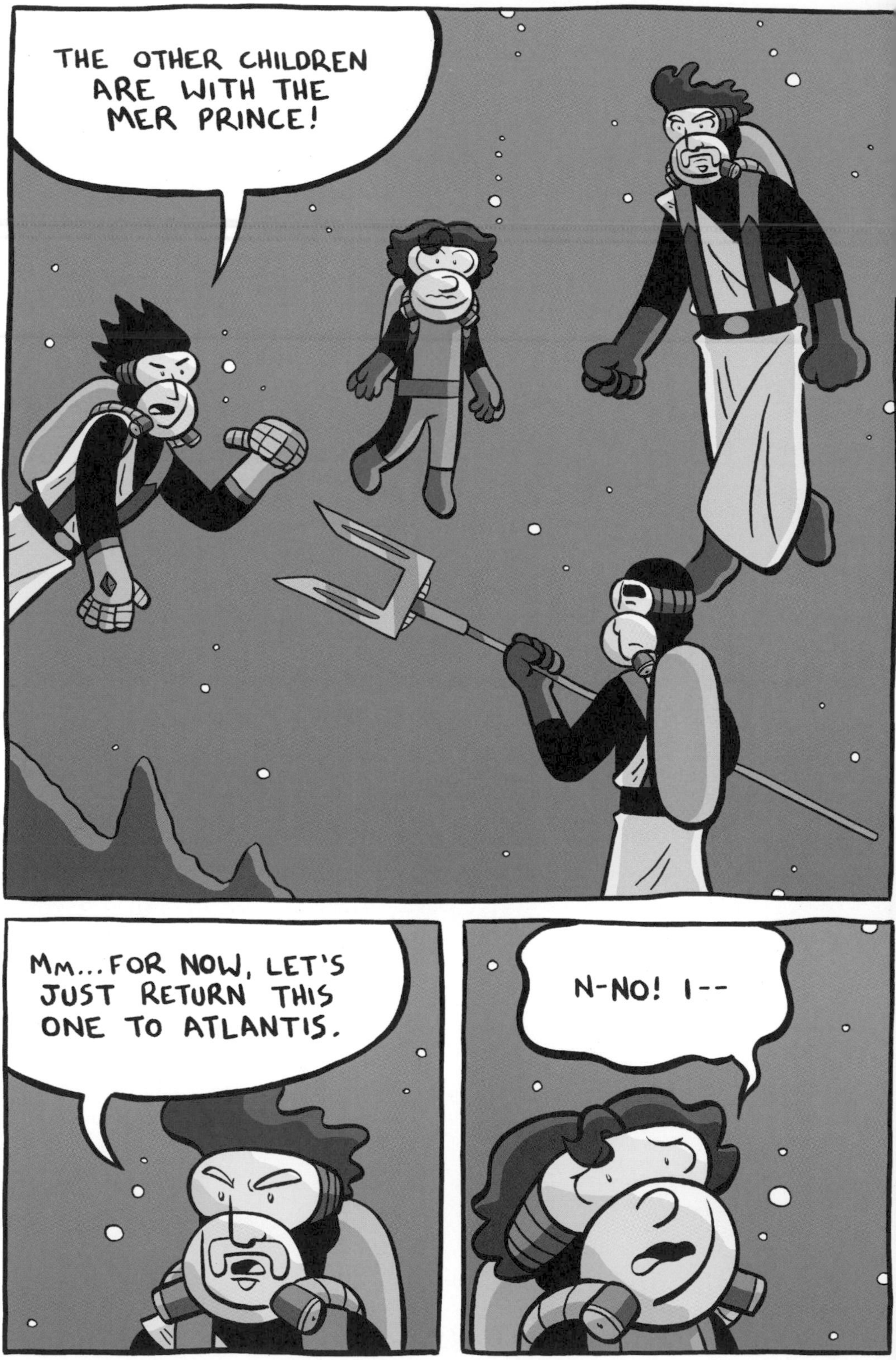
THE OTHER CHILDREN ARE WITH THE MER PRINCE!
MM...FOR NOW, LET'S JUST RETURN THIS ONE TO ATLANTIS.
N-NO! I--

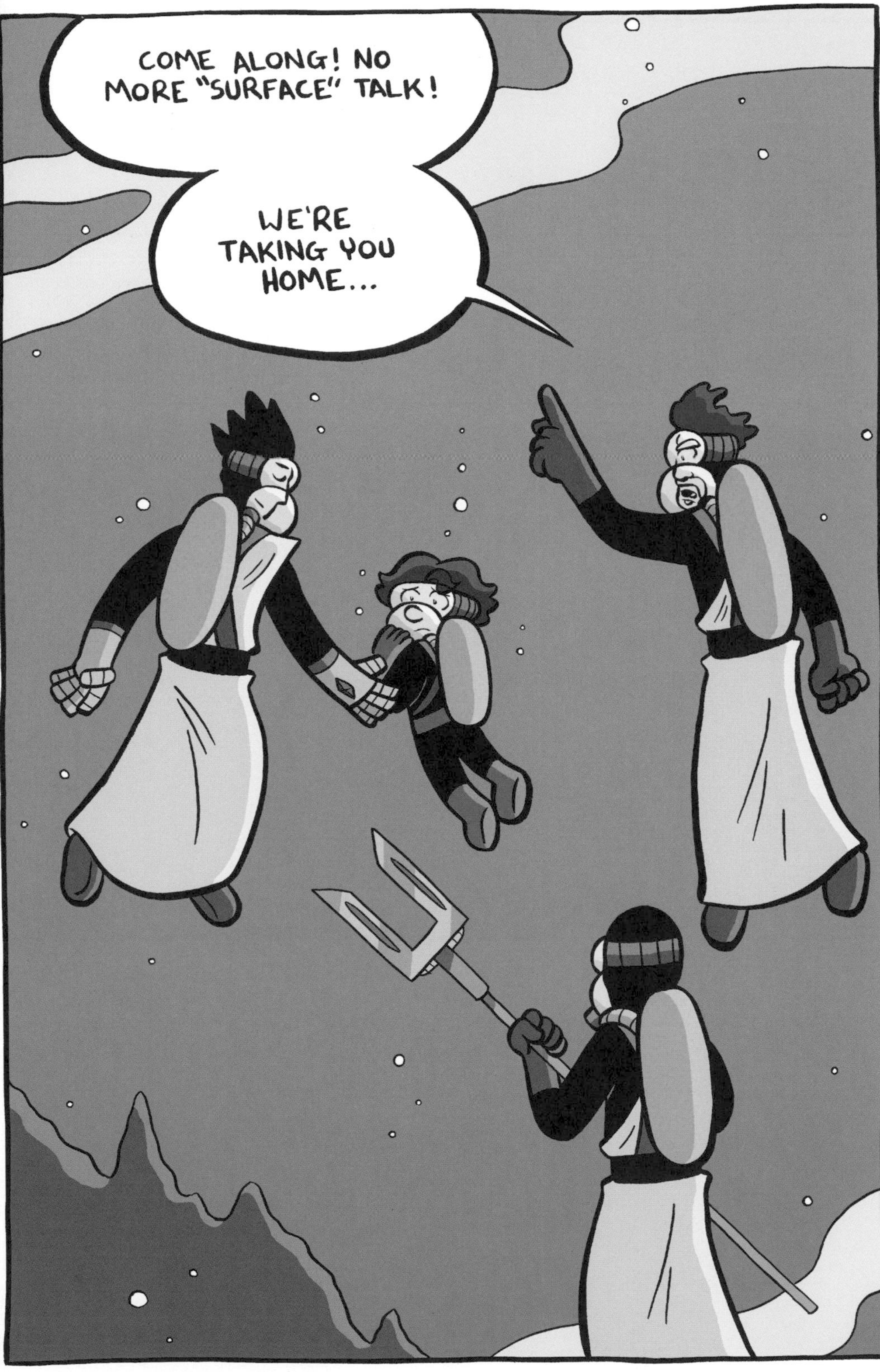
COME ALONG! NO MORE "SURFACE" TALK!
WE'RE TAKING YOU HOME...

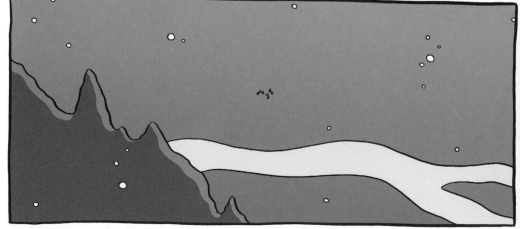

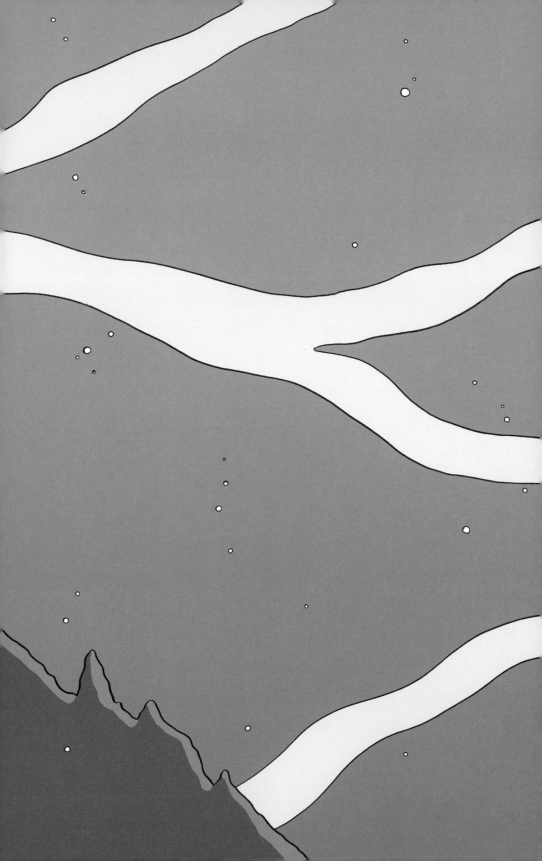

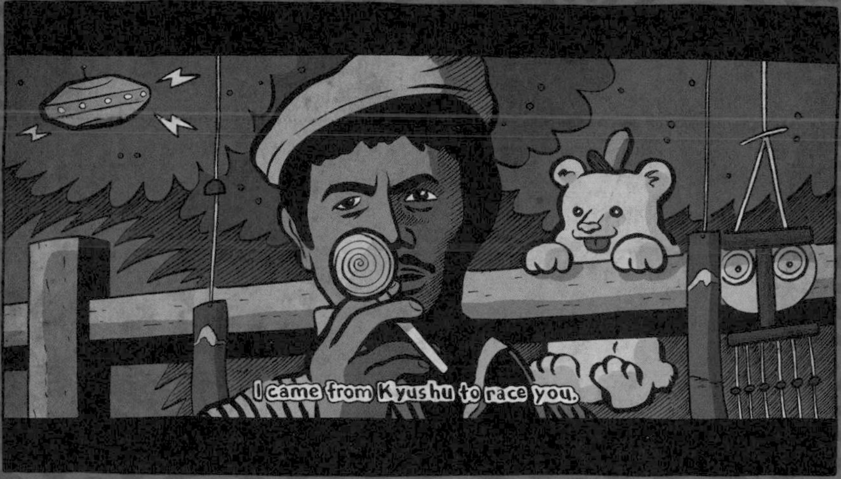
I came from Kyushu to race you.

Joey Weiser's comics have appeared in several publications including *SpongeBob Comics* and the award-winning *Flight* series. His debut graphic novel, *The Ride Home*, was published in 2007 by AdHouse Books, and the first *Mermin* graphic novel was published in 2013 by Oni Press.
He is a graduate of the Savannah College of Art & Design, and he currently lives in Athens, Georgia with his wife Michele and their cat Eddie.

OTHER BOOKS FROM ONI PRESS

MERMIN
BOOK ONE: OUT OF WATER
By Joey Weiser

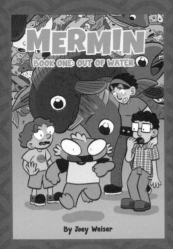

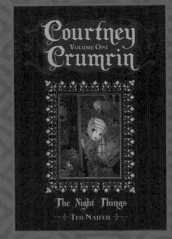

MERMIN, VOL. 1:
OUT OF WATER
By Joey Weiser

152 Pages, Hardcover, Color
ISBN 978-1-934964-98-9

MERMIN
BOOK TWO: THE BIG CATCH
By Joey Weiser

MERMIN, VOL. 2:
THE BIG CATCH
By Joey Weiser

144 Pages, Hardcover, Color
ISBN 978-1-62010-101-8

Courtney
Volume One
Crumrin
The Night Things
Ted Naifeh

COURTNEY CRUMRIN, VOL. 1:
THE NIGHT THINGS
By Ted Naifeh

136 Pages, Hardcover, Color
ISBN 978-1-934964-77-4

POWER
LUNCH
FIRST COURSE
J. Torres & Dean Trippe

POWER LUNCH, VOL. 1
FIRST COURSE
By J. Torres & Dean Trippe

40 Pages, Hardcover, Color
ISBN 978-1-934964-70-5

CROGAN'S
VENGEANCE
THE CROGAN ADVENTURES
by Chris Schweizer

CROGAN'S
VENGEANCE
By Chris Schweizer

192 Pages, Hardcover, B/W
ISBN 978-1-934964-06-4

SKETCH
MONSTERS
ESCAPE OF THE SCRIBBLES
JOSHUA WILLIAMSON • VINNY NAVARRETE

SKETCH MONSTERS, VOL. 1:
ESCAPE OF THE SCRIBBLES
By Joshua Williamson & Vinny Navarrete

48 Pages, Hardcover, Color
ISBN 978-1-934964-69-9

ONI PRESS
REVOLUTIONIZE COMICS
www.onipress.com

For more information on these and other fine Oni Press comic books and graphic novels visit onipress.com. To find a comic specialty store in your area visit comicshops.us.